NEVER SAY SE

"That's it, Violet! I'm calling your boss," Tiffany threatened. "And then the cops."

I held up my index finger in her direction. "Just give me a damned minute, Tiffany! You owe me that for stealing Jeff Wymonds away from me."

"What does Masterson have to do with this?" Reid asked.

"I'll explain it to you later. Right now I need to do my job, and you need to charm Jessica Rabbit up there with those big fireman muscles and the red-hot charm you hose-jockeys are famous for." I tried to pull free, but he held on.

"Sparky, you cannot go hunt that thing alone. Zo will kill me if anything happens to you on my watch."

"Aunt Zoe will kill me if I let anything happen to *you* on my Executioner watch." I pointed the ax toward the porch where Tiffany still hovered, a worried frown on her forehead as she glanced back and forth between the front door and us. "Please, Reid, you have to run interference for me. Take Tiffany back in the house and don't let anyone follow me into the trees."

Also by Ann Charles

DEADWOOD
MYSTERY SERIES

NEVER SAY SEVER
IN
DEADWOOD

Book 12

ANN CHARLES

Illustrated by C.S.Kunkle

For Sue Stone

What will I do without you?

You were there from early on in the Deadwood Mystery series, helping me get the local history right on the page.

Without you, the world has less sparkle and fewer smiles.

You will be missed more than words can say.

Never Say Sever in Deadwood
Copyright © 2021 by Ann Charles
Prescott AZ, USA

Cover Art by C.S. Kunkle
Cover Design by B Biddles
Editing by Eilis Flynn
Formatting by B Biddles

E-book ISBN-:13: 978-1-940364-79-7
Print ISBN-:13: 978-1-940364-78-0

Dear Reader,

Every now and then life kicks you in the ass. Sometimes, it kicks more than once. Sometimes, life keeps kicking even after you're face down in the dirt you've cried "Uncle!" repeatedly, and it won't stop until you stand up, brush yourself off, and tell it to go blow a goat.

Such was the reality behind the scenes during the writing of this story when Covid-19 came swooping in not once, not twice, but three damned times for our family. One would think we were out licking light switches in public bathrooms, sheesh! Turns out, even if you think you're being mindful, you still get that boot to the butt!

To make matters worse, during my last bout with Covid-19 while writing the end of this book, our 18-year-old cat died, breaking our hearts. Bamboo had been with us since she was six weeks old. We were fortunate to have so many wonderful years to create fun-filled memories with her. On a high note, tears work wonders to clear sinuses when you're sick. They should add that "tip" to those books about home remedies for everything under the sun.

Now, like Violet, I am back on my feet and ready to share another wild ride through the pages with you. As Violet's new career as a *Scharfrichter* continues, she is constantly learning and being tested (and getting kicked in the butt by life). This is how we grow to become wise, compassionate human beings, and this is how Executioners grow into smarter, better killers. Part of the fun of telling these stories is seeing how not only Violet's character develops, but how those around her change and grow, too. The rest of the fun is just hanging out with Violet on the page. She has a way of looking at the world that makes me chuckle.

As you travel along with Violet throughout this story, I hope you are able to escape from your daily troubles and share some laughs with me as we watch Violet and her team of misfits learn about the supernatural forces they face. Lift your glass and toast with me to another rough and rowdy tale. And while you're at it, never say "never" in Deadwood.

*"Some people **never** go crazy. What truly horrible lives they must lead."*
~Henry Charles Bukowski, American novelist and poet

Ann Charles
www.anncharles.com

Acknowledgments

I'd like to thank the following folks for helping me make it through another wild ride with Violet Parker:

My husband for holding my hand, helping me brainstorm scenes, and cheering me on daily.

My kids, Beaker and Chicken Noodle, stopping by to rub my shoulders and kiss my cheek as I pushed hard to finish the book.

My First Draft team: Margo Taylor, Mary Ida Kunkle, Kristy McCaffrey, Marcia Britton, Paul Franklin, Diane Garland, Michelle Davis, Vicki Huskey, Lucinda Nelson, Stephanie Kunkle, and Wendy Gildersleeve. You were especially patient this time as I struggled to reach "The End … for now." Your never-ending support book after book makes me smile.

Sue Stone for always being excited and ready to help.

My editor, Eilis Flynn, for helping me race toward the end at record speed and working around my crazy schedule. Your eyes are worth their weight in gold!

My WorldKeeper, Diane Garland, for help keeping track of everything and then some. You rock!

Michelle Davis for helping me pick a sneak peek excerpt.

My Beta Team for being so willing to help in such a short timeframe. I'm a lucky writer to have so much help.

My brother, C.S. Kunkle, for drawing my nightmares and for creating kickass cover art.

My graphic artist/cover designer/formatter (aka my husband) for putting together a finished product that sparkles.

My readers and friends for cheering me on with your excitement and positive words and reviews. The next round of virtual drinks are on me!

And as always, Clint (my younger brother), for swimming with me in jellyfish-infested waters off the Georgia coast and screaming every time you got stung. I'll never forget that day!

*"Things are **never** so bad they can't be made worse."*
~Charlie Allnut (aka Humphrey Bogart)
The African Queen

Chapter One

Almost midnight
Wednesday, January 16th
Central City, South Dakota

"Somebody needs to light a fire under Cooper's ass before I freeze mine off." I shivered deeper into my scarf, wondering if anything was lurking in the deep gloom under the surrounding pine trees. Watching. Waiting for me to lower my guard.

Or maybe I was just being extra paranoid tonight.

The frigid wind clawed at my coat, trying to tear the collar open so it could chill me clear through my bones. Another ten minutes in this sub-zero version of hell and my ears would ice over, shatter into pieces, and blow away into the inky darkness of the Black Hills forest, followed shortly by my kneecaps and nipples.

Before me, lit up by two sets of police cruiser headlights, sat a well-weathered wooden outbuilding leaning against a craggy hillside. Snow drifts crept partway up the board and batten siding. The rock-rubble foundation crumbled at the corners, and the tin roof sagged slightly in the middle. The place looked worn out from its slog through time. Downtrodden by gravity. Scarred from battles with the elements. Frightened by what might prowl out of the darkness next and reach for my … Wait, how did this become about me?

I scowled at the turn my mind had taken. Apparently, after a week of toiling with a shadowy devil and a slippery imp, my psyche wanted to have a pity party. Too bad. The roller coaster was just starting to pick up speed now. It was time to buck up. Time to charge Hell with a bucket of water and all of that battle-cry jazz. Time to …

Oh, please! Who was I kidding? I still screeched like a banshee when I walked through a cobweb.

"I knew I should've swung by my ranch on the way here," Old Man Harvey grumbled. He stood at my side, his shoulders scrunched. His gray beard glittered with bits of snow—or maybe that was frost.

"Why's that?"

"To grab a stick of dynamite. That would've warmed up this place in a single *BOOM*."

Normally, I'd gnaw on Harvey's hide about even going near the stash of old, unstable dynamite he kept in his barn, but tonight my teeth were chattering too hard to nibble, let alone gnaw. "It certainly would have loosened your nephew's sphincter a notch or two."

Cooper was Deadwood's rawhide and bristly version of a detective. The law dog had been all teeth and horns since we'd arrived on the scene of what he was already labeling another one of my "grand fuckups"—similar to the teeny-tiny blunder I'd made last week. While I'd argued that my freeing that troublemaking imp from the Sugarloaf Building had been an honest accident, the stubborn blockhead refused to listen to reason. He'd ordered me to wait outside in the pickup while he dragged my boyfriend inside the building to catch up with the other officers already on the scene.

Thankfully, Harvey had shown up to keep me company. After waiting in the truck for what felt like forever, we'd decided to join the others inside and see what was going on, but then chickened out halfway there and returned to stand beside the pickup and wait a little longer.

"It's not my fault the imp trashed three businesses up in Lead," I told Harvey, frowning at the outbuilding. "Why does Cooper always use me as his punching bag?" And here I thought we were on the fast track to being bosom buddies now that he was messing around between the sheets with my best friend.

"Ignore Coop, Sparky. He's just burnin' some powder and you're a fine target."

Another cold blast rattled me from teeth to toes. Maybe it was time to climb back inside the cab and warm up.

Harvey pulled the flaps of his fur-lined bomber hat lower over his ears. "Darn wind. I could eat a sheep for its wool alone 'bout now." He squinted in my direction long and hard.

I wrinkled my upper lip at him. "You lose something over here, dirty bird?"

"Besides my favorite hat that you took from my rig?"

I'd had no choice earlier while hunting a smoky devil up in Lead, since I'd forgotten to bring my own hat along. "I gave your hat back as soon as you got here."

He snorted. "Sure, but you ruined it."

"How?"

"It smells all girlie now, like peaches and cream."

That was called shampoo. "How about I wash your stupid hat later and then rub it in snips and snails and puppy-dog tails?"

He eyed me again, his eyebrows crooked. "You're lookin' as tired as a boomtown whore tonight."

I shrugged, too worn out to take offense. "I'd sleep on a barbed wire fence right about now if you'd promise to sing me a lullaby or two."

"Would you settle for a spirited drinkin' song about a well-endowed woman named Tatas Tig-ol-bitty?"

It took me a couple of blinks for her name to soak through the layer of permafrost surrounding my brain. I crossed my arms. "Don't you know any drinking songs that aren't X-rated?"

"Well," he said, tugging on his beard. "There was one tune I learned years back in a swanky joint just two hops and a skip over the Nevada state line."

My gaze narrowed. "Was it truly swanky? Or just really sweaty?"

"Actually, it was sweaty and spanky, so 'swanky' works on both counts." He wiggled his bushy eyebrows at me. "*Anyhoo*, this particular dirty ditty was sung to me personally during a titillatin' performance by a painted lady named Stinky Krinkle, and it starred her two favorite girls, the Jigglyhoohas." He cupped his hands in front of his chest in case my noggin was too popsicled to catch the underlying bawdy nature of his tale. "If you get my gist."

I rolled my eyes so hard they nearly popped free and bounced into a snow drift.

As self-appointed bodyguards went, I could have done much worse, I supposed. Most days, Willis "Ol' Man" Harvey would give Looney Tunes' Yosemite Sam a run for his money. Considering their mutual love of weapons and their colorful maxims, mottos, and metaphors, both rootin'-tootin' firebrands were a trigger squeeze from blowing a hole in someone's backside. But Harvey had bigger aims than a squirrely varmint, especially now that my Executioner dance card had filled up with all sorts of sharp-toothed menaces—some even back from the dead.

"Speakin' of spankin's," Harvey said, nodding toward the door of the building. "Here comes yer stallion. From that there thunderstorm brewin' north of his chin, I'm guessin' Coop and his pals weren't handin' out candy apples inside."

I watched Doc stride our way, searching his face above his dark, close-cropped beard for some sign that what happened here tonight was *not* my problem, so we could pack up and head home. Our bed had been calling me for the last ten numbing minutes like a drunken ex blowing up my phone.

But Harvey was right. Nothing about Doc's body language gave me a "hunky-dory" impression. Not his broad shoulders hunched in his thick coat, nor his grim expression spotlighted by the headlights. And especially not the way he frowned toward the inky black hillside while he crossed to where I waited for him with quivering knees.

He jammed his hands in his pockets when he stopped in front of Harvey and me. His dark eyes gave nothing away as they traveled over me before turning to Harvey. "When did you get here, Willis?"

"Oh, about two snaps and a wiggle ago. I brought Sparky's ride."

Doc and I had borrowed Harvey's pickup earlier for our Hungarian devil–hunting trip up to the Sugarloaf Building, leaving the old boy my SUV in exchange.

"Cooper called him on the way here about the suspected breaking and entering," I told Doc, glancing over his shoulder at the door of the worn-out building as a pair of cops stepped outside and huddled together. They looked around at the trees just as Doc had. Puffs of steam came from their lips, but they talked too quietly for me to hear.

"I decided to join the party," Harvey finished for me. He pointed toward the building. "What's goin' on inside Jonesy's taxidermy shop?" he asked Doc. "Coop gonna arrest Dorothy for disturbin' the peace?"

"Who's Dorothy?" I focused on Doc. His stocking hat sat crooked, like he'd run into something disturbing inside that had knocked it askew. Judging from his rigid posture and continued glances toward the trees, I had a feeling that whatever the "something disturbing" was, it might hit me even harder, sending me reeling backward, ass-over-teakettle.

"Dorothy is the stuffed, one-humped camel that Jonesy keeps on display," Harvey explained. "Swears his great-granddaddy brought her home from the Sahara Desert after the war. After Dorothy gave up the ghost, his great-granddaddy stuffed her so she'd keep him company while he worked. He sure did love that camel." Harvey snickered. "Wasn't a natural kind of love, though, if you ask me."

A stuffed camel? What other taxidermy works of wonder awaited me inside?

"So what's going on in there?" I asked Doc.

The lines around his eyes deepened. "You'll have to see for yourself, but the lights are out, so you'll need a flashlight."

Go inside a dark taxidermy shop at night? I shook my head. "I'd rather wait out here in the cold."

Doc sighed, reaching for my gloved hand. "It's not an option, Killer." His grip was firm. "Coop sent me out to get you."

After a check on the two cops, I leaned closer to Doc. "Was it that dang imp?"

"I don't think so. But I have a feeling we're going to wish it had been before this is all over."

I didn't like the eerie timbre in his voice. "Why's that?"

"Come on." He tugged on my hand. "I'll show you."

Uh oh. Show and tell was not my favorite game when it came to creepy things in the dark. I grimaced, letting him pull me along. God, I wished I was under the covers rubbing my icy toes on Doc's long legs instead of trailing after him into a shop full of stuffed dead things.

" 'Back home we got a taxidermy man,' " I said under my breath as we crossed the threshold, reciting one of my son's favorite lines from the movie *Jaws*.

" 'He gonna have a heart attack when he see what I brung him,' " Doc finished the movie quote, doing a much better impression of Robert Shaw. He clicked on a flashlight, aiming the beam at the floor.

The place smelled like a well-worn bowling shoe, musty with an underlying layer of sweat and chemicals. At least it was warm.

I tugged off my gloves and pocketed them. My cheekbones couldn't take much more of that arctic wind. I tucked away a few loose curls that had escaped my old chenille knit beanie that had showed up with Harvey. I stored the hat in my SUV during the snowy months, along with spare gloves, a blanket, and tire chains. Snowstorms in the hills tended to turn up at unexpected times, like a bad penny … or a depraved sister set on stealing what didn't belong to her.

I shook off all thoughts of the Bitch from Hell, aka my sister, before they could sink their claws in. Susan was a problem for another day. One pain in the ass at a time.

"You've been hanging out with Layne too much," I told Doc while we waited for Harvey to close the door behind us. Actually, Layne was glued to Doc's side lately, which was a good thing, considering my son used to see Doc as competition for the man-of-the-house role.

"I'm trying to get the kid to put in a good word for me with his mom." Doc caught my hand again and kissed my knuckles. "I'm hoping I have a shot with her."

His lips were nice and warm. I batted my eyelashes at the heartbreaker. "Make it a tequila shot, Candy Cane, and you'll be miles ahead of the competition."

He let go of my hand and crossed his arms. "Competition?" He looked over my shoulder. "Harvey, I'm going to need to borrow Bessie and a handful of rock salt rounds."

Bessie was Harvey's favorite shotgun. I'd met her double barrels up close and personal last July when I'd visited Harvey's ranch for the first time to see if he wanted to hire me as his real estate agent. Word at the office had been that he was looking to move closer to town. Unfortunately, his ranch came with disembodied human parts and much worse, making it not so easy to sell.

"Ahhh, true love in 12-gauge style." I toyed with the

zipper on Doc's coat. "You must really be soft on Layne's mom."

"Soft, you say?" He chuckled, his gaze hovering on my lips for a couple of beats. "Only on the inside, Vixen."

Harvey guffawed, patting Doc on the shoulder. "Sparky, this poor lovesick sucker has taken to you like a lean tick to a fat hound."

I stole Harvey's hat off his head and smacked him in the belly with it. "Call me 'fat' again, Willis Harvey, and I'll dye your beard pink while you sleep."

"There's no need to get in a lather, girlie. I didn't call you a heifer this time. I know how much you enjoy bein' compared to cows."

Doc chuckled, earning himself a wallop with Harvey's hat, too.

Harvey snatched his hat back and then turned to Doc. "What happened to the lights?"

"Whoever broke in cut the power," Doc explained, moving over to the long counter running the length of the wall with a cash register weighing down the far end.

I loosened my scarf while scanning the shadowy room. I sure wished I had that tequila shot—or three—to take the heart-palpitating potential out of this place. "Never have I ever been in a taxidermy store at midnight," I said, thinking of the drinking game I'd played too many times to count while downing alcohol with Natalie, my best friend since I'd stopped shoving crayons up my nose.

"I'd have to take a drink on that one," Doc said, leaning against the counter. He'd apparently played the game, too. When? With whom?

"You've been in a taxidermy store in the middle of the night before?" Harvey asked.

Doc nodded.

"Tell us more, Mr. Mysterious," I said.

Had he played the game with his ex, as in the red-haired

siren with super perky boobs who was trying to steal my realty job out from under me? Before the jealous ogre in my head could take another lumbering step, I knocked it down and hog-tied it. Then I knuckle-rubbed it into submission and locked the tyrant back in the closet where I'd kept it for the last couple of months.

Doc and I were solid now—not quite bedrock, but certainly stronger than sandstone. There was no room in our relationship for ogres or exes. As for my future selling houses for a living, my boss seemed happy enough for the time being, especially with the first of a three-episode series about our office on the *Paranormal Realty* show broadcasting in a few days. So, Doc's ex could go sit on something pointy and spin for now.

"It was a long time ago," Doc told us.

"How long?" I pressed, always interested to learn more about Doc's life before he came to Deadwood and made me fall for him ... literally.

"Back in college," he answered.

"In Colorado?" I pulled out my cell phone and tapped the flashlight option, shining the beam on the wall next to me while I waited for him to continue.

A huge moose head with black glass eyes deadpanned straight ahead. I cringed and took a step back, bumping into Harvey, who was eyeing something in a glass cabinet. Posed in a head-lowered stance on top of the cabinet was a coyote. His upper lip was frozen in a snarl. One of its ears was partly torn off and a chunk of hide was missing from its hind quarter.

"Yeah. My roommate's uncle was a taxidermist."

Before Doc could spin the rest of his tale, a door at the other end of the room opened and Cooper stepped out. He nailed me in the face with his flashlight beam. "Parker, I need you to come with me."

Sometimes it was nice to be needed.

This was *not* one of those times.

I shielded my eyes. "Lower the light, Detective. Unless you expect me to start performing a taxidermy-themed cabaret."

"I've always been a big fan of burlesque shows with plenty of feathers and not much else," Harvey piped up. "How 'bout you, Doc?"

"I'm more partial to belly dancing and those coin-covered bras that jingle with each little shimmy."

After a growl of exasperation, Cooper raised the beam to the ceiling, which lit up the room a bit more while deepening the shadows of all the creatures frozen in the afterlife.

I glanced around at the macabre zoo. Raccoons and rabbits, a bobcat and a beaver, to name a few. On the walls, sightless glass eyes stared at me from deer, elk, and pronghorn heads. A black bear crouched off to my right and a cougar sat on its haunches to the left, both still fierce in death. At the other end of the counter, a camel stood tall and regal—ah, Dorothy.

A uniformed cop wearing a puffy police coat, deputy hat, and thick utility belt filled the doorway next to Cooper, who was garbed in his off-duty leather coat and blue jeans. We'd come straight over to the taxidermy joint after saying *adios* to the Hungarian pest and dropping off a quirky ghost-whisperer at his apartment, not stopping off to change out of our devil-dealing duds on the way.

The cop headed my way, pausing in front of me with a shit-eating grin. "Nice black eye, 'Rocky' Parker. Did the other guy last the whole ten rounds, or did you knock him out in the first, like you did Detective Cooper?"

The badge-toting doofus was referring to the night I'd accidentally head-butted Cooper, who went down for the count with a broken nose. The officer didn't wait around for my answer, snickering as he closed the door behind him. I touched my bruised cheek. I'd forgotten about my black eye, a parting gift I'd received almost a week ago from a sweet librarian possessed by a crotchety ghost.

Cringing in anticipation of Cooper's reaction to being the target of his co-worker's joke, I hollered at the closed door, "Yeah, well, stink, stank, stunk to you, fuzz bucket."

"Nice parting shot, there, Grinch." Doc hooked me by the elbow. "Although a little late."

He led me past a mountain lion frozen in mid-lunge with what looked like a bite taken out of its leg. To my left, a toothy hyena loomed, its neck torn open with furry bits dangling. Front and center stood a scowling detective without even a shadow of a grin on his face. His short blond hair reminded me of a patch of spike strips meant to tear up anyone trying to roll past him. Fittingly enough, the prickly cop waited next to a wild boar's head mounted on the wall. Something had chewed along the end of its snout like it was corn on the cob.

"It's not my fault," I told Cooper before he could start pointing fingers.

His tired eyes narrowed. "What are you talking about, Parker?"

"I don't know, but when you look at me with that sourpuss face, I start sputtering alibis."

"I do not have a sourpuss face," Cooper said with a definite frown anchoring the corners of his mouth.

"It looks like you're chewin' on a mouthful of bitter berries, boy." Harvey took my side, both figuratively and physically.

"You're not helping, Harvey," I mumbled.

He grunted. "I call 'em like I see 'em." To Cooper, he added, "Now, are you going to get to the point here or keep two-stepping around it? My prostate ain't gonna wait all day."

"Christ, you two," Cooper snapped, adding a sigh as an exclamation mark. "Come on." He turned and headed through the doorway, lighting the way with his flashlight.

I followed first, then Harvey, leaving Doc to bring up the rear. We filed down a narrow hallway lined with shelves full of bottles and jugs of various chemicals and cleaners. At the other end, Cooper ushered us through a doorway leading into a square workroom. A fluffy-haired, wiry guy with a handlebar mustache sat on a stool behind a workbench, resting his chin on his hands. A kerosene lantern sat next to him, the flickering flame reflecting in his horn-rimmed glasses.

"Howdy, Jonesy," Harvey greeted the man, ambling over to shake his hand. "How's the critter-stuffin' business treatin' you these days?"

"It's a little slow now that Christmas is over, but otherwise, business as usual." The taxidermist pushed his glasses up his pointy nose. "Well, until tonight anyway."

Cooper took his favorite wide-legged cop stance. "Garth Jones, this is Violet Parker. She's the consultant Doc Nyce and I were talking about earlier. She needs to hear your story."

Consultant, huh? I raised my eyebrows in Doc's direction. He shrugged back.

I joined Harvey and Garth at the workbench, holding out my hand. "Nice to meet you, Mr. Jones."

His hand was dry and leathery, probably from all of the chemicals he worked with on a daily basis, but his grip was firm. He did a double take when he looked up at me. "What happened to your eye?"

"I ran into a stray elbow last week."

I glanced around, trying not to cringe at the taxidermist's works in progress. A pronghorn's head sat on the bench next to him, its eye sockets empty. A chunk of hide was missing from the black band running down its snout, and one ear was dangling next to its cheek. On the table behind Garth, a falcon lay tipped partly on its side, one wing spread wide with wooden dowels, the other ripped clear off and tossed on the table next to it. Over in the corner, the tarp covering a bighorn sheep was partially pulled away, exposing the head, neck, and front legs. The sheep's head was bent down, its curled horns ready to ram the wall. A large chunk of hide was ripped off its shoulder, exposing what looked like a jumble of wool, wire, and wood below.

Throughout the room on shelves, countertops, and under a bench were bottles and piles of rags and half-folded tarps. Some were stained with what looked like dried blood, others were stiff with some kind of lacquer or varnish or polyurethane—whatever taxidermists used to finish the job.

In the daylight, this place would have been a little bit unsettling, but at night with dancing shadows and glassy stares, it was downright hair-raising … and drafty.

Why was it so cold back here? Was there a window open? No, the two windows in the room looked closed, the droopy, burlap-like curtains were motionless. I looked beyond the carcasses, noticing a door near the corner of the room. One of the windowpanes down low looked darker than the others. Shards of glass glittered on the floor below.

"What happened, Jonesy?" Harvey asked, settling onto the stool next to the taxidermist.

Garth's brow lined. "Well, like I was telling your nephew and his crew, I was resting my eyes in my easy chair in the house before heading to bed when Beau here started growling and barking something fierce."

I hadn't noticed the bull terrier at his feet until the dog whined, lifting its fat head for a pat from Garth before lowering its snout back to the floor. Beau's shoulders and hind end were as thick as his head, and his nose was peppered with enough gray and white fur to tell me he was not a young pup anymore.

"Next thing I know, my pickup's alarm starts blaring. After I shut it off, Beau gets to howling and throwing himself at the kitchen door, making enough racket to wake the dead.

I grabbed my .22 and came out to see what had the old boy so excited." He twirled one end of his handlebar mustache. "I couldn't see much when I stepped out on the porch, but Beau made a beeline to the shop and tried to bust in the back door." He thumbed toward the door near the corner. "When I got closer, I noticed the broken window. Figurin' someone was trying to clean out my cash register, I snuck in back here and tiptoed out front, keeping my flashlight off. That's when I heard it." He paused and shuddered. Then he made a low, snarling, grunting noise.

Beau whined, burying his snout under his front paws.

"That's the sound you heard?" I asked, wanting to make sure he wasn't just clearing his throat. Lord only knew the damage he'd done to his lungs over the years inhaling the chemicals of his trade.

Garth nodded. "I stepped out into the front room with my gun at the ready, but it was dark. I hadn't realized the power was out until I tried to hit the overhead lights to surprise the son of a bitch." He winced and shot me a frown. "Pardon my French, ma'am."

Harvey waved him off on my account. "Sparky here can out-swear a longshoreman on a slow day at the docks."

I glared at my bodyguard. "I wasn't raised by a sailor."

"More like moonshiner," Harvey shot back, grinning. He nudged Garth's arm. "Sparky has a real looker for a momma. Pretty as a pie supper, and sweet enough to rot your teeth after just one nibble. Makes a man think about taking a bite, if you get my gist."

My glare tightened into a full scowl. "That's my mother you're talking about."

Harvey's blue eyes practically twinkled. "Would you rather I compare her to a fine heifer?"

"Finish your story, Garth," Cooper cut in, leveling a hard stare at his uncle and then me.

"Anyway, before I could click on my flashlight, Beau shot

past me and launched himself at the intruder. He sank his teeth into the guy, making him squeal like a stuck pig. Beau growled and snarled for a few seconds, and then he let out a yip and I heard something thud against the wall. I started toward the commotion, but the intruder rushed by me, shoving me into Dorothy in his haste to escape." Garth shook his head. "The bastard smelled like last week's roadkill and must have been about a head taller than Coop here. That shove of his sent me flying through the air for a few feet, so he was one strong sucker."

"Did you get a look at his face at all?" Harvey prodded.

"Nope. It was too dark." Garth shifted, rubbing his shoulder, which had probably taken the brunt of his landing. "Beau took off down the hall after him, though, so I scrambled to my feet and made chase, following the two of them out into the snow. The clouds were blowing through, so I could only catch glimpses during the moon breaks. The two of them were partway down the drive, spinning in circles. Beau had locked onto his leg again, this time below the knee, and he wasn't letting go. I raised my .22 and tried to get a bead on the guy, and that's when I noticed he was missing an arm."

"His whole arm?" Harvey asked. "Or just from the elbow down?"

"I think the whole damned thing." Garth rolled his sore shoulder. "The guy managed to drag Beau away from his leg and tossed him into the trees, like the old boy isn't fat as a hog during butchering season."

Beau let out a short, snarly bark.

Either Beau spoke English on the side, or he'd been called a "fat hog" before and didn't like it. I could relate. If Harvey called me a heifer one more time, I was going to bite onto his scrawny leg and not let go.

"And then the guy did the strangest thing," Garth continued, shaking his head as if it still baffled him.

"What?" I asked in a hushed voice, half afraid to hear his answer. I'd seen some strange things myself lately. The sort of sights that kept me wide awake and trembling under the covers many a night.

"He let out a howl that curdled my blood. Then he bent down onto all fours—well, all threes in his case—and loped off toward the trees like a three-legged bear." He shook his head. "I ain't never seen any man scamper off like that, 'specially not in the snow. It was downright disturbing to my mental well-being, and I've seen a thing or two in my time."

I bet he had, judging from the uncanny "pets" surrounding him day after day in here.

"Beau tried to give chase, of course," Garth told Harvey and me. "But the guy was too fast. He disappeared under the trees in two shakes. I stood there with my chin on the ground for what must have been a solid minute, not believing what I'd just witnessed with my own two eyes. Wasn't much after that I heard his howl again, only this time it was a ways off to the west, I think. Hard to tell for sure in the hills, though. Sound bounces off rock faces and the wind carries it this way and that."

I glanced at Doc. His eyes held mine, his mouth a thin pale line amidst his dark whiskers. Now I understood why he'd looked unsettled when he'd joined me outside, and the reason he'd kept searching the trees.

Garth sighed, pulling me back to his story. "The crazy part of it is the guy wasn't after the money in my cash register. Every single bill is still in there. But look at what he did to several of the pieces I was working on." He flicked the torn ear on the pronghorn's head next to him. "It's like he went around taking bites out of everything."

Bites, huh? I chewed on my lower lip. Well, shit.

"Including poor Dorothy." Garth pointed toward the hallway leading out front. "There's a big chunk out of her hump. What kind of man would do such a thing to a stuffed camel?"

I rubbed the back of my neck, avoiding eye contact with the taxidermist. I had a feeling this was no man, at least not anymore. My gaze shifted to Cooper, who stared back at me with a furrowed brow.

"Luckily, he didn't sink his teeth into the stag I just finished for a client over in Wyoming," Garth said, nudging his chin toward a big, partially tarp-covered deer over near the door.

"Musta been a hungry son of a gun to try eatin' your long-dead pals here." Harvey eyed the pronghorn and shook his head.

"Ms. Parker," Garth said. "Detective Cooper mentioned you might have had some experience with this sort of a troublemaker before."

That was one way of putting it.

"Do you think the guy was on some sort of hallucinogenic drug?" Garth asked me.

I wished it were that simple. Rather than lie outright to the poor taxidermist, I asked, "You're sure about that one-arm business?" There was one nasty *other* creature I knew about that was currently running around short an arm.

Garth nodded. "But ding-dang, he was strong. And he sure moved fast through the snow on just three limbs."

Of course it did. A *Nachzehrer* wouldn't be nearly as deadly if it were weak and slithered like a slug.

Fudge nuggets. I squeezed my clammy palms together and stared at the pronghorn's eye sockets. This year was off to a rotten start. First a Hungarian devil made of smoke and shadow, and now this dickhead.

With any luck there was only one flesh-eating, ghoul-like terror waiting for me out there under the trees. But with Mercury now gone retrograde in the astrological world and all sorts of trouble brewing, I had a feeling I was going to be chewed up, spat out, and stomped on before this was all over.

Chapter Two

S peaking of trouble …
A grizzle-faced detective and his gum-flapping uncle were
waiting for me when I finally dragged my sorry fanny out of
bed, pulled on my robe and slippers, and staggered
downstairs in search of brain fuel.

Harvey was kicking back at the kitchen table with his
stocking feet resting on a nearby chair. Wearing rainbow
suspenders over a white shirt, he looked as if he didn't have
a care in the world. Had he forgotten about last night's
macabre scene at Jones' Taxidermy already? Because I
certainly hadn't.

On the table in front of him sat two, heavy-duty, yellow
and black walkie-talkies. Where had those come from? My
dad had bought the kids a set a couple of Christmases ago,
but they were pretty rinky-dink, and if memory served me
right, Layne's had a cracked case wrapped in bright orange
duct tape thanks to Addy's fix-it skills.

"Mornin', Sparky," Harvey hollered at me even though I
wasn't more than three steps away.

I scowled at him, debating on turning around and
marching right back to bed. Burrowing under my covers
sounded like a great way to handle whatever had a usually
cranky Deadwood detective darkening my doorstep first

thing. Come to think of it, I probably shouldn't have gotten up in the first place. It was my one day off this week, and I was going to have a nice, relaxing morning, damn it.

"You look like you woke up foamin' at the mouth," Harvey continued in spite of my raised hackles. "Did you get bit in the booty by that three-limbed ghoulie when I wasn't guardin' your backside last night?"

Gah! I growled under my breath. I needed a few swallows of caffeine before I could handle too much sunshine and smartassery from the ol' boy.

Tightening my bathrobe belt with a hard yank, I aimed my feet in the direction of the coffee maker and ran smack-dab into Cooper's steely gray squint. He was leaning against the sink with his arms crossed, wearing blue jeans, a gray flannel shirt, and a crumpled brow. His hair was a mess of spikes and his jaw was prickly with stubble. Maybe if I turned him upside down, he'd come in handy as a foot scrubber.

Another yellow and black walkie-talkie was attached to Cooper's belt. I cast a second look at the two on the table. What was going on? What was with the walkie-talkies?

More important, why were Cooper and Harvey in my aunt's kitchen at the buttcrack of ... I checked the Betty Boop clock over the sink ... at the buttcrack of eight thirty-seven on a blustery Thursday morning? And where was Doc? My kids? Aunt Zoe? Elvis the chicken? Had I managed to stumble through an invisible door on my way downstairs and somehow crossed over into an alternate reality?

But first ... coffee. I moved my feet along on my quest.

Outside the window over the sink, I watched as a spiraling gust of wind swirled onto the back porch. It whistled through the door jamb and peppered the kitchen window with tiny pellets of snow. The meteorologist hadn't been kidding when he'd warned about that polar vortex blowing south and freezing the noses off the faces of the four presidents up on Mount Rushmore.

Lying across the bottom porch step was a pointed digging shovel with a blue handle—the one Layne had used to dig up my aunt's backyard last summer while playing archaeologist. Dang it, how many times had I told my kids not to leave stuff on the steps? Someone was going to trip and get hurt.

I opened the cupboard door and grabbed a mug, shooting a glare Cooper's way. He was standing too close to the coffee pot and I was still holding a grudge about his part in last night's "police business" rigmarole that had kept me out way past my bedtime.

"Who let you off your chain already, law dog?" I asked, coming out of my corner of the boxing ring swinging.

His bristly jaw tightened. His focus shifted to my hair, his eyes lining up a shot. "Did you just climb out of the backseat of a clown car, Parker?"

Harvey sucked air through his teeth. "Careful, Coop. Yer tiptoein' into a minefield there."

I set the mug down on the counter. "Are you making fun of my hair, pork chop?"

The son of a gun was foolish enough to grin. "Where's your big red nose, Bozo? Stick it in someone else's business one too many times?"

I was too tired to pull my punches and socked him in the shoulder before he could dodge and weave.

"Christ, Parker," he complained as he sidestepped, putting some space between us. "Nyce needs to work harder on taming you."

A snort came from the peanut gallery over at the table. "There's no taking a currycomb to Sparky, or any of her wild hairs."

"Yeah, what he said." I grabbed the coffee pot, peeking over at Cooper. "Besides, I barely hit you, big baby."

"We're supposed to be on the same side now, remember?" He smirked. "At least that's what your boyfriend keeps telling me. Maybe Nyce should invest in a muzzle for you."

"Keep it up, law dog," I said while filling my mug partway, "and I'll sic Natalie on you. She hits *and* bites."

"Oh, Coop knows all about that wildcat's fondness for bitin', dontcha, boy?" Harvey snickered. "Along with her slappin' and ticklin'. You should see how bruised up he is from the neck down after Nat spends the night with him."

Cooper and I shared a grimace, but twenty bucks said his cheeks were redder than mine.

"Where is Doc?" I asked to change the subject.

"He escaped to the Rec Center," Cooper said, nudging me aside so he could refill his coffee cup. "It takes a lot of strength to wake up next to you every morning and face off with that hair of yours."

When I threatened him with my fist, he chuckled and held up his hands in surrender.

Doc's almost-daily trips to the Rec Center had more to do with the stress of being a mental medium with a nose for sniffing out ghosts in a town notorious for its overcrowded ectoplasmic population than putting up with my crazy curls. Then again, thinking about the worry lining Doc's face in the dash lights as we drove home from the taxidermy shop last night, me and my "wild hairs" might be inspiring some extra adrenaline rushes for him these days.

"So, what's got you takin' up fisticuffs right out of the sack, Sparky?" Harvey pulled a chocolate chip cookie from Aunt Zoe's old Betty Boop cookie jar in the middle of the table and settled back into his chair.

I returned to my brain fuel, dumping enough sugar in it to light my rocket for a good hour or two. "It's your nephew's fault."

"What did I do?" Cooper frowned at me over his cup.

"Besides comparing me to a clown?" I took a sip of coffee and recoiled slightly. Holy hairy chest, that was strong stuff! Someone must have added an extra big scoop to the brew for more oomph. After yesterday's hoopla, I needed to soften the caffeine blow to my stomach.

"For one thing," I said on the way to the fridge. "You wouldn't let me leave last night when I wanted to get the hell out of there, insisting that I stay for an extra hour in the freezing cold while you played Sherlock Holmes."

"If the perpetrator who broke into Jonesy's shop had decided to return for more chew toys, you needed to be there, *Executioner*."

Cooper's reminder of my other job—killing troublemakers—drew a sigh from me. All right, so he had a good reason to keep me around until all of the other officers had cleared out, but still ...

"Couldn't you have waited until morning to be so dang thorough? Hell, I'm surprised you didn't pull on a pair of rubber gloves and check poor Garth and his fat ol' dog for polyps."

Harvey chortled and reached for another cookie while I grabbed the milk from the fridge.

"Welcome to Police Procedures 101, Parker." Cooper returned to his post next to the sink. "Unlike *your* investigation methods, which seem to involve pins, blindfolds, and donkey tails most days, I like to turn over every leaf before exiting a fresh crime scene."

I poured milk into my mug until the coffee almost spilled over the rim. "*Second*," I said through clenched teeth, "you're here in my aunt's kitchen right now instead of Doc, and he doesn't make fun of my hair."

"You started it today." Cooper crossed his arms. "You're just mad because I finished it."

"Yer stallion took the younguns to school so you could get some extra beauty sleep on your big day off." Harvey grinned and took another bite of cookie. "Judgin' from those red lines crisscrossing yer eyeballs, you could use another hour or two to get the job done."

I pointed a threatening finger the old buzzard's way before turning back to Cooper's steady stare. "And third, if you're in my face first thing in the morning …"

He scoffed. "It's almost nine o'clock, Parker. That's not 'first thing.' "

"*That* means you're here to piss on my parade," I continued. I didn't even get to take a victory lap last night after kicking some Hungarian devil ass, darn it. "Now I'm figuring that you probably came over here to order me to help you find your three-limbed 'perpetrator,' but since nobody got hurt last night, I have more important matters to deal with first."

His jaw tightened. "More important than heading off one of your damned *others* before we have another bizarre homicide on our hands?"

"They aren't *my* damned *others*, Cooper."

"You do realize that if someone gets killed, we'll have Detective Hawke lodged even farther up our asses, not to mention the FBI."

I made a face at the name of Cooper's partner in crime-solving. Detective Stone Hawke … a man whose ego would overshadow King Kong's.

Unfortunately, Hawke and I had gotten off on the wrong foot right out of the gate when I'd stomped on his silly pen. I probably shouldn't have threatened to grind his pea-sized balls into dust under my boot heel at the time, but in my defense, I'd been having a bad day, and he'd made the dumbass choice of insulting my hair along with my intelligence. Things between us had spiraled southward from there.

Currently, Hawke believed that I was the top suspect in several of the unsolved murder cases sitting on his desk. *And* that I was a witch—the ugly potion-making kind with grand plans to spread evil throughout the Black Hills; not the cute mini-skirt wearing ones who fixed spilled-milk messes with a nose wiggle and a blink.

Oh, and he was also under the illusion that I could see and talk to ghosts, but that misconception was partly Natalie's fault for encouraging me to …

"What could possibly be more important?" Cooper interrupted, bringing me back to the present. "Getting your nails done for your damned television debut on Sunday?"

"No, you big robot chicken." Oh dear, I needed more caffeine before I threw out any additional insults.

I swallowed a gulp of coffee, trying not to get sidetracked by my anxieties about the *Paranormal Realty* television show that mixed ghost hunting with house selling, in which I'd unhappily co-starred recently that could possibly be the end of my career selling real estate. Or at the least, the end of selling houses to normal people rather than ghost groupies.

"For your information, detective, I have an imp to catch, and from what I've been told that's not going to be—" The telephone hanging on the wall rang, interrupting my excuse for a moment. "Easy."

Coffee in hand, I headed over to the table and dropped into the seat opposite Cookie Monster's bearded twin. "What's the story on these walkie-talkies?" I asked Harvey.

I picked one up. It felt solid and sturdy, unlike the set my father had given the kids. The black rubber edging acted as grip protection against an accidental drop.

The phone rang again.

"Coop's frettin' about keepin' our chit-chats top secret. Says he don't trust cell phones much anymore, especially yours. Some nosy-nelly might be listenin' in."

Cooper had previously had me create a texting group, including Doc and me and a few others in our little circle of comrades, for emergency-only communication purposes when it came to dealing with possible "perps." Apparently, he'd leveled up to the paranoia zone in the game.

The phone rang again.

"So one of these is for me?" I asked, pushing the black buttons on the front of the device. The digital screen remained dark.

"Aren't you going to get that, Parker?" Cooper asked, thumbing toward the wall phone.

"No. If it's the school, they'd call my cell phone." I pushed a button on the side of the walkie-talkie, but nothing happened. "And Jerry gave me the day off, remember? In spite of your attempt to ruin my day before it even gets rolling, I'm going to sit here and enjoy my coffee along with your uncle's rated-PG company." I nailed Harvey with a gunslinger glare. "That means no cringe-inducing anecdotes about busty babes from any Nevada cat houses."

The phone rang for a fourth time.

I pulled my cell phone from my robe pocket and checked for missed calls just to be sure. Nope. If someone really needed to talk to me, like Doc or Natalie or one of my parents, they'd call my cell phone.

"What about a yarn from the poke parlor?"

"No." I stuffed my phone back in my pocket.

"Tales from the bunny ranch?"

"Still no." I pushed another button on the walkie-talkie. Nothing, same as before.

"How about eye-poppin' adventures from the bouncy house?"

The phone started to ring for the fifth time, only to stop midway through.

Either the caller had given up, or Aunt Zoe had picked up the call out in her glass workshop where she was working on another wedding order. This time, her creations were unique, rose-colored champagne glasses for each member of the bridal party, the bride and groom's families, as well as several of the guests. Apparently, the soon-to-be-married couple were counting on some extra rosy optimism to give their wedded bliss a boost.

Cooper came closer, looming over us like an ominous thundercloud. "Parker, we need to come up with a plan on how to catch whatever that thing was that broke into Jonesy's shop last night."

I sighed, scratching my thumbnail down the rubbery side of the walkie-talkie. "I told you already, I have an imp to catch."

"Is there some special Executioner rule that says you can only hunt one asshole at a time?"

"No, but I'm a little busy with all of the hoopla my boss is insisting we do to prepare for Sunday's TV premiere party."

We were down to just three more days until Jerry's big ghoul-themed shindig with all sorts of hoity-toity guests and several big-screen televisions where I would get to watch my career swirl down the crapper without needing to squint. I'd tried to bow out of it more than once, but Jerry had me by the collar and was dragging me into the limelight whether I liked it or not. Three more days. Crikey!

Cooper harrumphed. "Like I said, painting your nails."

I wrinkled my nose at him. "Don't you have a criminal somewhere to chase, law dog?"

Harvey leaned forward and fished out another cookie, offering it to me. "He's hopin' to chase some tail first." He winked at me. "You know, the female sort."

Grinning, I grabbed the cookie and dipped it in my coffee before taking a bite. The chocolate was soft and sweet— nothing like the detective breathing down my neck.

Harvey pulled out a cookie for himself. "Ain't Natalie supposed to be here soon?"

"Not until later. She had to run down to Rapid this morning."

Cooper snatched the cookie out of his uncle's hand. "You're confusing me for you, Uncle Willis. I'm here about

Jonesy's B&E. This has nothing to do with Nat's whereabouts." He took a big bite out of the cookie and grunted before stuffing the rest in his mouth.

Uh oh. Cooper didn't typically eat sugar or anything else that might sweeten his disposition. For him, all-out laughter was a sign that he was fraying at the edges. So, a cookie at breakfast meant one of two things—either hooking up with Natalie was having some weird chemical effect on his brain, similar to the Tin Man when he got a real heart; or Cooper had reached an all-new level of stress thanks to the three-limbed *other* starring in last night's crime scene.

The detective reached for a second cookie. "I don't give a shit about your fancy party, Parker. You're going to have to find a way to fit apprehending this three-limbed perp into your busy superstar schedule."

Cooper was right and I knew it, but was it asking too much to have just one damned day off before I started thinking about a creepy fiend that had gone around taking bites out of those poor stuffed critters?

I shuddered again at the whole freaky mess and took another drink of coffee while pushing one more button on the walkie-talkie. The screen lit up blue. "Hey, I found the 'on' button."

Cooper grabbed the walkie-talkie away from me. "We need to catch that thing before it takes a bite out of someone who's still breathing." He reached for the cookie jar. "That is far more important than any fucking—"

The back door flew open and Aunt Zoe rushed in along with a bone-chilling gust of wind. Her old work shirt and blue jeans were smudged with soot streaks and dirty palm prints. Several tendrils of her silver-streaked hair had escaped her leather tie and swirled around her face.

After a glance my way, she shut the back door. "Get dressed, Violet. We have to go."

Before I could blink, she rushed into the laundry room,

rustling around in there out of sight. Something clanged, followed by a grunt and then several curses.

What the hell?

I shivered and pulled my robe tighter around me, calling after her, "Go where, Aunt Zoe?"

"To Lead," she said, hurrying back into the kitchen while rubbing her elbow. She'd changed into a black cable-knit sweater and a clean pair of jeans. "That was Dominick Masterson on the phone. He has requested your presence." When I continued to sit there frowning up at her, she added, "And when I say 'requested,' I mean 'demanded.' You know how Masterson is."

I sure did.

Shit!

Dominick Masterson was trouble with a capital T. No, make that three capital Ts. He was an old spirit, and by that I didn't mean he liked watching black-and-white silent films and listening to 1920s ragtime music. For one thing, Dominick wasn't human. (I'd once heard him referred to as a "guardian," but I wasn't sure what that entailed.) For another thing, he wasn't simply a regular old *other* either. Slick, dangerously charming, and wily as all get out, he was neither my enemy nor my friend, but I had to work with him nonetheless.

Dominick had been around the Black Hills for a long time—how long? I had no idea and he wasn't selling his secrets. But something told me that he'd been here long enough to know the answer to why there was a three-limbed bogeyman running around the hills taking bites out of anything it could get its teeth on, so I should probably heed his call and find out what he wanted. Not to mention that it was his ugly little imp that I'd accidentally freed and had to somehow catch before it made an even bigger mess than it already had up in Lead.

However, there was the teeny-tiny fact that I'd just

executed his prized pet *lidérc* last night without his permission ... or even his knowledge. I'd hoped to have a bit more time to practice my game face in the mirror before Dominick figured out the Hungarian devil had gone missing from its ward-secured cage up in the Sugarloaf Building. But it appeared I'd missed the gravy train with its biscuit wheels this time, dang it.

I cowered slightly behind my coffee mug. "Do you think he already knows that I killed his smoky bastard?"

She shrugged. "He refused to clarify his purpose for calling while we were on the phone, claiming that eavesdropping had become a popular sport these days."

Eavesdropping? I frowned at the walkie-talkies on the table. Was someone trying to ear-hustle my phone conversations? As in a certain delusional detective who was probably trying to get a warrant at this very moment to prove I had a troupe of flying monkeys hidden away in Aunt Zoe's attic right next to a pentagram made with virgin's blood?

I squinted up at Cooper. "What aren't you telling us about these walkie-talkies?"

"That they take lithium batteries." He shrugged off my middle-finger salute. "The rest is police business, Parker."

"I'm going to cram your police business up your—"

"Violet," Aunt Zoe cut in, squeezing my shoulder. Along with a whiff of lavender soap coming from her, I could smell the familiar, musty scent of the thick, sleeve-like glove she used to protect her hand while heating the glass in the furnace. "Finish your coffee."

Calmed momentarily by her comforting scent, I lifted the mug to my mouth and swallowed the rest of my grumbling along with the last of my coffee.

"As soon as you're finished," she added, "you need to hurry up and get dressed. You and me and Harvey are going to see what that charming son of a bitch is up to now."

Lowering my cup, I hesitated for a couple of reasons. To

start with, it was my day off, damn it. To end with, Aunt Zoe had a history of extreme vulnerability when it came to Masterson's previous Don Juan endeavors.

Harvey took the cookie jar from Cooper, reaching inside for more sweets. "Why are ya draggin' me along? It's colder than a polar bear's toenails out there with that darn vortex swirlin' down from the North Pole."

"Yeah, what he said." I raised my empty mug in agreement.

She stole the cookie jar from Harvey, knocking his hand away as he tried to reach for it again, and set the jar back in the center of the table. "Because other than Violet and Doc, you're the only one I know who's immune to Masterson's mind games." She put the lid on the jar with a firm *clunk*.

One of Dominick's tricks was what I referred to as his "charm" spell. It didn't involve any fancy potions or magic, though. All it took was a simple smiling look from the slickster for women—and men—to become fawning zombies, happy to do whatever Dominick desired.

For some reason, though, that charm bullshit didn't work on Harvey. We had yet to figure out why that was, but for now it was to my advantage since the old trigger-happy boy was my bodyguard. When it came to Doc, his ancient Oracle bloodline shielded him from Masterson's powerful mojo.

As for me, Dominick's nearness alone spurred a warning reflex of revulsion mixed with a good dose of nausea. As secret weapons went, feeling the need to upchuck when my enemies came near wasn't very cool. Neither was the fact that those in my trade supposedly smelled of "death," according to some of the non-humans I'd met of late. I wasn't sure if that meant I reeked as badly as five-day-old roadkill, or if the scent I gave off was a little mellower, like a bin full of dirty socks and sweaty underwear. Or rotten eggs.

Why couldn't I smell like sugar and spice and everything nice like the other girls?

"I'm gonna freeze my twig-and-berries off, woman," Harvey groused, brushing the crumbs out of his beard.

"You sure this is a good idea, Zoe?" The line of barbed wire and fence posts across Cooper's forehead said there were plenty of reasons it was a bad idea in his opinion. "Maybe we should get Nyce to go in your place."

"Cooper's right," I told her. "Your history with Dominick makes me nervous about having you along." The asshole had shown more than once the power he had over Aunt Zoe with just the wink of an eye. I aimed my coffee mug at her. "Let's call that sneaky snake back and tell him we'll meet him when we're good and ready."

She snatched the mug out of my hand and glared down at me. "We both know that meeting with Dominick Masterson is never a good idea, but he insisted on *my* presence along with yours, so we're both going to talk to him and we're doing it now. Besides, this is a good test."

That must be why Dominick had called here at the house rather than on my cell phone. What was his angle with dragging my aunt along?

Cooper's face creased even more. "I think you need some backup besides Uncle Willis."

Harvey slapped his hand on the table, delivering his verdict. "Coop's right. I'll take Bessie. She's all spit-shined and ready for a good ol' Pecos promenade."

"Your shotgun is useless against Dominick," I reminded him.

"Maybe fer you, girlie, but Bessie gooses my gumption."

Aunt Zoe carried my mug over to the sink. "While I appreciate your concern, Coop, I'll have the best weapon there is against Masterson standing next to me." She returned to my side, smiling down at me. "Our very own *Scharfrichter*."

I groaned at the guttural-sounding German word for my killing trade along with the responsibility that came with the title.

Cooper seconded my groan. "Now I'm really worried."

"But Aunt Zoe, what about—"

"I'm done discussing this, baby girl." She grabbed my arm and hauled me to my feet. "Go get dressed. And don't forget to grab an extra backbone or two while you're at it." She nudged me toward the stairs. "There's no telling which way the mule is gonna jump."

Chapter Three

Speaking of mules …

"I don't want to do this," I told Aunt Zoe on our way out of Deadwood.

She spared me a quick frown from behind the steering wheel of my SUV, which I'd let her drive since she knew where we were heading.

Before she could finish that frown with a "Buck up, baby girl," or something else motivational about facing off with a slippery scoundrel on a blustery January morning, Harvey spoke from the backseat. "You remind me of a stubborn-assed hinny my aunt had back when I was still growin' potatoes behind my ears."

"Are you comparing me to a donkey now?" I turned in my seat to glare at him.

"I said a *hin-ny*," Harvey enunciated.

Aunt Zoe chuckled. "That's a step up from a heifer."

According to whom?

"A hinny is a mix between a stallion and a jenny," Harvey continued.

"Jennies are female donkeys," Aunt Zoe explained.

"So, you're comparing me to a hinny then." I continued my glare, not sure that was any better than a donkey.

Harvey grinned wide enough for his two gold teeth to show. "That hinny had the hardest hooves I ever did see. Kicked a hole clear through her stall door once after my aunt shut her inside for eatin' a path through her prized sunflowers. Woo-wee! I tell you, when that girl got herself in a lather, she raised hell and stuck a block under it."

I still wasn't certain if I was one step up from heifer yet in his assessment. "What's this have to do with me not wanting to go talk to Dominick?"

"Like that ol' hinny, you got yer hooves dug in this mornin'. Look at you, tuggin' at the rope and you don't even have a notion of what Masterson wants. For all you know, maybe he plans to pat you on the head and tell you what a good job yer doin'."

"So, you think I'm being stubborn?" He could have just said that. "Like your aunt's mu … I mean, hinny."

"Oh, that hinny was worse than yer typical stubborn mule, but a helluva lot smarter, too. She could smell trouble from a mile away, but wouldn't scare like any horse. Nope. She'd just lower her head and face whatever was comin'."

"So, you think I'm stubborn but smart and don't scare easily?"

"Nah, I've seen you jump at chickens in the dark."

Aunt Zoe laughed.

"That's not fair." I scowled at both of them in turn. "There was a juggernaut coming for me that night." Well, as far as I had it figured, anyway. That damned chicken of Addy's had nearly given me a heart attack. Elvis was lucky I didn't coat her in flour and fry her up for breakfast the next morning.

Harvey's grin reached his earlobes. "Beware of Elvis the killer chicken! You're such a big bad *Scharfrichter*."

"Shut it, old man." I wrinkled my nose at him before turning back toward the front, adding over my shoulder, "Or I'll feed you to that damned three-limbed ghoulie from last night."

"Now there's no need to get all het up about things." He sniffed. "All I was sayin' is that yer stubborn like that ol' hinny."

"Yeah, yeah, yeah."

"But what most don't understand," he continued, leaning forward over the center console so that his head butted into the front of the cab between Aunt Zoe and me, "is that hinnies and mules have a strong sense of self-preservation. They don't like to follow you into dangerous situations, a feelin' most folks confuse for stubbornness."

"That's definitely better than being a heifer," Aunt Zoe told me as we passed Gold Run Park on the left.

The park sat tucked away in the valley below the old Yates mineshaft headframe. I'd taken the kids there last fall to play around on the mining castoffs left over from yesteryear.

A century-plus of gold booms and busts had left plenty of scars behind in Lead, evident both on the landscape underneath the town's buildings and houses, as well as above. The terraced park now sitting where many of the Homestake Mine Company's buildings had slowly decayed for decades was a prime example.

Still staring out the window, I told my cab mates, "The hinny in me says this is a bad idea. If Dominick has already figured out that I executed his *lidérc* last night, he's going to want something in return."

At the least, I figured he'd ask for some sort of bizarre retribution. At worst, he'd want a life for a life, and that was where my hinny-ness would undoubtedly land me up to my hips in alligators. I highly doubted he'd hear me out on my reasoning for killing his deadly "pet." Nor would he understand why I refused to allow the *lidérc* to remain in its ward-lined cage, where it could escape yet again and come for me and mine.

Harvey grunted. "Did Masterson sound like he was in a horn-tossing mood on the phone, Zoe?"

"I couldn't tell. But he's very good at keeping his cool no

matter the circumstances. When Reid punched him during the Chamber of Commerce's Christmas party last month, the silver-tongued devil took the hit and kept on smiling, just as cold and smooth as the ice in his veins."

Aunt Zoe had come home from that party in a huff, ready to start throwing dishes at the wall, as well as at a couple of hostile males. Instead, she'd done as she always had when she needed to vent some steam—gone out to her workshop and fired up her glass furnace.

Out the windshield, the visitor center that overlooked the Open Cut came into view. Decades ago, after digging deep into the earth under the Black Hills in pursuit of gold, Homestake had opted for an alternate method of extracting the precious metal from the ground—open-pit mining. Many, many trips around the sun later, the Open Cut remained as a reminder of those golden days of the past. Now Mother Nature was at work instead of the miners, weathering the terraced sides of the huge pit year after year, working slowly but surely at softening the sharp edges the mining company had left behind.

Up on the hillside rimming the Open Cut I could see the beautiful historic house where a particularly crotchety ghost had resided for well over a century, supposedly waiting for me to show up and continue where she'd left off—executing troublemakers. Was Prudence watching over the huge hole in the earth from her perch up in the attic window? Could she sense I was near? Was there some connection growing between us that explained how she seemed to know more and more about what I was up to when she wasn't around?

"Hell, maybe Masterson just wants to shoot the shit with you two." Harvey leaned back. "His long life has gotta be lonely most days. There's only so much hard liquor and wild women a man can enjoy until there's nothin' else left to make your ticker giddy up and gallop."

I guffawed. "You don't really believe that, do you?"

"Not for a minute," he shot back without hesitation. "I've yet to get tired of wild women."

Harvey's reputation down at the senior center backed that statement. "I meant the part about Dominick looking for companionship."

"Maybe a wee bit, but mostly not."

"What about you?" I asked Aunt Zoe.

She glanced my way. "Your eye is twitching."

"That's not an answer."

Harvey leaned forward again, checking on me. "Sparky does look like she's chewing her bit more than usual."

"I do not look like I'm chewing ..." I finished with a growl and flipped my visor down, staring at my reflection in the lighted mirror. Okay, so my curls were poking out every which way below the red beanie I'd pulled over my bedhead mess. And maybe I should have spent a few minutes putting on some makeup to cover the blue, green, and yellowish bruises of my fading black eye instead of watching that funny video of cats freaking out over cucumbers that Natalie had sent me. I smiled wide in the reflection. At least I'd made sure to brush my teeth and wipe the cookie crumbs off my lips before leaving the house.

I slammed the visor up, aiming a mock glare at Aunt Zoe. "You should have given me more time to fix this up." I circled my hand in front of my face.

"You look as beautiful as always," she lied.

"Your nose is growing."

Grinning, she rolled along a few more blocks and then made a left turn and started up the steep hill behind the historic opera house.

"Almost there," she said.

"Almost where?" I asked, holding onto the dash as we bounced through a series of ovary-rattling potholes.

"You'll see."

Two turns later, she pulled into the deserted parking lot

of a weather-worn, three-story brick building. Thick gray clouds darkened the sky behind it, adding a hair-raising feel to the scene. No sooner than we'd parked, a swirling vortex of snow whipped through the chain-link fence edging the lot. It raced toward us, careening into my SUV and peppering the windshield with tiny pellets of ice and grit.

"Mother Nature needs to fire her welcoming committee," I grumbled, wondering if my paint job was now speckled.

I focused back on the crumbling stack of bricks and mortar in front of us. Creepy crawlies! Couldn't Dominick have chosen a meeting place that felt a little less like a mass murderer's lair?

Harvey popped up between us again. "Sort of looks like hell with everyone out to lunch," he whispered, frowning out the windshield. "You know, maybe Sparky is right about this here meetin'. Maybe we should call off this cat-and-mouse game on account of potential cardiac arrest."

"Was this a school?" I asked, whispering as well.

Aunt Zoe killed the engine. "It's the old middle school."

"Never did like this place," Harvey added. "Too many bitter memories chock-full of complex fractions and confusin' adverbs." He peered out the windshield. "Place has been closed up for a few decades. Probably dark as coffin air inside."

"Harvey, could you please refrain from trying to scare the crap out of me before we even step inside?" I sat forward, peering out at the old school.

The lower-level windows were mostly boarded up, except for the arched tops, which looked like dark eyes watching us. Several of the upper-story panes were smashed out, the sills rimmed with what my imagination decided were razor-sharp glass teeth. The brickwork on each story was stained rusty brown below broken downspouts and under fragmented pieces of what were once elaborate cornices.

Paint peeled from the rotting and sagging window and door frames. Large, spiderweb-like cracks lined the concrete steps and foundation around the two sets of red double doors chained closed on each side of the building. Dead weeds poked out through cracks in the foundation and surrounding sidewalk, while dirty patches of snow formed islands in the fractured-asphalt parking lot.

I crossed my fingers and toes that Dominick pulled a no-show on us. "If he isn't here in five min …"

A black Land Rover rolled to a stop a couple of car lengths away.

Oh, balls!

"Snap my garter and call me Pussycat," Harvey said. "Looks like the show's about to start."

Dominick stepped out of his vehicle wearing a long black trench coat, looking every bit as dark and dangerous as the Devil's shadow. His mirrored sunglasses hid his eyes when he glanced in our direction. Without a nod or a wave or a simple "Thanks for taking time during your day off to rush over here and play patty-cake with me in a heebie-jeebie-inspiring, probably haunted school," he headed toward the far set of red doors. Another gust of wind rocked the vehicle and then swirled along behind him, sweeping dust and snow from the asphalt as it trailed in his wake.

"Are we supposed to follow?" My breath fogged up the passenger window as I watched him make quick work of the chains securing the double doors.

"You two are," Harvey said. "As for yours truly, I think the wisest decision would be to stay put and hold down the fort. You know, keep the getaway vehicle warm and ready to roll."

I scoffed. "Try again, bodyguard."

Dominick pulled open one of the doors. He stepped inside the shadowy building and then turned, staring out at us as the door closed.

Jeepers! This was getting Scooby-Doo spooky.

"You ready for this, Aunt Zoe?"

"As ready as I can be."

I worried my lower lip. "What if he tries to use his charms on—"

"He promised on the phone that he wouldn't," she interrupted. "He said you'd fulfilled your end of the bargain when you captured the *lidérc*, so he would keep to the agreement."

"Yeah, but that was before I sent his *lidérc* to the hereafter that's specially reserved for really mean monsters."

"We'll cross that bridge when we come to it, baby girl." She reached for the door handle. "Let's go find out what he wants."

I joined her outside, pulling my collar tight when a blast of frigid air rocked me to my heels. Harvey was right—this was twig-and-berries freezing weather.

As Harvey eased out from the back seat, I told him. "Leave Bessie here for now. We don't need you shooting at shadows in there and somebody calling the cops with a 'possible gunshot' report." The last person I wanted to have to deal with on my day off was Detective Hawke. Dominick was enough of a pain in the rump.

Harvey huffed. "Fine, spoilsport." He slid his shotgun under the seat and shut the back door.

The three of us hurried across the lot. I held the door for my aunt and Harvey, but then had to struggle against a blast of grit-laden wind determined to drag the door back outside and me along with it.

"Holy crowly moly!" I took off my hat, shaking the dust and snow out of my curls after barely winning the tug-of-war battle. I waited for my pupils to adjust to the darkness, glad I wasn't standing alone in the murky hallway. "Is it just me, or does this school have some bad juju going on." I wiped off my face, wondering if buildings could have auras like people.

If so, I'd bet this one's was dark gray. "I feel about as welcome as a tornado on a trail drive."

Harvey let out a grunt. "Quit stealin' my lines."

"I borrowed that one from Natalie, not you." I pulled my hat back on my head.

A cold draft swirled around us, smelling of damp concrete and a mustiness left behind after years of wear and tear from generations of children.

"Yeah, well she stole it from me when we were down in Arizona over New Year's." He jammed his hands in his coat pockets, hunching his shoulders. "I sure hope I don't run into the ghosts of any of my ol' schoolmarms in here. I sorta had the tendency to rile the wagon master now and then, if you catch my meanin'."

Aunt Zoe rubbed her hands together. "I imagine putting socks on Elvis the chicken would've been easier than corralling you back then, Willis."

Farther down the hallway where the shadows were still too thick to see through, I could hear the sound of water dripping. Closer, on the right, a shaft of daylight spilled out through an open doorway.

Harvey sniffed, and then sniffed again. "Somethin' is startin' to smell sour in here. Sort of like a bagful of sweaty jockstraps."

"Oh, ick." I made a face at him. "How would you know what that smells like?"

"That's a silly question." He sniffed again. "It's gettin' stronger. Can you smell it?"

"I don't smell anything like that," Aunt Zoe said.

I could. Rotten potatoes came to mind, though, not sweaty jockstraps.

A small ripple of nausea spread up from my stomach. Hold on, I knew that feeling well enough. I squinted into the shadows, seeing something move ever so slightly.

I moved quickly, shielding my aunt with my body. "What

do you want, Dominick?" I spoke more harshly than usual, not in the mood for a game of hide-and-seek in what was most likely yet another haunted building in Lead.

"Relax, *Scharfrichter*." Dominick stepped forward into the light spilling through the open doorway, but his face remained half in the shadows. "We're not here to test your skills today."

"Then why are we here?"

He pulled off his gloves one at a time before speaking. "Join me." Then, without another word, he disappeared through the open doorway.

I hesitated, holding onto Aunt Zoe's arm, waiting for my gut to decide if this was some sort of trap or not. "I don't like this," I whispered.

"Neither do I," Harvey said next to me. "That's a math classroom he went into. My knees used to get shaky every time I stepped through that do—"

"Shhhh!" I cut him off, holding my finger to my lips. I thought I heard something coming toward us from the shadows farther down the hall.

There it was again. A quiet scuffing sound. Then the swish of something being dragged along the tile floor. Then another scuff.

What was coming our way? Was it dead or alive? And what was being dragged? Was it even human?

Never mind. I wasn't going to wait around for answers. "Come on."

I nudged Harvey toward the shaft of light and hauled Aunt Zoe along beside me, ushering them through the open doorway first. After one last hard look into the deep shadows, I joined them in a large, rectangular room with mouse-chewed boxes, a few wooden chairs, and several broken school desks cluttering the corners. Large chunks of plaster had fallen from the high ceiling, making a patchwork on the dusty, wood slab floor.

Veiled light glowed through the arched tops of several partially boarded-up windows running the length of one wall. Water stains splotched the warped, wooden sills under them. A long, rusted radiator filled the space between two of the windows, its heating days long gone.

In the far corner, Dominick sat on the edge of a school desk near a stack of boxes that were hemorrhaging faded textbooks from gaping seams. With his ankles crossed and his hands in his coat pockets, he appeared to be at ease. But there was a cagey glint in his gaze that said differently.

Harvey moved over to a pile of books near one of the windows, leaning down for a closer look.

"Why did you choose to have us meet you here?" I asked Dominick, catching sight of a mouse darting from one of the boxes over to the radiator.

He shrugged. "I wanted to ensure our privacy and I needed to look into a situation here. The best course was to kill two birds with one stone."

I preferred that killing be totally off the table today. After all, it was my day of rest.

A high-pitched screech came from the hallway.

I aimed a wrinkled brow toward the open door, waiting for something to lurch into view. Was that Dominick's "situation" or something else? I should have brought a weapon with me. At the least, a baseball bat or a …

Something slammed, echoing throughout the building.

My heart scrambled up into my throat. My bladder was probably one more scare away from springing a leak. Damn it! I wasn't in the mood for this haunted school baloney.

I focused back on our host. "Okay, Dominick. You snapped your fingers and we jumped. What do you want?"

He eyed me for several seconds. "You're not much of a morning person, are you, Violet?"

"Mornings are for the birds, especially in the winter, and I've been told somewhat recently that I'm more of a mule."

"I said a 'hinny,'" Harvey corrected, returning to my side. "Yer too ornery to be a mule."

The hinny in me tried to poke him in the ribs, but the old mongoose in him dodged just in time.

"Got yer tail up, don't I?" He snickered. "Now stop tryin' to kick holes in stall doors and pay attention. I have a feelin' that Masterson is about to talk a blue streak any minute now, and I'm not sure how long my prostate will hold out in this chilly nightmare."

Dominick waited for us to finish and then turned to Aunt Zoe. "You brought extra company, darling. You disobeyed the instructions I gave you on the phone."

"Willis is Violet's shadow," Aunt Zoe explained in a tone that was meant to put an end to further discussion on the matter.

He raised one black eyebrow in my direction. "And where is the rest of your entourage?"

"Here and there." That was none of his concern. "Enough with the chitchat, Dominick. Why are we here?"

He pulled his hands from his coat pockets and clasped them together. "It has been brought to my attention that you have a formidable problem looming, *Scharfrichter.*"

Chapter Four

A formidable problem? *Just one?!!*
My snort of disbelief sounded loud in the mostly empty classroom. I had a full-on, Level 5 on the Fujita scale, clusterfuck of problems brewing, according to Prudence-the-dead-Executioner.

And Prudence wasn't the only one who'd spoken of doom and gloom in my future. No sirree. I had bad omens playing chicken with me more often than not.

Take old Ms. Wolff, who'd warned me about too many cages being opened last fall. I didn't fully understand what that "cages" business meant at the time, nor did I now, but I got the gist of her shit's-about-to-hit-the-fan message. It'd been hard to miss while she was blackmailing me into executing her so that I could assume her Timekeeper skills. Skills supposedly needed for the upcoming battles with especially problematic troublemakers. Skills that I had yet to figure out how to use in order to save my own ass, let alone anyone else's.

Then there was … never mind. Now was not the time to stroll down memory lane.

Ignoring Aunt Zoe's raised eyebrows, I told him, "I'm flush with problems, Dominick."

Although less so than I had been before I took care of his damned *lidérc*. At least I'd thought so before this little classroom meeting. However, judging by the tension visible on his usually schooled features, I might have escaped the frying pan only to land in the fire.

"Which problem in particular has you calling me at the buttcrack of dawn?"

"It wasn't really dawn when he called," Aunt Zoe said.

"Some of us had been up long enough by that time to need a catnap," Harvey added.

I shushed both of them at once.

"I'm referring to the situation involving a local taxidermist," Dominick said.

I tried to keep surprise from showing on my face. Hell, it hadn't even been 24 hours since I'd left the scene of that crime. "How do you know about that?"

"I have my ways, *Scharfrichter*. Same as you."

Same as me? Ha! He must not know about my tendency to seek counsel from my Magic 8 Ball.

He zeroed in on Aunt Zoe and said something in a foreign language that went in one of my ears and out the other. I did manage to recognize two words, though: *magistra* and *Nachzehrer*.

Magistra was the Latin word for a female teacher. It was also a title handed down through our family line, given to those who were enlisted to train a *Scharfrichter*. His use of that particular word had me wondering if Aunt Zoe had let it slip about her family "duty" at some point last month when he'd wooed her with his charming spell. Or had he somehow read her mind? And was his familiarity with this term even something I should be concerned about?

As for the other word I'd picked up, since he knew about last night's events at Jones' Taxidermy, I wasn't really surprised to hear him talk about the *Nachzehrer*.

I watched my aunt, waiting to see if she replied in Latin or in plain old English so that Harvey and I could follow along.

Her blue eyes held mine for several seconds before she

said, "There is not much written about that particular foe. Violet knows that according to German folklore, the creature is similar to a vampire, only it consumes human flesh rather than drinks their blood."

Dominick raised one dark eyebrow. "That is the extent of your knowledge in this matter?"

"Not quite. It's written that the creature is a reanimated human corpse, although there is no cause listed to explain the occurrence."

I watched Dominick for some sort of reaction to her words, but he held his cards close to his vest.

Aunt Zoe continued, "There was also one account that claimed if you are bitten by a *Nachzehrer*, you will turn into one as well. Although this borders on implausible if you ask me."

I snorted yet again, drawing all three pairs of eyes.

"Is there something wrong with your nose, Violet Lynn?"

"Yer startin' to remind me of my momma's favorite pig, Lulubelle." Harvey pursed his lips. "That girl always had her snout buried in somebody else's shi—"

"Harvey!" I cut short his Old MacDonald tale of yet another alleged spirit animal of mine. For chrissake, why couldn't he compare me to something less barnyard-ish like a cheetah? Better yet, a unicorn.

Returning to my aunt and Dominick, I held up my hands. "Doesn't anyone else find this *Nachzehrer* crap far-fetched besides me? I mean, we're basically talking about zombies here as if they're real."

"A *Nachzehrer* is no voodoo-created monster from Haitian folklore, *Scharfrichter*," Dominick said without a hint of mirth. "Nor is it some fictional, brain-hungry fiend from Hollywood." He shook his head slowly. "These particular terrors that you must hunt and execute are remarkably more menacing and savage. They would like nothing more than to gut you and revel in your blood and entrails."

"Oh, is that all?" I barely held in a third snort. "And here I was worried that a *Nachzehrer* would want to cuddle with me under a blanket next to a campfire and maybe sing a few verses of 'Kumbaya' *a cappella*."

Harvey snickered. "I think Bobby Pickett's 'Monster Mash' would be more likely to tickle their turnip, don't you, Zoe?"

"It'd be a graveyard smash," Aunt Zoe shot back a line from the song.

I rolled my eyes. "You two are about as funny as a block of wood."

Dominick cleared his throat. "Is this the extent of your knowledge, *Magistra*?"

Aunt Zoe shrugged, tugging off one glove. "According to an old book I found on mythical creatures, it is believed the *Nachzehrer* eats its own death shroud immediately upon re-awakening." She took off her other glove and stuffed both in her pockets. "Truth be told, though, I have trouble believing that it would eat a burial cloth."

"Don't forget about havin' to cut off its head and to shove a copper coin in its mouth to kill it," Harvey chimed in. "Or maybe it was the other way around—first you put the copper coin in its mouth, then you have to cut off the head." He scratched his chin through his beard. "Although it might be tough to put the coin in the bugger's mouth if it's still chompin' away. Sort of like tryin' to pet a shark when yer wearin' chum-dipped mittens."

I frowned in his direction.

He winked back.

Dominick moved over to the shelf-like windowsill, sitting partway on it, one foot dangling. His black pants were made of fine wool, I could tell in spite of the ten feet or so separating us. And those shoes of his were most likely Italian-made. His whole ensemble was rather extravagant, especially for a visit to a derelict middle school in Lead. If he was going to keep calling clandestine meetings like this, he really should try to blend in better.

He fiddled with a broken piece of plaster on the sill next to him. "I find it amusing how facts are twisted over time until they resemble nothing even close to the truth." He didn't look amused, though. More disgusted, judging from that curl in his upper lip.

"So the myths are wrong," Aunt Zoe snapped. "Unless you insisted we rush up here to rub our noses in our ignorance, stop wasting our time and share what you know about Violet's newest problem."

Dominick's gaze turned downright predatory. "I do admire the fire in you, Zoe. We could have been extraordinary together."

Aunt Zoe's eyes narrowed. "No more game playing, Dominick. You gave me your word."

He faked a pout for a moment before continuing. "It is correct that a *Nachzehrer* is a reanimated terror of human origins, but it does not have the tendencies of the fabled vampire. I suspect that part of the myth came from an unlucky observer who witnessed one of the creatures claw its way out of a grave."

Yikes! I'd seen enough zombie movies to picture that scene with bone-chilling clarity. "And the thing about it eating its own death shroud?"

"It is not an actual shroud." He brushed the piece of plaster onto the floor. "Think of it more like a cocoon."

"A cocoon?" Harvey shot me a wrinkled brow. "What sort of critter are we dealin' with here?"

"One with astounding vigor and an insatiable hunger," Dominick answered.

Harvey leaned closer and said in my ear, "Reminds me of you when yer in heat and yer stallion rides into town."

My face warmed. I gave the buzzard the evil eye before focusing back on Dominick. "Go on."

"*Der Nachzehrer* is the final form of an ancient pest left over from a time when violence was a way of life. Back then, survival was a constant battle."

How was that time different from the here and now? Since moving to Deadwood and finding out I'd come from a long line of Executioners, I'd been dodging violent killers left and right.

"Final form?" Aunt Zoe asked. "Explain that."

"They are parasitic in nature." He crossed his arms. "You must think of what we are dealing with here *not* as merely a dead human brought back to life, but rather a 'host' that has experienced a metamorphosis."

I didn't like the words "parasitic" or "host." Both conjured the idea of tapeworms and maggots, which were high on my list titled "Horrific Shit to Avoid at All Costs."

"Are you saying a *Nachzehrer* is like some kind of mutant being?" I asked, though I wasn't a big fan of the word "mutant," either. I preferred talk of kitties and puppies. Hell, even chickens.

" 'Mutant' fits, I suppose." Dominick's foot swung slowly back and forth. "You see, a *Nachzehrer* will progress through stages before emerging in its final form. The process is really quite intriguing. They start very small, in an egg form, much like a fly."

Harvey and I exchanged a look of disbelief, but we both kept our lips closed and let Dominick continue.

"This egg is carefully implanted in a human host, usually through the ear or nostrils."

I cringed. Crap, I had a feeling this biology lesson was going to give me nightmares.

"Why a human?" Aunt Zoe asked.

"Because they are the easiest to catch and have the least genetic resistance as a host."

I bristled at his tone of superiority, but kept my mouth shut.

"Once secured inside the host, the egg will hatch."

Oh no, please don't say …

"A larva then emerges and begins to devour."

I tugged at my right earlobe, feeling an empathetic itch inside my ear canal.

"Devour what?" Harvey asked.

I made a face at him. Did we have to go there?

"The host, of course, from the inside."

"Dear Lord!" Aunt Zoe covered her mouth.

The itching sensation moved deeper. I rubbed the skin where my cheek met my ear to no avail.

"The soft organs are consumed first," Dominick said without even a twinge of revulsion. "This is because the larval form of a *Nachzehrer* instinctively knows what parts to eat and when so that it can keep its host alive as long as possible." He shifted, his foot stilling. "While it eats, the larva excretes a type of mucus that acts as a stimulant, reinvigorating the damaged tissues, prolonging the death of the host."

The itch moved again, settling in the back of my throat. I swallowed hard a couple of times, trying to make it go away.

"Within a relatively short time," Dominick said, "the host grows weak, appearing more and more ill, until eventually the human collapses into a coma. Soon enough, breathing stops, and the heart, too, so the host appears to be dead. But the host is still alive. Well, in a manner of speaking. This signifies the end of the larval stage."

I cleared my throat once, twice, and then again.

Dominick paused, his brow lifting slightly.

"Sorry. I have an itch in my throat." I stuck my pinkie in my ear and shook it, rattling the itch away.

"Maybe somethin' planted an egg in your ear last night," Harvey said under his breath, wiggling his eyebrows at me.

I shuddered and then waved for our teacher to continue his lesson.

"At this time, the larva goes through a metamorphosis,

which in turn spurs a chemical change within the host."

Aunt Zoe groaned. "Let me guess, it becomes a pupa."

"More or less. This change causes a thin viscous coating to form on the outer layer of the skin. Over several days, it quickly thickens until the whole body appears to be wrapped in a cocoon."

"The death shroud," she said, earning a nod in return.

"Inside this cocoon, more changes are occurring as the creature takes on its final 'adult' form—*der Nachzehrer.*"

"So, it busts out of the grave and gobbles up its own cocoon?" Harvey asked, sounding skeptical.

"Sort of like a butterfly," Aunt Zoe said.

Dominick frowned. "More like a parasitic wasp."

"Holy shit." I scratched a new itch on the back of my neck.

"It is my understanding that the viscous coating is actually full of nutrients the creature needs to sustain itself until it can begin to feed on something else."

"You mean *someone* else." Aunt Zoe's eyes reflected the revulsion now lodged in my chest.

"Correct." Dominick flicked another piece of plaster off the sill. "As I said before, they are voracious. They need food often in order to sustain their strength and keep their host from decomposing. Their speed is exceeded only by their strength."

I covered my face with my hands. "This is madness."

"And if one of them critters takes a bite out of …" Harvey trailed off.

"It could become infected like any other bite, but you will not turn into a *Nachzehrer.* As I said before, transformation requires the implantation of an egg."

My skin wanted to crawl off my bones and go hide under the bed.

Harvey let out a gargling sound. "Reminds me how a coffin fly will burrow down into a grave to lay its eggs near a corpse."

I lowered my hands and glared at him. "Really? You had to go there?"

"Where do the eggs come from?" Aunt Zoe pressed, her face slightly pale when she glanced my way.

"Another realm. It is my belief that they have been transported here to create a 'pack' needed for a hunt."

"A hunt for what?" Harvey asked.

I knew the answer even before Dominick looked my way, but still winced in anticipation.

"A *Scharfrichter*, in this case."

Last November, a partially burned body was found out by the trees along the Mickelson Trail, an old railroad line turned recreational playground. Knowing what I did now, I wondered if someone had tried to burn the body to stop the metamorphic process.

After doing a crime scene song and dance, the authorities had collected the charred body and stuck it in the meat locker behind Mudder Brothers Funeral Parlor—aka the interim morgue. A short time later, the burned body disappeared after someone (or *something*) had made short work of the thick cooler door and its heavy-duty lock.

Fast forward to early December. Cooper stopped by Aunt Zoe's one evening to tell us about a case of hit-and-run, only in this instance, the driver didn't "run" after hitting the victim—except for hightailing it to the police after the partially burned victim stood up and growled at him. Then its arm fell off. Then it rushed the poor driver, trying to claw its way into the car with its remaining arm.

At that point, Aunt Zoe had informed us we most likely had a *Nachzehrer* on our hands, but the only help she could offer was how to kill it. However, if the myths were wrong about its origin, then …

"How do you kill a *Nachzehrer*?" I asked Dominick.

"You must sever the head from the body."

Come on! "Can't I just burn it?"

"That has been tried before. Unfortunately, the creature's flesh contains some sort of fire retardant. The skin will smolder, but fire will not destroy the creature."

That explained what was found on the Mickelson Trail. "But it can lose a limb?"

"That limb will regrow with time and the proper nutrients." He stood, pulling a pocket watch from inside his coat. He glanced down at it before tucking it away again. "The only way to execute a *Nachzehrer* is by severing the connection between the spinal cord and the brain."

"And what about placing a copper coin in its mouth?" Aunt Zoe asked. "Is that necessary?"

Dominick sneered. "A silly fable."

"When you say 'pack' …" I began, returning to the reason a *Nachzehrer* was currently roaming about the Black Hills.

"How many are we talking?" Aunt Zoe caught on to my train of thought.

"Typically…" he paused, rubbing his jaw. "I'd say no more than three. Although I once heard of a pack of four."

"Why so few?" Harvey asked. "Wouldn't they be of the more-critters-the-merrier notion?"

"Well, for one, *Nachzehrer* eggs are extremely difficult to obtain, not to mention transport. There are only a handful of known queens in existence, and it takes years for them to produce what tends to be a small cache of eggs."

There was a queen *Nachzehrer*? Eek. I really needed to find a new vocation.

"For another, the creatures can be a touch unruly."

I scoffed, thinking of the taxidermy shop and all of the bites taken out of the animals' hides.

"The bounty hunters that opt to use *Nachzehrer* for the hunt can control only a few at a time. When there are too many in the pack, they have been known to turn on their master and devour the hunter as well as the hunted."

Served the bounty-hunting bastard right. "Are they used solely to hunt Executioners?"

"No, they will hunt other hybrids and purebreds alike. However, it is a well-established fact that the blood of a *Scharfrichter* is a rare treat. It will stir a frenzy in many different breeds of pests and demons."

I'd heard that before, only it came from a certain uppity *Scharfrichter* who'd been dead for well over a century and had recently saved me from a demon-copulation disaster.

Dominick pointed at me. "You must find the *Nachzehrer* that was spotted last night."

Now he was starting to sound like Cooper, damn it.

"You must use the creature to lead you to the bounty hunter that bred it, along with any other pests brought into this realm. We cannot have this vermin running loose. It will bring more trouble to the Black Hills."

"You mean due to more law enforcement showing up?" I asked. Deadwood and Lead certainly weren't big enough for more than one Detective Hawke trying to pin crimes on my ass.

"I mean before more hunters show up to join the hunt. Killing a *Scharfrichter* is an impressive feat." When I stared at him, he added, "You cannot let the number of your enemies grow beyond your ability to keep them in check."

Yeah, I'd heard that warning before, and experienced the same tightening in my gut then as well.

I looked at Aunt Zoe. "This is nuts, you know. Parasitic creatures using human hosts like some kind of macabre puppet. You can't make this shit up."

She put her arm around my shoulders. "Be that as it may, you have a job to do."

Harvey was still eying Dominick. "You think there are more than one of those critters runnin' around these hills?"

"It is possible. As I said, three is the typical pack size."

"Along with a hunter leadin' the charge?" Harvey pressed.

"Correct."

Harvey turned away, muttering, "Gonna need me some more dynamite."

"Or not." That thought made my gut tighten, too.

Aunt Zoe gave me a squeeze and then stepped away. "Will the hunter require decapitation as well?"

"Not necessarily, but removing the head does tend to be the most reliable method for eliminating life from most creatures."

I let out a high-pitched laugh. "A decapitation a day keeps the *Nachzehrer* away."

"Yer losin' your vertical hold, Sparky."

Harvey didn't know the half of it. "Why are you helping me, Dominick? What's in this for you?"

"Your skills will be needed for what I believe is yet to come our way."

I smirked. Of course. My kind were merely tools in his eyes. Weapons to be used when necessary and then tossed aside. "And how will I catch a *Nachzehrer*? Using bait?"

I'd used bait in past hunts, including putting my own butt on the line when it came to catching the *lidérc*.

"That is up to you. You should know, though, that the creatures can smell *Scharfrichter* blood from a great distance."

A screeching sound came from out in the hallway, drawing Dominick's gaze for a moment. And then his frown. "You will start the hunt for them today," he said, rising and ushering us toward the doorway.

"I will not," I said to him in the hallway. "Today is my day off. I will start the hunt tomorrow."

Or maybe Saturday. Then again, I had a busy weekend coming up with that dang *Paranormal Realty* premiere on Sunday. Monday would work better.

"Waiting is foolish," he chastised, standing in the light

spilling out through the classroom door.

I held my ground, both physically and mentally. "When I hunt is my decision, Dominick."

Harvey opened the outside door and held it for us while Aunt Zoe lingered at my side.

"Besides, I still need to find that damned imp of yours."

He shook his head as he backed deeper into the shadowed hall. "Imps are very tricky. You'd be better off starting with the *Nachzehrer*. They will be a less challenging foe, even as a pack."

Really? A pack of voracious parasites were easier to catch and kill than one little imp?

"Who I execute first is also my decision, not yours."

He needed to understand that I would not heed his orders now or in the future, nor would I be his tool to use when and where he chose.

"Your stubbornness will be the death of you," he growled as he stepped back into the murky shadows, leaving me with one final warning. "Time never waits for anyone, *Scharfrichter,* and neither do bounty hunters."

Chapter Five

Two hours later of "time" having to hold its horses ...

Violet, are you still in the tub?" Aunt Zoe's voice came through the bathroom door. "You have a phone call."

I lowered the book I was reading about a female mountain climber struggling to make a round-trip summit of K2, the second-highest and the deadliest peak in the world. Like the heroine, I wondered if I would survive to tell my tale after my toils here in the Black Hills were all over. If it would ever be over, of course. Judging from the multiple volumes of my family's horror-filled history, I wasn't so ...

"Violet!" Aunt Zoe knocked this time. "Are you okay?"

After checking to make sure I had enough bubbles to hide my hills and dales, I placed the book on the floor outside the tub and grabbed the washcloth hanging nearby.

"I'm reading a book," I said in lieu of an answer while draping the cloth over my chest. "The door is open."

Aunt Zoe stepped inside, closing the door behind her. She looked at the book on the floor. "*Cold Horizon*? You're reading that in the middle of winter?"

"It's exciting." And romantic.

"You're supposed to be relaxing on your day off."

"I am. Climbing mountains is less stressful than hunting and killing monsters."

"If you say so." She brought my cell phone over. "He

says it's urgent. It's muted."

"Is it Doc?" I asked as I took the phone, unmuting the call.

She shook her head and moved over to the sink counter, apparently intending to hang out and listen in on the call.

Sending another questioning look in her direction, I hit the speaker button. "Hello?"

"Who is this?" Cornelius Curion's voice came through the speaker loud and clear.

"You called me, Spirit Miser." I used the name Prudence had given him after she'd paid a visit to the locked-away parts of his psyche and found a prison filled with ectoplasmic degenerates there.

"Are we sure about that?" he asked.

Were we …? Actually, I wasn't since I had been enjoying a bubble bath when the actual connection was made.

"There is the possibility that you used remote viewing to visit me mentally," he continued. "And then instigated a telepathic link to communicate your need to talk to me. We cannot be positive who really called whom without further investigation and testing."

I pinched the bridge of my nose.

Of course, Cornelius would be the one to interrupt my bath. The eccentric, deep-pocketed, pied piper of ghosts must have sensed that my aura was taking a smoke-break. Or that my third eye was snoozing. I sank lower into the bubbles. Or better yet, that I'd taken my chakras to the cleaners. If I had known the first time he'd walked into Calamity Jane Realty that he would become my partner in tiptoeing through spooky haunts and dark realms, I would have insisted on a higher commission rate.

"Why is your voice coming out of my phone's speaker, Cornelius?"

"Would you prefer a verbal explanation of how soundwaves travel? Or should I come over and draw you a diagram?"

"If you come here, I'm going to poke you in the eye."

"Which one?"

"For the love of Elvis!" I growled.

Aunt Zoe made a calm-down gesture with her hands.

"You sound tense, Violet," he said. Something crashed in the background, followed by the sound of sporadic hammering. "Have you considered trying some breathing meditations to relax? Sudarshan Kriya is very powerful, but it can be quite difficult for amateurs."

"That name sounds like a Bollywood movie," I told him, sticking one of my bubble-covered feet out of the water and envisioning kicking him in the butt with it. "For your information, I'm taking a soothing, lavender-infused bath right now." *Hint, hint.*

At least it was soothing until he'd called.

"Oh, then don't even try either of the two forms of Tummo. They should never be practiced near water."

Why not? What was Tummo?

No, I wasn't going down that rabbit hole.

"A better choice would be Buteyko," he continued. "It's said to be great for anxiety attacks." The hammering in the background of the call stopped, only to be replaced by the sound of a high-pitched drill that made my shoulders tighten. "I myself prefer the art of nose singing to release nitric oxide for widening the capillaries in my nasal passages and increasing oxygenation."

What in the heck was nose singing? The puzzled expression on Aunt Zoe's face confirmed I wasn't alone in my bewilderment.

"Listen, Corn—" I tried to get a word in edgewise.

"Speaking of coitus," he said in a loud voice, nearly yelling.

I grimaced at the phone. "I don't believe we were, and I'm one hundred percent certain we shouldn't go near that topic moving forward."

The only person I ever talked sex with while bathing had texted me on my way home from the school in Lead to say that he'd be working through lunch today because one of his newer clients needed some tax-related paperwork help ASAP. Since Doc was already buried in work, I'd skipped filling him in on Dominick's biology lesson. All that could wait until we were face-to-face, partly so I could see if Doc's ear itched like mine had when hearing how *Nachzehrer* came to be, but mostly because bad news was best delivered when he could hug away my frets afterward.

The commotion on Cornelius's end of the line quieted, but his voice didn't. "Did you know that the tissue inside your nose is an erogenous zone and thought by some to be the most easily aroused part of your body? In fact, it's quite similar to erectile tissue and can become engorged with blood the same as a sexually aroused pen—"

"Nin-gah!" I shouted at the phone, unable to form a solid English word in my rush to stop him. Talking to a ridiculous Abe Lincoln lookalike about the male anatomy while sitting in a warm bubble bath with my aunt only a few feet away was not helping me relax on my day off, damn it!

Silence came through the line for a moment, then, "Are you speaking in tongues again, Violet?" he asked in a much quieter voice. "Are you channeling another parasitic ghoul?"

Frickety-frack in a pink Cadillac. I kicked my foot, splashing water over the side of the tub. I'd had enough talk about parasites to last me a lifetime.

A cacophony of hammering and drilling and some other repetitive pounding came through the line, louder this time.

I shot my aunt a scowl and hit the mute button, speaking in a steely undertone. "I swear I told you and Harvey both that I didn't want to talk to anyone for an hour unless it was an emergency having to do with the kids or Doc."

She pointed at my phone. "Cornelius claimed this was a

Doc-related emergency."

Screeeeeech! My heart did a double take. I scooted up the edge of the tub, leaning closer to the phone, and unmuted the call. "What's wrong with Doc, Cornelius?" I tried to talk above the commotion coming from his end of the line.

"ARE YOU REFERRING TO AN ISSUE WITH THE TALL MEDIUM'S ERECTILE TISSUE?" he yelled back.

A steamy scene popped into my head of Doc and me and our recent use of his particularly pleasing erectile tissue.

"No! Doc doesn't have any ..." I pinched my lips together to keep from finishing that sentence.

A snort of laughter came from over by the sink.

My face began to roast. "I'm referring to the reason you called me today," I explained into the phone. "You mentioned some emergency having to do with Doc."

"OH, YOU MEAN THAT," he yelled louder.

I winced and turned down the volume. "Yes, that."

Whatever *that* was.

The commotion on his end of the call quieted again, but that didn't stop him from yelling into the phone, "YOU NEED TO COME TO MY HOTEL IMMEDIATELY!"

"Why?"

"THERE IS A BLOCKAGE I NEED YOU TO—"

The phone cut out.

"Cornelius?" I moved closer to the microphone. So did Aunt Zoe. "Cornelius, can you hear me? What do you mean a blockage?" And what did that have to do with Doc?

Silence continued from his end of the line.

"Cornelius?"

Static for a moment, then silence again.

"CORNELIUS!" I yelled, making Aunt Zoe jerk in surprise. *Sorry*, I mouthed to her.

More static. I was about to end the call when ...

"Violet." His whisper sounded like he was talking into a plastic cup. "You need to come to the hotel immediately, before it's too late."

"Too late for what?" Aunt Zoe and I asked in unison.

But we were too late. The big bunghole had hung up.

* * *

I was still damp from my bath and the sweat I'd built up rushing to dress, tame my hair, and zigzag through the streets of Deadwood, when I pulled into the parking lot behind The Old Prospector Hotel. Teeth-chattering gusts tore at my coat as I dashed along the sidewalk lined with dirty snow and big salt crystals to meet with Cornelius.

If he'd used Doc's name merely to lure me to this so-called emergency of his, I was going to …

I turned the corner and ran into a solid body. "Oof!"

A hand reached out to catch me as I stumbled backward, slipping and sliding on snow.

"Careful, lady," a gruff voice said as I righted myself. A familiar voice, at that.

"Jeff?"

"Hey, Violet Parker." Jeff Wymonds, my former client and the father of my daughter's best friend, was still holding onto my arm. With his wind-tousled blond hair and wide toothy smile, he looked younger than his almost forty years. His shoulders seemed broader, too, in his brown canvas work coat. "Where are you heading in such a rush?"

"Ahhh …" I searched for an answer other than the truth, which would sound bizarre to a beer-and-potato-chips kind of guy like Jeff. I needed a response that had nothing to do with ghosts or other-worldly parasites or breathing relaxation methods or Doc. Especially not Doc, as last I'd heard Jeff was having some kind of torrid fling with Tiffany, Doc's ex.

Actually, the word "fling" might be too long-term in their particular case, since my understanding was that Tiffany had offered sexual favors in exchange for Jeff ripping up the listing agreement that he'd signed with me and taking her on as his agent instead. Who knew the real estate world could be such a reality shitshow?

I licked my lips. "I need to see a guy about …" *a mule— no, about a hinny. Shush!* "Umm … something."

Okay, so coming up with lies on the fly was not in my wheelhouse today. It appeared that my brain was taking this day-off deal seriously, even if nobody else was.

"Hmmm, that sounds mysterious." Jeff was still hanging on to my arm, which he now used to pull me closer while sniffing in the general area of my head. "You smell good. Who's this 'guy' you're meeting? Are you back on the market?" He wiggled both blond eyebrows at me. "Does that mean Doc Nyce is no longer petting your cat?"

I frowned. "Petting my cat?" What did Bogart, our vegetarian cat, have to do with Doc?

Jeff leaned in for another sniff. "I'm really good at petting cats, too."

Oh, dear Lord! My brain had finally dipped low enough into the gutter to catch Jeff's meaning. I shoved him back a step. "Doc is still petting my …" *No! Just walk away, doofus.*

I started to do just that, but then stopped and turned back. In case Tiffany was going to be hearing the play-by-play of my run-in with Jeff, I wanted to clarify things so the red-headed siren wouldn't get any ideas about trying to steal Doc away from me. We'd done that song and dance before, and there would be no encores on that score.

"Doc Nyce is still my boyfriend," I announced. Sheesh, "boyfriend" was such a silly word for a woman my age. "I mean, we're a definite couple in *all* the ways."

Jeff grinned. "Which ways are those?"

"You know, the 'couple' ways." When he just stared at me with a dumb grin, I added, "Boom, boom, out goes the lights."

His laughter rang out loud and clear, catching the

attention of people on the opposite side of the street. "I'm not sure if you know this, Violet Parker, but that old song actually refers to landing a knock-out punch."

Thinking back on all the times I'd pinched, elbowed, and tackled Doc, including the black eye I'd accidentally given him, I shrugged. "Sex with Doc is amazingly physical. He's a real heavy hitter under the sheets, delivering a solid one-two sock-'em every time." I wasn't sure what I was alluding to by this point, but I kept throwing out boxing slang to fill the void. "I'd give you the real dirty blow-by-blow, but we don't sell ringside tickets for our wild sex matches."

His jaw gaped. "No kidding?"

Before my big mouth unleashed another round of idiotic sex-boxing ambiguities, I said, "See you around, Jeff."

I couldn't scuttle away from the train wreck fast enough.

Ignoring the sign taped to the glass that read "Temporarily Closed: Under Construction," I pushed through the double front doors of Cornelius's hotel. Inside, the casino floor was abuzz with construction workers going here and there, some with arms full, others arms empty, reminding me of drones at a busy beehive. A wave of warm air settled any last shivers I had but did nothing for my nerves. Neither did the banging and screeching and pounding.

I scanned the room. Where in the hell was Cornelius? I wanted to get in and out of here and back to reading my book as soon as possible so I could escape from my troubles until the kids came home from school.

All of the slot machines in the front room of the casino had been herded together off to the side. Where they used to sit, the gold-colored carpet had been torn up, leaving behind a concrete floor lined with glue tracks and numbers written in chalk. The matching gold wallpaper had been torn off in spots, leaving a few strips behind along with more chalk scrawls. Overhead, the glass chandeliers and gold-painted ceiling tiles were dulled with a coat of dust. I would be too if I stood around much longer.

I headed for the front desk in search of my summoner.

"Howdy doody, Socrates," I said, pausing in front of the full-sized stuffed mule who'd stood in the lobby for decades.

A drop cloth covered all but the mule's head, the thick fabric sliding off his hind end. I paused to pull the cloth back in place, wondering if Jones' Taxidermy had a hand in Socrates' stiff-legged display here in The Old Prospector. Maybe Garth's dad or grandfather had done the work on him. The old mule looked plenty worn now, the fur rubbed clean off his nose. At least he didn't have a bite out of him like the other poor critters at Garth's place.

Dang *Nachzehrer.* I shoved aside those thoughts and returned to my search for Cornelius. Instead of running into my old séance-loving pal, Safari Skipper, in her usual place manning the front desk, I found a note with my name at the top and a single order written under it: *Join me in the basement.*

The basement, huh? I guess that was better than his usual suite on the third floor. I hadn't been looking forward to taking the stairs where Doc and I had once run into the ghost of a young prostitute. Of course, taking the elevator was out of the question after my experience of riding down from the third floor in the dark with a freaky-ass clown doll possessed by a vindictive spirit.

The Old Prospector Hotel had been around for many, many trips around the sun. During oodles of those trips, prior to it sheltering tourists for the night, its rooms had housed a brothel. Unfortunately, not all liaisons that occurred here had been fun romps, which was nothing new in the business of selling sex. Several had ended in murder, many of them rather brutal.

Cornelius claimed that there were several ghosts still floating through the halls in this place, including the young prostitute. I had no qualms about hanging my hat on his claim after having multiple séances here myself with and without Doc.

I stuffed the note in my pocket and headed for the wide stairwell leading down into the hotel's furnished basement. I'd been downstairs a couple of times already. The first visit had been during the initial tour of the hotel with Cornelius and Doc's ex, Tiffany-the-client-stealer, back when the hotel was on the market. The second had been with Doc when he'd dragged me downstairs to look at a picture from over a century ago featuring a frighteningly familiar face.

"Violet," Cornelius called as my foot touched down on the last step. "Over here."

I looked to my right, seeing him sitting at the old bar that ran most of the length of one wall. He was dressed in his usual black pants and sweater ensemble, except for a cornflower blue scarf draped around his neck that matched his eyes.

Things had changed since the last time I'd been down in the basement. Before, the room had been filled with tables and a sound stage, all set up to be rented for parties and receptions. Now there was barely room to walk between the rolls of plastic-wrapped carpet and wallpaper, crates and boxes of who knew what, and stacks of slot machine stools. The place smelled the same, though—slightly musty with a hint of lemon-scented furniture polish and stale cigar smoke.

I joined Cornelius, frowning at a partially burned white candle and his Viking helmet sitting on the bar nearby. Those were séance tools. "What's going on here?"

"My hotel is being upgraded."

I scoffed. "I know that. I meant what's going on with that." I pointed at his helmet.

"My lucky helmet?"

"Yes. Why is it sitting there?"

"Would you rather it be sitting somewhere else?"

I held up my fist, threatening to bop him.

"I see your lavender-scented bath was ineffective. Did you try breathing the right way?"

"You mean in and out?"

"Oh, it's much more complicated than that."

I sighed, long and loud.

"You have the 'out' part mastered, it appears," he said with his usual crooked grin that often left me wondering if he was smiling or still suffering from a case of Bell's palsy. "We'll have to settle for that baby step for now."

"Cornelius, why am I here? And don't give me one of your roundabout answers this time. If there's a problem that involves Doc, I need to know now."

He slid off the barstool, grabbing his helmet but leaving the candle. "Come with me and you'll understand why I interrupted your bubbly-tub time." His expression sobered. "Although, if my hypothesis is correct, the answer you seek may be one that you wish you had not learned."

My heart did a little hop-skip-panic-hop jig. I tried to chuckle away my unease, but it sounded like I was choking a frog. "You remind me of one of those cryptic fortune-teller machines at the county fair that spits out oddball advice on a slip of paper."

"I prefer cartomancy when it comes to peeking into the future. My grandmother was amazingly accurate when she read the cards." He stopped and looked back at me, his gaze narrowing. "When we're done down here, I could do a reading for you to see what your future holds."

No way! Fortune telling gave me the heebie-jeebies. And after my talk with Dominick this morning, I didn't want to know that answer. It was hair-raising enough just living with what the present had in store for me.

"Not on my day off." I nudged him forward again, following him through the narrow passageway of remodeling riff-raff. A worrisome thought occurred as I skirted a stack of light fixtures. "Please tell me you didn't convince Doc to cancel his afternoon appointment and join us for a séance."

"I did not contact the Tall Medium."

He led me into a short hallway crammed with more boxes on each side. A set of steel doors were at the other end. One of them was open, allowing a glimpse of darkness inside.

I slowed, hanging back a bit. I'd had enough fun in the shadows this morning after tarrying in what was probably a haunted school.

"I have a suspicion that the medium's presence could be more risky than beneficial," he added, stepping into the dark.

I didn't follow him.

His footfalls continued, stopped, and then returned. He leaned out into the hallway. "You need to join me in here."

"Not until you turn on the lights."

One black eyebrow rose. "How long have you been afraid of the dark?"

"Since the first time you taught me how to reach into it and something licked me."

His smile lifted both sides of his mouth this time. "That was an exciting afternoon."

Terrifying was more like it.

"What am I doing down here, Cornelius?"

"I need you to help me clear a channel." He reached to the side and the overhead fluorescent lights flickered to life.

"If this is something to do with a malevolent ghost, I'm not interested."

"I believe you will find this especially intriguing." He took a step backward into the room.

"Is what you're talking about alive or dead?"

Another step. "That is yet to be determined."

"Can it hurt me?"

"Psychologically speaking …" He paused, stroking his pointy goatee as he thought. He shrugged. "We would have to read your fortune for that answer."

"Cornelius," I warned.

"Quit being such a fussbudget and come along." He turned his back on me and walked out of view.

I hesitated for a moment longer and then joined him in the room. Tall cabinets and shelves lined the walls, the same as the last time I'd been in here. Plato, the mothballed ancestor of Socrates the mule, had been moved to the far corner, a tarp covering most of his worn form. Several stacked filing boxes leaned against his back hindquarter. A rack of what looked like framed art pieces blocked him from going forward.

"Close the door behind you," Cornelius ordered.

As much as I didn't want to, I did as told and then headed over to where he stood. A couple of steps away from him, I stopped short.

In the center of the room was a circle drawn on the concrete in the same white chalk I'd seen used upstairs on walls and the floor to note measured lengths. In the middle of the circle sat another candle, this one fatter and made of black wax. The candle flame was lit and burning steadily.

What had he told me was the difference between a white candle and a black one the other night in the Sugarloaf Building? White candles were for cleansing, if I remembered right, and black candles were for protection. So, what did we need protection from in this room? When I'd been in here before with Doc, he hadn't picked up the scent of any ghosts.

While the sight of a circle and candle had me reluctant to go any farther, the item that lay on the floor next to the candle made me want to race back home and lock the door behind me.

"Cornelius, why is there a pair of handcuffs in that circle?"

He stepped carefully over the chalk line, bending to pick up the item in question. "These aren't handcuffs. They're a tethering device."

"No, those are most definitely handcuffs." And I was

most definitely allergic to them, especially after Cooper had unrightfully cuffed me and hauled me to jail, a bone of contention I hadn't let go of even though we were managing to share space in a room these days without hissing and growling ... at least not too much.

"I assure you, their purpose is to tether. Without the Tall Medium here to guide us, we need to have a secure connection." He stepped out of the circle and walked past me, shutting off the lights.

As my eyes adjusted to the dim candlelight, I listened for the sound of anything in here other than the two of us. The good news was that it appeared we were alone. The bad news was that he returned with the cuffs still in hand and motioned me to follow him into the circle.

I resisted, holding my ground. "Guide us where?"

"We will know that answer after we begin."

I shook my head. Every hair on the back of my neck was rising up in rebellion, pitchforks and shovels at the ready. "Cornelius, you need to explain why I'm here in clear, non-cryptic speak or I'm hitting the road."

His lips pursed as he nodded. "How interesting. The prickly detective told me you would be averse to this. I was unaware that he had the psychic ability to read thoughts as well as see apparitions."

The prickly ... "You mean Cooper?" Cooper had a hand in this séance setup?

"Do you know any other bristly, ghost-seeing grumbletonian who solves crimes for a living?"

I grinned. "I dare you to call him that to his face."

"And risk being bitten? I'd rather not."

"Are those Cooper's handcuffs?"

"Yes." He pulled a familiar-looking walkie-talkie from his back pocket. "The detective dropped this off as well, but we don't need it for this particular undertaking." He placed it on the floor outside the circle.

But we need handcuffs? I frowned, still trying to wrap my mind around the fact that Cooper had been here before me today. It wasn't like him to be so cooperative when it came to playing with ghosts.

"Why was Cooper here?" I asked.

"To see."

"To see what?"

He looked at me as if I'd recently fallen off the turnip truck. "To see ghosts. Why else would he stop by?"

"Maybe you two are bosom buddies now for all I know."

"Not yet, but he's warming up to me," he said with a wink and then waved me closer. "Join me in the circle, Violet, but don't step on the line."

I held back. "I'm allergic."

"To chalk?"

"No, to handcuffs. Being shackled makes me foam at the mouth." When he stared at me as if a daisy had just sprouted from the top of my head, I added, "I thought Cooper told you I have an aversion to handcuffs."

"That is incorrect. He informed me that this was your day off and you were being, and I quote, 'a bit of an ass' about helping others in need."

I harrumphed. "Cooper's the ass."

"Donkeys aside, we need to do a bit of eavesdropping while the voices are still audible." He lowered into a cross-legged sitting position and patted the concrete next to him. "This shouldn't take long, if everything goes right."

What voices? "And what if this goes wrong?"

"Then it will not be going right, of course." He patted the floor again. "Come now. Don't be shy, channeler. You need to clear the airwaves for us."

I moved closer, hesitating at the edge of the circle. "Shouldn't we wait for Doc to be safe?"

"If I'm hearing the voices correctly, the presence of the Tall Medium could be a grave mistake."

I wasn't sure if he meant "grave" as in super serious or "grave" as in having to do with the no-longer-living.

He held my stare, all jesting aside. "Trust me."

Trust a man who was hearing voices in the walls of his hotel? I shrugged. I'd witnessed crazier shit. I crossed into the circle and sat down next to him.

He took the handcuffs and secured one around his wrist, offering me the other.

"Show me the key first." I wasn't going to spend the remainder of my day off shackled to him because he hadn't thought ahead about how to get uncuffed.

He pulled a small key out of his pocket. When I tried to swipe it, he pulled back, closing his fist over it.

"It is imperative that I hold onto it."

I frowned. "Why you and not me?"

"Because you tend to wander during séances. This way you'll have to drag me along."

"Like an anchor."

"Precisely. The Tall Medium has warned me repeatedly never to let you wander without a tether."

"You mean Doc knows what we're about to do?" If so, why didn't he call me and give me a heads-up?

"Absolutely not. If he did, he'd insist on being here."

"But that's a bad thing," I clarified, because usually Doc was a good person to have on hand when I messed around with channeling ghosts and whatnot.

"Yes, as I specified before. Did you hit your head on the way over?"

"No, but I wish I had. I sort of feel like we're dabbling where we shouldn't here and I want to make sure I'll still be breathing when we're finished."

"As I said before, trust me." He grabbed my wrist and locked the other handcuff around it. "Now quit delaying. We must get started."

"Because of the voices?"

"Because I have a meeting with my general contractor in approximately thirty-seven minutes."

I huffed at him.

"Are you trying to blow my house down?"

"Maybe I am."

"Your shoulders are very tense. It appears you took the wrong kind of bath."

I knew how to take a dang bath. "The water was hot."

"Did you use enough magnesium salt?"

I glared at him. "I'm done talking about baths with you."

"Great. We'll get started before time runs out."

"For your contractor."

"For the Tall Medium."

I sobered. "What have you been hearing?"

He pointed at the black candle. "Listen for yourself."

I watched the candle flame flicker for a few breaths, listening, feeling Cornelius shift and squirm since my wrist was cuffed to his. I heard a few muffled bangs overhead, praying none of the construction crew came down and found us in here fooling around with ghosts.

When my circle partner stilled again, I whispered, "Am I supposed to picture one flame or two this time?"

He lifted his hand between us. In his palm was a small dark mound of what looked like pepper, but I couldn't tell for sure what it was in the candlelight.

"What's that?"

"Cedar ashes."

"What do they do?"

"Protect you."

"From what?" And how?

"Not what, whom. Now close your eyes."

I closed them, wondering how a pile of ashes in his hand could protect me.

A poof of air hit my face. I jerked back and sucked in a breath, smelling wood ash and something slightly fetid. My nose tickled. I reached up and scratched it, my fingers brushing over grit. What the heck? Did the big goose just blow those ashes in my face?

I took another breath and my nose itched again, on the inside this time. I wiggled it, but the itch spread into my sinuses, triggering a sneeze.

And then another.

And then another.

When I sniffed and caught my breath, a ringing racket filled my head. I winced, wondering what was going on overhead. Was the construction crew hammering on a huge brass bell?

The ringing grew louder, making my head rattle. I tried to plug my ears, but it did no good. The ringing volume increased, sending a stab of pain through my skull. I had to get out of here before my head cracked in half!

"Cornelius!" I tried to yell above the commotion. "I need to go!"

I tried to open my eyes but my eyelids wouldn't budge. I tried again, but still I couldn't lift them. It was like they were glued shut.

I pushed to my feet, blindly panicking, trying to make my escape, but something tugged on my wrist and yanked me back down. I shifted to my knees and tried to rise again, but another tug dragged me back onto my butt.

The ringing faded, the pain in my skull easing. I sat huddled into myself, struggling to think beyond my pounding heart and head, waiting for the racket to grow deafening again.

But it didn't. Instead, I heard a voice speaking far off in a loud whisper. It was too far to really comprehend what was being said, though.

"Who's there?" I asked, clambering back onto my knees.

"Violet, sit still," Cornelius insisted, tugging me back down. "You must stay in the circle."

Of course, the dang handcuffs. In my dark-filled panic, I'd forgotten he was tethered to me. Relieved that I wasn't alone, I did as told, scooting closer to him.

"Where are we?" I whispered.

"On the other side of the wall," he replied just as quietly.

"Why did you blow that stuff in my face?"

"To seal your eyes shut so you couldn't rely on them to see and to clear your ears so you could hear."

"Yeah, well, it stinks."

"Next time I'll mix it with rosehips and jasmine essence."

"Really? You'd do that for me?"

"No. Now be quiet and listen."

I sat with my lips pinched, resisting the urge to wipe away the grit on my face with the back of my sleeve. All around me, murmuring voices swirled closer, first encircling us, then bearing down on us, trying to breach the circle. At least that was what it felt like. I struggled to make out what was being said, but there were too many voices. So much that it merged into waves of hisses.

"What am I listening for in particular?" I asked.

"You will know when you focus enough to hear it."

I listened some more, getting nowhere. "Focus on what, though?"

"The Tall Medium."

Oh, that was easy. I thought of Doc. His dark eyes, the smile warming his face when he walked in the door, the feel of his whiskers on my neck, the sound of …

A familiar voice came through to me above the rest.

I leaned forward, trying to single it out, thinking I'd heard it wrong.

Nope, there it was again.

What was it saying, though? I focused, straining my ears.

The words seemed louder this time: *Listen, Killer, I know you are hell on wheels.*

I sat back, my heart thudding. Had I heard that right?

I focused and listened again, catching more of it this time: *Listen, Killer, I know you are hell on wheels in other realms, but ghosts are my specialty.*

My memory stepped forward, trying to locate the source of that line and stamp it with a time and place.

It was at the old Hessler house, wasn't it? Alone in the dark. Only not really alone. Standing at the base of the stairwell.

No, wait! It was prior to that. Back at the start of the séance in the root cellar. We'd been preparing to free Cornelius from the hold of the ghost of Wilda Hessler. Before Cornelius and I had gone under, Doc had pulled me aside and given me a pep talk, saying that very line to me.

But why was I hearing it here? Were the voices spurring it in my memory?

Through the whispers another high-pitched, chanting voice caught my attention. This one gave me chills.

Violet, the one that I love.

Violet, the one that I love.

Violet, the one that I love.

I shivered clear to my toes.

Wilda's ghost had repeated those lines previously on numerous occasions, including right here in this very hotel.

Cornelius leaned toward me. "Do you hear?"

"Yes. That little bitch is back."

"No, you're not listening."

"What do you mean?"

"Stop fighting it, take a deep breath, clear the channel. Really listen."

I tried to relax my shoulders and fine-tuned the dial of my internal spirit box. The words kept repeating, but then something happened. Something that made me hold my breath and *really* focus. And listen.

The voice repeating the words was changing, slowing down, the timbre deepening. I exhaled and drew in a full breath clear to the bottom of my lungs, holding on to it.

Then I heard it. The line was the same as before, but this time it wasn't coming from a little bratty girl bent on destroying everything good around her. This time the voice speaking the words was the same one that had guided me through terror-filled darkness more than once. The one that usually soothed me when I fretted and warmed me when my feet were icicles.

Violet, the one that I love.

It was Doc speaking now.

Why was I hearing him repeat those dreadful words over and over?

"You hear it now?" Cornelius asked.

"Yes. I hear him."

"Good. That makes two of us. Now hold on. We need to leave before it finds you."

Before *what* found me? My arm jerked hard, and then I was being dragged forward across the cold, hard floor.

"Open your eyes, Violet," Cornelius said at full volume.

I couldn't because of the … I opened my eyes.

We were still in the storeroom, only no longer in the circle with the lit candle. I sighed in relief and sat up, brushing my sleeve down my face.

After a soft clink, my wrist was free.

Cornelius hit the lights.

"Why was Doc repeating Wilda's favorite line over and over?" I asked him as he returned and held out his hand to help me up.

"That wasn't the Tall Medium you heard." He hauled me to my feet.

"Yes, it was. Believe me, I know Doc's voice well."

"It might have sounded like him, but it was not."

I brushed off my backside. "Then who was I hearing?"

"A mimic."

I frowned at him. "You mean someone was mimicking

Doc's voice?"

"I believe so."

"Who?"

"The answer to that I have yet to decipher, but if I were to guess, I'd say it was the changeling we were hearing."

By "changeling," he meant Wilda's poor twin who suffered from a birth deformity that left her limbs and face contorted. Wilda's mother, Mrs. Hessler, would dress the disabled girl up in a clown costume whenever she took the child out in public in order to hide her from public scrutiny. This was for Mrs. Hessler's benefit, of course, not the child's, being her family had owned the local jewelry store and was flush with money. Society couldn't know their family was anything but perfect.

Cornelius's and Doc's theory was that the changeling had been manipulating Wilda's ghost for decades. Now it appeared it was up to something new from the sounds of what we'd just heard.

I grimaced. "The changeling, huh? That's creepy."

"Unsettling, for sure, but I fear the *why* is more worrisome than the *who*."

Okay, I'd bite. "Why do you think the changeling was mimicking Doc's voice?"

"I'm not positive, but one hypothesis is that it heard him speak that night in the root cellar before we detached Wilda from me."

If his guess was correct, then it not only heard Doc talk, but it eavesdropped on the private pep talk he'd given me.

"So, you think this changeling is practicing voices?" To what end? Was it like the *lidérc* in some way, which tried to use replication of a recently deceased loved one as a lure?

He shrugged. "Another hypothesis is that it's trying to locate the owner of that voice once again, practicing to keep the tones fresh in its ectoplasmic memory."

"Why would the changeling want to locate Doc?" Ever

since the séance at the Hessler house, Doc had been worried the changeling would come for me, not him.

"Time will likely answer that for us." Cornelius frowned toward the circle. "At least we know now that the changeling is still nearby."

He said that as if we should be high-fiving about it. "Oh, goodie."

"The question is, how do we keep it from possessing the Tall Medium when he helps us with an exorcism?"

Chapter Six

Did Corny actually call it an exorcism?" Natalie asked a half hour later as she and I slipped and spun our way up Burnham Avenue on the north end of Deadwood under dark, snow-fattened clouds.

I'd received a phone call from my long-time partner in mischief right after I'd left Cornelius and his haunted hotel. She'd wanted to know where I was because she needed my help with a "little job." My opt-out due to needing to pick up my kids from school didn't fly since she'd already called Harvey and asked him to give them a ride home. When I reminded her that this was my day of "no-jobbing," she pretended the phone cut out right after telling me she'd be by in two shakes. Now, here I was on this usually wide street narrowed by piles of snow. Thankfully, we were the only ones risking our lives on the lone set of tire tracks at the moment.

"Or did he say 'exotism,' " she continued, "and you heard him wrong?"

" 'Exotism'?" I repeated, darting a frowny glance her way while maintaining my death grip on the dashboard.

"Yeah, you know." She paused to downshift. "Something with exotic qualities."

"I know what 'exotism' means, birdbrain."

"If you say so, numbskull, but you always sucked at English in school, so I wasn't sure if you'd need me to spell the word, too."

She was right. High school English classes were the closest I'd ever come to prison life—well, except for a few stints in jail, but I was innocent every time, damn it. Okay, except for that one time. Anyway, I'd rather spend an afternoon of thumbscrew torture than squirm and sweat at a school desk labeling sentence parts; or worse, analyzing long-dead literary authors' words to try and figure out what they truly meant in every freaking line they jotted down. Bleck! Maybe the line "It was a dark and stormy night" was just a weather report by a wannabe meteorologist.

Shit, where was I?

Oh, yeah, holding onto the dash for dear life while my best friend tried to give me a heart attack.

"Sucking at English class was better than what you sucked back then with those baby inner-tube lips," I shot back, managing a grin in spite of the now slightly sideways crawl of her rig up the icy hill as her pickup's back end fishtailed hard to the left.

Natalie laughed, giving me a loud, lip-smacking air kiss while keeping her eyes on the road.

I probably should tap my kidneys before we slid back down this icy hill, or I might leave a puddle on her front seat by the time we skidded to the bottom and plowed through the traffic down on Highway 85. Hopefully, we'd stop before taking a nosedive into Whitewood Creek.

I looked across the cab at my best friend while she maneuvered our way back to the straight and narrow. With her fuzzy pink earmuffs and double Dutch braids, she looked almost young enough to still be in high school. But the faint wrinkles that fanned from the corners of her eyes, creased her forehead, and curved along each side of her full lips couldn't hide the truth—she'd lived a bit of life, sunny with laughter and rainy with heartaches. But she'd survived. And now, she was determined to put my life at risk on this damned street under a sky that threatened to unleash more icy doom any minute.

I tried to focus on something besides this wild sled-run from hell. "Why on earth would Cornelius be worried about an *exotism*? That doesn't even make sense."

"I don't know. A lot of what Corny says most days doesn't make sense."

She had a point. That bit he told me about nostril erections still had me scratching my head.

"He definitely said 'exorcism.' And when I told him that I wasn't interested in reenacting that *Exorcist* movie—"

"Yuck." She made a face. "So much projectile vomiting."

"He called me a namby-pamby."

She slanted a glance in my direction. "Namby-pamby, huh? I like that boy's spunk. Did you pinch him hard enough to bruise after that?"

"He dodged my fingers." The stick insect was as quick as he was quirky.

The whole pickup started to slide sideways as Natalie made a left turn onto a side street, but she steered out of the spin with much-practiced ease.

I breathed a sigh of relief, happy to be rolling along on a flat surface again. "Isn't there a cemetery up this way?"

"St. Ambrose," she confirmed. "An old Catholic cemetery." She pointed out the windshield. "It's just ahead of us over that hill."

It seemed like Doc told me about that cemetery once. It was established in the late 1800s and closed officially some years back after a restoration. Most of the graves were over seventy years old now, with many of the older ones dating back to the late nineteenth century.

"Please tell me we're not going there today for this 'job' of yours." The snow looked knee-deep around here.

"What? You don't want to say hello to some old friends?"

"Not in these babies." I pointed down at my suede ankle

boots.

She scoffed at my foot attire. "What were you thinking, wearing those on a snowy day like this?"

"I was thinking that it was my day off and I was going to stick to shoveled sidewalks and a torn-up hotel, not go traipsing through the snow-covered hills like some frontierswoman."

She slowed to a stop in front of a square, single-story house with yellow siding and a green tin roof. Mounds of snow barricaded the place, except for a somewhat recently shoveled driveway. The windows were dark, though, and no smoke came from the chimney.

She shifted into park and then turned to me, her eyes practically sparkling with excitement. "Speaking of Coop, what time are we meeting tomorrow?"

I did a double take that ended with a frown. "We weren't speaking of Detective Cooper."

"You sure about that? Because I was certainly thinking about him." The saucy grin filling her cheeks gave me the notion that Cooper probably wasn't fully clothed in those thoughts of hers.

"I'm positive, Miss *Single White Female*. You're obsessed."

"I'm not obsessed, and your reference is all wrong. In *Single White Female*, she was obsessed with her roommate, who was a girl, not a guy." She snorted. "I love you to pieces, babe, but not enough to don a blond, curly Dolly Parton wig and go on a killing spree."

Dang, she was right. "Fine, then you're Miss *Fatal Attraction*."

"Bzzzt. Wrong again. There's an affair in that one, and Coop was single coming into this pocket-rocket rodeo. Besides, I like Bugs Bunny too much to play that part with the rabbit."

I flipped through movies about obsession in my memory, skipping past those involving extramarital affairs. Criminy, there were a lot of those, though. How come Hollywood had so many affairs end with the woman going nutso? When I caught the kids' piece-of-shit sperm donor boinking my sister way back when, I didn't go bananas and reach for the butcher knife. Sure, I poked holes in my old Ken and Barbie dolls one night after too much tequila, but my witch doctor skills have always been amateur at best.

Wait! I had a good one. "You're Miss *Misery* then."

She blew out a raspberry. "Coop is no writer, and while my fantasies have included bondage, I'm not into breaking bones."

"How about *The Hand That Rocks the Cradle*?"

"Seriously? Can you see me breastfeeding some other woman's kid on the sly ever? I mean, I'm all for breastfeeding, don't get me wrong, and I know that wet nurses can be lifesavers, but my girls probably aren't even big enough to feed a newborn kitten, let alone a whole baby."

Who was she kidding? Her rack was plenty big. She was forgetting that pregnancy could turn oranges into cantaloupes. I frowned down at my chest. And then sad, bitter lemons when everything dried up again.

I held my hands in front of the warm air blowing out the vent. "What about *Play Misty for Me*?"

"That's a little more on the mark." She stared out the windshield, looking a bit dreamy eyed. "But I don't want to stab Cooper. I just want to get him down to his birthday suit and spread Italian meringue caramel buttercream frosting all over him."

I raised one eyebrow. "That seems weirdly specific."

She scrubbed her hand down her face, blew out a breath, and then focused back on me with slightly rosy cheeks. "Clint Eastwood was early 1970s hot in that movie, though, with his wavy hair and thick sideburns."

"Maybe, but I like him better with a beard and hat, like in *Two Mules for Sister Sara*." I snapped my fingers. "I got it.

The Crush."

Natalie wrinkled her nose. "She was 14 years old. I'm 36." She shook her head at me, feigning a sad look. "Really, Vi, just stop. You're embarrassing yourself now."

I stuck my tongue out at her. "You're the one who failed at your year-long sabbatical from men, not me."

"Hey, I made it a long time without a guy."

"Five months was not even halfway there."

She shrugged. "It's not my fault. Coop chased me clear to Arizona and proceeded to woo me with billiard balls and bullet holes. What's a girl to do?"

"*Not* sleep with a cranky law dog. That's what a girl is supposed to do."

She eyed me for a couple of beats. "You sound like my cousins. At least two out of three of them, anyway."

"I'll take that as a compliment. They're smart women."

I'd grown up next to Natalie's cousins down in Rapid City. The Morgan sisters were always one step ahead of the law … at least they had been until they moved down to southeastern Arizona and the oldest of the three had started monkeying around with the county sheriff.

I reached over and poked Natalie's shoulder. "At least *they* know well enough to lay low when the cops are around."

"I lay low sometimes when Coop's around." She batted my finger away. "Other times I prefer to be on top."

I covered my ears. "Stop or I'm going to projectile vomit all over your dashboard."

She laughed. "I'm kidding. Kind of. Or maybe not. But Cornelius is right, you're a namby-pamby." She yanked my hand closest to her away from my ear. "What time are we heading down to Spearfish?"

Tomorrow was Cooper's birthday. Unbeknownst to him, we were having a little party of sorts at an old mansion in Spearfish that was built well over a century ago by a lumber baron. The main part of the sprawling house had been renovated recently and was now used for weddings, company parties, and more. However, back in the early twentieth century, a large wing had been added on to the rear of the mansion that was used as an overflow jail throughout the decades. Inside that rear wing, the new owners had repurposed the jail space, which was supposedly haunted like everything else in the Black Hills, but I had a feeling that was a marketing ploy. They'd made it into an escape room game, where money-paying guests, aka prisoners, had to figure out clues hidden throughout the various floors in order to find the key to escape from the jail wing back into the mansion.

I'd made it known from the start that I'd been against this whole birthday party idea. First of all, I'd spent enough time in jails to know there was nothing fun about trying to escape from them. More important, though, Cooper had threatened to shoot anyone who dared to throw him a birthday party of any kind, complaining that birthdays brought nothing but bad luck for him. Being that he liked Natalie, Doc, Cornelius, and his uncle far more than me, I figured he'd take aim at my hind end first. But Natalie and Harvey had blown off my concerns, going forth with their plans to celebrate Cooper's birthday anyway.

"Doc is going to leave after work tomorrow, pick up Cooper, and head straight to Spearfish for some happy hour drinks."

"Good. Remind him to pour at least two whiskeys down Coop's throat to soften him up before bringing him to the mansion."

I had a feeling it would take a whole bottle of whiskey to relax that steely hardass.

I continued with the plan. "Harvey is going to pick us up a little after six, and then we'll meet Doc at the mansion about quarter to seven." Seven was our start time in the escape room game.

She rubbed her hands together. "This is going to be so

much fun."

I guffawed. "I've solved mysteries with your lover boy before. More than once, actually. Every time, I ended up bruised and walking with a limp."

"Wow. Sexy. Giddy up." She wiggled her eyebrows at me. "Did he use handcuffs or silk neckties?"

"I meant metaphorically, you oversexed orangutan."

She reached over and patted my head. "Don't be such a party pooper, babycakes." She shut off her pickup and pocketed the keys. "Coop said he didn't want a big party and we're not giving him one. This is a *small* party with only a few friends to celebrate, that's all." She opened her door, flashing me a grin. "Oh, and you, of course."

"He's going to blame me," I called as she shut the driver's side door.

"Come on," she hollered through the window and headed toward the tailgate.

I shoved my door open, scowling at the snowflakes drifting down around us. Apparently, the sky had finally decided to let loose. "I'm going to put out an ad for a new best friend," I said, stepping carefully onto the curb.

"Didn't you learn anything from *Single White Female*?"

I pulled my coat hood over my head and joined her at the back of the pickup, grimacing as I sank an inch through the crusty snow with every step in my suede boots. "Just do me a favor and make sure Coop has no bullets in his gun."

She sighed. "For the umpteenth time, he is not going to shoot you for partaking in his birthday party."

"You can't guarantee that." I watched her untie the back corners of the blue tarp covering the bed of her rig.

"If he threatens to fill you with lead, I'll stand in front of you." She winked at me. "It's really sexy when he uses that police lingo on me."

I pretended to stick my finger down my throat. "Really, please stop this carnality talk involving Cooper before my brain barfs out my ears."

She laughed, lowering the tailgate and rolling back the tarp. "Now, hold out your arms."

I frowned at the pieces of firewood filling the bed of the truck alongside a well-used ax with a wooden handle, and then back at her. "Please tell me that unloading firewood isn't the reason you dragged me up here."

"I said I needed your help with a job." She tried to hit me with a serious stare, but then a smile cracked through. "I'm kidding. I just wanted you to hang out with me on your day off, Outlaw Curly Bill."

I smiled back. "Of course you do. It's because I'm so crazy cool, right?"

She grabbed a piece of firewood. "Right. Still crazy after all these years."

After loading up with several more pieces of wood, she carried them up the shoveled drive to a small carport angled off the side of the house.

When she returned empty-handed, I asked, "What's the story here?" I nodded toward the house. "It doesn't look like anyone is home."

"She's not." Natalie collected several more pieces of firewood. "This place belongs to Ms. Gaucho, my old history teacher. Last week she had her hip replaced and is currently in rehab at the hospital."

"When will she be home?"

"In a few days." She started up the drive.

I stared after her and then looked down at my tan cashmere gloves. I'd have to make do without them. I yanked them off and stuffed them in my pocket. Hefting a chunk of the firewood in each hand, I followed Natalie, taking care to step where the snow had been somewhat recently shoveled to protect my suede boots.

"Did you shovel her drive?" I asked after we'd returned to the pickup.

"No, another one of my classmates did. A bunch of us from school decided to work together and get her place all set up for her return." She grabbed more firewood. "I volunteered for *this* job. This wood came from that dead tree at my parents' place, the one that blew down last fall." I placed another log on her load. "This is about a quarter of a cord. It should last her a few weeks. Put one more on top."

I did, then followed her up the drive with a couple more pieces myself. "That's really sweet of you guys."

"It's the least we can do."

I tossed my pieces on the pile and helped her unload.

"She was a wonderful teacher who liked to give good grades just for trying," Natalie said as we headed back to her truck. "Her two kids live over in Montana, so they can only come every so often. Besides, you know how it is in a small town. We all have to take care of each other."

The snow was coming down harder now, coating the exposed chunks of firewood in the truck bed. Natalie brushed the snow off of a couple before snagging them. When I tried to pick up a piece with my left hand to stack it on top of the others in her arms, it slipped from my fingers. A jagged spike left over from a broken branch sliced across my hand, cutting into the meat of my palm.

"Son of a beaver!" I said, trying to shake off the pain.

"Here, let me see." Natalie dropped her load on the tailgate and caught my wrist. She held my palm up for inspection, frowning down at the now bloody gash. "Why aren't you wearing any gloves?"

"Because the ones I brought are cashmere."

"Suede boots and cashmere gloves." She shook her head.

"How was I to know I'd be hauling firewood this afternoon?"

"You should have said something before about the gloves. I have a spare leather pair in the cab."

I winced as she pressed on the skin around the wound,

making more blood well up. "You're lucky I'm not wearing the cashmere coat Doc gave me for Christmas, or I'd still be sitting in the cab and you'd have missed out on my stellar company."

She rolled her eyes at me. "Good thing you left your crown jewels at home, Princess Parker." She scooped up some fresh snow, washed off the blood, and then pulled a white handkerchief from her coat pocket. "How about I wrap this around your hand until we can get you home and fixed up?" When I eyed her makeshift bandage suspiciously, she added, "It's clean, I promise."

"So you say."

I watched as she wrapped my hand and tied a little knot with the tails to secure it.

"Does it hurt bad?" she asked.

The stinging had dulled to a low throb already. "No."

"Good. Hold it above your head and wait here while I finish up."

I leaned against the back fender with my wrapped hand held up in the air as she tromped back and forth with load after load. The snow continued to fall quietly, adding a fresh white layer to the world.

I did my best to keep Natalie company in between silently fretting about that voice I'd heard down in the basement of The Old Prospector Hotel. I really didn't want to participate in any sort of expulsion of evil spirits from anywhere if I could help it. The last time we'd messed around with exorcising the Hessler clan, shit had gone from bad to worse.

Fifteen minutes later, my hand no longer hurt at all and Natalie was carrying the last load of wood over to the now chest-high pile next to the teacher's house. The sky had darkened even more while the snow continued to fall, creating a world of muffled sounds and murky shadows. I stared up at the sky, watching big flakes swirl down toward me. Maybe Cooper's party wouldn't be so bad. Maybe he would actually …

A shiver trickled down my spine, only instead of chilling me, a rush of heat flowed out to my toes and fingertips.

I pulled my right hand from my pocket and frowned down at my fingers, wiggling them along with those on my bandaged hand. That was weird. They tingled still, although the heat had ebbed slightly.

My wound began to throb, worse than when I'd first cut it. I unwrapped the now-stained handkerchief, expecting to see fresh blood welling up again, but the skin had mostly closed over the cut. I gently poked around what was now a dark pink slash.

I'd always been a quick healer when it came to cuts for the most part, a characteristic that I'd recently learned had more to do with me being an Executioner than merely good genes. These days, though, my cuts were healing faster than ever. If only my bruises wouldn't take so long to fade.

Another shiver zinged through me, this one leaving the hairs on the back of my neck standing. I pulled up my coat sleeve. Goose bumps dotted my arm. I could feel them down my legs, too.

"What in tarnation?" I muttered and sniffed, catching a whiff of something unpleasant under the cold, fresh air. I sniffed again. It was still there. Something rotten, definitely. I looked down to see if I was near a sewer vent, but the public sewer lines didn't come this far up the street. Maybe there was a dead animal nearby under the snow.

Thump-thump.

I sniffed again, shuddering when the stench hit the back of my throat. Where in the heck was that smell coming from? I checked the bed of Natalie's truck, seeing nothing but her ax and a plastic gas can, along with clods of dirt, wads of pine needles, and pieces of bark.

Thump-thump. Thump-thump.

What was that thumping? I pulled my hood off and

cocked my head, listening, hearing nothing but Natalie's breathing, a trickle of water somewhere under the snow, and my steady heartbeat.

I stepped away from the pickup, looking high up in the limbs of the two pine trees lining the driveway. That sound was like clumps of snow falling from a tree or rooftop.

Thump-thump. Thump-thump.

There it was again. I stepped carefully through the snow, trying to keep it from packing down inside my ankle boots. I reached out with my good hand to touch the bark of the taller of the two trees and then hit the trunk twice, using the wadded-up handkerchief around my hand to soften the blow. The soft *whap-whap* wasn't the same as that *thump-thump*. A peek up through the tree limbs found them empty.

I stuffed the handkerchief in my pocket and frowned back toward the pickup.

Another flash of heat rocketed through my veins. The skin on my skull tingled now, as if I'd rubbed a balloon over my head and static electricity had turned me into the bride of Frankenstein.

Thump-thump. Thump-thump. Thump-thump.

The sound was louder now. Rhythmic. I looked toward the house, hoping it was just Natalie stomping off her boots.

Off to the side of the house, movement higher up the hillside under the trees caught my eye. I squinted through the falling snow. Was that a coyote? No, it was bigger than that. Maybe a cougar.

"Uh, Nat," I called out.

A blast of adrenaline lit me up. My muscles tightened all the way up my spine. My heart started to gallop. I zeroed in on the shape moving under the trees while the snowflakes falling around me seemed to slow, almost hovering in the air.

I watched the trees and caught a glimpse of whatever it was as it skulked closer, keeping to the shadows. What I saw spurred me to take a step backward in the snow.

What the shit? That was nothing like any of the usual predators found in the hills.

Thump-thump. Thump-thump.

Whatever was up there was making its way closer through the snow. I leaned forward, listening, and heard it breathing. Ragged, growling huffs. The stench in the air was thicker now, sticking to the back of my throat.

A check on Natalie found her midway down the drive, walking in slow motion toward me as she brushed off the front of her canvas coat. Her mouth was moving, but the low, whooshing sound in my head drowned out everything but the *thump-thump* that was growing louder and louder.

I returned to the trees on the hillside behind the house in time to see a long-limbed figure clear the tree line. Whatever it was, it was coming fast, even in my slow-motion world. Its loping, *thump-thump*, four-limbed stride kicked up whirls of snow as it headed straight for me. Its guttural, raspy breath rumbled in my ears.

Holy fucknuts! I needed a weapon. Something to swing at it. Something to …

Natalie stepped front and center into my vision, her forehead creased in worry as she stared at me. "Violet?" Her voice came from far away, as if she stood high up on White Rocks across the gulch instead of six feet away in the driveway.

I leaned to the side, watching the creature coming down the hillside behind her. I could see it more clearly now. It sort of looked like a … a human. I cringed. But not human. Its arms and legs were too long and gangly, along with its neck and face, reminding me of a piece of licorice that had been stretched a little too far. It moved all wrong, too. Unnatural, with an odd, loping gait through the snow on its elongated arms and legs.

Thump-thump. Thump-thump. Thump-thump.

Shaking out of my shock, I yelled, "Natalie! Run!" and

started toward her so I could shield her. But the toe of my boot caught on a clod of icy snow. I stumbled to my knees.

An ear-piercing yowl cut through the growing darkness, sending a fresh batch of heebie-jeebies crawling over my skin.

Natalie flinched and turned toward the creature. Her eyes widened, her jaw dropping in horror.

I struggled back upright and rushed toward her. "Get down!" I yelled, diving for her as the long-legged creepster lunged into the air.

We crashed into the snowy yard with me on top, her pink earmuffs flying off her head. I heard her *Oof* at the same time I saw the creature reach for me. I bowed my back, feeling its long fingers brush across my coat. But they didn't make purchase.

The thing came down with a hard thud on the other side of the drive, its arms and legs tangling as it tumbled and smashed head-first into the pine tree I'd been pounding on moments ago.

Crack!

Globs of snow and pine needles rained down on it.

"What the fuck?" I heard Natalie say from under me.

Snowflakes were falling at regular speed again. Normal sound had returned to the world.

I rolled off her and pushed to my feet. "Did that thing crack its melon open?"

Before she could answer, the creature pushed up on all fours again, shook its hairless, deformed head several times, and then cough-snorted out something dark and globby onto the snow.

"Oh, gross," Natalie whispered behind me.

I scowled back at her, saying under my breath, "You need to get out of here before it attacks again."

"I'm not leaving you with that ... that ..." She slowly moved up next to me, her shoulder bumping mine. "What the hell is that thing?" She kept her voice so low it was hard to hear her. "It almost looks human."

I knew exactly what it was even though I'd never seen one before. "That's because it used to be human. It's a *Nachzehrer.*"

And boy howdy was this one ugly bogeyman.

The creature shook its head again, like something was loose inside. Then it looked skyward and pulled its lips back, showing off an impressive set of pointy choppers as it hissed up at the falling snow.

Natalie took a step back, hauling me with her. "Do you see all those teeth?"

"The better to eat you with," I whispered.

We both took another step back as the *Nachzehrer* stood upright on its legs.

"Jesus! It must be eight feet tall." Natalie's voice had a slight quiver.

"Or more." Even its toes were gangly, moving like individual fingers.

"What's it wearing?"

"Saggy skin." So saggy, in fact, that everything south of its nipples and north of its knees was nothing but folds of flesh. Although the skin looked dried and scraped, jerky-like. An old leather sofa left out next to the curb too long came to mind.

"That doesn't look like skin to me," Natalie said.

"Fine. Why don't you go touch it and tell me what it is, then?"

She elbowed me in the ribs. "How are we supposed to kill it?"

It took a lumbering step toward us, its teeth still bared, its huge hands swiping aimlessly at the open air.

"There is no *we* about this," I said, trying to remember if Dominick had mentioned the creatures having a weak spot during his history lesson this morning. "You need to get the hell out of here and let me handle it."

"As if I'm going to leave you alone with this … this …"
She pulled me back another step.

"*Nachzehrer*," I finished for her.

"More like nightmare."

The *Nachzehrer* swiped at the air again, reminding me of
King Kong taking swings at airplanes from the top of the
Empire State Building. It took another lumbering step into
the yard, sinking to its ankles in the snow. The fiend's head
whipped side to side. A long, pink tongue pushed out
between its meaty lips, pointing in one direction and then
another. The end of it curled slightly as it bobbed up and
down.

"What is it doing now?" she whispered.

"I don't know. I'm not a freakin' monster-ologist."

But if I were to guess, I'd say it was "sniffing" the air like
a snake.

" 'Monster-ologist'?" She huffed quietly. "Is that the best
you can do?"

"Until my brain is done hiding under the bed, yes."

The *Nachzehrer* blinked repeatedly as it looked left and
right. It reached out again, swiping the empty air. Then with
a grunt, it lowered onto all fours. It stood completely still,
aiming its long slimy tongue toward the trees and then the
house.

"I don't think it can see us now," I whispered. "That hit
to the tree trunk must have knocked something loose and
temporarily blinded it."

"Hey!" Natalie yelled suddenly, making me almost wet
my pants. "Asshole!"

"Shhh!" I turned into a statue, waiting for the *Nachzehrer*
to turn our way. Instead, it took another step toward the
forest, reaching out blindly in front of it.

My breath rushed out as relief made my knees rubbery.
"What the hell is wrong with you?" I asked without looking
her way.

"I was testing its hearing. The sucker didn't even flinch. It must be deaf and blind."

"How can that be? It must have heard us unloading wood and come for us."

"Maybe it was just passing by and saw us."

I frowned at her. "I don't think so. This thing is trained to hunt Executioners. It must have picked up my scent somehow." I reached in my coat for my cell phone, but I'd left it in the pickup. "We need to radio the others. I don't suppose you have your walkie-talkie handy?"

Her gaze was still glued on the creature. "What walkie-talkie?"

"The one Coop wants us to use now to communicate instead of our cell phones."

It was her turn to frown at me. "He didn't say anything to me about a walkie-talkie."

Oops. Maybe he didn't intend to give his girlfriend one, which was a really dumb move on his part if that were the case. Super dumb after not including her previously in our group texts.

"What about your cell phone?" I took a different tack.

"It's in the truck. Did *you* get a walkie-talkie?"

I hesitated as the *Nachzehrer* turned in our direction, its tongue curling in and out as it "sniffed" the air, or whatever the hell it was doing.

"Did you?" she pressed.

"Yeah, but I left it at Aunt Zoe's." I thumbed toward her rig. "We need to step lightly and make our way back to your truck."

"What about that thing?" She plucked her earmuffs from the ground and hung them around her neck. "We can't just leave it here at Ms. Gaucho's place as a 'welcome home' pet."

"It will probably go back up in the trees." At least I hoped it would. I was not prepared for a cage match at the moment, not with Natalie's life at risk if I failed at my job.

"Violet!" She growled out my name. "You have to kill it right now."

"According to Dominick, killing a *Nachzehrer* requires severing its head." I grimaced at the leggy beast as it took another step toward the trees.

"Decapitation it is," she said, as if it was a done deal and I should sign on the dotted line.

"I don't want to."

"Why not?"

I held my arms wide. "Because it's my day off."

"Oh, for the love of all things hairy." She grabbed me by my coat lapels and hauled me close until we were nearly nose-to-nose. "We are not leaving until you kill that thing."

"Your pupils are really big right now, Nat. It's kind of creepy."

"Quit trying to change the subject."

"Fine! What am I supposed to kill it with? I left my weapons at home and my patented laser glare needs new batteries."

"We'll have to improvise."

She pointed toward the woodpile. "You could bash its head in with a piece of firewood."

I recoiled, pulling free of her grip. "Jiminy Cricket, Natalie. Do I look like a basher of heads?"

"Oh!" She held up her index finger. "What about my ax? It's in the bed of my pickup."

I rubbed my jaw. "I don't know about that. I've never been much of a lumberjack."

But it was too late. Natalie was already tiptoeing through the snow toward her pickup.

I cursed under my breath, following her. "I'm not dressed for a decapitation."

She made it to the truck and scowled back at me. "Do you hear yourself?" she chastised in a loud, bossy voice.

We both looked at the *Nachzehrer* to make sure it still

wasn't hearing or seeing us. The thing was about to round the corner of the house and disappear from sight.

"Snot bucket! This is going to ruin my good boots." Not to mention my supper if that thing exploded like the chimeras back in Slagton when I'd killed them.

She scoffed at me. "All of the killers in your family line just rolled over in their graves, even the lousy ones that died young."

I narrowed my eyes. "That's a low blow."

"Zoe is going to kick your ass if you don't do your job right now."

"Fine. Hand me the stupid ax."

After I took it from her, she pointed at my hand. "Where's your bandage?"

"The bleeding stopped so I took it off." I reached into my coat pocket and pulled out the blood-stained handkerchief, holding it out to show her.

A loud screech pierced the air.

We both whirled toward the *Nachzehrer*.

It was loping toward us on all fours again, its tongue pointed straight at me.

"The handkerchief!" Natalie yelled at the same time I shouted, "My blood!"

I dropped the handkerchief as the nightmare bore down on us.

"It's coming too fast, Violet!" Natalie reached for me, but I shoved her aside with enough force to send her stumbling into the snow.

She was right. The son of a bitch was going to hit me hard. I hefted the ax and planted my boots, readying for the collision. A warm calm rippled through me, filling me with steady confidence. I focused on the *Nachzehrer*, hearing its rasping breath, along with the crunch of snow with each step.

The thing grunted as it pushed off the ground, flying through the air with its long arms and fingers outstretched.

Its tongue had pulled back into its mouth, leaving pointy teeth bared in a face-stretching snarl.

I gripped the ax, locking my jaw.

But before I could swing, something slammed into me from the side, sending me flailing into the snow.

The *Nachzehrer* careened toward the back of the pickup, crashing into the open tailgate. The metal hinges ripped free with a loud screech.

I sat up, digging snow out of my collar. "Dammit, Nat! I had that."

"No way. It would have smashed you into my truck, leaving you flat as a pancake."

She scrambled to her feet and held out her hand for me, checking out the back of her truck. "Ah, shit! It took off my tailgate. Those aren't cheap, ya gangly cocksucker."

I took her hand and let her pull me upright. Grabbing the ax out of the snow, I crept over to where the *Nachzehrer* lay in a tangled heap of saggy flesh on the road behind her truck. More blackish goo oozed out of a huge gash in its shoulder. Its right arm dangled by just a few muscles and strips of leathery flesh.

"You have to kill it, Vi." Natalie joined me. "Remember the partially burned one Coop said was hit by a car and its arm fell off? That one got right back up and tried to attack the driver." She squeezed my shoulder. "It won't stop until it kills you."

I blew out a breath. "I know."

"Yeah, well hurry up before it gets its second wind."

I gripped the ax. "Step back."

After she'd moved a few feet away, I lifted the ax over my head. Wincing in advance, I closed my eyes and swung.

The ax connected with a sickening, squelchy sound. I waited for an explosion or splattering or something else vile.

The thing gurgled.

"Oh jeez, Vi." Natalie crunched through the snow

behind me. "You closed your eyes, didn't you?"

"Maybe," I said, opening them.

The ax had missed its mark, landing in the sternum instead of the neck. More black goo oozed out onto the snow. A lot more.

The *Nachzehrer* warbled out a growl and rolled to the side with its jaws snapping. Its sharp teeth scraped over the toe of my boot. I hopped back, leaving the ax still stuck in its chest.

"You did close your eyes." Natalie bumped me aside. "You always close your eyes when you chop wood." She dodged the creature's long fingers and yanked the ax free.

It gurgle-growled again and took a swipe at her, but she moved away in time.

"Okay, maybe I did close my eyes a little."

She handed me the ax, pulling me out of the way when the *Nachzehrer* tried to grab my leg. "This time, keep your eyes open when you swing."

"I'll try."

"And hurry up before something else catches a whiff of your blood and comes looking for its next meal."

I shook the tension out of my arms, stretched my neck side to side, and then raised the ax overhead again. "It's supposed to be my day off."

"There's no rest for the wicked, toots."

The *Nachzehrer* hissed and lunged up toward me, its teeth snapping.

"Violet! Now!"

Keeping my eyes wide open this time, I swung.

Chapter Seven

An hour plus a shower later …

And then the *Nachzehrer* withered away in the snow, leaving behind nothing more than a dusty shadow," I said, taking the freshly cleaned and rinsed dinner plate Doc held out to me. "Like when you smash a moth against a window."

"Christ, Killer." Tension lines crisscrossed Doc's face. "You need to start carrying your mace with you."

I agreed, but the mace he was referring to was long with several sharp points on the business end. "It's going to be tough to fit that in my purse," I said with a smile, trying to use a little humor to ease some of his worries. "Maybe you should switch places with Harvey and play bodyguard until we catch them all."

"I'd rather keep you tied up in the bedroom."

He leaned closer, his eyes sliding to my lips with obvious intent, but a certain annoying detective interrupted us before I could finish what was on Doc's mind.

"You shouldn't have killed it," Cooper said as he set a stack of dirty bowls on the counter on the other side of Doc, who was wrist-deep in sudsy dishwater.

I nudged my head toward the kitchen table, where Natalie, Harvey, and Aunt Zoe were relaxing while Doc and I did our part cleaning up after a meal of hearty beef stroganoff and a sweet berry cobbler that still had me licking sugary goodness off my lips.

"Tell that to your girlfriend. She insisted I finish the job before we hightailed it out of there."

Or rather fishtailed it out of there, being that all of the fresh snow made for a slippery slide back down the hill. I'd left a finger indentation—or four—on Natalie's dashboard by the time we'd skidded onto the main drag.

"What was Vi supposed to do, Coop?" Natalie came to my defense, of course, same as she always had since our pre-training bra days when we'd see how many pieces of bubblegum we could stuff in our mouths at once. "Handcuff the gangly sucker and bring it down to the station for some stale doughnuts and burnt coffee?" She crossed her arms over her bib overalls, scowling at him. "Or maybe Vi should have asked me to get hold of you on the old walkie-talkie so *you* could tell us what to do with the thing. Oh, wait. That wouldn't have worked because I'm not part of your little walkie-talkie club, am I?"

Cooper took her scowl and cranked it up to a full-on glare that he aimed at me instead of her. With his finger-plowed hair sticking up like rows of shark teeth, and not one, but two muscles clenching in his cheek, he looked a heartbeat away from popping his top.

"What?" I raised my hands in surrender, holding the mostly dry plate between us as a shield. "I told you she'd be pissed if you didn't invite her to be part of our posse."

He groaned rather than growled, surprising me into lowering the plate. "There is no damned posse, Parker." An uncommonly soft sigh followed, then a single shake of his head before he turned to Natalie. "I have a valid reason for not giving you a walkie-talkie."

She set her jaw. "Let me guess, it's something to do with protecting fragile li'l me."

"Partially, yes." He crossed to the refrigerator.

Two red blotches appeared on Natalie's cheeks. Uh oh. It appeared his answer had lit a fire inside of her. Cooper had best back slowly out of the room. And then run.

Harvey snorted. "Coop, did you leave your brains in your back pocket?"

Cooper grabbed two bottles of beer out of the refrigerator, pointing one at Natalie. "But not in the way you're probably thinking, Beals, so you can stop giving me that go-to-hell look."

I took a clean bowl from the sink and started drying it, glad the focus was off of me for a moment. I'd been in the spotlight since we'd finished supper and the kids had headed upstairs—one to take a bubble bath, the other to read his newly acquired library book about cannons throughout history. I had a feeling Harvey had something to do with Layne's reading choice, what with his recent purchase of an actual old cannon.

Anyway, I'd started story time with what Aunt Zoe, Harvey, and I had learned from Dominick earlier at the old school, filling in Doc, Natalie, and Cooper so that my ending tale of the *Nachzehrer* had more oomph. I'd skipped the part of my day showcasing Cornelius and the weird voices, giving Natalie a warning look when she seemed about ready to bring it up. That unnerving segment was something I wanted to save for later when Doc and I could hash out the who, how, where, why, and what-the-fuck answers.

Aunt Zoe glanced up from the leather notebook opened on the table in front of her, tucking a few strands of hair behind her ear. She still wore her jeans, but had exchanged her work shirt for a clean sweater.

She'd been adding to her earlier notes about the *Nachzehrer* as I talked, drilling me for several minutes about its apparent lack of hearing and sight. Although, after weighing Natalie's take on the creature's impairments, we were all pretty sure the blindness was only temporary due to cracking its noggin on that pine tree.

After focusing on Natalie for a moment, Aunt Zoe chuckled. "That's more like a you're-full-of-crap look, if you ask me."

Natalie touched her finger to her nose and then pointed at Zoe with a slight smirk. "Bingo."

"I'm not full of shit." Cooper used the edge of the counter next to Doc to quickly knock the bottle caps off both beers. He took a drink from one and set the other down on the table in front of the smirker. "I didn't give you a walkie-talkie, Nat, because you live under the same roof as Detective Hawke. We all know how sound travels through the vents in that place."

Natalie and Hawke were both staying in apartments at Galena House this winter, which was owned by Freesia Tender, one of my clients. Officially, Hawke was more of a squatter, having taken over the late Ms. Wolff's place, aka the crime scene, insisting someone needed to stay there to protect more police evidence from being stolen by burglars. In particular, by "burglars," he meant me. The detective's paranoia about me these days seemed to know no bounds. The irony was that while I was very interested in the buttload of old German Black Forest clocks hanging on the walls in that apartment, it wasn't me who had been sneaking in and taking them.

Natalie lived right above Ms. Wolff's apartment and was trading her handywoman skills for her one-bedroom digs. When she wasn't helping Freesia fix up the place in order to make it easier for me to find a buyer, she'd taken to playing nosy neighbor. Hawke appeared clueless that his phone conversations were coming through the vents loud and clear. Well, mostly anyway.

Cooper returned to the seat next to Natalie. "I'm just trying to keep Hawke from hearing about Parker's guano-psychotic life and dreaming up any more witchy-witch ideas about you two." He clinked his bottle against hers and then tipped it back for another swallow.

" 'Guano-psychotic'?" I spelled that word out in my head.

"Batshit crazy," Doc supplied, pulling the plug on the dishwater.

I cut Cooper a glare while handing Doc the dishtowel so he could dry his hands. "I'm not crazy."

"I was talking about your life, not you. Although if you want to split curly, crazy hairs …"

"I think Violet's pretty damned badass-tastic," Natalie said. "But she could use some coaching on planting an ax."

"I did just fine." At her raised eyebrow, I added, "I mean, the second time. The first was a warm-up swing."

Harvey scratched his beard. "Did you put a coin in that critter's mouth before lopping off its head?"

"Why would she put a coin in its mouth?" Natalie asked.

Aunt Zoe spoke while writing a couple of words on the page. "There is a myth that said you have to put a coin in its mouth when you kill it. Masterson debunked it, but …"

"Hmm." Natalie sat forward, leaning her elbows on the table. "Maybe that's a rule for non-*Scharfrichter* types."

"I've made a note here that no coin was used." Aunt Zoe's blue gaze shifted to me. "But maybe next time you could try slipping a coin in its mouth before you kill it just to see if it makes a difference."

I guffawed. "Natalie, you saw the sharp pointy teeth on that sucker. I'll lose a finger trying to put a coin in there."

Doc kept the towel, nudging me aside and reaching for a rinsed bowl. "We can try the coin if I'm there. Otherwise, just turn it to dust."

"I don't want you to lose any fingers either." I shoulder bumped him, batting my lashes at him. "Your fingers are magic," I said for his ears only.

"Metal is metal, Sparky," Harvey said. "Screw the coin.

Just jam Bessie's 12-gauge barrel in its maw and yank on the trigger. Same difference at a safe distance."

Natalie turned to Cooper. "I thought you aren't supposed to 'yank' on a trigger."

He shrugged. "Up close like that, yanking will work, too."

"For the record," I said, hopping up on the counter. "Since you see ghosts now, Cooper, your life is as much of a crap carnival as mine."

"Not quite," Doc said.

Cooper pointed his beer toward us. "What he said."

"Hey." I lightly backhanded Doc's shoulder. "Whose side are you on?"

"Yours, Boots. Always." Since he used that particular nickname for me, which was usually followed by pleasurable activities involving his hands and mouth, I let him lean over and steal a kiss. "But you have to admit that seeing ghosts is not on the same level as having to decapitate a parasitic bogeyman that has matured by being deposited in a human's ear canal so that it can devour not only its host's innards, but transform it at a cellular level, too." He returned to drying bowls. "A ghost is child's play compared to a *Nachzehrer*."

I cast a frown in Doc's direction when he wasn't looking. I wasn't so sure he was right after what Cornelius and I had heard this afternoon. For all we knew, cannibalistic hosts might be a fun-filled fiesta compared to the horror that was perfecting Doc's voice in the walls of The Old Prospector Hotel.

"So what's the plan?" Natalie asked. "Should we head out at dawn and begin the hunt?"

Aunt Zoe looked up again from her notes. "The hunt for what?"

Natalie thumbed in my direction "The other *Nachzehrer* hiding in the hills waiting to attack Violet. The partially burnt, one-armed bastard that Coop told us about before."

"Bad idea," Cooper said, earning an eyeroll from her.

"What're we gonna use for bait?" Harvey asked.

"I'm not going anywhere at dawn, except to the shower," I told them, leaning back against the upper cupboard doors.

"I'm glad to hear it," Doc said, finishing up the dishes. He draped the towel over the faucet and then stepped between my knees, resting his hands on my thighs. His gaze dipped below my chin. "Maybe I should follow you into the shower," he said quietly. "You know, do some backup bodyguarding."

I grinned. "Is that what the kids are calling it these days?"

"Are you going to just sit around, Vi, and wait for the other *Nachzehrer* to surprise you?" Natalie asked. "We were lucky today. The one we dealt with was clumsy, and I had an ax handy. Next time might not go so well."

"Sure as shootin', sittin' around whistlin' up the wind isn't gonna do us much good," Harvey agreed.

At least I thought he was taking Natalie's side.

"Do you two have some kind of death wish?" Cooper asked, setting his empty beer bottle down with a hard thud. "The last thing we need to do is go tromping through the hills in all of that snow where these creatures can move twice as fast as us."

"Or more," I added. "Let me get through this weekend's parties and then I'll go out searching with you guys. But not at dawn. Never at dawn."

Doc's back was still turned toward the rest of the group, so they didn't see the wince he made at my words.

But I did. I paused and retraced my last …

"What *parties*?" Cooper's gaze was locked onto me tighter than a choke collar. "I thought there was just the one party for your work."

Uh oh! I'd been thinking about his surprise birthday party tomorrow *and* Sunday's big release shindig. I licked my suddenly dry lips. "I meant 'party,' as a singular noun. It was a slip of the tongue. That's all. I swear."

His eyes narrowed to gunfight-at-high-noon slits.

Yikes! "Sheesh, Cooper. Chill out. There's no need to take me down to the station and tie me up in the interrogation room. Actually, I don't think you're allowed to tie up a suspect, are you?" I was sinking into a pool of bibble-babble, but couldn't seem to stop. "Sometimes my mouth doesn't listen to my brain, and I accidentally make my nouns plural, like 'What's up, Docs,' and 'I'll have some bacons, Harvey.' It's just a fluke, really. Right, Nat?"

Natalie squeezed her lips together and rolled them inside, giving me a pointed stare that said I should follow her example.

"Parker, if you are covering up for—"

"Maybe Harvey and I will go out hunting on our own tomorrow morning." Natalie interrupted before he could finish what was probably a jail-themed threat. "Violet has to work, so we can go do some pre-hunting prep work. You know, tracking, asking a few questions here and there. That sort of detective work. What do you think, Harvey?"

He grunted. "We'll put out the fire and hit the trail before it gets too cold."

Cooper frowned across at his uncle. "No, you won't. We need to do this methodically to reduce risks."

Whew! Natalie's diversion had worked. At least I hoped it was just a diversion. She and Harvey didn't need to go looking for trouble on my behalf.

"How do you propose we start, Coop?" Aunt Zoe asked.

"We lay out a map of the northern Hills and track all known past locations, like the taxidermy shop."

Doc settled against the counter next to me. "I'd like to return to Jones' Taxidermy for another look around. You think that can be arranged, Coop?"

"Why?" Aunt Zoe set her pen down and leaned back in her chair. "Did you notice something odd when you were there last night?"

I scoffed. "Besides all of the creepy stuffed critters watching us with those glass eyes?"

"I noticed Coop," Doc said.

"What about him?" I looked to Cooper, waiting for him to deny whatever Doc was implicating, but he didn't.

"Did you see somethin', boy?" Harvey asked his nephew.

Cooper made a pained face. "You had already left," he told his uncle. "And Parker was in her vehicle waiting for Nyce, who was talking to Jonesy. The other officers had taken off and I was doing one last sweep around the perimeter."

"Alone?" Natalie asked, her expression showing exactly how she felt about him taking that risk.

"Not completely. I had my firearm."

"What did you see?" I echoed Harvey's question. Had the *Nachzehrer* that broke into the taxidermy shop been hiding in the trees, watching us? Waiting for the right moment to attack? Or had it been something else? A bounty hunter?

"Someone was standing in the shadows just out of reach of the headlights."

"That's creepy," Natalie whispered. "What did you do?"

"He didn't see me, so I held back, watching to see his next move." Cooper shrugged. "Then he passed right in front of me, not three feet away, and disappeared into the side of the hill abutting the shop."

Ah, so it was a ghost.

"Did you recognize him?" Aunt Zoe asked.

"Was it Jonesy's grandpappy?" Harvey hooked his thumbs in his suspenders. "You remember him, dontcha? He wore a patch over one eye. Supposedly lost it in the war. Was the left one, I think."

Cooper shook his head slowly. "I'm not sure."

"Why not?" Harvey's bushy eyebrows drew together.

"Because he was missing something that would have helped me determine his identity."

"What?" I asked, wondering if he'd been skinned like that poor guy we'd found in Harvey's barn months back.

"Most of his head."

I covered my mouth.

"Oh, my." Aunt Zoe cringed.

"Jeez." Natalie reached out and touched Cooper's arm.

"That explains the expression on your face when you rejoined Jones and me," Doc said.

"Shocked," I suggested.

"More like sucker punched," Cooper told us, rubbing his eyes.

"So, this here ghostie was just wanderin' around without his top nut?" Harvey shook his head as if things weren't adding up right. "Sort of reminds me of that headless corpse ol' Red dug up back in my graveyard. Makes me curious if that fella is still wanderin' around my ranch, lookin' for something to rest his hat on."

"Not that I've noticed," Cooper said. He turned to Doc. "Why do you want to return to the taxidermy shop? You think you can interrogate a nearly headless ghost? We already know the perpetrator was one of Parker's parasitic pals."

"Nice alliteration, Hot Cop," Natalie said with a purr in her voice.

He gave her a wink. "You inspire me, Beals."

She trailed her fingers up his arm. "I could do more than that to you."

"Like what?" Harvey asked with a slick grin.

"I can't tell you. It's police business," Natalie shot back.

Aunt Zoe was still looking at Doc. "Do you think there is some clue to the location of the *Nachzehrer* or the bounty hunter that supposedly commands them over at Jonesy's?"

"No. Maybe. I don't know." He rubbed the back of his neck. "It's probably nothing."

I rested my hand on his shoulder. The tight muscles under his shirt told a different story.

"Coop, is there any way to find out who the headless guy is?" Harvey asked. "Somethin' you have down at the station that could help clue us in?"

"Would Jonesy know?" Aunt Zoe said, taking a sip from the cup of coffee she'd been nursing since dessert.

"Maybe." Cooper shrugged. "But it's tricky. Questions like that can fuel rumors and conspiracy theories. Plus, I don't need any of this ghost shit getting back to the station. I'm under a microscope with Hawke as it is." He looked specifically at me after that last sentence.

"Your partner's paranoia is not my fault."

"Quit acting like you're one hundred percent innocent, Miss Spellcaster."

"I could dig through some records at the library," Doc offered. "Old newspaper articles on microfiche, maybe."

"You don't have time for that," I told him. "Your work schedule has you running at full speed already. Maybe I should look into this for us. Things are slow at work right now outside of a few listings up around Terry Peak." The ski resort was hopping with all of this snow, bringing in buyers who daydreamed about log homes near the slopes.

"I could help with that," Natalie offered. "Vi and I could pay a visit to Mudder Brothers and go through Eddie's old undertaker records again."

Doc and Cooper both groaned in unison. My history at Mudder Brothers Funeral Parlor was filled with macabre escapades that nobody would like to repeat, especially me.

"What?" Natalie looked back and forth between the two of them. "Vi and I promise not to get into any more trouble with pale-faced juggernauts."

Cooper pushed back from the table. "If Detective Hawke catches wind of Parker near the morgue, he'll haul her into jail and slap some asinine crime like trespassing on her."

"Hawke is such a dickwad," Natalie said to her beer before finishing it off.

I seconded her opinion of Hawke. To Cooper, I said, "I want to go back to the taxidermist's place with you two." When he seemed to hesitate, I added, "What if that *Nachzehrer* comes back for seconds while you're there? You'll need my help."

"You don't think Nyce and I can handle one *Nachzehrer* on our own?"

"Maybe. But what if there are still two out there and they team up on you?"

"I'd like Violet to be there," Doc said. "She might sniff out something I can't."

I doubted that, but him wanting me along made me want to kick my feet and grin like a starstruck groupie. "Can we go during the day this time? That place at night is spookier than a haunted clown hotel."

Cooper took Natalie's empty bottle and set both on the counter next to the sink. "Let me see what I can do tomorrow on that front." He eyed me with a suspicious glint. "Or is this something else that has to wait until after your 'parties' this weekend."

I flipped him off. "And kiss my ass while you're at it."

Doc chuckled and caught my hand, holding it hostage in his. "That's my job, Boots. Leave poor ol' Coop be. He has his hands full with a headless ghost and a hot-headed partner."

"Don't forget his pissed-off honey badger here," Harvey added, pointing across the table.

Natalie grinned. "That's right."

"Why are you pissed off again?" Aunt Zoe asked her.

"He's not sharing his walkie-talkie love with me."

"Sounds like a prostate problem to me," Harvey said, snickering. "They have a pill for that, ol' man."

Doc laughed out loud.

Cooper didn't. "Real funny. And you all are supposed to be my friends. I'd be better off hanging out with a pack of jackals."

Grinning, Natalie went over and grabbed Cooper's elbow, tugging him toward the dining room. "Come on, birthday boy. Let's sneak over to your place for some hard-driving negotiation work and see if we can come to a mutually beneficial outcome on this walkie-talkie hankering."

Cooper let her pull him along. "But it's not my birthday yet."

She stopped and looked up at him, flirting under her long eyelashes. "Soooo, you don't want your present early?"

He stood stock-still for a few ticks of Aunt Zoe's Betty Boop clock, then he scooped her up, tossed her over his shoulder, and carried her out of the room.

A squeal of laughter followed in their wake. "See you guys tomorrow," she shouted right before the front door slammed.

Harvey reached for the cookie jar. "Zoe, how do you feel about puttin' me up for the night in exchange for me makin' breakfast come mornin'?" He pulled out a chocolate chip cookie and broke it in two, offering half to her. "Those horny toads will be busy hangin' from the chandeliers and testin' the mattress springs for half of the night. I need my sleep in case one of Sparky's ugly critters comes callin' out of the blue."

She took the half cookie, popping it in her mouth, then grabbed her pen. "What did you have in mind, Willis?"

"Looks like yer fridge is full up on bacon and I saw some taters in the pantry. How about I make Sheepherders Breakfast?"

"You know where I keep the spare pillows and blankets." Pen hovering over her notebook, she nailed me with a pointed look. "Now, Violet, how about you tell us your story again, and this time don't leave out the part about the séance Natalie told me that you had with Cornelius down in the basement of The Old Prospector Hotel."

Chapter Eight

Buttcrack of dawn
Friday, January 18th

W e need to have another séance with Cornelius in the basement of his hotel," Doc said.

I opened one eye, frowning up at him from my pillow. He was shirtless, fresh from the shower by the looks of his wet hair and the towel draped around his shoulders. My one-eyed perusal drifted southward, meeting an unhappy ending at the waistband of his black pants.

"You're dressed." My voice was rusty. So was my brain.

He glanced down at his pants, as if they were a surprise to him as well. "Partly."

A two-eyed peep toward the window furthered my grief. It was still dark out. "The sun isn't up yet."

"Have faith, it will rise again." He hung the towel on the hook on the back of my bedroom door, closing it and shutting out the faint sounds of Harvey belting out Charley Pride's old 1970s tune, "Kiss an Angel Good Mornin'," down in the kitchen.

I groaned and turned away from the rest of the world, tugging the covers up over my head and closing my eyes.

I'd stayed up late last night, long after Doc and Aunt Zoe had gone to bed, watching a revenge-fueled Western with a strong female lead. Harvey had fallen asleep in the recliner partway through the movie, but I'd stayed awake, looking for inspiration from the tough-as-nails heroine.

After the film was over, sleep had remained elusive, sort of like that damned imp, hiding out of reach long into the early morning hours. Finally, the sandman had come knocking, and I'd tiptoed upstairs, sliding into bed without waking Doc.

I hadn't had any coffee after supper, nor had I stayed awake fretting about the *Nachzehrer* or Detective Hawke or any of my other Executioner problems. All I could figure was that I'd suffered from a post-killing adrenaline rush that kept my motor running long after I should have been snuggling under the covers next to Doc.

The mattress sank behind me. "What time did you come to bed?"

"Around four."

His hand found me under the covers. His fingers glided over my bare back above the top of my camisole, spurring delicious shivers down my spine. "Why so late?"

I shrugged. "I couldn't sleep."

"Were you worried about something?"

"No more than usual."

"Scoot over."

I did as ordered, moving into the middle of the bed. The covers lifted behind me. A draft of air hit my skin, and then Doc was there.

"Come here, Tish." He pulled me back against him, curling around me.

I popped my head out from under the covers, cozying up to his heat, breathing in the clean, spicy scents of his cologne and shampoo. Ah, this was the good life. I could stay right here for days and let those *Nachzehrer* roam the hills, hunting to no avail.

He pushed the covers lower, exposing my shoulder to the cool air and then his warm lips. "Talk to me," he whispered against my skin.

I sighed. "How about we fool around instead, and then I go back to sleep?"

"Tempting, but I heard your aunt waking up the kids as I left the bathroom."

"Buggers."

Addy and Layne had sort of grown used to Doc being in my bed, but in their minds Doc was just camping out next to me since all of the other beds were full and there wasn't anywhere else for him to sleep. They had yet to fully understand how the birds and bees worked, and neither Doc nor I wanted to burst their innocent bubbles. That meant we had to save any fun beneath the sheets for late at night or super early in the morning.

He rolled me onto my back, his palm resting on my hip. "Open those beautiful eyes, Boots."

It took me a few blinks, but I managed to pry my peepers open. He was resting up on his elbow, staring down at me. My gaze started with his freshly trimmed beard, traveled up over his strong lips and nose, and ended at his dark eyes rimmed by even darker lashes.

"It's not fair that you look so good without any makeup," I told him, reaching up to run my fingers over his bearded cheek. "Nice. It's way softer than the hair on my legs." He must be using the conditioner I'd noticed in the medicine cabinet.

He cracked a smile. "Quit flirting with me and tell me what's causing those little lines on your forehead."

I touched my brow, feeling the wrinkles for myself, and then tried to rub them away. "I don't want to have a séance in Cornelius's hotel."

"Why not?"

The answer to that was tricky. I didn't want Doc to think I doubted his abilities, which was the basis of the disagreement we'd had last night after I told Aunt Zoe,

Harvey, and him about the voices Cornelius and I had heard. When Doc had mentioned wanting to repeat the experience while he was there with us, I'd put my foot down and refused to budge in spite of his frustration with my "hinny-ness," as Harvey had called it.

Instead of answering, I switched to something else I'd worried about in the middle of the night. "Who do you think Reid was talking about when he told Aunt Zoe he couldn't come over because he had company in town?"

Doc's eyes narrowed. "You're trying to distract me."

Yep. "Did you see the way Aunt Zoe scowled when she told us about his reason for declining her supper invite? She was jealous, I could tell."

"Violet." His voice was low and growly.

Under the covers, I took his hand and slid it up inside my camisole. "You don't think Reid has another girlfriend, do you? I don't want him to give up on Aunt Zoe yet."

He looked down at the covers, under which his hand now rested on one of my fun-bags. "And that is distraction number two."

I moved his palm around in a circle over my left lung-bongo since he wasn't taking the bait. I pasted on my best blank look. "Why, Doc. I don't know what you're talking about."

"Boots, listen. The changeling is not going to possess me." He stubbornly resisted my subject switcheroo, but his hand started moving on its own, not requiring any more assistance from me.

"We don't know that for certain. You said yourself that you haven't dealt with an entity before that has this much power."

"Outside of Prudence," he said, reminding me of the qualification he'd made during our disagreement last night.

"Prudence doesn't count."

"Why not?"

"Because she was an Executioner. We tend to have additional skills outside of killing assholes."

His gaze dipped to my lips, his smile positively predatory. "You do have an extremely talented tongue."

Now who was trying to distract whom?

I clasped his hand, stopping his fingers from further teasing. "For all you know, the changeling or its ghoulie parasite could possess both of us. Or worse, it could open up that locked door in Cornelius's head that you and Prudence peeked into and then let something even worse out into the world."

He tugged his hand free of my grip and relocated it to the other side of my chest, spreading his attention equally. "That seems a bit over the top."

I pushed up onto my elbows. "Doc, you're an Oracle. A hybrid species left over from ancient times when your kind were used by those who were hungry for power to conquer and devastate legions."

At least that was the gist of what I'd learned about Doc's ancestors from the elusive Mr. Black, who I had a feeling had also been used as a tool by those craving dominance—and still might be.

"That seems a shitload 'over the top,' in my opinion," I continued. "We don't know what the Hesslers or their sinister pals want with you. Nor do we know what capabilities these entities might have if they are able to latch onto you like the one did with Cornelius."

His hand under the covers stilled. His gaze held mine. "We can't just ride out this changeling situation. It won't go away on its own."

"I know that. All I'm suggesting is that we wait a little longer so we can bone up on this sort of infestation or whatever you want to call it. Then we go into it with more backup plans in place in case the séance takes a hard right, as it undoubtedly will."

When he continued to stare at me without speaking, I reached out and cupped his chin, leaning toward him. "I'm just scared of something getting its ectoplasmic claws in you, *mon amour.*"

He sighed, resting his forehead against mine. "Okay, Tish. We'll wait a little longer."

"Thanks," I whispered, dropping back onto the bed in relief. "I'd just like to have a normal day for once. You know, go to work, try to sell real estate, pick up my kids from school, go out with my friends to celebrate a birthday, and then come home and go to bed with my boyfriend."

His hand slid south over my stomach. "And then what?"

I looped my arms around his neck, wrapping my leg around his under the covers. "I'd show you, but you're overdressed for the occasion."

"Damn it, Boots." He pulled me closer. "We don't have enough time."

"We never do, but we could make it really quick." As I closed the distance between our lips, a knock rat-a-tat-tatted on the bedroom door.

"Mom?" Layne called out.

"Son of a biscuit," I muttered.

Doc groaned under his breath, and then untangled from me, sliding out of bed.

"What do you need, Layne?" I called out, pulling the covers up to my chin.

"Can I come in? I need to talk to you."

I sent a raised brow look at Doc, who was sliding on his shirt. He nodded, walking over to the window.

"Sure, Layne."

Still wearing his dinosaur pajamas, which were about a size too small now, Layne stepped into the room, leaving the door open behind him. His dark blond hair was sticking up on one side. He glanced from Doc to me and then back at Doc, a grin surfacing. "I told you Mom was a bed hog."

Doc laughed while buttoning his shirt. "She sure is."

"If you're going to keep sleeping at our house," Layne continued, "you should buy her a bigger bed."

I shot a surprised look at Doc. Was that my son's version of a thumbs-up on Doc and me taking the next step in our relationship?

"Or you guys could get two twin beds like on those old TV shows. Then Mom wouldn't knee you during the night anymore." He eyed me with a half-pinched face. "Or we could put the extra bed in my room and you wouldn't have to sleep near her at all. But my room is smaller, so it would be a tight fit."

Right. So maybe that wasn't an official green light from Layne, but at least he wasn't making a big deal of Doc getting dressed in front of me.

Low in my stomach, a pinching pain off to one side made me flinch slightly. I rubbed my belly and the pain eased almost as quickly as it had started. That was weird.

"I don't know, Layne." Doc tucked his shirt in his pants. "I've had to sleep alone for a long time. I sort of like sharing a bed with your mom. She smells really nice and is good at making me feel better after I've had a rotten day." He glanced my way with a grin. "Although, when she rubs her cold feet all over me, that separate bed idea appeals."

"Her feet are the worst," Layne agreed.

"Hey, now!" I stuck one leg out from under the covers and pointed my sock-covered toe at Doc. "My frozen tater tots are dutifully swaddled, so quit bawling, you big babies." I followed with a yawn that morphed into a stretch.

Doc's gaze crawled up my otherwise bare leg, then he blew out a breath, shaking his head. "We should let your mom get a little more sleep. She was up late last night hanging out with Harvey."

"Okay. I just wanted to know if she could take me to the police station sometime today."

What!? "Why do you want to go there?"

I shuddered at the mere idea of stepping foot inside of the cop shop. I'd had too many bouts of inquisitional indigestion thanks to Cooper and Detective Hawke in the past six months.

"To see Coop."

Oh, of course. "I told you we could deliver the birthday gifts Addy and you made for him at Doc's place after school." According to Natalie, Cooper had the day off and planned on working on a few things at home before Doc took him out for happy hour drinks.

"This isn't about Coop's birthday present."

I pushed up onto my elbows. "It's not?"

"Why do you want to go to the police station, Layne?" Doc asked while buckling his belt, his lined brow mirroring the tension brewing inside of me.

Before Layne could answer, Addy came rushing through the door, her straight blond hair pulled back in a ponytail, her glasses slightly askew. Unlike her brother, she was wearing blue jeans and a kitty-covered pink sweater. "Did you tell them, Layne?" she asked, mumbling around her toothbrush.

"I was just about to."

"Tell us what?" I asked, sitting fully upright now.

Addy looked at me and her eyes widened. "Your hair is crazy this morning, Mom."

Cooper was rubbing off on her, dang it.

She took a step closer. "What's wrong with your eyes?"

"They look freaky, don't they?" Layne added.

Crazy hair and freaky eyes. So far, my "normal day" was off to a stellar start.

"Adelynn Renee, you just drooled toothpaste on the rug." I turned to her brother. "Layne, tell us why you want to go to the police station right now."

"We want to report a missing rooster."

* * *

"A missing rooster?" Mona, my coworker-slash-mentor, asked a couple of hours later as I settled in behind my desk at Calamity Jane Realty.

"Yeah. Only it's not really a rooster." I tucked my purse in my desk drawer, shoving it closed with an extra kick of frustration.

"What is it, then?" She watched me from over the rims of her rhinestone-edged reading glasses as she stirred some sugar into a cup of coffee.

Dressed in a cropped, black and white striped blazer over a black silk tank top and knee-length leather skirt, Mona would be an excellent choice for the cover girl of *Sophisticated Sirens* magazine, if there were such a periodical. She'd left her auburn hair free and flowing today, with big casual waves that spilled over her shoulders like a smooth lava flow.

Hell's bells. Next to Mona, I felt like a ragamuffin with a bird's nest for a hairdo, sticky fingers, and Kool-Aid stained lips. Add to it my pink tweed jacket and black knit pants, and I could blend in with a row of flamingo lawn ornaments. I really needed to hire someone to dress me, comb my hair, and send me off to work with a sack lunch.

"Rooster is a stray dog," I explained. "It turns out they've been feeding it behind Aunt Zoe's and my backs, so it kept coming around for more." At least it had until three days ago, having since been a no-show, which prompted their request to submit a missing-dog report over at the police station. "Addy named it 'Rooster Cogburn,' so that I'd be more willing to let them keep it when I found they'd unofficially adopted it."

Mona chuckled, heading back to her desk. "There's never a dull moment in your life, is there?"

She didn't know the half of it. Well, actually, she did know some about what I dealt with—the ghostly stuff, anyway. Mona also knew that Doc was a mental medium and that Cornelius was able to hear ghosts, and he and I had dabbled with multiple séances. Mona had even joined us, along with Cooper and Natalie, when we'd tried to reach out to our old boss, Jane Grimes, whose ghost haunted the building. She just didn't know about my Executioner gig on the side, or about all of the *others* that roamed the hills these days.

I walked over to the coffee maker to pour myself a second cup of much-needed caffeine, catching the sweet scent of Mona's jasmine perfume in the air. After Doc's hands-on wakeup call and my kids' pet collecting escapades, I'd joined everyone down in the kitchen for Harvey's belly-filling Sheepherders Breakfast. It turned out I'd been even more hungry than tired. But the one cup of coffee I'd wolfed down along with breakfast wasn't going to cut it today.

"It gets even better." I dumped cream in my coffee. "Addy had the bright idea to teach 'Rooster' my scent as well as hers, so she'd sneak my dirty laundry from my bedroom and wear my clothes while she fed and petted the dog."

Which explained the long white hairs I'd noticed on my yoga pants and cable knit cardigan when I did laundry earlier this week.

"Smart girl," Mona said, leaning against her desk as she cleaned her reading glasses. "The dog would be all lovey-dovey with you from the get-go, making it even harder to turn it away."

"Smart and scheming." I shook my head. "That girl takes after me a little too much for comfort."

"And Layne was in on this, too, huh?"

I returned to my desk. "Yep. Addy has him convinced Rooster would be officially his pet, since she has Elvis, the real chicken of the two."

"Oh, dear. Have they thought about the fact that the dog might want to eat poor Elvis?"

"Yeah. They were using Addy's stuffed chicken toy to teach Rooster that chickens are friends, not food."

Her laughter was interrupted by the sound of the back door opening.

When I looked around to see who had joined us, another pinching pain struck low in my gut. I winced and pressed on it. What the hell? Had I gotten food poisoning somehow? Was this the start of a stomach flu? It almost felt like a premenstrual cramp, but it was too soon for that, wasn't it? Same as earlier this morning, the pain eased as quickly as it had come.

"Violet?" Jerry called, striding into the front room, looking fresh from a workout and shower at the Rec Center with his damp hair, untucked shirt, missing tie, and freshly shaved square-cut jaw. "I need you to do me a fa …"

Jerry's voice trailed off as he gaped at Mona, who'd stood to greet him. His eyes practically bulged as they roved over her curvy form. I wouldn't have been surprised to see his tongue roll out and start lapping up dust bunnies from the floor.

"Oh, damn," he said in a high, creaky voice, which sounded funny coming from a six-foot-eight, Thor-lookalike. He cleared his throat, speaking in a much deeper voice when he said, "Morning, Red."

Jerry had spent his early years playing pro basketball, wowing television audiences, and slam-dunking his press interviews. After our previous boss died last fall, Jerry had shown up to pick up where Jane had left off, turning a four-person real estate crew into a five-man, all-star sales team. Currently, our "team" was down a player, but Jerry was determined to not let the loss of one agent interfere with his goal to be the top-selling real estate company in all of western South Dakota. This champion ambition was his reasoning behind volunteering our office to be the focus of the *Paranormal Realty* television show.

"Good morning, Jerry," Mona replied smoothly before settling in behind her desk. At first glance, she seemed oblivious to her effect on him, but then I saw a small quirk of her lips as she pulled on her reading glasses.

Ah ha! That was who she'd dressed to impress today.

"You need something from me, Jerry?" I asked, wondering if he was able to hear above the sound of his panting libido.

He blinked several times, turning my way in slow motion. "I was just ... Umm, I could use ... What?"

"I believe you were going to ask me for a favor."

"Oh, right." He glanced at Mona again before continuing. "I was wondering if you could help me out with an appointment. I have some clients interested in attending an open house up near Mount Roosevelt this morning. It's in the Bountiful Big Pines housing community. They asked if I'd go through the house with them, but I need to take care of a pressing matter down in Rapid City."

"So, you want me to drive them to the open house?"

"No, just meet them there and do the walk-through with them. They like a little extra hand-holding."

"When?"

He checked his watch. "I'm supposed to meet them at the house in about an hour."

"Sure, I can help."

I had no appointments today and was happy to escape the office for a bit. Maybe I could sneak in a quick visit over at Doc's office on my return. He should be done with his morning appointments by then.

Ten minutes later, I slid in behind the wheel of my SUV. I'd decided to leave early so I could check out the place on my own, talk to the agent staging the open house, and prepare for whatever questions Jerry's clients might have for me. I'd just pulled out of the parking lot behind Calamity Jane Realty when my cell phone rang.

I accepted the call via my vehicle's speakerphone. "Hello?"

"Hey, Sparky," a deep, gravelly voice said.

"Hi, Reid. We missed you at supper last night."

"Even Zo?"

Uhhh … "Yep."

"Are you crossing your fingers while you tell that lie?"

I uncrossed my fingers. "No. She did. For real."

At least I assumed that it was missing him that spurred that jealous gleam in her eye when she'd told me Reid hadn't come to supper due to having out-of-town company.

"I need to talk to you, Sparky."

"I'm on my way to an open house."

"In town?"

"A few miles out from it. Up by Mount Roosevelt."

"Can I meet you there? This will only take a few minutes."

Was this going to be about Aunt Zoe? Did it have anything to do with whoever his mystery company was? Was he going to practice his it's-not-you-it's-me speech on me, stomping on my hopes for them sharing a future?

"Sure," I said, hiding my anxiety behind a dollop of bravado. "I'm a little early, so if you can meet me there in the next twenty minutes that should work."

"Great. Give me the address."

I rattled off the street number and name.

As I hung up, a full-on cramp tightened down low in my abdomen. I rubbed it, wincing until it passed.

What was today's date? The 18th, right? I counted backward on my fingers. It couldn't be here already, could it? I stopped off at Jackpot Gas-N-Go on the way out of town so I could use their bathroom to see if what I suspected was true.

It was, damn it.

Aunt Flo had come calling a week early and I wasn't

prepared. The timing was weird, especially considering that the birth control pills I'd been taking for the last year sometimes had me skipping periods altogether. Not to mention the cramping like I was having hadn't happened since I'd started this particular brand of pills.

Maybe all of the stress from that *lidérc* and everything else going on screwed up my cycle. At least I wasn't pregnant. I quivered at the thought alone. I'd rather face off with another Hungarian devil. Although the thought of having Doc's kid had crossed my mind now and then, but usually my pregnancy amnesia kicked in only when I was good and drunk.

The bathroom vending machine didn't offer much choice. Holy menstrocity! Football players wore smaller pads than what came out of the box. But this would cover me until I could stop by home after this open house business. I bought an extra pad as a backup, figuring I could keep it under my car seat in case I accidentally cut off one of my arms someday and needed to staunch the flow of blood.

"So much for my normal day," I muttered as I crawled back behind the wheel. I popped a couple of ibuprofen I found in my purse to ease the cramps and headed back down the road. At least I was wearing black pants today.

A few minutes later, I pulled up in front of an open house sign planted in front of a two-story log home with a wraparound porch. Its angled tin roof still sported a thin layer of snow, probably left over from last night's extra-thorough dusting. Its lower story had been dug into the hillside and was fronted with a river stone façade. Or maybe the stone walls were real. I'd see for myself when I walked through the place. The house still looked somewhat new, considering it had been built about ten years prior.

Off to the side of the house sat a detached, A-frame, three-car garage with tan-colored siding and dark green doors. According to the sales listing, this outbuilding included a fully furnished mother-in-law apartment upstairs. The garage backed up against the forest, separated from the hillside covered with pine trees by a cedar rail fence that was obviously more for looks than privacy.

The half-circle drive had been plowed, but I decided I'd park near the end of the drive to give potential buyers the closer spots.

I steered past the two vehicles currently sitting in the drive—a pickup and a Subaru. As I passed the garage, I noticed another vehicle parked back out of view of the road. I did a double take, hitting the brakes.

"Shit!" That was Tiffany Sugarbell's Jeep.

What were the chances that she was only visiting the place and this wasn't her open house? I looked around for the For Sale sign that should be near the end of the drive, finding it behind a mound of plowed snow. Sure enough, Tiffany was listed as the agent to contact.

Growling at the idea of facing off with Doc's gorgeous ex, I parked my SUV and shut off the engine. I pulled down the visor and peered in the light-up mirror on the back. Eek! I should have worked harder on my eye makeup this morning. Or at least brushed on some cover-up powder. I looked red-eyed and blotchy with a shiny nose and forehead, as if I'd come straight over from holding a spot in a police lineup. Scrubbing off my T-zone with a tissue, I painted my lips and retouched my mascara, pinching my cheeks a few times in place of blush. Sadly, that would have to do for this round of Violet "Rocky" Parker versus Tiffany "Perky-tits" Sugarbell.

I closed the visor mirror and checked the time. Still no Reid in sight. Blowing out a breath, I grabbed my purse and pushed out into the cold. I might as well get this reunion with Tiffany over with before I had company. It would be better to hiss and snarl at each other without too many witnesses.

The wind was stronger up here in the hills above

Deadwood. The pine trees surrounding the place shivered and bent in the stiff breezes that tore at my coat and blasted through my wool pants as if they were made of a single layer of cheesecloth. At least my knee-high boots were doing their job of gripping the ground in spite of the packed snow. A falling on my ass display in the driveway would fill the red-haired viper inside with a fresh spurt of venom.

I'd made it up onto the porch when Reid's dually pickup rumbled into the drive. I waved as he circled in front of me before parking behind my SUV.

Bracing against the wind, I walked back down the porch steps and along the drive. A strong gust hit me halfway there, ramming me into the knee-high snowbank ringing the drive.

"Asshole!" I shouted at the sky and returned to the plowed path, brushing and shaking the snow off my pants before continuing over to his driver's side door.

Reid rolled the window down, his easy grin reaching clear up to his deep blue eyes. "Howdy, Sparky. Is that mean ol' wind bullying you around?"

As firemen went, Reid was one of the finer specimens. In spite of the decades of wear and tear he had compared to the newer recruits down at Deadwood's station, the fire captain could probably hoist ladders and wield hoses as well as the rest of them. He had that rip-cord sort of strength that reminded me of cowhands stuck out on the range for weeks at a time. It didn't hurt with the local female population that he looked a bit like Sam Elliott in his younger days, including the salt-and-pepper mustache and swaggering gait.

"Keep it up, Reid, and I'll have Aunt Zoe hit you with another uppercut."

Reid had one somewhat hindering flaw that my aunt had discovered by accident long ago—he had a glass jaw. Off and on over the years, Aunt Zoe had used that Achilles heel of his to her advantage, bringing the big strong fireman to his knees … and then sometimes leaving him flat on his face.

He held up his hands in surrender. "Down, Sparky."

"That's more like it." Another gust pushed me up against the side of his pickup, leaving my black pants smudged with dust.

"Oh, come on!" I swiped at the dirt. Now I'd have to face Tiffany while looking like I'd ridden in on a dust devil.

"Sparky, why don't you hop in the passenger side while we talk? You need to get out of the wind."

Grumbling about being Mother Nature's punching bag, I stalked around to the passenger door and crawled up inside.

Reid's rig was warm and smelled of his musky-scented cologne and fresh oranges, the latter probably having to do with the air freshener hanging from his rearview mirror. I sniffed again, checking for a hint of a woman's perfume, but came up short. If his out-of-town visitor was female, she must not have ridden in his pickup lately.

"How are you doing?" he asked as I settled into the leather seat.

I eyed him warily. "Why? What have you heard?"

He laughed. The deep, baritone sound eased the tension from my shoulders.

"You're as prickly as your aunt today."

"Did you go see her?"

"No. I called."

"What did she say?"

"When I asked her what she was up to, she told me to go to hell and then hung up on me."

I chewed on my lower lip. She'd seemed fine during breakfast this morning. A little withdrawn, but quick to smile.

"That's why I need your help."

"I've already hidden her shotgun shells, Reid. She just keeps buying more. You should probably buy a bulletproof vest and duck for cover after you knock on her door."

His forehead creased as he stared out the windshield. "I love that girl's spunk, but she has one hell of a bite."

"Well, at least she's stopped filing her teeth when she knows you're coming around, so we're making progress."

He sighed. "Yeah, about that. I want to introduce her to someone, but I'm worried about how it will go."

My heart sank. I didn't want Reid to move on. I'd been rooting for him to win over Aunt Zoe for months, keeping my fingers crossed he'd eventually beat down the walls she'd built.

"If this 'someone' comes equipped with mammary glands and a pair of X chromosomes, I recommend you reach out to Aunt Zoe via pen and paper, and then leave town for … I don't know, maybe six months to a year."

I had a feeling that in spite of Aunt Zoe's repeated claims that she wasn't going to fall for Reid again, she was already halfway to the ground. A solid nudge would send her crashing the rest of the way down.

"It's my son," he said quietly.

"Your son?" I'd forgotten Reid had a kid. Well, he wouldn't be a kid anymore.

He nodded.

"Is that who your out-of-town company is?"

"Yeah. He's thinking about moving here to be closer to me. He knows a little bit about my recent history with Zo and wants to meet her, but I'm nervous about bringing him around."

Only the recent stuff? "You think she won't like him?"

"Yes. No. Who knows?" He gripped the wheel with both hands. "I just want the two people I love to hit it off right out of the gate."

I could relate to that. Bringing Doc into the kids' life hadn't gone near as well as I'd hoped, but time was smoothing out the burrs. If only my kids' biological sperm donor—the no-good son of a bitch—would take a rocket to the moon and leave us alone so we could finish forming a tight-knit, happy little family.

"What do you need from me?" I asked, checking the time. Jerry's clients should be showing up in another fifteen minutes or so. I flipped down the visor to have another look at myself after battling with the wind.

"I guess I was hoping that you and I could put our heads together and figure out a way to grease the wheel."

"I'm game. Do you want me to talk to Aunt Zoe about your son?"

I tipped the visor a bit, trying to get a better look in the mirror at my hair. The wind had done a bang-up job of messing it up after the wrangling I'd done. I leaned down and turned slightly, checking to see what remained of my French coil.

I saw something move in the reflection back near the trees behind the garage.

Crud, was Tiffany coming out to check up on us? She'd probably noticed my SUV and Reid's pickup by now.

"I think we might have company." I turned in the seat to get a better look through the back window.

Reid followed my lead, peering out the back along with me. "I thought your clients weren't here yet."

"They're not. I think it's … " my voice squeaked in my throat at the sight of a gangly, long-limbed creature loping along on all fours on the far side of the cedar rail fence. "You gotta be fuckin' kidding me," I said under my breath.

"What in the hell is that?" Reid's windpipe sounded strangled.

I faced forward, my breath coming fast, my body tingling with a sudden bolt of energy. I could feel the adrenaline ramping up in me again, shooting through my veins like a fireball. The urge to kill the creature as soon as possible took over my thoughts, followed by a rush of anticipation. I had to go find it. Chop it to pieces. Turn it to dust. Now, before it was too late and someone else saw it.

I reached for the door handle, but out of the blue another

cramp gripped me, low and fierce, making me double over. I groaned in pain.

"Violet!" Reid reached out and touched my back. "What's going on? Are you okay?"

Wincing, I looked at him. "I don't suppose you happen to have one of those heavy-duty fireman axes in your truck that I could borrow."

He nodded. "Yes. Why? What is that thing in the trees?"

"A *Nachzehrer.*"

His face paled. "You mean the used-to-be human Zo talked about? The thing we found burnt next to the Mickelson Trail last fall?"

"I saw two arms and two legs, so this isn't the one you found, but it's just like it, only not so crispy." I sat upright as the cramp began to fade.

He swiveled, looking out the back window again. "What the hell is it doing here?"

"Looking for me." I reached for the door handle again. "Now, where's that ax?"

Chapter Nine

What are you going to do with my ax?" Reid asked as he followed me up the drive.

"I'm going to take care of that thing before it kills anyone. Especially you and me."

As we neared the house, the front door opened and Tiffany rushed out onto the porch. She was dressed to the nines in a shape-hugging pristine white suit. Everything else on her was red, including her stiletto heels, belt, lips, and hair.

Damn it. As usual, Tiffany looked drop-dead sexy, and I just looked dead, or at least recently back from it. Pale and blotchy with wind-whipped hair and a fading black eye, I was no match for her polish and shine today.

"Violet!" she snapped, planting her hands on her tiny, non-child-widened hips. "What are you doing with that ax?"

Oops! I lowered the weapon and pasted on a big, glossy smile, trying my best not to act the part of a psychotic killer rushing off into the trees to decapitate someone—or rather, something.

"What ax?" I played dumb.

Her scoff echoed off the side of the garage. "If you touch my Jeep, I'm going to—"

"I'm not going to touch your stupid Jeep, Tiffany," I snapped back at her. To Reid, I whispered tersely, "Go take care of *that* problem."

"Me? No." He kept stride with me. "I can't let you go

after that thing alone. It was huge. Easily twice your size."

"I know," I said. "I just killed one yesterday."

He grabbed my coat sleeve, tugging me to a stop. "You what?"

"Violet!" Tiffany hovered at the top of the porch steps shivering in the wind, her arms wrapped around herself. "Don't make me call the cops on you."

"Reid." I stared hard up into his dark blue eyes. "I need you to go distract her now. I can't have Detective Hawke racing out here and threatening to burn me at the stake in front of everyone."

"Coop will protect you."

"He has the day off for his birthday, remember?"

"Shit. That's right. You guys are doing that murder-mystery thing tonight, right?"

"The escape room, yes."

"But Zo is staying home with the kids?" At my terse nod, he asked, "Should I bring my son over tonight?"

I shot a glance at the trees and then Tiffany, before leaning closer to him. "Do you think we could bookmark this conversation and get back to it after you go distract Tiffany and I go kill the *Nachzehrer*?"

"Sure." When I started to turn away, he grabbed my sleeve again. "What's your plan?"

I looked down at the ax and then back at him. "I figured I'd start with removing its head, per Masterson's instructions."

"That's it, Violet! I'm calling your boss," Tiffany threatened. "And then the cops."

I held up my index finger in her direction. "Just give me a damned minute, Tiffany! You owe me that for stealing Jeff Wymonds away from me."

"What does Masterson have to do with this?" Reid asked.

"I'll explain it to you later. Right now I need to do my job, and you need to charm Jessica Rabbit up there with those big fireman muscles and the red-hot charm you hose-jockeys are famous for." I tried to pull free, but he held on.

"Sparky, you cannot go hunt that thing alone. Zo will kill me if anything happens to you on my watch."

"Aunt Zoe will kill me if I let anything happen to *you* on my Executioner watch." I pointed the ax toward the porch where Tiffany still hovered, a worried frown on her forehead as she glanced back and forth between the front door and us. "Please, Reid, you have to run interference for me. Take Tiffany back in the house and don't let anyone follow me into the trees."

"Christ!" He scrubbed his hand down his face.

"Reid." I gripped the front of his canvas coat, pulling him down to my level. "This is what I do. Now go play fire captain and put out that fire." I shoved him toward the house.

A shriek pierced the air, making my shoulders tighten. It came from the hillside, but higher up. The *Nachzehrer* was either running away from me or luring me into the trees where it might have the advantage.

Tiffany took a step backward, her worried brow now aimed at the hillside behind the house. "What the hell was that?"

"It's a cougar," I heard Reid say as he walked toward her, his baritone voice steady and calming. "How about we get you inside, darlin', before you catch a chill?"

Without a backward glance, I hurried past Tiffany's Jeep and around the back of the garage, slipping and sliding out of sight. I leaned my back against the wall, taking a couple of deep breaths, focusing on the tree-covered hillside beyond the cedar rail fence.

The *Nachzehrer* wasn't anywhere to be seen, but I could smell something rotten in the air. The scent was strong back here. I sniffed again, grimacing. Why couldn't my enemies smell like fresh-baked cookies?

The prickling of my skin told me the danger was still near.

The tingling throughout my limbs assured me I was ready to fight.

The pounding of my heart warned me to take care during the hunt. I had two kids depending on me to not die this morning.

I scoured the trees, searching for a sign of my enemy while I listened for further sounds of its loping footfalls or ragged breaths. But the weather was working against me, the wind rushing this way and that, making the pines whisper so loudly they were practically humming. The gusts made it hard to catch any telltale movement, what with branches swaying and dropping clumps of snow. The whole forest had come to life, both beautiful and sinister at the same time.

There was no getting out of this—I was going to have to chase the creature down. I cursed under my breath. It turned out that Natalie and Harvey had been right after all—this morning I would be going on a hunt.

With one last check for trouble to my left and right, I eased through the cedar fence rails and started up the hillside, taking shelter under the pine trees from prying eyes and the worst of the wind blasts. The cold wasn't so biting inside the protection of the trees, nor was the snow as deep, only coming up above my ankles in drifted piles here and there. I quickly learned where to step as I climbed up the hill, using the ax as a makeshift cane now and then. Above me, the crowns of the trees whipped to and fro, dropping snow bombs like aerial missiles.

Thirty feet or so into the forest, I found the creature's trail. At least I was pretty sure that only a *Nachzehrer* could take such long strides. The individual tracks themselves were too big for the other animals in the forest, since most of them had hooves.

I continued up the hill, pausing every so often to stop and listen, sniffing the air repeatedly like a bloodhound.

Pulsing with energy, my legs wanted to give chase at a sprint rather than a cautious walk. This was the polar opposite of normal, which involved a lot of lazing around on the couch under a blanket while my hand did all the work feeding my face. Maybe this *Scharfrichter* gig would pay off on the diet front, saving me from having to cut back on carbs once spring came and it was time to drop some of my winter insulation.

Farther up the trail, the creature's stride shortened. It had moved more slowly through here, or maybe it had been cautious. Another fifty feet ahead of me, I could see a tall outcropping of rocks. The weathered remnant of an ancient peak or solid cliff, maybe. Throughout the outcropping there would be wide cracks and narrow, shallow caves, providing several places to hide. The height difference would offer an excellent ambush opportunity. The higher ground was always preferable in battle.

The tracks in the snow headed in the direction of the rocks. I didn't follow, listening to my gut instead, which told me I was being led into a trap.

Just how smart were these things? Was there a bounty hunter waiting for me up by those rocks, too? Could the *Nachzehrer* simply be the bait?

As I stood contemplating my next move, the ax gripped firmly in my hand, I heard the snap of a small branch behind me down the hill. I hid behind a tree, my breath held. A rush of heat under my skin kept the cold at bay as I bided my time and waited to see if the *Nachzehrer* had managed to sneak around behind me.

A breeze whipped through the trees, carrying a familiar spicy-sweet scent. That was no mythical monster, although Aunt Zoe might disagree depending on the day. I stepped out from behind the tree, spying Reid before his gaze locked onto me. He was moving stealthily, his brown canvas coat and salt-and-pepper hair blending in with the forest far better than my getup today.

I attempted a bird-like whistle. It came out a little too shrill, but it drew his gaze. At the sight of me, I could see the relief spill over his features. He rushed toward me, almost tripping on a broken tree limb partially buried in the snow.

"Sparky," he whispered when he reached me, pulling me in for a quick, hard hug. Then he pushed me back and patted my shoulders and arms, checking to make sure I was still in one piece, no doubt.

"I'm fine," I whispered back. Although if this *Nachzehrer* was like the one from yesterday, it might not be able to hear or see us, so all of this stealthy fun and games was for naught. "What are you doing up here?"

"I told you I wasn't going to let you hunt alone."

"What about Tiffany?"

"I convinced her that you and I were going to come up here and scare off that cougar. Told her she didn't need it hanging around during an open house. The big cat might deter potential buyers."

"Smart thinking. Tiffany is all about the almighty dollar."

He scowled down at me. "Sparky, I know you've come from a long line of killers and all that jazz Zo talks about, but hunting alone is always dangerous. You should have waited for me."

I would have liked to, but having him along added a liability. My aunt would kick my ass if anything happened to him, even though she swore she wasn't starry-eyed for him anymore. Plus, I liked Reid a lot. I didn't want him to get hurt any more than she did. But truth be known, I was relieved to have company. Maybe that made me a lousy Executioner—and I had no doubt Prudence would call me a big chickenshit for this—but right here and now under these trees with that creepy sucker wandering around, I didn't give a shit.

"Thanks for following me, Reid." I squeezed his arm and then pointed toward the rock outcropping. "My gut tells me our troublemaker is prowling around up in those rocks."

He eyed the towering rocks, shaking his head slowly. "If we go up there, we're sitting ducks. It could be hiding right above us and drop down on our heads."

"Right. So how do we get it to show itself?"

A cramp hit me hard, making me gasp and bend partially over. Son of a kraken! What the heck was going ... Oh!

I finally figured it out.

Well, duh!

Reid grabbed my shoulder. "What is it? What's wrong?"

"I ... uh ..." I stood upright, grimacing more at how to explain my realization to my aunt's not-boyfriend. The truth was slightly embarrassing and exceedingly bizarre, but I was pretty sure I now understood why the Red Army was on the march south a week earlier than usual for me.

"Did you fall and hurt yourself on the way up the hill?" He frowned down at where I was gripping my side. "If you landed on a branch or rock, you could have a fractured rib or done some other internal damage."

"I didn't fall."

His eyes returned to mine. "Then what's wrong?"

The pain ebbed as a breeze blew up through the trees, rippling past us toward the rocks.

"I suspect that my body is working its own magic and providing an irresistible lure via cramps."

His frown deepened. "What do you mean?"

Before I could answer, a screaming howl rang out from above us.

I cringed, turning toward the rocky outcropping. As I watched, the creature stepped out from a shadowy crevice up near the top.

"Look!" I pointed at the sneaky bastard.

The *Nachzehrer* leapt into the air, crashing down on the forest floor, sending snow and rocks scattering.

"Holy shit," Reid said in a strained voice, sounding like

he'd had the wind knocked out of him. "It's like a daddy-long-legs spider covered with human skin."

It sniffed the air, its face contorting. Then it took a step toward us. Its jaw unhinged, gaping wide.

And wider.

And even wider.

"Jesus, look at all those teeth," Reid said, taking a step back and pulling me with him.

The creature let out another screaming shriek that made my neck hairs bristle along with the rest of me. I tightened my grip on the ax handle.

"Should we run?" Reid asked.

I shook my head. "It's faster than us. We have to stand our ground." I raised the ax.

The *Nachzehrer* lowered its head, its dark eyes locked onto me. This one certainly seemed to be able to see us and looked to be preparing to charge.

"Get behind me, Reid," I said, not bothering with whispering now. "It's picked up the scent of something it can't resist."

"You mean human flesh?"

The *Nachzehrer* stuck out its long, snake-like tongue. It writhed in the air for a second before pointing directly at us.

"No." I took a steadying breath and bent my knees, planting my feet. "*Scharfrichter* blood."

In a blink, the creature sprang at us, coming fast and hard. Its lips were pulled back, and those sharp-toothed jaws opened wide in a howling screech.

A loud "pop" exploded next to me, followed by a sizzling hiss as a flare flew through the air toward the thing. I tried to see if it hit the creature or not, but a close grouping of trees blocked my view for a second.

The *Nachzehrer* cleared the trees but then stumbled before losing its footing entirely. It tumbled down the hill toward us with sparks shooting out every which way. I stepped aside as it rolled past me, gangly arms and legs flailing, and watched it slam into a downed, dead tree.

I turned to Reid, who was holding a bright yellow flare gun out in front of him. "Where did you get that?"

"I grabbed it from my truck before I came to find you."

The *Nachzehrer* was still shooting sparks, putting on its very own fireworks show. It rose up onto its knees, its saggy skin draping like an apron over its thighs, and clawed at its throat as flames shot out of its mouth.

"You nailed it right in the kisser. That's impressive shooting, Tex." I wasn't joking either. That thing had been coming at us fast.

"I was aiming for the eye," he said, cutting me a quick grin. "Thanks, though. I've spent lots of time at the shooting range with Coop. I guess it paid off today."

We eased closer as the *Nachzehrer* fell backward, its jaw opening and closing as it thrashed in the snow.

Another breeze swirled around us. Even while its throat was burning, the creature picked up on the scent of my blood and reached for me, making desperate swipes at my legs with its long, bony fingers.

I stared into the creature's dark eyes, searching for signs of the human that used to be in there, but they were like two black pieces of obsidian. I moved my hand back and forth in front of it. Those black eyes followed the movement.

"Apparently, this one can see okay."

"It certainly seemed to have a bead on us when it raced down the hill."

"Can you whistle loud?" I asked him, dodging its attempt to kick me in the midst of its struggles.

"Uh, sure."

"I mean really, really loud."

"Well, I'm no match for a train, but I can certainly get attention when I need to."

"Good. Do it."

He gave me a look as if I had a train smokestack growing out between my eyes. "Right now?"

"Yes. And hurry, the flare is dying out."

He licked his lips and then let out a loud, piercing trill that left my ears ringing.

The *Nachzehrer* didn't even flinch or glance Reid's way.

"I don't think this one can hear either," I said more to myself than him.

He pulled another shell from his coat pocket and loaded it into the chamber of the flare gun. "Stand back, Violet." He pointed the gun at the creature. "At this close of range, it can't possibly live through another hit."

"Don't shoot, Reid," I said as the sparks fizzled out. "Another flare might kill it, but it won't finish off the body so that we leave no trace of this thing behind. Then we'll have to figure out how to hide the carcass so Cooper doesn't end up with another bizarre murder case on his desk." That would surely result in him putting a cap in my ass out of sheer frustration.

He lowered the gun. "Then how do we put it out of its misery? And ours?"

I raised the ax. "Like this."

* * *

"You closed your eyes again, didn't you?" Natalie took a bite out of her peanut butter and honey sandwich, giving me and my freshly showered hair that know-it-all look.

"Only the first time." I dished up some leftover berry cobbler from the refrigerator. After the morning I'd had, I needed a whole casserole dish of sweetness to make me feel better, but my hips could only handle a plateful.

"Was that green stuff on your pants blood from the *Nachzehrer*?" Aunt Zoe asked. She sat across from Natalie at the kitchen table wearing her work shirt and jeans, but both were clean so she must have been sketching out new designs in her shop instead of getting her hands dirty.

"I thought they turned to dust when you executed them," Natalie added, her voice slurred from the peanut butter.

"That wasn't its blood," I said to Aunt Zoe. "And they do turn to dust when I kill them," I added for Natalie as I took a seat at the table. I stuck a forkful of sweet berry yumminess in my mouth, swallowing before explaining, "The ax missed its mark on the first swing, landing an inch deep in its shoulder, partly because it tried to dodge my swing."

Natalie pointed her sandwich at me. "But mostly because you closed your eyes again."

"Shut up, Paul Bunyan," I grumbled and scooped up another bite of cobbler. "Before I have Babe the Blue Ox jam one of his horns up your ass."

The cobbler was missing a key, uplifting ingredient. I returned to the fridge, carrying a can of whipped cream back to the table.

"What was that green sticky stuff then?" Aunt Zoe asked.

"Some kind of vomit." I sprayed the whipped goodness on my cobbler, making an upside-down cone with it.

"Oh, gross." Natalie pretended to gag a little. At least I thought she was pretending.

"After I missed its neck, I was struggling to yank the ax free from its shoulder. But it was really stuck in there. I pulled hard enough that the *Nachzehrer* came up off the ground some, and that's when it spewed that green vile stuff on my pants and boots."

I didn't mention the bits of fur and chunks of its last meal that had come out along with the green slimy gunk. The memory of that moment almost made me lose my appetite, but then I added a final spritz of whipped cream to my cobbler and I was good to chow down again.

"It threw up on you," Aunt Zoe noted and then frowned down at her *magistra* notebook, which she'd brought downstairs after I'd finished my Silkwood sterilization shower and started the tale of my open house nightmare.

Thankfully, the couple I was supposed to take through the open house flaked out on me. Or, I should say they "snowflaked" out. According to Mona, who had texted me while I was trying to clean the green gunk off of my pants and boots with snow and pine needles, Jerry's clients had called the office to cancel today's visit. They'd claimed that last night's snowfall had them nervous about driving up into the hills on the slick roads and rescheduled for tomorrow afternoon, when Jerry would be back and able to show them the place.

Considering the state of my pants and boots at that moment, which were going to have to be burned, not to mention my urge to smear green *Nachzehrer* vomit all over Tiffany's pristine white outfit, not having to play real estate agent was a relief. I'd informed Mona that I was going to take a long lunch and headed home, careful not to let my pantlegs touch my vehicle during the drive.

I'd called Doc as soon as I made it home but got his voicemail, so I'd just told him I missed him and to call when he had a moment free. Some stories were better told in person with a lot of animated body language and a few angry gestures, so he'd have to wait until I could stop by his office for this one.

Aunt Zoe looked up at me. "Was vomiting on you a defense mechanism, or a reaction to pain from the ax blow?"

It was funny how much Reid and she thought alike. He'd asked the same thing while helping tug off my boots. Between the sharp-toothed human spider and vile-smelling vomitocious ferocious, the fire captain had stood solid by my side. I owed him big time, which I'd told him when we reached his pickup. He'd nodded and asked for one thing in return—my help softening up my aunt. A handshake had settled the deal.

"Reid thought it might have been some sort of defense. Like when a skunk sprays its enemy." I thought back to that moment when the green stuff had gushed from its mouth and cringed. "Only the smell was more like rancid meat and spoiled cabbage than the acrid stink of rotten eggs that comes from a skunk's blowhole."

Aunt Zoe returned to her journal. "So, this creature was deaf, like the first one you killed, but not blind."

I nodded even though it wasn't a question, and then filled my mouth with berries, cobbler, and whipped cream.

"And you believe it picked up the scent of your blood in the air, same as the way the first one was drawn in by the cut on your hand."

I nodded again, mumbling around my mouthful, "The bloody handkerchief."

"How is your hand?" Natalie asked.

I showed her my palm. A fine white line was the only evidence of yesterday's cut.

Aunt Zoe scribbled something on the page. "And you weren't supposed to begin menses for another week."

"Right." I swallowed. "And I had cramps, which I normally don't thanks to the pill I've been taking. But all of that stopped after I killed the creature." I paused, fork in midair. "It was as if it were Groundhog Day and my uterus looked out and saw its own shadow, then returned to its burrow for another six weeks."

Natalie snorted. "You're such a dork."

"Said the world's biggest goob," I shot back, flashing her a purple-toothed smile.

After sticking out her peanut butter–covered tongue at me, she asked, "Zoe, are there other stories from your family's history about the hoo-hoo flu being used by a *Scharfrichter* to lure a bloodthirsty enemy?"

"Hoo-hoo flu?" I chuckled. "Where did you hear that one?"

"Grandma Ford used to call it that." Her smile grew melancholy. " 'You're biting at flies today, Natalie,' " she said in a high-pitched voice, mimicking her grandma. " 'What's wrong, sweetie? The hoo-hoo flu cramping your style?' "

"I always liked your grandma," I said, swirling my cobbler and the whipped cream into a purple work of art. "She made the best monster cookies, hands down."

"Yeah, she was something," Natalie said, but a shadow passed over her face.

Before I could ask about that shadow, Aunt Zoe piped up. "There was one story I remember about a *Scharfrichter* who was able to somehow stop her heart for several minutes when needed in order to play dead long enough to fool her enemy."

"Like an opossum." I took another bite of cobbler. "That's not the coolest superpower, but if it works, so be it."

Aunt Zoe chewed on the tip of her pen. "I question if she actually stopped the organ, or just ingested a natural herb that slowed her heartbeat dramatically, and then others mistook her for dead."

Natalie popped the last of her sandwich in her mouth, swallowing it before continuing. "If these suckers are lured by the scent of your blood, then why did that three-limbed one go on a rampage in Jones' Taxidermy? You'd never been there before, right?"

I shook my head.

"So there was no chance of your blood being there. Yet the thing took bites out of all sorts of stuff, including Dorothy the camel."

"How do you know about the camel getting bitten?" I hadn't mentioned anything about that.

"Coop told me."

"He talked to you about the camel?"

"Sure, why wouldn't he? It's not like Dorothy is a top-secret agent on loan from INTERPOL, here to capture taxidermy terrorists."

"Because it's police business and Cooper tends to hoard those kinds of details. Especially from me."

"Well, that may be true for you." She leaned back and crossed her arms, a small smile playing on her lips. "But I have a leg up when it comes to interrogating the dreamy detective."

"Cooper is not dreamy." I stabbed at the last of my cobbler. "I find him more of a nightmare most days, especially when he's barking at me from the end of his chain."

"Just one leg up, Natalie?" Aunt Zoe asked with a twinkle in her eye. "Or two?"

Natalie screeched. "Zoe Parker! What a dirty mind you have."

"I may have been around a bit longer than you girls, but sex isn't a new sport. Women have been winning gold medals in it for a long, long time."

Chuckling, I pushed my plate away. "Speaking of hot fireman sex," I started, staring at Aunt Zoe.

"We're not going to go there, Violet," Aunt Zoe interrupted. "So don't even mention his name."

"Fine, but don't you want to know why he-who-will-not-be-named joined me today at that open house?"

"No."

"Yes, you do, and you know it."

"I want to know," Natalie said. "So, tell me. Zoe can listen if she wants to or not."

I made a point of focusing on Natalie and only Natalie. "He wants Aunt Zoe to meet someone very important to him, but he's nervous about it. So, he asked me to help clear a path for this meet-and-greet."

Natalie and I both looked at Aunt Zoe, who was working furiously at drawing little circles in the margin of her notebook. Or maybe they were bullet holes.

"Oh, really," Natalie played along, resting her chin on her hand. Her eyes were extra wide, as if my story was sure to make tomorrow's headlines. "And who is this VIP that Reid is super excited to introduce to your aunt?"

"His son. He is the reason Reid didn't come to supper last night."

Natalie pursed her lips. "I wonder what his son is like. You think he looks like Reid?"

"If he does, he's sure to break some hearts around town."

Aunt Zoe slammed her leather notebook shut. "I do not want to meet Reid's son."

"Why not?" Natalie beat me to the question.

"Because I don't want to give Reid any big ideas on a future together, and meeting his kid feels like a step closer to commitment." She sighed, settling her frown on me. "I told Reid a couple of weeks ago that I was willing to be friends at this point, but that's it."

"Yeah, but—"

"No 'buts,' Violet. Reid and I skipped over friendship when we were together years back. We went straight from strangers to bedfellows and then basically back to strangers again after I kicked him out. I'm of the age when having someone to help warm the sheets is great, but true friendship is more important."

"Yeah, but—" I tried to get a word in on his behalf again.

"No 'buts,' and I mean it." She rested her forearms on the table. "I don't know if I *like* Reid, you see. I know I can love him because I did before, but that's not enough anymore." She glanced at Natalie and then returned to me. "Does that make sense?"

I nodded slowly. "But won't seeing Reid with his son show you a side of him that has nothing to do with you loving him? You'll be able to see the kind of father he is and determine if you like *that* side of him."

"You two are getting in deep now," Natalie said, rubbing

her neck. "Much further and we're going to need some tequila therapy to climb back out of this."

I grinned. "Lord knows I could use some after the morning I've had."

"I'll think about it," Aunt Zoe finally said to me, giving an inch.

Unfortunately, I needed a mile at this point. "Well, you have only a few hours to make a decision."

Her gaze narrowed. "Violet Lynn, what have you done?"

I rattled out really fast, "Reid-and-his-son-are-coming-to-supper-tonight." Then I cringed and waited for the mushroom cloud to form over Aunt Zoe's head.

The walkie-talkie chirped instead, drawing all three of our gazes to where it sat on the counter.

"Come in, Violet Parker," Cornelius's voice rang out from the speaker. A slight crackling sound followed it, then another chirp, then, "Do you copy? Over."

I pushed back from the table, rushing over to the walkie-talkie. I pushed a button on the front. That didn't feel right, so I pushed it a few more times. "Hello? Can you hear me, Cornelius?"

"That's the channel button, spudnut," Natalie said, joining me. "Here, push this one."

I pushed it and held it in.

"Now talk," Natalie whispered.

"I'm going to, sheesh. Hold your horses. I'm trying to decide what to say."

"Just answer him and then let your thumb off the button."

"Stop bossing me around, cheese ball," I said to her. I held the walkie-talkie close to my lips. "What do you want?"

"That's not how you talk into these things." Natalie took the walkie-talkie from me. "Go ahead, Cornelius. Over."

"That's basically what I said," I muttered.

"Quit your bawling, baby."

"Where did you learn walkie-talkie talk?" I poked her in the side. "Trucker college?"

"Your timekeeping apparatus appears to be functioning, over," Cornelius said abruptly.

"Functioning over what?" I asked, frowning down at the gadget. "Is that code for something?"

"Not 'functioning over,' " Natalie explained. "He means *functioning*, then a comma, then *over*."

"I knew that."

"Your nose twitches when you lie, Vi."

I poked her again, making her laugh.

"Do you copy, Violet?" Cornelius said through the speaker. "Over."

"Yes, I'm copying. But I don't understand what you mean. What the hell is my 'timekeeping apparatus'?"

"You're supposed to say 'over' after each transmission," Natalie said.

"I'm gonna knock you over after each transmission," I growled back.

"I think he means your clock is working."

"Oh! What's the code word for 'I get it'?"

"Are you serious, woman?" She smacked her forehead. "It's '10-4.' "

"Oh, yeah." I pushed the button. "10-4, good buddy."

Natalie burst out laughing.

Wait a second. My clock was working. I pushed the button again. "Do you mean the Hellhound clock is now ticking?"

"Say 'over,' " Natalie reminded me between giggles.

"Shut it." I threatened her with my closed fist.

Natalie laughed even harder, fanning herself as tears filled her eyes.

"Affirmative," Cornelius said. "Over."

If the clock was ticking, that meant a traveler had passed through a gate and was now in this realm. And by traveler, I meant another bounty hunter was here to collect my head.

"Shit." I looked at Aunt Zoe. Her face was a whirlwind of worry. The same whirlwind was spinning in my chest.

Natalie took the walkie-talkie from me, sobering quickly as the weight of the situation settled over the three of us. "We'll be there in a few, Cornelius." I nodded at her questioning look. "Over and out."

Chapter Ten

Over and out," I repeated several hours later as I stood staring in the bathroom mirror at Calamity Jane Realty. The coiffed blonde staring back at me looked surprisingly calm and collected, considering the fact that she now had a ticking clock, figuratively, hanging over her head. Literally, too, being that the clock was in the apartment Cornelius was staying in located above the office.

I finished washing and drying my hands and then returned to my desk, pretty much falling into my chair. I was alone in the office this afternoon. Jerry was still down in Rapid City, Mona was out shopping for a few items in preparation for Sunday's release extravaganza, and Ben had the day off. That left me plenty of time to wallow in my worries.

I was quickly learning that being a Timekeeper was more of a pain than a blessing. It would have been nice last fall if Ms. Wolff had given me more than a few panic-filled seconds to weigh the pros and cons of keeping track of the clocks, which acted as some sort of between-realm gate monitoring devices, before forcing me to play Executioner and take her totally out of the game.

I drew a little alarm clock on my desktop calendar, adding a frown on the face of it, while trying to remember the rules of timekeeping. A ticking clock meant that more trouble in the form of a bounty hunter or something even worse had popped into my jurisdiction. Although I wasn't sure what could be worse and hoped not to find out anytime soon.

I hadn't yet been schooled enough by Mr. Black, the other Timekeeper who had been working with Ms. Wolff at the time of her demise, to understand the nuts and bolts of how the clocks worked, but I knew that no ticking was a good thing for me.

Chiming and cuckooing were another matter. These actions could be good or bad, depending if the traveler represented by the particular clock was coming or going through the gate between realms.

I always preferred going.

Cornelius wouldn't have heard either the chimes or cuckoos, though. Only Timekeepers could hear anything other than the ticking of a clock.

I tossed my pencil aside and walked over to the coffee pot, staring down at my mug. The last thing I needed was more caffeine. The zings of leftover energy from this morning's frolicking in the snow with a parasitic menace still crackled under my skin. I grabbed a packet of ginger tea instead and filled my mug with hot water.

Stupid ticking clock. As if a pack of *Nachzehrer* out there sniffing around for me and my blood wasn't enough of a headache. Now something else had come to join in the fun.

"And let's not forget I still have that damned imp to catch," I told the empty room, ripping open the tea packet and dipping the little bag into the hot water.

The bells over the front door jingled.

Pasting a smile on my face, I turned to greet my visitor. Only the door was closed and the office was still empty.

Huh.

Had I imagined the bells?

Leaving my tea to steep, I walked over to the door. An envelope lay on the floor in front of it.

An envelope that had my name scrawled on the front.

I picked it up and checked the door, making sure it was latched. Maybe the wind had blown open the door enough to make the overhead bells jingle.

Sure, and then it delivered this envelope while it was at it.

"Nobody asked you," I told the smartass in my head and tore open the envelope. Inside was a folded sheet of paper. I unfolded it and read:

> You've really fucked things up now, Blondie! They're following me! You had to go and run your big mouth!! THIS IS ALL YOUR FAULT!!! Fix this shit or I'll tell them the truth about you!!!!!!

Damn. Someone had a hard-on for exclamation marks.

Blondie ... There was only one person who called me by that name: Ray Underhill, aka the egotistical asshole who used to sit at the desk across from me. The same backstabbing bastard who'd insulted me daily for months and ended up getting fired for helping Tiffany Sugarbell steal Jeff Wymonds away from me.

I lowered the note. Well, well, well, it appeared Ray was back to his old blame game and I was his current target.

A shadow passed in front of the plate-glass windows. I looked up, watching as a pair of teenage girls giggled along on the sidewalk. My focus moved beyond them, searching for Ray. Was he out there somewhere now? Watching me read his note? Hoping to cause a stir? If so, he was going to have to try harder than dropping off a mere letter littered with exclamation marks.

I returned to my desk, grabbing my cup of tea on the way. Sitting in my chair, I pretended to be focused on a listing report while keeping an eye out the window. Unless Ray had binoculars, there was no way he'd be able to see through my act.

Before long, my watchfulness paid off. Across the street, Ray eased out from behind one of the silver maple trees that stood in front of the courthouse. The big dork was wearing all black, including sunglasses and a beanie hat, looking like he'd gone shopping for his outfit at Cat-Burglars-R-Us. He spared one last glance in my direction, then hustled off around the side of the courthouse and out of sight.

What in the ever-loving hell? Had getting fired from his job here at Calamity Jane Realty fried some fuses in his noggin? Or was someone—or something—really following him?

Last year, Ray had dipped his fingers in some shark-filled pools, partnering with the late George Mudder to run some sort of shipments via huge crates through the back doors of Mudder Brothers Funeral Parlor. George had ended up dead soon after, and Ray had been on the chopping block when I'd found him and saved his ungrateful hide. Maybe there was more to this story yet to be told, this time starring Ray and a new terror bent on revenge. Or maybe it was as simple as one of Ray's ex-girlfriends deciding on a bit of payback in the form of stalking. Knowing Ray's off-the-charts standing on the asshole scale, the possibilities were endless.

The question was, how was I supposed to fix whatever was going on with Ray? And what truth did he have to tell about me? He didn't know about my killer vocation. At least I didn't think so. The only secret he'd ever had on me was that I was dating Doc, but that was common knowledge now.

The screen on my computer flickered, and then a new note window with a blank page appeared. The cursor blinked at me, waiting, as if it expected me to have some answers instead of more questions.

Huh. That was kind of weird.

I shrugged, returning to my quandary. I could make a list of possibilities. Cooper and Detective Hawke were always jotting down their suspicions in their little notebooks. Never mind that they were erroneous when it came to crimes associated with me most of the time, especially when Hawke was the one doing the writing.

My hands hovered over the keyboard, but before I could start typing, some of the keys started moving up and down slowly on their own. I frowned down at the keyboard, trying to make sense of what I was seeing. Then I looked up and my jaw dropped. Words were forming on the screen before my very eyes.

NOT … ALONE

Several thoughts slammed into me all at once:

Jane the ghost was back.

Jane was trying to tell me something.

Jane was using my keyboard.

Jane had always liked to use all caps to get her important messages across.

Jane must be sitting in my chair at the moment.

I was sitting in my chair at the moment!

Did that mean she was sitting on me? Or was I on her?

Or was she hiding inside of my skin, wearing my face like a ghoulish mask the same as that dead prostitute had in the stairwell of The Old Prospector Hotel months ago?

Goose bumps peppered my arms. I leapt out of my chair and took several steps back. Jane might be my old boss, but I drew the line at sharing skin.

I cleared my throat. "What do you mean, Jane?" I spoke out loud. "You said the same thing before when the *lidérc* was in the office with me. Please tell me that smoky bastard hasn't somehow returned for more hide and seek games."

More keys moved up and down.

I … MEAN … RAY

If memory served me right, Jane had said something similar about Ray before in an email message to Mona back before Jerry had fired the pompous douchebag in December. Was someone still tailing Ray?

"Ray said he's being followed in his note." I picked up the folded note on my desk, scanning it again. "But who is following him?"

TOO … DARK … TO … SEE

I frowned, wishing Jane wasn't feeling so cryptic this afternoon. If she couldn't see whatever was following Ray, had she just sensed it then? I had no idea how things worked for the ectoplasmic crowd, nor did I want to find out any time soon.

I glanced out the window again, searching for Ray's alleged shadow. The silver maples swayed in the breeze. A snowplow rolled past on the street, blocking my view. By the time it was out of sight, the trees had stilled along with the rest of the world for the moment.

The keys on my keyboard started moving again.

RAY … IS …

Jane paused.

I stared at the screen, waiting for her to finish. When the cursor kept blinking and blinking, I took it upon myself to finish the sentence for her. "Ray is what, Jane? A jerkweed? A giant tool? A limp-dick sandwich? A misogynistic ass clown? A spray-tanned monkey fucker? A colossal dope on a rope?" I crossed my arms. "I could go on like this for days. I had months and months to come up with names for the butthead while putting up with his constant bullying in this very room."

The keys began to move again, but more slowly now, as

if she were tiring.

B ... A ... I ... T

"Ray is bait?" I repeated. How would she know that if it was too dark to see what was following him?

Y ... E ... S

"Bait for who?"

W ... H ... O ... M

I rolled my eyes at her for correcting my English. Before I could tell her where to cram her editing, my cell phone started ringing.

I reached for my purse. A glance at the phone screen made me smile in spite of the unsettling foreboding still coiled in my gut thanks to Ray's note.

I accepted the call. "If you're looking for love in all the wrong places, you've called the right number."

"Coop and I just got off the phone with Reid," Doc said.

I cringed. Hearing the juicy tale about my rendezvous with the *Nachzehrer* secondhand probably hadn't gone over well with Doc. He preferred such news face-to-face from *moi*. "I was going to tell you, but—" I hesitated, wanting to choose the right words that would smooth any ruffled feathers.

"But your phone wasn't working?" he finished for me.

"*But* I was waiting until tonight so I didn't interrupt your work. I know you have a lot on your plate right now."

Doc's business was really taking off, ramping up with tax season on the horizon and people looking to invest in some money-saving write-offs.

A deep growl rumbled from his end of the line, making

it clear how he felt about my excuse.

I tried to lighten up the mood. "Is that a grizzly bear in your pocket, or are you just happy to hear me?"

"I'm happy to hear you're still alive. Reid said you planned to take on the *Nachzehrer* all by yourself."

"I didn't want Reid to get hurt. Besides, you know how Aunt Zoe feels about me using him as a carrot."

"According to him, you were the carrot this time."

Damn, Reid had really spilled the beans. "Yeah, this one was smarter, I think. It lured me up into the trees and set up an ambush, but Reid and I didn't fall for its trap."

"Tell me the whole story."

I lowered my rump onto the corner of my desk in case Jane was still sitting in my chair with plans to finish her cryptic warning. I shot a glance toward the wall adjoining our offices. "Are you back at work?"

"No. I'm at my place waiting for Coop to get out of the shower. We'll head down to Spearfish shortly, but I have time to hear your version, so talk."

Knowing how fast Cooper took showers from back when he was temporarily living at Aunt Zoe's, I talked really, really fast and told Doc about the whole shebang, including the parts about Tiffany even though talking about his ex made me want to beat on a teddy bear with a rubber hose. Then, for an encore, I filled him in on the ticking clock at Cornelius's place, Ray and his note, and Jane's puzzling message as a grand finale—leaving out the part when she corrected my grammar. Doc thought I was smart. There was no need to pull the rug out from under that notion this afternoon.

"That was impressive," he said when I paused to take a breath.

"You mean how Reid and I took out the *Nachzehrer*?"

"I meant how fast you can talk. I knew you had a talented tongue, but damn, woman."

I stuck my tongue out at the phone. "Shut up, Candy Cane."

"Come over here and make me, Boots."

"So, who do you think is following Ray and in what way are they using him for bait?" I asked, scooting my buns farther onto my desk.

"Forget about Ray. I'm more worried about you running into another *Nachzehrer* at the moment."

"What about that ticking clock?" Lord only knew what bounty hunter had come to join in our fun and games.

"What about *her*?"

It took me a half-beat to catch on. "Funny guy, but I'm not ticking."

"My heart won't be either for much longer if these blood-sniffing creeps keep trying to ambush you when I'm not around to watch your backside, damn it."

Short of me hitching a ride on Doc's back all day long like a baby chimp, there wasn't much we could do about keeping that from happening again. I appreciated his need to protect me, though.

"I like it better when you watch my frontside," I flirted, trying to take my mind off the growing darkness outside and the distance between the back door and my SUV. I should probably carry a weapon now whenever I was out and about.

"Actually, I am quite fond of both of your sides. Not to mention totally smitten with your lips, but quit trying to distract me, vixen. It appears that whether or not you consciously want to hunt these creatures, your subconscious rules and will do whatever is needed to lure them, including using your body against you."

I winced. Reid must have told Doc and Coop about my temporary foray into menstruation land. What a bloody embarrassment. Three grown men comparing notes on my surprise visit from Aunt Flo.

My cheeks grew warm. This was almost as bad as when

my parents walked in on that S&M party I'd accidentally hosted and found two strangers demonstrating a rather perplexing pain-inducing position in my father's favorite recliner.

"Uhhh, yeah." I fanned myself with my notepad. "But I stopped bleeding, though." Not a drop of blood had appeared since the hunt was over, nor any cramps.

"For now. I have a feeling this will keep happening until you've fully finished the job. You should probably be prepared for the bleeding to start again."

"Right." I fanned harder. We really needed to stop talking about me sailing the Red Sea. "So, what do you propose we do in the meantime?"

"I lock you in my bedroom to keep you safe."

"Will you be in there with me?"

"Of course. I'll need to guard your body day and night."

"You are very good at taking care of me." Doubly good. Often even triply good.

He growled again, low and sexy. "*That* was the grizzly in my pocket."

I laughed. "Should we send Cooper and his favorite gun out to hunt down the remaining *Nachzehrer* for us while we work on our mattress mambo moves?"

He scoffed. "Who gives a damn about Coop?"

"Kiss my ass, Nyce." I heard the law dog's voice come through the line loud and clear. He must be finished with his shower.

Doc chuckled. "Not even on your birthday, sunshine."

"Does Cooper have any clue about what we're up to tonight?" I whispered, in case Cooper's bionic ears were cranked up.

"I don't think so."

"Is he pissy after hearing about Reid's and my adventure this morning?"

"Initially there was some swearing, but there doesn't

appear to have been a lasting effect."

"That's surprising. He usually chews me up one side and down the other about this kind of trouble."

"Well, I believe Natalie spent the night here."

"Ahhhh. That explains his lack of bristles today. I should have paid her to start sleeping with him months ago."

"*And* she brought your kids over to give him the birthday presents they'd made."

With Harvey's help, and several supplies from his ranch, Layne had made Cooper a small tank out of bullet shell casings for his desk at work; and Addy had taken an old ammo storage box, painted it black, and decorated it with police dog stickers, adding a clear coat over it as a sealant.

"Did he like their gifts?"

"He smiled when he thanked them."

"Wow." Gratitude and a smile at the same time from the law dog. I glanced out the window. Were pigs flying, too, this afternoon?

I heard Cooper's voice rumble in the background.

"Okay," Doc replied to him. To me, he said, "It's time for me to take the birthday boy out for a celebratory drink."

"Good. Get him fully schnockered, please. If he can't see straight, I have a slight chance of not ending up with a bullet in my ass."

"Don't worry. Your ass is mine tonight, Boots."

I smiled. "I'll see you in a couple of hours."

"Yes, you will. Hey, Killer, do me and my heart a favor and try not to execute anything in the meantime."

"I give no guarantees."

"I'm serious." His timbre echoed his words.

I held up my left hand. "I solemnly swear not to kill anything else today. Cross my heart and hope to die, stick a needle in my eye," I said, reverting to one of my childhood vows often pledged to Natalie.

"Sure, you say that now, but then I get phone calls," he

teased.

"Admit it—I keep your life exciting. You never know what's going to happen next."

His chuckle warmed me through the line. "That's true. Phone calls from you make my heart pitter-patter faster for more reasons than one."

"Life is not all lovely thorns and singing vultures, *mon cher*," I said, repeating one of my favorite Morticia Addams quotes.

"Ah, Tish, that's French," he said, playing along.

"Son of a— Jesus, Nyce!" I heard Cooper snap. "You two are like rabbits, I swear. Now give me that damned phone."

There was a shuffling sound on the other end, followed with Doc laughing. "See you later, Killer," he called out and then the line went dead.

I set my phone on the desk, still smiling. Then I looked out the window at the darkening sky and my smile flipped upside-down as reality settled back onto my shoulders. My focus returned to Jane and her cryptic messages.

"Are we done here, Jane?" I asked, watching my computer screen to see if any new words appeared. "Is there anything more you can tell me about Ray's shadow or why you think he's being used as bait?"

The fluorescent light over my desk flickered.

"I take it that's a no."

It flickered again.

Fudge nuggets. "Okay, but if you see or learn something more, let Mona or me know."

The streetlight outside the plate-glass windows glowed to life while the shadows deepened.

How many more *Nachzehrer* were hiding out there, waiting for me to let my guard down? One? Two? Or even more, in spite of what Dominick said about pack sizes?

I puffed my cheeks and blew out a long sigh. Before this

was all over, I was going to give ol' Lizzie Borden and her ax a run for her money.

A glance at the clock spurred me off the desk. It was time to head home and grab something to eat before heading down to Spearfish for Cooper's birthday fun. Maybe I'd get a chance to meet Reid's son before we took off, if Aunt Zoe hadn't called the whole dinner off.

As I locked up and collected my keys and purse, my thoughts returned to that infamous rhyme about Lizzie Borden and her gruesome whack-job.

"Violet Parker took an ax," I sang under my breath while heading down the hall toward the back door. "And gave the *Nachzehrer* forty whacks." I grabbed my coat from the wall peg. "When she saw what she had done," I said, pausing to slide my arms into the sleeves, "she gave the next bastard forty-one."

With a final glance at the empty office where Jane used to spend her days and sometimes nights, I said "Good-bye" to her and walked out into the dark.

Chapter Eleven

"Why's it so dark in here?" Cooper whispered from behind me. And then he hiccupped. "Parker, hit the lights. I can't see a damned thing."

Pluck my duck! What in tarnation possessed Natalie to partner me with Detective Whiskey-on-the-Rocks tonight? Having to work with a hammered law dog to escape from a rusty old jail had to be some kind of sadistic payback for me declaring squatter's rights on her man "claim" last August when she had a crush on Doc. Why else would she choose to torture me like this?

I paused partway down the creaky basement stairs and turned, shining my flashlight at Cooper, who was leaning against the wall several steps up. "It's dark because that's part of the game, remember?"

The lack of lighting throughout the three-story jail had been one of the line items listed on the "Escape from Jail" instruction sheet we'd found on the "sheriff's" desk next to six flashlights—one for each of us.

He shaded his eyes from the light. "Oh, yeah."

"You do recall insisting on reading the instructions aloud to all of us after prattling on and on about having the most experience with solving mysteries, don't you?"

He hiccupped again. Still leaning against the wall, he took a step down. His coat scraped along the cement, undoubtedly leaving scratches on the black leather. Knowing Cooper's and my tendency to exchange bruises when forced to work together, I'd probably wind up with several marks, too, before this night was out.

"I didn't prattle," he whispered. "I've never prattled in my whole life, and I certainly wouldn't do any such thing in front of Nat."

Oh, he definitely prattled, ostentatiously even, trumpeting about his detective skills loud and clear for all the land to hear. A little too much whiskey had turned the sullen detective into a regular chatterbox. Lucky me.

"Fine," I conceded so we could finish with our detecting down here in the damp, musty basement. "You waxed eloquent. Your presentation of the subject was clear and succinct, and I believe several of us in the crowd experienced knee-buckling awe." More like knee-buckling boredom.

"Damned straight," he whispered, and then hiccupped yet again.

"I told you upstairs that we don't need to whisper."

"Oh, yeah," he whispered and slid down another step, adding more scratches to his coat. "I forgot that, too."

"I think you're too drunk to remember your own name, Coop, much less what you read on that instruction sheet."

Doc and Cooper had arrived at the timber baron's historic mansion over ten minutes later than our agreed-upon time. At our collective raised brows about their tardiness, Doc explained that Cooper hadn't wanted to leave the bar, refusing to vacate his barstool until Doc told him where they were going. The truth had gone over like a Sherman tank—with a lot of rumbling and grumbling. In the end, it'd required a bit of finesse along with some brute strength to get Officer Tanked to leave the bar.

With only minutes to spare before the six of us—Doc, Cooper, Natalie, Harvey, Cornelius, and *moi*—were scheduled to sign in, there had been no time to work on drying out the whiskey-soaked detective before the game started. So, we'd all filed in through the front double doors of the mansion, pooling together in the sconce-lit foyer where we were met by a stooped docent who looked timeworn enough to have been around when the century-plus-old house was built.

After reading through a short history of the place, including details about when the jail was added on and how many people had died within its walls over the years—three prisoners and a guard in a fire on the third floor, and one guard in a skirmish during an attempted escape—the docent had led us into a brightly lit kitchen with modern appliances and marble countertops. Then he'd opened a steel door next to the pantry and ushered us into a room decked out as the sheriff's office, closing and locking the door behind us.

According to the game instructions, we had an hour and a half to escape before the docent would come to our rescue. Since it was Cooper's birthday, Natalie had let him take the reins, which would have been fine and dandy if he hadn't been filled to the gills with liquor.

I continued down the basement steps, waiting at the bottom of the stairs with my flashlight beam showing him the way. The last thing I needed was for the half-corned Sherlock to fall and break something down here—especially if he landed on me.

"I'm not that drunk," he whispered yet again when he joined me on the packed-dirt floor.

"You're slurring."

"No. I'm. Not." He emphasized each consonant, speaking loud and clear.

"You are, *and* you smell like the inside of a shot glass."

"I do not." He lifted his shirt and sniffed it, wrinkling his slightly crooked nose. "Okay, so maybe I do a tiny bit, but that's only because I accidentally spilled some of my drink on my shirt at the bar."

According to Doc, Cooper had hurriedly dumped his last

glass of whiskey down his gullet, spilling a good amount of it down his chin and using his shirt to mop it up before being dragged out of the bar.

"A whiskey-smelling shirt does not mean I'm drunk. I'm just happy is all." He gave me a big sloppy grin as demonstration, pointing at his white teeth. "See?"

"You happy?" I guffawed. "That only happens when you lock me up behind bars."

He let out a loud laugh. "That's true. Your face gets really twitchy when you're mad. It's funny."

I growled at him. "How many fingers am I holding up, Coop?" I held up my middle finger right in front of his face.

He knocked my hand away. "You know what, Parker? You're kinda mean. Did anyone ever tell you that?"

"I'm not mean." Well, unless you ask my sister, Susan, but I have years' worth of good reasons for snarling at the Bitch from Hell.

He poked me in the shoulder with his pointer finger. "You're like a stray dog who snarls at me through the fence, but then takes off running when I try to get near."

I crossed my arms. "This coming from the guy who's routinely told me that it's not his job to be warm and fuzzy when I could use a little compassion at his crime scenes."

His chin lifted. "That's right. I'm a cop, not a teddy be—shhhh!" He put his hand over my mouth, cocking his head to the side. "Do you hear that?" he whispered.

His hand smelled like soap, which was a relief since he'd visited the bathroom up on the main floor before we'd started down the basement steps.

I rolled my eyes and tugged his hand down. "It's just the floor creaking under Natalie and Cornelius while they check for more clues."

"Oh, yeah." He nodded a few too many times, giving a decent bobble-head impression. A frown added shadow lines to his face. "Why did she choose Curion as her partner instead of me? I'm her boyfriend now."

Oh, Lord. I'd rather snarl and circle with the law dog than console a boozehound.

Natalie had set up the sleuthing partners during the reservation process. When I'd found out earlier in the foyer that I was going to have to search for clues tonight with Detective Whiskey-on-the-Rocks instead of Doc, I'd threatened to give her a reverse mohawk haircut the next time she slept over, especially if Cooper ended up shooting me before the night was done.

"Natalie put us together because she wanted to torture me. Plain and simple." That was my theory and I was sticking to it. I'd objected when Doc suggested that this together time with Cooper might help me learn some detective skills, and I stood by that objection still.

"That makes complete sense," Cooper said, grabbing my flashlight from me and shining it around the open room.

I followed the beam of light, taking in the few items down here, including a water heater, a four-tier shelving rack, a metal 1950s-era table and chairs, and a rusty-looking two-drawer filing cabinet. There couldn't be many clues hidden here, judging from the sparse furnishings.

"Why does that make sense?" I asked, glancing his way.

"Because Nat is a dominatrix in the bedroom."

Cooper appeared not to notice my total body cringe at that keyhole peep into their sex life. Jeez-n-crackers, the guy needed to warn me the next time he was going to drop an X-rated bomb like that so I could plug my ears in advance.

I scrubbed my hand down my face, trying to wipe away the image of my best friend decked out in a black leather catsuit cracking a whip over Cooper while he lay strapped to the bed with a silk scarf muffling his big, bossy mouth.

"I'd use a ball gag to shut him up," I muttered. One of those gags with an extra-large ball.

He shined the light in my direction. "What?"

"Nothing."

He lifted the beam to my face. "It sounded like you said something about a ball gag."

My scoff turned into a snort and ended with me blowing a raspberry.

"Are you choking on a hairball, Parker?"

"Shut up, Coop."

The beam of light moved away from me. "Okay." He puffed out his chest, shifting into cop-mode. "Let's fan out and see what clues we can find down here. We'll figure out who committed this murder in a jiffy."

"There is no murder, Mr. Magoo." I stole my flashlight back. "We're looking for clues that lead us to the key that fits in that door we came through from the mansion." When he just stared at me, I added, "The door in the sheriff's office that leads back into the kitchen. You do remember walking through that door and the old docent wishing us good luck in making it back out alive, right?"

"You mean the leprechaun?"

Come again? "You're seeing leprechauns tonight?" I'd had a lot of wild tequila nights in my time, but I'd yet to have a leprechaun show up on the scene.

He let out a weary sigh, as if talking to me was akin to carrying the blocks of stone needed to build the Great Pyramid of Giza. "Not an actual leprechaun, Parker. The man was just tiny, wearing a green suit, and had a green clover pin stuck in his lapel."

I hadn't noticed the clover pin. I'd been too busy fretting about having to partner with Cooper at the time.

"Got it. Not a real leprechaun." I shined the light toward the shelving rack. "I'm going to go look for clues now."

I started to walk away, but Cooper caught me by the elbow before I got far. "Give me back the flashlight."

"No, it's mine. Use your own."

"I can't."

"Why not? Are the batteries dead? Is it broken? You didn't drop it, did you? We'll have to replace it if you did, or at least leave some money for it."

"You ask too many questions too fast." He reached for the flashlight again. "I lost mine and I need yours to see."

I gaped at him. "Are you fucking serious? We just started the game. How could you have lost yours already?"

He held his hand out at me like a traffic cop. "You really need to work on controlling your potty mouth before you corrupt your kids."

Of all the ... "Who do you think you are? Chief Coop, top dog of the swearing police?" I tugged him along toward the shelves since he was still holding onto my elbow. "So, maybe I cuss a teeny-tiny bit." I ignored his guffaw. "But we both know that you rattle out curse words like an auctioneer, especially when you're pissed at me."

"Nope. But that's mostly your fault."

Huh? I shook off his confusing answer and focused on my part in it. "That's hogwash. It's your own fault for being so crabby most of the time."

He stumbled over his own boots, dragging me sideways a few steps. "I don't know if you realize it, Parker, but you can be very frustrating. Just ask Nyce," he slurred out Doc's last name.

Why? What had Doc told him? Was it something recent? *Wait!* No. I wasn't heading down that road tonight.

"Don't drag my boyfriend into this."

Cooper sighed. "Your boyfriend is nice, like his name. Isn't that funny?" He started to laugh but then hiccupped.

I shook free of Cooper's hold. Maybe someday I'd look back on this evening and smile. And maybe, with the help of hard liquor, I'd actually laugh about it. But right now, I settled for reaching up and flicking him on the forehead.

"Ow!" He rubbed where I'd flicked. "What did you do that for?"

"Because you need to focus on finding clues, not on Doc, not on leprechauns, and not on Natalie tying you to the bed and tickling your toes with a feather."

His face crinkled. "Who said anything about a feather?"

"Not that you'll be much help when it comes to playing detective while you're drunk off your ass."

"Not drunk," he whispered. "Only a teensy bit tipsy."

"You're ham-sandwiched."

He pursed his lips, shaking his head. "I'm just a little sauced. No ham."

"Who are you trying to kid, Coop? You're plum pickled and I don't need a breathalyzer test to prove it, you know why?"

He held out his hands as if to say, *duh*. "Because you're a Schraft … a Sharkfricker … a Sharpener."

I shook my head. "Please stop."

"A Shrackner."

I shined my flashlight directly in his rummy eyes, making him recoil and use his fingers to deflect the beam. "Are you done?"

"Maybe." He squinted at me over his hand.

I lowered the beam to his chest. "I know you're toasted because I've called you 'Coop' several times tonight, and you've not corrected me once."

"It's just like you, Parker, to take advantage of a poor guy when he's feeling down and out."

I headed over to the shelving rack. It was about five feet wide and secured to the wall with metal straps and some impressive cobwebs. The water heater sitting a few feet away was coated with a thick layer of dust. I was tempted to draw a smiley face in it, but stayed on task—finding clues, which meant focusing on the rack and its stuffed shelves.

"So why are you down and out?" I asked when he came up right next to me, his shoulder brushing mine as he teetered sideways a few degrees. "Is this about your birthday and turning another year older?"

"Nah. Age is just a number."

"Then what could possibly be wrong with your life? You have a good job," I said, starting a count on my fingers.

"Yeah, I like busting criminals."

I raised another finger. "And you get to carry that stupid gun you love every day."

"I like carrying my gun."

"You have a smart, funny, beautiful girlfriend."

"She's so hot." He sounded almost drooly about Natalie.

I counted off a fourth finger. "And you have several great friends."

"Very great," he agreed.

"Including me."

He grunted. "Well, let's not go overbo—*oof!*"

After I removed my elbow from his ribcage, I repeated, "Including me."

He groaned and rubbed his side. "With friends like you, I miss my enemies."

I patted his shoulder. "Yeah, but you're not feeling so down and out anymore, right?"

"True. Now I'm just feeling bruised."

I smiled and took a step closer to the shelving rack. The various contents lining the four shelves reminded me of my dad's workshop. Dust-covered jars, cans, and small cardboard boxes were scattered here and there, holding screws, nails, nuts and bolts, as well as insect repellent, mouse traps, work gloves, and more. Mixed in with all of this was some plumbing riff-raff, electrical whatnot, several cans of assorted oils, and four rubber duckies—red, yellow, black, and green, each sitting on a different shelf.

I reached toward the black duckie on the third shelf down, but Cooper caught my arm.

"Look with your eyes, Parker," he said, "and *only* your eyes when you're searching for clues at a crime scene. As soon as you touch something, you've contaminated the scene."

I pulled free of his hold and crossed my arms. "Then how are we supposed to see if there's a clue in those boxes and jars?"

"We start by looking for something that doesn't fit in."

"Like four rubber duckies?" I said, pointing at the yellow duckie sitting on the second shelf down.

"Yep, but those are too easy. They're obviously planted." He took the flashlight from me and shined it on the red one. The beam wavered slightly. A glance at Cooper found him wavering slightly, too. "Look, they aren't even dusty like the rest of the stuff on the shelves."

They did look fresh out of the tub.

"In fact," he continued, "all of the items on these shelves are probably staged to distract us."

He was most likely right, but I didn't give the know-it-all the satisfaction of hearing me say it.

"There isn't much else down here." I took the flashlight back, directing the beam around the large room. A set of dilapidated folding chairs sat in the far corner opposite the stairs we'd come down. They looked like they'd seen action in a couple of wars. There was nothing distracting about them. "Maybe there's something taped to the underside of those."

Dodging low-hanging cobwebs and ducking under a pair of pipes running the length of the room, I went to check them out. The chairs held no clue, though, just a few spots of rust and a smattering of light blue paint.

"Nothing, dang it."

Cooper joined me long enough to take the flashlight back. "I think we should take a closer look around that old water heater."

Without waiting for me to agree, he headed back toward the heater, listing to the side as if the room was tipped.

But the water heater held no clues, either.

However, the rusted two-drawer filing cabinet was locked, which started us on a new quest—to find the key to open the drawers.

I took charge of the flashlight and shined the beam up on the ceiling, walking around, peering up through cobwebs at the floor joists overhead.

"That key has to be down here somewhere," I said, extracting a cluster of sticky webs from the tip of the flashlight, before continuing.

"Or not." Cooper sounded muffled. "They could have hidden it on one of the other two floors. That's how these games work, I think."

Something creaked over his way. I aimed the beam toward him, finding him leaning against the edge of the 1950s table with his hands covering his face.

"Are you okay?"

"Everything is spinning. That last drink was a mistake."

I chuckled under my breath. Been there, done that.

His sick-sounding groan spurred me to take a step back. "Please don't throw up on my watch."

"Why not?" He peered at me from between his fingers. "It's only fair after you threw up on me and my favorite tie."

"That was the past," I said, swirling my hands in the air like I was washing it away. "Let's wipe away that memory and replace it with a happy one, like when we stayed up late watching old black-and-white Westerns together."

"That's a happy memory? You were having horrible nightmares at the time and I was too stressed to sleep because I was having to babysit you 24/7 to keep Hawke from throwing your ass in jail."

Oh, right. I kept swirling my hands anyway. "We're wiping it all away, see?"

He covered his eyes and groaned again.

While Cooper stayed in one place trying not to lose his

cookies, I searched the basement's dirty windowsills, the shadow-thick corners, and the web-infested backside of the water heater. I even "looked" closely with my eyes—not my hands—over the four shelves, but there was no file drawer key to be found.

I sighed, nudging the red rubber duckie, making it wobble sideways. "I think you're right, Coop. The key isn't down here."

"Und-ra-wares," he mumbled from behind his hands.

I frowned, trying to make sense of what he'd said while straightening the duckie. "What about your underwear?"

"Why are you asking me about my underwear?" This time his words were clear.

I spotlighted him. "You're the one talking about them, not me."

He blocked the beam. "I said 'under the stairs,' Parker, as in go look under there." He pointed toward the staircase with a healthy amount of attitude.

"Okay, okay, Detective Bossypants. I like you better when you're a sappy drunk."

"Call me sappy again and I'll lock you away in one of those cells upstairs."

"Speaking of overbearing assholes," I said on my way to the shadow-filled alcove under the staircase. "Ray stopped by my office today."

"Ray Underhill?"

"The one and only."

"What did he want?"

"He slipped me a love note under the front door."

He grunted. "That guy has only ever loved himself. What did it say?"

"Something about being followed and that it's all my fault." I squatted and shined the light in the far corners, finding more cobwebs and a small nest of shredded paper. "Even more interesting, Jane weighed in on his visit. She typed a few short messages on my keyboard, claiming that Ray wasn't alone and is being used as bait."

"Did she expand on either of those?"

"Nope." I looked up along the wall, following the underside of the steps upward. "What do you think?"

"I think I should have eaten something before letting Nyce pour all of that whiskey down my throat."

"I meant about Ray."

"He's an asshole."

"I know that. What about his claim of being followed and Jane sort of confirming it?"

He sighed. "I think we need to find whatever clues are down here and go back upstairs, so I can sit behind the sheriff's desk while the rest of you figure out how to get me out of this damned jail."

Fortunately for him, I hit paydirt under the stairs. "Ah ha!" I lifted a small metal key that was hanging from a nail pounded partway into one of the stairsteps.

"What is it?" Cooper trailed me over to the filing cabinet.

"A key." I nudged him to the side, kneeling in front of the drawers. "You were right, Detective."

"What did you say?"

"I said you were right about checking under the stairs."

"One more time, Parker, louder and clearer."

I looked up, finding him grinning at me. "I said I'm going to cram this key up your crooked nose, Coop."

He laughed, and then held his palm to his forehead and cursed.

"Learn your lesson, law dog? Give me trouble again and I'll make you cry like a baby. Just ask your buddy, Detective Hawke, about my propensity to conjure wicked curses."

Focusing back on the file cabinet, I stuck the key in the slot. The lock turned with a clunk.

"Bingo, baby," I whispered and opened the top drawer. It was empty except for a couple of pencils and an old lighter that didn't work. The second drawer had a single piece of paper in it. I held it up and shined the light on it. Five shapes were drawn on it.

"Are those letters of the Greek alphabet?" Cooper took the paper and the light from me.

"Yep." I kicked the file drawer closed. "I think we found a clue, but to what?"

He rubbed his jaw. It was so quiet in the basement that I could hear the scratch of his whiskers on his hand. "Let's go back upstairs and see if any of the others found something requiring a sequence of five Greek letters."

I looked around the shadow-filled room. "You think we're done down here?"

"One thing most detectives learn early on, Parker, is that you are rarely ever fully done with a crime scene, which is why I told you to stay out of Ms. Wolff's place. But did you listen? Oh no, not super-sleuth Violet Parker."

I jammed my hands on my hips. "My becoming a Timekeeper was Ms. Wolff's doing, and you know it. You were there. I had no choice but to finish the loop."

He rubbed the back of his neck. "And now Hawke is going to stupid lengths, like round-the-clock drive-bys and sleeping on the floor in Ms. Wolff's apartment, to keep you and any other nosy-nellies away so that the crime scene remains undisturbed until her case is either solved or listed officially as a 'cold' case that will probably never be solved."

Wow, that was a mouthful from the soused detective. He must be starting to sober up. "My fingers are crossed for the latter."

"Mine, too, Parker, believe me."

He started toward the stairs with a slight list. Hmm. Not too sober yet. My flashlight weaved along with Cooper. I followed, ready to catch him if he started to fall.

He slowed as we neared the stairs. "But if those clocks keep disappearing from Wolff's place and end up on your doorstep, you could wind up behind bars again. No game this time."

I joined him at the bottom step. "Only one of Wolff's clocks showed up on Aunt Zoe's porch and you know it."

"Yeah, well, that's one too many in my book." He latched onto my upper arm and pointed the light up the steps. "Now, help an old man out of the basement."

"Where'd you leave your leash, law dog?" I teased, pulling him along. "If you're a good li'l doggy, I'll give you a treat at the top. Would you like that? Huh?"

"Keep it up, you crazy-haired clown, and I'll shoot you as soon as the floor stops trying to buck me off."

"Shucks, Coop. And here I was hoping you and me would be best friends forever before the night was over. Maybe even get matching BFF tattoos."

"It's only whiskey, not magic." He stumbled up a step, leaning onto my shoulder for support.

I laughed. "You're just a big ol' drunk teddy bear, Coop."

"Shut up, Parker," he said as we continued up the stairs. "And that's 'Cooper' to you."

Chapter Twelve

Natalie blocked the doorway when we reached the top of the stairs. She shined her flashlight down on Cooper and me. "Ah, look at you two, hugging like long-lost best friends."

The law dog had been leaning heavily on me the last couple of steps, making my knees work double time. "It is the opinion of my spine that this birthday boy does not need another 'one to grow on.' He's grown too heavy for both of our good." We lumbered up another step together, him with a grunt, me with a groan. "Nat, get your ass down here and help me."

Natalie hopped down the few remaining steps like a bunny rabbit. She looped her arm around Cooper's back from his other side. "Here I am, Hot Cop. What are your other two wishes?"

He chuckled. "I can't say them right now because Parker's listening."

"Maybe later after I get you home and undressed." She giggled. "I mean comfortable."

"Definitely later," I said. "When I'm a few blocks away and the windows are closed."

We made it to the top much quicker with Natalie joining in the fun. Once there, I stepped away from the two of them, following as she led Cooper toward the sheriff's office. He seemed much steadier on his feet now that we were on a flat surface, and much more smiley to have Natalie by his side.

"Where's Cornelius?" I asked. He was supposed to be looking for clues alongside Natalie.

"Upstairs with Doc."

"I thought Harvey was with Doc," I said as the three of us filed into the sheriff's office.

"Somethin' didn't sit right with me up there," the man in question spoke up. He was kicking back in the comfy leather chair, his boots resting on top of the desk.

"You seem to be sitting just fine right now," Cooper said.

"Damned straight." He hooked his thumbs around his suspenders and grinned wide enough to show his gold teeth. "There's a new sheriff in town."

Natalie left Cooper leaning on the sideboard along the wall, joining me in front of the desk. "I brought you a mighty fine deputy, Sheriff Harvey," she said with a twangy accent. "He just needs to park in here with you until the whiskey fumes have done burnt off."

A glance at the clock told me we had about forty-five minutes left until the old docent sprang us from this jail. I wondered if Doc had unearthed anything that would explain the Greek letters written on the slip of paper Cooper and I had found in the basement.

I eyed Harvey. "Your job tonight was to help Doc look for clues, you ol' mule. Not sit behind a desk with a thistle-eating grin on your face."

"I'm better at bein' head honcho. Besides, yer stallion has Corny at his side now. Between the two of 'em, they're sure to find any needles in the haystack."

True, but with Cooper too dizzy to search for clues and Harvey now playing sheriff, we were down to four players left to finish the game. "I thought your nephew was supposed to be head honcho tonight."

Harvey looked up at Cooper. "Him? Naw. He looks like somebody wrung him out of a bartender's rag." He aimed his thumb at the steel door that divided us from the mansion. "We need a teetotaler to study the clues and figure out where that door key is, and tonight, Sheriff Harvey is yer man."

"I'm not that drunk," Cooper muttered.

"You couldn't even climb stairs on your own just a few minutes ago," I reminded him.

Cooper crossed his arms. "Okay, maybe I'm still radioing in as a 10-56, but the world isn't spinning as much anymore."

"What's a 10-56?" I asked.

Harvey snorted. "Code for drunk as a skunk."

"Not quite," Natalie said. "But close enough."

Cooper aimed a raised eyebrow her way. "When did you learn police codes?"

She gave him a cheeky grin. "I have the right to remain silent."

Cooper's eyes widened for a moment. Then his gaze narrowed, heating up, sliding down Natalie's chest and lower, blazing a path along the way.

"What's that supposed to mean?" Harvey asked.

Natalie chuckled low and sexy. "It's a private joke between Mr. Hot Cop and me." She winked at Cooper before turning back to me. "Did you two find anything in the basement?"

"Surprisingly, yes." I pulled the slip of paper with the Greek letters out of my pocket and put it on the desk in front of Harvey. "This was locked away in a file drawer."

Harvey's boots hit the floor. He leaned over the paper. "These look Greek to me."

I couldn't tell if he meant that saying literally or not, so I pointed at each letter, one at a time. "That's omega, delta, beta, alpha, and ..." I scratched my neck. "Crap, I can't remember that last letter."

Natalie leaned over the desk. "That's phi."

"I know." Harvey squinted up at me. "As I said before, they look Greek to me. But what're we supposed to do with them?"

I shrugged. "That's your job to figure out, *Sheriff*. My job is to go find more clues." I nudged Natalie in the arm. "You want to come help me while Harvey babysits Cooper?"

"I don't need babysitting," Cooper growled. He pushed to his feet, only to grimace and sink back down again. "I just need a few more minutes for the merry-go-round to come to a stop."

"Here's what Cornelius and I found so far," Natalie said and dug in her coat pocket, pulling out a keyring with a set of long skeleton keys dangling from it. She dropped them next to the paper with the Greek letters. "We also found this taped to the underside of a chair." She drew a small screwdriver from her pants pocket. "It has a star-shaped head, which isn't real common."

Harvey picked up each item, jotting down some notes on the small pad of paper the docent had given us to keep track of our clues. "Duly noted."

"I haven't checked out the restroom yet," she said.

I smirked. A certain detective and his flashlight had.

"You think we'll find a clue in there?" I asked, not looking forward to peeking in hard to reach places in a strange bathroom.

"The old guy out front said that if a room wasn't locked, there might be something hidden in there for us, so we should go check."

I nodded, focusing back on Harvey. "Has Doc found anything upstairs?"

He shrugged. "I was only up there with him for a few minutes when I felt the need to come back down and take care of business. I appointed myself sheriff after leaving the head." He scratched his beard. "I did find another flashlight by the sink in the bathroom. Not sure if that's a clue or not."

"It's not a clue," Cooper spoke up. "It's mine. I left it by mistake. Did you grab it?"

"Nope. Yer always sayin' not to touch things at crime scenes."

Cooper scoffed. "Now you listen to me, but at my actual crime scenes you and Parker are always messing with shit."

"Quit yer bellyachin', boy." Harvey leaned back in his chair and pointed at me. "Sparky, grab the flashlight when you pass by there in case we need it."

I saluted him. "Will do, Sheriff."

"Parker, you don't salute a sheriff."

"Coop's right," Natalie said. "This is more true to course for you and me when it comes to addressing the law." She scratched her nose with her middle finger.

I chuckled. "I like it when you pretend to reel your middle finger up."

"You mean like this?" she demonstrated, aiming the bird at Cooper.

His hand snaked out to grab her.

Natalie dodged, laughing. She pulled on my arm. "Let's go before Coop sobers up enough to chase us down and handcuff us."

"Ha!" I said, letting her tow me away from the desk. "As if you would run from him." I'd heard enough about their love life tonight to know better.

"Well, I might run a little," she said with a wink in Cooper's direction. "Thrill of the chase and all that."

We left the slightly intoxicated cop and the newly self-appointed sheriff, taking a short hall into the jail's reception area. According to the docent, the inmates were first processed here back in the day. It was a mid-sized room with an L-shaped counter close to a door that led out to a parking lot. That door had two strips of crime-scene tape barring it tonight, though. According to the instruction sheet, we couldn't use it for our escape game. Against one of the walls, four aluminum chairs with army green vinyl cushions that looked to be refugees from the 1960s were lined up like prisoners. On the wall above them hung a corkboard with wanted posters plastered all over it. Some of the posters were a few layers thick.

"Did you check out the posters on this corkboard when you and Cornelius were in here before?" I asked Natalie, who had stepped behind the L-shaped counter. From the sounds of things, she was checking for clues in drawers below it.

"A little. Mostly I searched underneath the chairs to see if anything was taped to them. That's where I found the screwdriver." Another drawer opened and closed.

"Who found the skeleton keys?" I kneeled on a chair and scanned the various wanted posters. Most looked like something I'd see on the set of an Old West movie. I wondered if any of them were real leftovers from the past.

"Cornelius found them in the storage room next to the bathroom. They were hanging in plain sight on the wall, though, so we weren't sure if they were a part of the game."

They were old school, unlike the lock on the door in the sheriff's office. "What do you think they go to?"

I heard the sound of another drawer sliding open.

"I'd guess the jail cells," she said. "But when I zipped upstairs at the start of the game, all of the cell doors were blocked open with bricks, including the outer door at the top of the stairs. That's what made Cornelius and me think they might not be used in the game."

I lifted one of the wanted posters to see what was behind it, finding another poster starring two criminals: Rosie "Rails" Turner and Ted "Blue-belly" Jones. Both were wanted for armed train robbery. A whopping $2,000 reward awaited anyone who brought them in, dead or alive.

"So getting accidentally locked in a jail cell like Deputy Barney Fife on the old *Andy Griffith* and *Mayberry* reruns probably isn't supposed to be part of the fun."

"Exactly." She chuckled. "You and I have had enough so-called 'fun' behind bars in our time."

"You can take that to the bank." I flipped past another wanted flier. *Just watch out for the bank robbers ... and killers,* I thought as I read about a three-time murderer with a $5,000 reward named Fat-fingers Frankie. "Hey, Nat. I think this is one of your old boyfriends. Remember that guy you dated who had bratwursts for fingers?"

"God, don't remind me." She leaned on the counter. "He was a thumb sucker."

"Did he have a blankie, too?"

"No, I mean he got off on sucking women's thumbs." She joined me at the corkboard. "At first I tried to keep an open mind about it. I mean the guy had muscles upon muscles and he was sexy."

"Sexy? We're talking about the same guy, right?"

"Yeah. Sexy like a circus strongman in a leopard onesie sort of way. He even had one of those fun mustaches."

I glanced her way. "You mean a handlebar mustache?"

"No, it wasn't that big. It was thinner with more of a hook on the ends. I think he waxed it sometimes."

My laugh was more of a snort. "You date weird men."

"Said the woman currently sleeping with a mental medium who comes from an ancient line of Oracles."

"*Touché.* But Doc has better fingers."

"Longer, maybe," she conceded with a shrug.

I flipped up Frankie's flier to look at the wanted poster below him. This one was a group shot, but clearly a clue.

"Are those rubber duckies?" Natalie asked, pointing at the sepia-colored picture of four ducks lined up on a shelf. Each duck had a word written below it, along with a reward amount, obviously added by a graphic artist.

"Yep."

"I don't get it." She leaned closer. "Ol' Yeller, Big Red, Greenback Bill, and Black Bart. Is that supposed to be their names?"

"Apparently for the game, it is. I think we need to

remember something about this wanted poster. I found these four duckies in the basement sitting on different shelves, but Cooper told me not to touch them."

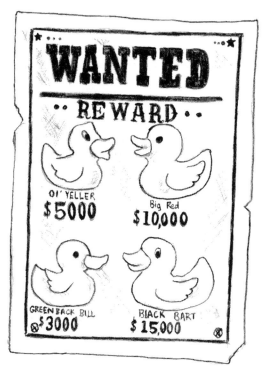

Natalie stared at the poster for a few more seconds before saying, "Okay, I got it memorized."

I glanced at her. "Since when have you had a photographic memory?"

She shrugged. "I'm a visual learner. That's why I always preferred looking at the pictures of naked guys in those magazines Claire would sneak from her mom's closet. You, odd duck that you are, preferred reading the sexy stories rather than checking out the men."

And I still liked reading sexy stories while Natalie preferred looking at men—some things never changed.

I stepped back, grimacing at her. "Those dirty magazines were Claire's mom's? I always thought your cousin snuck them from the head shop around the corner."

"Nope. Aunt Deborah acts all uppity and sophisticated, but there's a lot of fire beneath that icy surface. I think she and my uncle were having some problems with their marriage even back then, and she was using the magazines to spice up their lives with wild monkey sex."

Images of Claire's mom and dad, my childhood neighbors who'd joined us for many backyard barbecues, doing some kinky, hokey-pokey moves flashed through my thoughts. If my grimace sank any deeper, I had a feeling my face might cave in.

"Kate also found—"

"No!" I held my hands up in surrender. "I don't want to hear any more about your cousins or your aunt right now. Especially when it comes to sex."

"Fine, but you're going to miss out on some of Aunt Deborah's juicy sex-capades down in Arizona with her new hubby."

"And I'm one hundred percent fine with that."

"You're such a wuss." Natalie pointed her flashlight toward the exit leading farther into the jail. "Let's finish going through this level and then go see how Doc and Corny are doing upstairs."

"Lead the way, Deputy-up-to-No-Gooder."

According to the old leprechaun docent, after the criminals were done being processed in the reception room, they were escorted down the hallway Natalie and I were currently walking through. I tried to imagine what it would have felt like to be led along this hall, most likely handcuffed—if not in leg chains—facing days, weeks, even months of cell life ahead of me. I shuddered. No, thanks.

My time behind bars had been measured in hours so far, and each visit to the clink had left me rattled for days after I was sprung. That was all the more reason for me to avoid Detective Hawke, who seemed to have made putting me behind bars the top spot on his to-do list.

The hall dumped us out into a larger room with light blue walls and a staircase on the far side leading up to the cells. Together, Natalie and I checked out each of the rooms lining the edges that were tucked away behind unlocked closed doors.

One door led to the bathroom where Cooper had left his flashlight, which Natalie found when she zipped inside to use the facilities.

Another door opened to a storage closet full of mops, cleaning supplies, and other maintenance necessities. This was the room where Cornelius had found the skeleton keys, according to Natalie.

A third door led to the basement. We opted to skip going down there since Cooper and I had already scoured it. Although Natalie did take a quick run down the stairs to check out the rubber duckies while I waited up top.

The fourth door was marked as an emergency exit. It was solid steel and secured with an alarm and the proper signage to meet modern fire codes. In the old days, before fire safety measures were a requirement, it had probably been locked up tight to keep any prisoners from making a quick escape.

We felt around the thick door frame but came up empty. Natalie won the coin toss for who would play "stepstool," so I got down on all fours and let her climb up on my back. She took her sweet damned time feeling along the top of the lit exit sign. The new bruises I'd undoubtedly gained from our efforts were all in vain.

"Well, shit." She helped me to my feet. "I guess that's all the clues we have down here. Seems like there should be more. Do you think they plant different numbers of clues depending on how many people are playing the game?"

"Maybe." I brushed off my hands and knees, following

her out into the center of the room. "Could be there are a bunch of clues to where that key is up in the jail cells."

She walked over to the base of the metal staircase and looked up the stairs. "That's weird."

"You're weird." I joined her, looking up the stairs.

"I know you are, but that's what makes you special in my heart." She pointed at the door on the landing at the top of the stairs. "The door is closed."

"Good observation, Sherlock." The heavy-duty steel door with a small square window was indeed shut. "That must be why we haven't heard any sounds from Doc and Cornelius."

"But didn't the docent say that door was to be left open?"

"I remember him saying not to close the cage doors in the jail, but not anything in particular about that door."

"The door was blocked open earlier, though. Why would they close it?" She turned to me. "Something isn't right here."

My heart picked up speed, starting to jog along. I craned my neck, listening. It was quiet up there, really quiet. How thick was that door? Thick enough to be soundproof?

"I don't like how quiet it is," I told her. "Let's go see how they're doing." I hurried up the twenty or so metal steps, the thud of my boot heels echoing throughout the big first-floor room as I climbed.

Natalie kept up behind me. "Maybe I should go get Coop."

"Let's do a drive-by of the crime scene before we call for backup."

"You've been spending too much time with Coop. Now you're starting to sound like him."

"It's your fault. You partnered me with him."

When we reached the upstairs landing, Natalie tried the door. "It's locked."

I pounded on the slab of steel. "Doc? Cornelius?"

Nothing happened.

We both went up on our toes to peek through the small square window. The room on the other side was too dark for me to make out details, of course, being that the game was meant to leave us in the dark.

"Can you see anything?" I asked, going up on my tippy-toes for another look.

"No, it's too da—wait! I think I see a light at the other end of the room." She held up her flashlight, shining it through the glass. "Damn it, I'm too short." She aimed her light at my chest. "Get down on your hands and knees again."

"You get down this time. Your heels hurt my kidneys."

"Fine, but take off your boots before you step on me. The tread on those babies is too meaty." She dropped onto all fours.

I sat down on the metal grate flooring and started to slide my boots off, but then paused. "This steel grate is going to kill your knees, Nat. Maybe we should go look for a stepladder."

"There's no time for that. Quit dicking around. Get up on my back and check on the guys."

Fine! I stripped down to my socks and then carefully stepped up onto her, leaning into the door for support.

"Move your boney heel off my spine, bigfoot," she growled.

I readjusted. "Better?"

"A little." She grunted, shifting slightly under me.

I wobbled, clutching the small window's frame with my fingertips to keep my balance. "Hold still."

"I am."

"You need to stop wiggling or you're going to dump me off."

"Yeah, well you need to stop shoving two helpings of cake down your piehole in the future," she said in between grunts.

"Shut it, mouth," I growled back at her.

Slowly and carefully, I lifted my flashlight.

"What do you see, Vi?"

"Not much. You were right about the flashlight on the floor at the far end of the room." I aimed my light in that direction, leaning closer. There was something dark on the floor. Big and dark, with an arm sticking out from one side. Was that a ...

"Oh, shit," I whispered.

Natalie grunted, shifting under me again. "What?"

"We've got a man down." I pressed my nose against the glass. "I think it's Cornelius."

"Where's Doc?"

I shined my light around, catching a glimpse of a light beam coming from my far, far right.

Natalie grunted again, louder this time. "Vi, you need to get down. My old knee injury is throbbing like a son of a bitch. I don't know how much longer I can hold you."

"Just a second."

"Hurry!"

I leaned farther to the side, shifting my light as far to the right as I could.

"I found Doc!"

He was sitting on one of the inmate beds in the group cell. His flashlight lay at his feet, the beam aimed toward the far wall. I dipped my light down over his stiff profile. Something definitely wasn't right here.

"Is he okay?" Natalie asked.

"I don't think so."

"What do you mean?"

"It looks like he's covering his ears."

"Hear no evil," she said, shifting again and then cursing in pain.

"Doc!" I pounded on the door, but Doc remained frozen in place with his head down and ears covered. My heartbeat sped up, going from a jog to a long stride.

"Vi! Down! Now!" Natalie said through gritted teeth.

"Shit!" I stepped down onto the metal grate floor. "We have to break in there, and we need to do it now."

She held out her hand for some help up. "Why would Doc just be sitting there if Cornelius is hurt?"

I hauled her to her feet. "Remember how the docent joked about this place being haunted?"

"Yes." Natalie leaned against the wall and rubbed her knee, her face tight with pain.

"I don't think it was a joke." Nor was the *haunted* label a marketing ploy, as I'd previously thought. "I'd bet my mom's Janis Joplin record collection that there's a ghost in there with Doc and Cornelius." I tugged on the door handle again to no avail. "And I'm guessing that ghost isn't some sweet young mail clerk who delivered letters from loved ones to the prisoners."

I tried pounding on the door again.

"You think it's a deranged King Kong–sized inmate wearing a clown mask with a manic grin wielding a bloody cast-iron pipe?"

I turned to her, my jaw dipped low. "Jumpin' Jehoshaphat, Nat! Why did you have to go and make him so scary?"

"I don't know. That image just popped into my mind."

"Well, think of a less creepy ghost next time. One with a geeky bowtie and highwater plaid pants."

"Why would an inmate be wearing a bowtie?"

"Just do it!" I went back to banging on the door.

Behind us, footfalls thundered up the stairs, matching me pound for pound on the door.

Chapter Thirteen

"What's all of the pounding and yelling about?" Cooper asked, joining us on the landing. His focus shifted. "Who closed the door?"

"We don't know, but now it's locked." Natalie reached out to him when he swayed slightly, but he kept her at bay with a shake of his head. "Doc and Corny are trapped on the other side."

"I think there's someone in there with them," I said in a somber voice as I put my boots back on. "Someone who shut the door and locked it. Someone no longer breathing."

Natalie smirked. "Nice job, Vincent Price. Queue the ghostly 'oooohhh' groans."

Cooper frowned from me to Natalie. "What the hell are you two talking about? What makes you think there is anything going on here other than the obvious—the door closed and accidentally locked?"

Rather than waste my breath, I pointed at the window. "Look in there and tell us what you see."

He took my flashlight and bumped me aside, staring through the window. Unlike Natalie and me, Cooper was tall enough to not need to go up on his toes.

"What's Curion doing on the floor?" he asked.

"Please tell me he's breathing," I said.

"Definitely breathing. Is he taking a nap or rebooting his third-eye chakra again?"

I blew out a breath in relief at Cooper's still-breathing assessment. "Your guess is as good as mine, but I don't think he's taking a nap and it's too early for his bedtime." I tapped the right side of the window. "Doc's over in the group cell sitting on one of the beds."

Cooper aimed his light in that direction. "Yeah, I see …" He jerked, the flashlight clattering against the glass. "What the fuck?"

I knew there had to be someone in there that Natalie and I couldn't see. An ectoplasmic visitor was the only explanation I could think of for the scene on the other side of the glass—and for Cooper's reaction.

"What does the ghost look like?" I asked.

"There's more than one," he said under his breath.

Natalie shot me a worried look. "How many?"

"I count four," he said, moving the beam of light around. "No, make that five. Three are inmates, judging from their clothes. The other two appear to be guards, but their uniforms are slightly different. Maybe they're from different eras in the past." He shifted, angling to get a better look at Doc. "What's he doing?"

I tried to see, but his head fully blocked my view. "Who?"

"Nyce. He's rocking back and forth with his head bowed and his ears covered. I've never seen him do that."

I hadn't either, although I'd witnessed him convulsing during a séance before.

Crap. I wrung my hands. Had he been rocking when I peeked in at him? I hadn't been able to watch him long enough to tell.

"If I were to guess, I'd say he's either trying to keep those five ghosts from swarming him; or they've already swarmed him and he's fighting to keep his head above water as he relives their deaths."

"Relives them one at a time or all at once?" Natalie asked.

I shrugged. "One at a time he could probably handle, but

five at once would overwhelm him for a bit."

"Christ, Parker." Cooper stepped back, turning to me. "Didn't you look into the history of this place before letting two mediums waltz into a haunted jail?"

"Cornelius isn't a medium," I said defensively.

"I was talking about *you*. Or have you forgotten about playing Chatty Cathy with my great-grandfather out at Uncle Willis's ranch?"

"There might be another 'great' or two in there," I said, correcting him on his ancestor's place in the family line.

His eyes narrowed into a squint. "You know who I mean, damn it."

I did, of course. One doesn't quickly forget a shotgun-happy, hooch-lovin', old flirt who jawed about breeding hips—mine, in particular.

Natalie squeezed in between us, nudging Cooper back enough to give me some breathing room. "There weren't any details online that confirmed the 'haunted' rumors were true." She crossed her arms. "And don't go blaming Vi for this. I'm the one who had the bright idea to come to an escape room for your birthday. This is my fault for not digging deeper on the history of the place."

His expression softened. "Don't beat yourself up. I hadn't heard anything about the place either."

"What the hell!" My jaw dropped. "No fair! You're taking it easy on her because she's sleeping with you."

"Of course I am. And we're doing more than just sleeping," Cooper said before turning back to the window.

I wrinkled my nose at Natalie. "You need to sober your boyfriend up. He's way too loose-lipped about your sex life when he's drunk."

She gave me a crooked smile. "I kind of like him with his inhibitions out to lunch."

Cooper tried the door handle again. "We need to figure out how to get them out of there without raising any alarms.

Nyce wouldn't want this to make front-page news."

He was spot-on there. Doc had plenty of clients in Spearfish. They didn't need to know that the guy handling their money partied with ghosts during his time off.

"I could try to do my medium trick from out here," I suggested. "But I usually have Cornelius or Doc to help keep me from making a wrong turn in the dark." Not to mention that there were things hiding in that shadow-filled realm that liked to lick and bite. "And that steel door might be a game changer even when I'm in here." I tapped my temple.

"Shizznit," Natalie muttered. "I really cocked this one up." She went up on her toes to peek through the glass. "I shouldn't have let Cornelius join Doc up here."

I squeezed her arm. "How were you to know?"

She frowned my way. "Now you're going easy on me, too. Both of you need to stop treating me with kid gloves and hold me accountable as one of the team. It's not like I'm new to all of this supernatural shit you've been dealing with the last few months." She poked Cooper in the shoulder. "I didn't hold back on you when you nearly got Violet killed back in Slagton, did I?"

I shrugged at Cooper. "She's got a point there." She'd read him the riot act in front of me on Aunt Zoe's front porch.

"Fine, Beals." Cooper rubbed his eyes. "You fucked up. You should have considered Nyce's abilities and Parker's tendency to cause a huge clusterfuck when you set this up."

I did a double take. "Hey, I think I resent that."

He continued, ignoring me. "Now let's fix the problem at hand. That's what you keep telling me you do best. Fix broken things."

"He's right. You are good at fixing things, Nat." I hit her with an extra-wide, blinding smile. High school cheerleaders had nothing on me.

She held her hand up in front of my face. "Stop it. That

smile would scare the piss out of a battle-scarred veteran."

"She's right." Cooper blocked my face, too. "Beals, didn't you give Uncle Willis an old set of keys that Curion found?"

Natalie gasped. "The skeleton keys!" She took off down the stairs two at a time, hollering, "I'll be right back," as she reached the main floor.

Left alone with Cooper, I crossed my arms. "I find it ironic to be standing next to you of all people while trying to break *into* a jail." I leaned back against the wall. "At least you're a little nicer when you're drunk." Although a tad too vocal about his sex life for my liking.

"I'm nice all of the time, Parker." Cooper returned to peering in the window. "Just not to you."

"That's not fair."

"Life's not fair, but I know you're a tough cookie and can take more ribbing than most."

I tilted my head. "Did you just compliment me, Cooper?"

"I don't know. I'm drunk, remember?" He pulled away from the glass. "I think the ghosts know we're out here. They keep looking over this way."

That meant they weren't just some sort of haunting, which Cornelius had taught me was like an old movie clip from the past that played over and over without any interaction from the stars of the show. These ghosts were more like Jane, which was good and bad. Although seeing as they were all surrounding Doc, it was probably mostly bad. They must know he could interact with them on some level, the same as Cooper, only ... wait!

"Do you think they realize *you* can see them?" I asked.

He scowled at me. "How in the hell am I supposed to know that? You want me to call them on the ghost phone and ask?"

"No, smartass. Listen, my point is that *you* could distract them from Doc. They're obviously drawn to his energy. I've seen Prudence and other ghosts do the same thing to him—

as if they are trying to connect with the living. To feel alive again in some way. If the ghosts realize you can see them, you might be able to stop them from draining Doc, which will give me time to get him out of there."

"I thought you said they swarm him."

"Same difference. You know what I mean."

He closed his eyes and squeezed the bridge of his nose. "Their deaths weren't pretty."

I cringed on his behalf. I would hate to have Cooper's ability to see ghosts as they had been at death, especially the gruesome ones. "You've seen worse, though, right?"

His eyelids snapped open. "That doesn't mean I want to see something like that up close and personal."

"Yeah, but you're a tough cookie," I said with a smile.

His steely eyes narrowed. "Copycat."

"And you're protected by a layer of whiskey right now."

"No, I'm slightly queasy because of too much whiskey dumped on an empty stomach. Getting a closer look at those dead guys in there is going to make matters worse."

"Empty stomach? What were you thinking? Why didn't you eat before you left with Doc?"

He sighed, rubbing the back of his neck. "Because it's hard for me to get a buzz when I have food in my stomach. I figured Nyce and I would be going to the bar for some drinks and shooting the shit all night, along with playing a game of pool or darts, and that was it. I didn't expect to be dragged by the collar to a haunted jail, forced to partner with a crazy-haired harpy on a sleuth mission, and then pressured into playing nice with ugly ghosts to save my friends."

"I'm going to ignore that hair insult," I told him, "because you're still drunk."

He grinned. "Not that drunk."

"Drunk enough, plus it's your birthday. My parents always told me I had to be kind to *old* people."

He reached out and flicked my forehead.

Chuckling, I rubbed where he'd flicked. "Seriously, it's nice that you consider Cornelius your friend. He's a bit quirky, but he means well and will only resort to using a tiny bit of blackmail to help you when you're in a pinch."

He shrugged. "I like oddballs. They're more trustworthy than slick bastards."

I pointed toward the window. "How ugly are we talking in there? Tell me what you see."

"You sure you can handle it?"

I smirked. "I kill monsters in my spare time."

"True. One must have been burned to death. Half of his face is partially melted and the other side pretty charred."

"Oh, God." I hoped that Doc had not been forced to relive that one's death. The sight of a human torch would leave me mentally scarred for a long time. Then again, the little I'd learned about the deaths Doc had suffered during different medium experiences had taught me that he was a super-duper tough cookie.

Cooper peered through the window. "And the burned guy is not even the worst. One of the guards has an eyeball dangling."

I covered my mouth in horror.

Natalie came pounding up the stairs, two at a time again, interrupting Cooper's ghostly exposé.

"Here!" She handed Cooper the set of skeleton keys. "Harvey is going to run interference in case that docent dude decides to come check on us."

"Good," Cooper said, giving me back my flashlight. He tried one of the keys in the lock. Nope. He found the right key on his third attempt and turned it. Something clinked in the locking mechanism.

I pulled on the handle, but the door didn't budge.

"Step aside, Parker." He gave the door a hard tug.

It still didn't open.

"What the hell?" Natalie tugged on the handle next. "I

heard the lock *clink*. You guys heard it, too, right?"

I nodded.

Cooper twisted the key back the other way. The lock clinked again, but the door still wouldn't budge.

I watched as he tried turning it back and forth again, pulling on the handle to no avail. "It's like Jane's ghost holding that closet door shut in Jerry's office. Not even Nat and her crowbar could budge the sucker until Jane decided to let us inside."

And for good reason, too, it'd turned out. Just the other morning while brushing my teeth I was worrying about that red-armed monster reaching for me through the hole in the courthouse basement wall. My poor gums had taken a beating that morning and were sore the rest of the day.

Cooper pulled out the key and glared at the door handle. "Son of a motherfucker!"

"It's too bad you aren't a killer robot from the future disguised in human skin like I'd initially had you pegged. We could really use some laser vision right about now to burn a hole in that steel door."

"You watch too many movies, Parker."

"That's blasphemy, Coop." Natalie took the keys from him and pocketed them. "Movies encourage us to dream big in life." She shined the beam of her flashlight around the door's frame. "I'd say we could try to remove the door itself, but these hinges are welded to the steel plate surrounding the frame. Somebody didn't want to have any prisoners escape on their watch."

I chewed on my knuckles, thinking back to Jane and that closet door. "I think we have to convince one of the ghosts to open the door from the other side, but how? Cooper, you said they can see us, right?"

"Yeah."

"We could try flashing them." Natalie winked at me. "But the window is too high. Cooper will have to let us stand on his back."

"Nobody is flashing anyone," Cooper told her. "Especially not you."

"Nat does have some pretty great hooters," I said. "They could probably even wake the dead."

He gave me a "no-shit" look. "I know, Parker. Beals and I are sleeping together, remember?"

"And then some," Natalie quipped.

"I think I liked the chatter between the three of us better when you two were both sexually frustrated and I was the only one getting some." *Chatter* ... that word stuck in my head as an idea surfaced. I frowned at the window. "Hey, Cooper, if they can see you, then you can interact with them."

"I'm not going to play pattycake with them, if that's what you're thinking."

"Pattycake? Jeez, would you sober up already."

"I'm sober enough."

"Good. Then I want you to convince one of the ghosts to open the door for us."

"And how in the hell am I supposed to do that?"

"You said two of them were guards, right?"

He nodded.

"They're officers of the law, same as you. Use your law dog lingo and get them to help us out."

His head dipped, one eyebrow inching up. "My law dog lingo?"

"You know what I mean, Cooper. 'Hook 'em and book 'em' and 'berries and cherries' and all of that cop talk crap." I pointed at the window. "Now, stop wasting time and get one of those guards to open up for us. We need to get to Doc before they drain him dry. And keep your fingers crossed Cornelius is just taking a cat nap and doesn't need to go to the hospital."

Cooper glowered at me for a handful of seconds. "Fine. I'll try for Nyce's and Curion's sake."

I clapped my hands together. "You can do this, Cooper. I just know it."

"Nat, duct tape Parker's mouth, please."

Natalie chuckled and then handed Cooper her flashlight.

Cooper aimed the beam through the glass. "Hey! Guard!" he shouted in a deep, commanding voice. "Come over here."

I snorted. "They teach you to talk like that in cop camp?"

He spared me a glance. "Zip it, or I'll throw you behind bars when we get inside."

"*If* we get inside," Natalie said. "What's happening now?"

Cooper stared through the window. "One of the guards is coming this way."

"It worked!" I cheered silently, pumping my fist. "Now be careful. Sometimes these ghosts can be persnickety. You'll need to be tricky when you talk to it."

"Tricky how?" Natalie asked.

"Like use mind games on it. Pretend you think it's still alive." I poked Cooper in the side. "Whatever you do, don't let them know you're here to help Doc. You should probably think of something random in case he can read minds. I know, mentally picture your gun lamp or your uncle's cannon."

"Would you be quiet, Parker!" he growled.

"Now what's happening?" Natalie asked up on her toes, trying to look through the glass along with Cooper.

"The guard is standing on the other side of the door staring out at me."

I shrunk back against the wall. Ghosts creeped me out even after all the times I'd been around Prudence. Hell, it was probably because of all the times I'd been around the pushy dead *Scharfrichter* that spurred my fears. She taught me that ghosts can hurt the living, and apparently I made a good punching bag.

Cooper pulled out his wallet.

"What are you doing?" Natalie whispered.

"I have an idea." He flipped open his wallet and held it up against the window. "Police!" he shouted through the glass. "Open up!"

I rolled my eyes. "Sheesh, Cooper. Now who's been watching too many movies. You need to be more creative than that if you want to trick a ghost into …"

The door creaked open.

Cooper gave me a cocky grin. "You were saying?"

"Stuff a sock in it and get inside before the ghost guard changes his mind."

Cooper pulled the door open farther, casting a glance in Natalie's direction. "You need to wait out here, Beals."

"What? No. Why?"

"Because if they close the door again with Parker and me on the inside and won't let us out, somebody needs to go for help."

She crossed her arms. "That's a load of bullshit, Coop."

"Actually, it makes sense," I said. "I'm allergic to jail cells. If I wind up stuck in this one with those ghosts, I want you to bring the cavalry along with Harvey's cannon and get me the hell out of there."

She squinted at me and then Cooper. "Fine, I'll stay out here, but you two better tell me every single detail when this is all over."

"I'll make it up to you," Cooper said, leaning down and dropping a kiss on her lips.

"You better, birthday boy." She palmed the sides of his face and pulled him back for a longer, wetter, noisier kiss.

I wrinkled my nose. "You two are really loud kissers." I tried to nudge them apart. "Come on, this isn't a mint gum commercial. Wrap it up."

Finally, she detached from his face and turned to me. "Sorry, he tastes good."

"Eww, Count Dracula." I spit in my palm and held it out to her for a shake. "Promise you'll spring me if I get stuck in there."

She recoiled and pushed my hand away. "I told you back in second grade how gross that is and I still stand by that today."

I shrugged, wiping my hand on my pants. "Your loss. My spit is magical—just ask Doc."

"You're cocoa bananas," she said and hugged me. "Don't let anything happen to either of you," she whispered in my ear and gave me a quick kiss on the side of my head.

"Bleck." I wiped off where she'd kissed me. "You just traded spit with Cooper and now you rubbed his saliva on my hair."

"That's right, baby." She blew me an air kiss. "Now you have Cooper cooties, too."

I batted her kiss away. "I'll try not to let the ghosts lock up Cooper for all eternity, but I give no guarantees."

"Come on, Parker," he said, gripping me by the wrist. Handcuffs were no match for his hold as he towed me over the threshold and into the jail behind him.

As we passed through, the door started to swing shut, but something blocked it. I glanced down and saw Natalie's boot in the way. She always had been a quick thinker.

"Maybe we should have brought her along," I said to Cooper as we hurried along the walkway between the jail cells to where Cornelius lay toward the back of the room.

I shined my light on Doc as we passed the group cell. His eyes were closed, his skin pale with a glisten of sweat on his forehead. Shitballs. That wasn't a good sign at all.

"No way in hell," Cooper said, tugging on me when I tried to head in Doc's direction.

I tugged back. "Why are you still holding onto me?"

"Because Nyce always worries about you taking side trips when we're playing friendly with the wispy folks. I'm going to make sure you stay right here by my side."

"You should have brought your handcuffs along."

"Maybe next time. Now come on. Nyce is obviously still breathing just fine. We need to make sure Curion is, too."

When we reached Cornelius, Cooper dropped to his knees, pulling me down with him. Cornelius lay on his stomach with his head turned in our direction. Cooper shined the light on his face, lifting his eyelids one at a time while I checked for a pulse, which I found with ease. It was beating at a smooth, regular rate.

"His pulse is strong and steady." I sat back on my heels.

"His pupils contracted when I checked." Cooper held his hand in front of Cornelius's nose. "He seems to be breathing fine, too."

"Okay, so it appears Cornelius is just taking some sort of mental break." Oddly enough, this wasn't the first time I'd found him in this state, or at least something similar to it. "Now let's go help Doc." I tried to stand but Cooper wasn't having it.

"Let's turn him over on his back first. Check for other injuries. He might have fallen on something."

Together, we made fast work of the task and then sat back to have a look-see with our flashlights. Cornelius looked peaceful, as if he were taking a snooze in a hammock, not checked out in a haunted jail.

I reached down and ran my fingers through his hair feeling for injuries. "Hmm."

"What is it?" Cooper asked. "Did you find a lump?"

"No, but his hair is softer than I expected. I always figured it would be coarse since it's so thick."

Cooper cursed at me six ways from Sunday.

"I beg your pardon, Officer Pottymouth!" I poked him in the shoulder. "And you need to take that last one back."

"I'm not taking anything back. Now is not the time for horsing around, Parker."

"Are you kidding?" I snapped. "We're in a haunted jail surrounded by five menacing ghosts most likely drawn out from the woodwork by our pied piper pal here who is conked out on the floor while my boyfriend sits locked away over there in a cell going through who knows what hellish mental shit because I can't get to him to pull him back to safety." I huffed at Cooper's silent stare. "Now is the best frickin' time for horsing around, because at this moment I'm one rotted corpse breath on the back of my neck away from screaming these walls down."

His hold on my wrist loosened a little. "Okay, calm down. You're right. The situation in here is a bit tense."

I nodded, breathing hard. "Where are the damned ghosts right now?"

He glanced behind me. Half of his face squinched. "You don't want to know."

Goose bumps prickled down my spine. I gulped and focused on Cornelius. "He's breathing and doesn't seem to be physically hurt, which could mean one of these freaky phantoms must be exerting some kind of specter-spell on him."

"You have a real way with words, you know it?"

"I try my best."

I dared a peek over my shoulder all the while cringing, fearing I'd suddenly be able to see whatever it was that Cooper didn't want to tell me about. Thankfully, I remained ghost-blind. However, movement in the group cell made my breath catch. I shined my light at Doc, jerking back at the sight of him staring back at me with wide, dark eyes. At least his pupils looked extra black from here.

"Doc?" I whispered. "Cooper, look." I nudged my head toward the group cell.

"Why are you whispering?" Cooper asked. "It's not as if the ghosts can't hear you."

"Now you're chastising *me* about whispering? Oh, that's rich."

"Stay back!" Doc interrupted our bickering. His voice

was raspy, tired sounding, but stronger than the times he'd gone head to head with Prudence.

Why was he just sitting in there? Had the ghosts locked him in the cell the same as they'd locked us out, or had he done it to somehow protect himself from whatever knocked out Cornelius?

Cooper stood slowly, pulling me up with him. "Are you talking to us or the ghosts, Nyce?"

"I'm talking to her," he answered, pointing in my direction.

Her? Oh shit, what had these ghosts done to his mind? Didn't he recognize me? "Doc, it's me, Violet. Cooper and I are here to help."

"Not you, Killer."

Relief flooded through me. Good, his brain wasn't totally gone. Now to get him out of that cell.

"So loud," Doc said and groaned, closing his eyes and lowering his head into his hands. He took a deep rattling breath before continuing. "Coop, there is a banshee behind Violet. She's sitting on Cornelius."

My shoulders tightened up in a snap. Holy heartstopper! I slowly turned back to the pied piper of ghosts. How in the hell did he hook a banshee? And from where? Weren't they usually over in Ireland or Scotland? I always thought banshees were made up. Fairy women from fairy tales. Then again, why should I be surprised to find a banshee roaming around in the Black Hills? After all, I was currently being hounded by parasitic, long-limbed ghouls with a penchant for my blood. A banshee couldn't be too bad, could she?

I shined my light all around Cornelius. "I can't see her," I whispered to Cooper. "Can you?"

"No," he said, stepping away from Cornelius and dragging me with him. "But I think I can hear her wailing now. It sort of reminds me of when you were in jail."

"Not funny, Cooper."

"Sure, now you don't want to horse around." He towed me farther away from Cornelius—or tried to, but my right boot was caught on something.

I tugged, but my foot was stuck fast. What the hell?

Cooper pulled again. "Quit screwing around, Parker."

"I'm not screwing around. My boot is stuck on something." I shined the light down on my foot.

"There's nothing there," Cooper said.

"I know that." I tugged again. "But I'm telling you, it's stuck."

A cold, tingling sensation started at my toes and quickly moved along the arch of my foot, over my heel, and up my calf. My pulse rocketed. "Something isn't right here," I told Cooper as the tingling chill climbed over my knee and up my thigh.

"What's wrong?"

"I have to get this boot off," I cried, frantically tugging at my frozen leg with my hands. "Help me, damn it."

Cooper let go of my arm and wrapped his arms around my waist, trying to haul me free while I worked to slip out of my boot with no luck.

"Coop!" Doc's shout made us both jump and look over at him. Coop lit him up with the flashlight. He was standing at the bars of the cell, his face lined with pain. "You need to let go of Violet."

The tingling cold fingers climbed over my hip, moving up my back while another chill started down my other leg. I was panting now, struggling to catch my breath. What the hell was going on?

I needed to focus. Slow my breath. Center myself. I closed my eyes and saw a single candle flame in the dark flickering brightly.

"Let go?" Cooper asked, but held tight to me, which was good because if he let go now I was going to fall as both of my legs seemed to be frozen. "Why?"

"Because the banshee is sinking its claws into her."

It was doing what?

A blast of panic shot through me. The flickering candle flame in my mind's eye flared big and bright, exploding like a firecracker in the dark.

The tingling cold filled my chest and raced up my neck.

"Let go or she'll take you with her!" I heard Doc yell, but his voice seemed small and distant.

A blood-curdling, long-winded shriek rang out, going on and on and on, piercing my head.

I screamed in pain, lashing out in the darkness.

The shriek stopped as quickly as it started.

My ears ringing still, I opened my eyes.

"Oh, no!" I scrambled to my feet. "She got me."

Chapter Fourteen

She got me, too, damn it!" Cooper growled.

I looked down. He lay flat on his back on the tiled floor. Under the bright overhead lights, I could see a vein pulsing in his forehead. His eyes were hard and sharp like two silver daggers aimed up at me.

But I didn't care. I was happy to see I had company, even if it was a bristly law dog. "How'd you get down there?"

"How in the hell did I get *here*, wherever the fuck we are?" He pushed to his feet and then poked me in the shoulder. Hard. "This is your fault, Parker."

Ouch. I rubbed my shoulder. Apparently I was back to feeling something other than the cold tingling touch of the banshee. I could hear Cooper loud and clear, too, including the underlying fury clipping off the end of his words, so my sight, sound, and touch senses were still online.

I grimaced at him. He was obviously still waiting for an explanation. "Oops."

Cooper probably should have let go of me when Doc told him to.

" 'Oops'? Is that all you have to say for landing us ..." he glanced around. "Where the hell did you take us?"

Rather than bask in the glow of his huffiness, I took inventory of our surroundings, trying to figure out myself where we'd ended up. It didn't take more than a glance to see we were in the same place—the top floor of the old jail, but things felt slightly different. Brighter for one thing, with the lights on and white light blaring in through the barred windows. Also, the walls were painted a cool mint green instead of sea blue, giving the jail a fresh, sterilized feel. The place smelled musty, same as before, but with hints of sourness underlying a coating of ammonia or some other nose-burning disinfectant.

"It's clear where we are," I told him. "The better question is *when* in time are we at this moment. Or is it the same timeline, only a matter of some other plane or realm?"

And where was the banshee? Had I left her behind?

"Christ." Cooper plowed his fingers through his hair. "This supernatural shit makes no goddamned sense."

"Tell me about it."

I spun in a slow circle. It was easier to see the size and layout of the place in the light. There was one group cell that would sleep four men. This was the same cell Doc had been sitting in when we'd entered the jail room. This group-holding pen was almost twice as big as one of the cells in the modern-day Deadwood police station. I knew that from first-hand experience, thanks to the big bozo grumbling next to me.

On the opposite side of the large cell were three narrow single cells, including the one we were standing next to, and one slightly roomier caged area with an open shower stall and sink. That must have been where the prisoners showered, right here in front of one and all. Each of the cells had a stainless-steel toilet and a small sink as well. I cringed at the lack of privacy, something I had experienced as well while waiting to be sprung from Deadwood's jail months back.

Cooper pocketed his flashlight. "What are we doing here, Parker?"

"I don't know."

"How do we get out of here and back to the others?"

"I don't know that either."

He cursed under his breath. "What *do* you know?"

I sucked air through my teeth. "That I panicked back there when that banshee was crawling up my leg and I played my physical medium card, same as I did when I ran into the Bone Cruncher in the graveyard out behind your uncle's barn."

"Okay, so how did you get back to the regular world *then*?"

I frowned down at my hands. "I don't know that either. One minute I was in that other realm watching the Bone Cruncher take bites out of a skull. The next thing I remember is you calling my name, and then *shazam-balam!*"

" 'Shazam-balam'? Did you say those actual words?"

"No, I was just using that to … never mind. Let's leave it, as I somehow managed to bring the Bone Cruncher back to our realm with me by accident."

"You really have a talent for screwing up, Parker. You should win awards for this shit."

"Screw you, Cooper. You're the one who dragged me into that jail room because you were too chickenshit to face off with those five ghosts on your own."

"I wasn't chickenshit, I was drunk." He rubbed his palm down his face. "I still am, for that matter. At least I think I am. Maybe I passed out and this is just a horrible nightmare and I'll wake up in my bed next to Nat."

"With a big red ball gag in your mouth," I finished the scene for him, and then realized I'd said it aloud and squeezed my lips together.

"What is your fascination with ball gags tonight, Parker?"

Instead of answering that, I reached over and pinched him.

He jerked back. "What'd you do that for?"

"To test your theory. See, this is not a nightmare." Although I didn't think it was total reality either. I had a feeling we were trapped somewhere in between two realms, like an elevator stuck mid-floor. I just had to figure out how to get us back to where we'd come from.

"That doesn't make me feel any better." He rubbed where I'd pinched him. "What happened to the banshee?"

"I've been wondering that myself." I looked around, listening. The jail was quiet. Too quiet. "Maybe I lost her when the candle exploded."

"What candle?"

"The one I use to center myself during séances."

He rubbed his jaw. Just like in the basement during what seemed like another lifetime ago, the rasping of his fingers over his beard stubble seemed extra loud. "Is this the same candle Curion has you picture when you're going into that dark place?"

"Yep."

"But that candle blew up this time?"

"Like an M-80 firecracker. *Ka-boom!*" I demonstrated with my hands.

His brow tightened. "Jesus, Parker. What did you get us into here?"

"Hey, I had a banshee trying to claw her way under my skin, so I used a previously tested tool to escape."

He snorted. "You're the tool."

"Yeah, well, Doc told you to let go of me but you didn't listen to him, so it's *your* fault you're here with me. You need to listen better and do as you're told."

In spite of his complaining, I was still really glad he hadn't listened or done what he was told.

"Shut the hell up and figure out how to get us back to the others."

"Fine." I dropped onto the floor, sitting cross-legged.

He walked over to the door with the little square window, peering out.

"What do you see?" I asked.

"Nothing. It's like a whiteout. I can't make out the stairs

or anything."

He tried the door. It didn't budge. No surprise there.

"It looks like we're stuck in this place for now."

"Let me see if I can reach out and find Doc."

I took a deep breath and closed my eyes, trying to ignore the lead weight in my chest. Locking onto Doc in the dark was not something I'd had much success with before. He always came for me when I was in that creepy-crawly place, and more than once it took him a little too long to locate me. My fingers were crossed that he was in a mental state where he could focus on finding us. But if that banshee was still with him …

Okay, enough negative thinking. Time to focus on how to get out of here. I thought back to things Doc and Cornelius had talked about when it came to my physical medium abilities, trying to remember words they'd used.

There was something about me being a psychophoner and using telepathy, but that had to do with Doc transferring information to me and then me acting as a fancy microphone of sorts for Harvey's long-dead relative. Or was that something to do with retrocognition?

Damn it, I'd heard these words bandied about enough by Doc and Cornelius that I should have the meanings down, but spoken words tended to go in one ear and out the other.

Whatever the paranormal professionals wanted to call it, I was somehow able to move between realms and take others with me. It didn't matter if the "other" I dragged along was a dangerous creature like a Bone Cruncher, or something much, much worse, such as a half-crocked, crabby-pants detective.

I took another deep breath, letting it out slowly through my nose.

Back to the graveyard with the Bone Cruncher … I hadn't even been trying to do any physical medium voodoo tricks that night and pulled it off, so this should be a breeze.

A woman laughed hysterically in my head. *Shut up.* I stuffed that big red ball gag in her mouth. Now focus!

"Hurry up," Cooper said, returning to my side.

I growled. "You're not helping." I opened one eye to glare up at him.

"Then tell me what I can do and I will."

"First of all, sit your ass down and make sure you're holding on to me." I'd hate to leave the birthday boy behind. Natalie would pluck all of the hairs from my nose one by one just for starters, and then she'd go into full-speed revenge gear.

I held out my hand. Cooper did as told and took it.

"You have a lot of calluses," I said.

"I work hard."

"At what? Shuffling papers on your desk?"

"Would you fucking focus on getting us out of here."

"Okay, okay."

Truth be told, I was dragging my feet because I was afraid of where we'd end up after I went back into the dark with Cooper, especially without Doc around to guide me in that in-between world. I didn't have the best track record when it came to this medium shit. On top of that, I'd run into some really freaky shit in the dark.

"Here goes." I closed my eyes again.

Focus …

Ignore the scratchiness of Cooper's palm.

Focus … I took a deep breath through my nose.

Ignore that sour smell underlying the disinfectant.

Focus … I conjured up a black candle in my mind, the one used for protection, not cleansing. Although depending on what I ran into in the dark, my underwear might need some cleansing when this was all done.

Ignore the fact that I don't know what the hell I'm doing and could run into an orange-eyed, pustule-covered demon with a hard-on for revenge after I blew up a stick of dynamite in his face last time we played hide-and-seek together in the dark.

Damn it, focus!

I lit the black candle, centering on the flame, watching it sway like a belly dancer in the slight breeze. The teardrop bottom undulated in opposition to the pointy tip while the flame swelled and shrank several times.

I took another deep breath, reaching out with my mind but not my hands, as Cornelius had warned in the past. Reaching, reaching, reaching into the dark. Searching for a way that felt right.

Up ahead, I saw something. A gray form emerged from the dark. I brightened the flame to see it better. It looked like … a silver-haired woman. She was dressed in a long gray cloak and looking off to the side.

I edged nearer. I was wary after that damned Hungarian devil had played tricks on me in the past involving a cloaked woman, trying to use my great-grandmother to lure me within reach.

As I slinked closer, I could see her profile. This woman looked different than my grandmother. Younger. Taller. Striking. Not to mention she had no rune stones clacking in her hands.

I tiptoed forward, wondering if she was another Clockmaker. She kind of reminded me of the one Cornelius and I had met previously. They had the same build and both were young.

"Who are you?" I whispered.

She turned to face me. Her features were a swirling blur. The only thing I could see clearly were two bright red eyes staring at me. A dark circle appeared where her mouth should be, and then a high-pitched wail rang out. The blaring screech blasted me onto my ass.

I cried out and opened my eyes.

Son of a mother-humper! I was still in the frickin' jail, only now the room was draped in thick shadows. Outside the windows, the world was dark. And it was quiet. A thick, cottony quiet that made me want to tip my head to the side and see if water dribbled out my ear.

I fumbled with my flashlight, aiming the beam toward the big cell. *Please, please, please let Doc be here.*

The cell was empty.

"Shit!" I hunched over in defeat.

Then I realized Cooper's hand was no longer in mine. "Cooper?" I whispered.

"Who's that in the corner?" He spoke in a normal volume.

Oh, thank God. He was still with me.

In fact, he was standing behind me. "Which corner?"

He pointed his light toward the cell with the shower. The beam spotlighted a huddled figure.

It looked like the same woman I'd seen in the dark, only she was crouching now. Her long silver hair pooled on the ground around her feet. A gauzy veil shrouded her features under the hood of her cloak. "I think it might be the banshee. I ran into her in the dark. I must have brought her along for the ride this time."

"That's just great, Parker." He grabbed me by my coat sleeve and hauled me to my feet. "Now we're still not back to where we should be *and* we have a banshee for company."

"I'm trying to get back to our regularly scheduled program, Cooper. I swear." I whirled on him, shaking my finger in his face. "Maybe you could try to motivate me with some positivity for once. I know I'm a general fuckup most days, so I certainly don't need your help kicking my self-esteem."

We squared off nose to nose for a few breaths before he sighed and shook his head. "You're not a fuckup, Violet. Trust me, I understand more now than I used to about the shitty hand you've been dealt when it comes to this supernatural crap. I'm just …" He paused, his face crinkling.

"Just what? Pissed off? Frustrated? Mad as a hatter?"

"That last one means crazy."

"I know that. It rolls off my tongue nicely, though."

"I'm not crazy."

"Then what are you right now?"

"I'm worried. What if we can't get back?"

"Doc will find us." I wish I felt as confident about that as I sounded. Truthfully, though, my understanding was that the dark was a vast playground full of bullies and monsters. Extra vast. Doc probably had a better chance of finding a black cat in a coal cellar.

"What if Nyce can't find us?"

"Welcome to my world, Cooper. Every time I help with a séance and step into that dark hell, I don't know for sure that I'll be able to come back out. I have to blindly trust that the Oracle will find me." I shook free of his grip on my coat.

"What are you doing?" he said as I turned my back on him.

"I'm going to see what she wants." I pointed my light toward the banshee. There had to be a reason for her to be hanging out in that cell.

Cooper grabbed my arm before I'd taken two steps, stopping me. "Parker, this is a bad idea."

Sheesh, he was grabby tonight. Must be the whiskey making him act more human. "What do you know about banshees?"

He shrugged. "They're from Irish or Scottish mythology, I think. Or is it Celtic? I don't know."

"I mean, what do you know about what a banshee wants from the living?"

"Aren't they supposed to predict an upcoming death? Like a harbinger of doom."

"Yeah, I think so." I nodded toward the stooped figure. "I want to find out why she was in that jail room with Doc and Cornelius. I want to know if the pied piper picked her up with his ghost magnet somewhere along the way. Or if she'd been there from the start and had something to do with the five ghosts in there with her."

His brow lined. "Or if she came to warn one of us that death is coming soon?"

"God, I hope not." But, yes, that was another reason I needed to try to make contact with the banshee. "You stay right here while I go see if she's feeling friendly." I tried to pull free of him, but he held tight.

"That makes no sense, Parker. We should go together. That's how partners work during a bust."

"No, we shouldn't. Remember when we were in the Galena House with Mr. Black and Ms. Wolff that last time? Doc said he struggled to find you when you were too close to me. Maybe if I step away from you, he'll be able to pick you up on his radar."

That was assuming Doc was somewhere out there searching for us in the darkness. I didn't want to think about how things might go if he wasn't. Who knew where we'd end up the next time I sat down and started thinking about that dang candle flame.

"Okay." He let go of me. "But don't go in the cage with her. Who knows what she's capable of besides screaming her head off?"

I tiptoed toward the banshee, keeping the light on her. Her wailing started when I drew closer, growing louder with every step. The gauzy veil seemed to breathe along with her cries.

I stopped in front of the cell bars, not sure I wanted to go any farther.

"That's far enough, Parker," Cooper said.

"Yep." We were surfing the same wavelength.

I cleared my throat. "Why are you here?" I asked in a gentle voice, using honey instead of vinegar with the fairy woman.

Her keening stopped.

The hairs on my arms and legs quivered, along with my knees. I gripped the cell bars to steady myself. "Are you here because someone died or because someone is going to die?"

Her head moved slightly, the veil shifting, masking her face. I wasn't sure if she was nodding or shaking her head or just dancing to her own beat.

"Ask her who she's here for," Cooper ordered.

I frowned back at him. "I'm getting there, Bossypants."

Something soft tickled my knuckles.

When I turned back to the cell, the banshee stood just on the other side of the bars. Her veil brushed against my fingers.

I let out a shout of surprise and stumbled backward a couple of steps, bumping into the cell door behind me.

The banshee pressed her face against the bars. The white veil pulled tight, outlining her chin, mouth, and nose. "You arrrr …" Her high-pitched, screechy voice trailed off.

I was what? I was the reason she'd come tonight? I was the one who was going to die? But wasn't I supposed to be Irish or Scottish for a banshee to get involved with the process? According to everything I'd learned from Aunt Zoe, I'd come from a long line of *German* Executioners, so I didn't fit the bill.

"I am what?" I whispered in the sudden quiet.

"I think you need to get your ass back over here," Cooper said, his voice tense.

He sounded closer, but I didn't look back to see. I was too mesmerized by the way her veil billowed in and out over her mouth.

"Maybe she's the key to returning to Doc and the others," I told him.

"Or maybe she's the reason we can't get back. Step away from the bars, Parker."

I held up my index finger for him to give me a minute. There must be a reason she was at the jail tonight, and if it were something to do with *my* death, Cooper needed to hold his damned horses.

Ever since I was a kid, I'd had an irrational fear of rune casting and other types of serious divination, such as palmistry, cartomancy, and scrying, to name a few. Astrology and feng shui and other lighter-weight fortune telling I could handle in small doses, but thanks to my great-grandmother's obsession with rune stones and her hair-raising comments about me smelling like death and carrying hidden dangers, I decided early on to take each day as it came and let the future be a surprise.

But now, standing face-to-face with a harbinger of doom, I wanted to know if this was all going to end for me.

"Am I going to die soon?" I asked her. And would it be

due to one of those damned *Nachzehrer*? Or did this have to do with the new bounty hunter in town that started the Hellhound clock ticking?

"You arrrrrrr," she wailed. The veil trembled until her voice died out again.

My chest tightened, making it hard to breathe. I tried to relax, shaking my shoulders looser. A deep breath in. A deep breath out. *Now face death head-on.*

"I get it," I told her. "I'm going to be taking a dirt nap soon. But if you could give me a hint about how it's all going to go down, I'd really appreciate it. I have two children that I'll be leaving behind." *Two wonderful, smart, loving kids.* I had to pause to swallow a lump in my throat. "And a kind, generous man who has taught me what it means to be loved, so if I could have an inkling of how much time I have left, that would be—"

"You arrrrrrr," she interrupted me, wailing louder this time. Her mouth was stuck in an O shape long after the words died out. She sucked in her white veil, then blew it out. Then did it again. And again.

I stood watching, hypnotized. What was that about?

"What is she doing?" Cooper asked, his voice coming from far away.

She did it again.

"Parker!" His harsh commanding tone made me jump to attention.

I looked around to find him standing next to the door with the little square window. "She's breathing, I think."

"Isn't she dead already? Some sort of fairy ghost?"

"Well, I would think so, but maybe banshees are somewhere between the living and the dead."

"You arrrrrrr!" the banshee wailed even louder.

I covered my ears through the middle of it, catching what sounded like a tongue trill at the very end.

"I think you need to step back farther," Cooper said

when her keening died down.

I glanced his way. He was looking out through the window in the door. "You think she can get through the bars?"

"Trust me, Parker. It's best to interrogate a dangerous suspect from a safe distance."

For once, I agreed with him. I took several backward steps toward Cooper and the door. Something about this banshee didn't feel right, besides the fact that she was supposed to be a mythological fairy but was now standing right in front of me. I wondered what Dominick would have to say about her kind.

"How much time do I have left?" I asked her, trying once more to get some details about my death.

"You arrrrrt!" she outright shrieked, and then her hands shot through the bars. Her long, curling fingernails clacked together like crab claws as she tried to catch hold of me.

I leaned safely out of her reach, but held steady. "Cooper, did she add a 't' or 'd' to the end of it that time?"

He didn't answer.

I looked toward the door and he was gone.

"Cooper? Where are you?"

Still no answer.

Spinning this way and that with my light, I checked in the corners and under the beds. What the planets! Where did he go? Had he gone out the door? Why didn't he wait for me?

I rushed over to the door, but it was locked. I pounded on it, calling out his name, going up on my tiptoes to try to see out the window. Shit! I needed something to stand on.

Taking a few steps back, I tried to think of what to do. I could try the candle flame trick again. But what if Cooper were still here and I left him behind and we couldn't find him again?

"Cooper!" I yelled, fighting back a blood-pounding rush of panic.

The room was silent.

Except for the slight whisper of cloth across a concrete floor right behind me.

Oh, no.

A cold breath of air curled along my neck and tickled its way across my collarbone. It smelled of damp dirt and rotting flowers, and it chilled me from the inside out. I shivered with fear more than cold. With creaking slowness, I turned around.

The banshee was no longer in her cell. Her white, gauzy veil puffed in and out mere inches from me.

I gulped, my heart kicking at my rib cage with both feet, trying to break out and run for its life.

Maybe now was when I checked out of this world. I could see my tombstone:

Here lies Violet Parker.
She died from having the living shit scared out of her
too many times.

The banshee reached up and snagged her veil with one long, curling fingernail. The material slowly lifted.

I should run. I should race to the door, yank it open, leap down the stairs two at a time, and crash out through that emergency exit. I should not stop until I made it home to Aunt Zoe's, and then hide in my closet with my eyes closed until all this was over. I should …

But I couldn't, because the stupid, cock-sucking door was locked. Not to mention that my aunt's place was not of this realm.

The gauzy material climbed higher, revealing a rounded chin. Next came a pair of full lips. Then a narrow nose that turned upward at the tip. Long lashes lined her closed eyelids. Delicately arched silver eyebrows framed the top of her face. And finally, a high forehead creased by thick, silver hair that fell in soft waves around her heart-shaped face.

I drew in a sharp breath. Good golly, Miss Molly! She was gorgeous. Angelic even.

And then she opened her red, glowing eyes and screamed, "YOU ARRRRRRT!"

The shrilling screech sent me reeling backward. I slammed into the bars of one of the single cells. My flashlight crashed to the floor, the beam spinning wildly. Hot pain ripped through my head and sent ripples of agony down through my chest and arms and legs. My knees buckled, but I clung to the metal bars and held myself up.

She glided over to me, bending down until her gaping mouth was right in front of my eyes. Her shrieking wail droned on and on. Spikes of pain jabbed my ears, making my head spin.

I kicked out at her, my boot snagging on her cloak but not making purchase.

I had to get out of here!

With a grunt of effort, I stumbled toward the door. She followed, still screaming her head off. I grabbed the handle, only to have my legs give out. The door handle turned as I collapsed to my knees. When I teetered backward, the door gave way from the weight of my fall.

How did it get unlocked?

Never mind! Just get up and out!

Struggling to my feet, I lurched over the threshold and onto the landing.

I was screaming along with her now. I couldn't help it. Everything inside of me was burning and stinging and aching all at once. Before the banshee could follow me, I closed the door and leaned back against it, praying she didn't know how to use a door handle.

Oh God, what if she could float right through the door?

Her shrieking continued, growing louder in spite of the steel separating us.

I needed to move, but I couldn't. The sound was deafening, bearing down on me, making me dizzy.

"Cooper," I whispered, wondering what she'd done to him. Where she'd taken him.

My legs gave out again and I slid down the door, crumpling onto the floor. Pulling my knees to my chest, I closed my eyes and covered my ears. I rocked back and forth to ease the pain, but there was no blocking the high-pitched wail. She was inside of my head and I needed to cast her out. I needed to focus. I needed to … *just breathe.*

Right, right. It all started with the breath. That's what Cornelius had told me more than once. I inhaled through my nose, holding it inside my chest for a count of five, and then released it. I took another breath. And another. And another.

When my pulse had finally slowed and the pain had eased slightly, I pictured a candle flame in my mind.

What about Cooper?

Tears filled my eyes. I'd have to try to come back for him later. Right now, I had to get away from the banshee.

I fixed my thoughts on the black candle. The sight of the small, flickering fire surrounded by darkness soothed my nerves. As I stared into the dancing flame, my shoulders relaxed, my pulse slowed, my heart …

Long bony fingers reached out of the darkness. They wrapped around my arms, gripping me tight. I tried to pull free while fingernails bit into my skin.

I shrieked, matching the banshee note for note, as something dragged me kicking and screaming into the darkness.

Chapter Fifteen

A hand covered my mouth, muffling my screams. I thrashed and kicked out in blind panic, struggling to escape.

"Stop her ... kicking," I thought I heard, although the ringing still echoing in my head from the banshee's wails made the actual words hard to make out.

The bony fingers let go of me only to be quickly replaced by a firm weight on my sternum that flattened me on the tiled floor, forcing me into submission. The faint smell of ammonia filled my sinuses as I gasped for air.

"Violet."

Did somebody say my name? It had sounded as if I were being hailed from the other side of a valley.

I froze in the dark, listening. The ringing was fading, along with the stabs of pain in my head. I could hear my heart pounding in my ears like a big Hawaiian drum. *Boom-boom! Boom-boom!* The beats reverberated clear to my toes.

The hand lifted from my mouth.

"Violet." This time the voice was closer. "You are ..." Something clanged. "... Dead."

Dead. A whimper escaped my throat. That stupid banshee bitch! I didn't get to say good-bye to my kids or Doc or Nat or ...

"Why in the hell did you tell her that?"

The voice spoke right above me this time. Actually, it

sounded more like a growl.

My breath caught. I knew that growly voice. Cooper! I found him! Or he must have found me somehow.

But his fingers weren't long and bony like the ones that had come out of the darkness. Those looked more like …

"So she could mourn," Cornelius said. "Violet." Something poked me in the cheek. Twice. "Why isn't she opening her eyes? Did she hit her head on the other side?"

"Not on my watch," Cooper answered. "But I wasn't there at the very end." The pressure on my sternum eased. "Parker!" Something snapped me in the forehead, right above the bridge of my nose.

"Ouch!" I reached up and rubbed the spot. "That stings."

"Then it worked. Now open your eyes. We have company."

Still rubbing my forehead, I did as Cooper ordered, blinking in the semi-darkness. Cornelius's narrow face with his pointy goatee loomed over me. I smiled up at him. "Hello, Prince Charming. You're a sight for sore eyes. I think I left my glass slipper back at the Banshee Ball."

He frowned across at Cooper, who was looking down his crooked nose at me. "The banshee must have broken her brain."

Cooper scoffed. "I think it was broken long before tonight."

Cornelius shined his flashlight in my eyes. When I squinted and turned my head to the side, he reached down and plugged my nose.

I gasped for air, slapping both of his hands away. I glared up at him. "What did you do that for?"

"I was making sure you were breathing."

"Of course I'm breathing. I was talking to you. You can't talk if you're not breathing."

"I beg to differ. Ghosts talk to me all of the time, and they aren't breathing." To Cooper, he said, "She's breathing, but I'm not sure which nostril she's using."

"Good." Cooper sounded distracted. He stood and walked away.

"I'm using both nostrils." I craned my neck to check out my surroundings, relieved to see I was back in the jail cell. Cornelius had said something about me being dead, but the floor was hard under me and I could smell the underlying musty mix of urine and dust.

But where was Doc? I looked over at the larger cell. Shadows shrouded the back corner, but the beds were empty, and as far as I could tell so was the rest of the cell.

"I doubt that's true, Violet," Cornelius said.

"Why wouldn't it be?" I asked, breathing just fine out of my nostrils now that he wasn't pinching them shut.

My gaze shifted to Cooper, who was peering out through the window in the steel door. *Déjà vu*, I thought with a smirk. I wondered if he could see anything. I couldn't from my spot on the floor. It was dark on the other side of the glass, same as two of the last three times I'd tried to look through the dang thing.

But where is Doc?

Something fluttered in my stomach. I tamped it down. Everything was going to be fine. There was no visible reason to freak out. And in spite of Cornelius's talk about death, I seemed to be alive and kicking still. Well, not kicking at the moment, but I had been a few minutes ago. Besides, Cooper and Cornelius were here with me and the banshee wasn't.

I glanced back at the shady corner in the group cell, watching for any movement in the shadows. At least I hoped she wasn't here.

"I'll tell you why your statement is likely not true." Cornelius readjusted so that he was sitting cross-legged next to me. "It is a well-known fact that human nostrils divide the job of breathing so that only one nasal channel is fully open at a time. I'll demonstrate." Cornelius plugged one side of his nose and then the other, breathing noisily so I could hear the difference. "You see, it's called the nasal cycle. While you breathe through the clear nostril, the tissue in the other nostril is flooded with blood. This is a similar physiological occurrence as an erection, when blood rushes into the penis and causes it to engorge to a size nearly two to three times that of its normal flaccid state."

"Great balls of fire!" I covered the upper part of my face with my hands, pressing the meat of my palms into my eyes, attempting to block out the imagery going on behind my eyelids.

"This has nothing to do with testicles, Violet."

I lowered my hands to glare at him. "I told you yesterday during my bath that you and I are never going to talk about erections. Ever."

Cooper shined his flashlight back at us, putting us both in the spotlight. "You two were talking about erections while bathing?"

"It wasn't like that." I pushed up onto my elbows.

"Violet was the only one in the tub," Cornelius explained. "I was just giving her relaxation advice."

Cooper lowered his light to the floor. "So, Parker was bathing and you were helping her find ways to relax?" He chuckled. "That's not legal anymore in Deadwood."

"Shut up, Cooper." I turned back to Cornelius. "You're supposed to check if my chest is moving up and down, not plug my nose."

One of his black eyebrows cocked upward. "Where does it say that in the rule book?"

"What rule book? I'm talking about CPR."

"You mean a common-pool resource?"

"No. The other CPR."

"Conditional pre-payment rate?" His mouth twitched, giving away his game.

I held my fist in front of his nose. "Now you're just

messing with me."

"Maybe, but it's good to see the snap back in your garters, as my grandfather used to say."

Cooper strode over and grabbed me by the elbow, hauling me to my feet in one quick tug. "Let's get out of here before I give in to the voice in my head telling me to lock you both up in a single cell and toss the key out the window on my way home."

"Give me a second." I held onto Cooper for a few beats as I steadied myself, looking around the room to make doubly sure the banshee wasn't with us. I paused on the empty group cell. "Where's Doc?"

"He's downstairs with Nat and Uncle Willis."

Doing what? Something was odd about this setup.

Cooper turned my chin in his direction and aimed his flashlight at my eyes.

I recoiled. "What are you doing?"

"Checking your pupils. Curion was too busy plugging your nose to make sure you're not in shock."

"I'm fine." I pushed his light away.

"Are you sure?"

"Yes, Cooper. I'm sure."

He pointed his light at where I was holding onto him. "Then why are you digging your fingernails into my arm?"

"Sorry." I loosened my grip, but still held on. Until we made it out of this damned room, ghost- and banshee-free, I wasn't sure I wanted to let go.

"Maybe the banshee is inside of Violet and trying to claw her way into you next," Cornelius joked and aimed his flashlight at my eyes, too.

I shoved his flashlight to the side. "Shine that in my eyes one more time, Spirit Miser, and I'm going to light up your prostate with it."

Cooper laughed. "Okay, she's proven she's the one and only pain-in-the-ass Parker." He unhooked from my grasp.

"Hold steady here a second." He returned to the door, peering out the window again.

"What's going on?" I asked.

"We're hiding from the law," Cornelius explained, shining the light beam through his fingers. "I think my bones are growing. Does that seem normal to you?"

"It does if you're a *Nachzehrer.*" I frowned toward Cooper. "Why are we hiding from the law?"

"We're not hiding." He returned to where Cornelius and I were waiting. "We just need to get out of here before trouble finds the three of us together."

Who was going to find us? And why hadn't Doc been waiting here for me when I came out of the dark? He was usually the first one I saw when I opened my eyes.

I rubbed my temples. Nothing about my current situation was anything close to normal. I'd like to go home now, hug my kids, and forget this whole banshee bullshit ever happened with the help of Doc and chocolate or tequila. And maybe a handful of cookies. Probably all of the above.

Focusing on Cooper, I asked, "When you say 'trouble,' are you talking about those five ghosts?"

He shook his head. "They already know we're in here."

"You can still see them?"

"Yes, Parker."

"All of them?"

He cut me a glare. "Do you want me to draw you a map showing where each one is standing?"

I narrowed my eyes. "Maybe I do, darn it, because I don't understand what's going on here, and you two have done a crappy job of filling me in." I pointed at Cornelius. "And why on earth did you say I was dead?"

His brow crinkled. "I didn't say anything close to that."

"Yes, you did. After you dragged me out of the dark, you said, 'You are dead.' I didn't dream that." At least I didn't think so. Although the banshee had been saying something similar to me before her siren scream made my ears practically bleed and my head nearly explode.

"I said, 'You art is dead,' which is entirely different."

I huffed. "No, it's not."

"It is. There's a distinct 't' at the end of my version."

Huh. The banshee had added a "t" to the end, too.

"So why are you putting a 't' at the end of 'you are'?"

"Because it's not 'you are.' " Cornelius pointed at his mouth. "The word I'm saying is spelled e-w-a-r-t, but pronounced 'ewe-art,' not 'you-are.' As in 'Ewart is dead.' "

I blinked. That was about as clear as a slice of meatloaf.

"Okay, I'll play along. What is ewe-art? Is it some kind of new-age art fad specializing in adorable baby sheep paintings or quilts? And why is it dead? I wouldn't think that sheep go out of style."

"Actually, a baby sheep is called a 'lamb.' A ewe is an adult female sheep. I'm surprised you don't know that with your extensive background in wool fashion."

Of course I knew that! I pinched his arm through his black wool coat.

"Ouch!" He stepped back. "What did you do that for?"

"Quality testing the thickness of the wool fibers in your coat, smartass." I turned to Cooper, who'd been observing our asinine vaudevillian act with his hand unsuccessfully covering his grin. "What in the ever-loving hell is a 'ewart'?"

"Ewart is the last name of the docent who locked us in here," he explained.

"You mean the little old guy in the foyer with the green suit and clover pin?"

He nodded. "And at the risk of starting your Abbott and Costello comedy routine again, I'm going to clear this up in four words: Mr. Ewart is dead."

My hand flew to my chest. "You're kidding? He died while we were in here searching for clues?"

He nodded. "He had a heart attack, but managed to call

911 before he died."

How horrible! Here we were having fun and the poor guy was dying all alone. Well, I wouldn't actually call our time in this old jail *fun*, especially after we ran into the … The banshee's wailing voice echoed in my memory: *You-arrrrt!*

"Ohhh! That's it!" I told Cooper. "That's what the banshee was saying all along when I was asking her who she'd come to warn. It was *Ewart*."

Cooper nodded again. "I realized that, too, after Nyce pulled me out of that place and Nat told me that the medics were out front trying to revive him."

I smacked my forehead. So, true to the myths, the banshee had been here to warn about an upcoming death—as in the death of Ewart, the docent. Not my death.

Lordy, I was such a bonehead.

On the other hand, Doc had pulled Cooper out. That meant he'd found us "out there" and been able to save my bacon yet again. It sure was nice to have an Oracle on our side.

I puffed my cheeks, blowing out my breath as I checked the shadows again for the banshee. "What are the chances of this happening at your birthday party, Cooper?"

"Surprisingly good. I have bad luck when it comes to my birthday."

I remembered Natalie mentioning something about Cooper saying that. "As bad as what happened tonight?"

"Last year, I got shot on my birthday." He patted his shoulder. "It was just a graze, luckily. The year before that, I was breaking up a bar fight and caught a Bowie knife in the thigh. Four years ago, I got bit by a stray dog I was trying to rescue. Seven years ago—"

"Okay, I got it. Lesson learned. You need to be wrapped in bubble wrap and locked in the basement when your birthday rolls around next year."

"You need some salt," Cornelius said out of left field.

When Cooper and I both gave him a confused look, he added, "Bathing in salt water is said to remove negative energy from the body."

I snorted. "Cooper would need an ocean's worth of salt to pull that off."

"Do you two really expect me to buy into any of this hoodoo bullshit?"

"Oh, this has absolutely nothing to do with the hoodoo religion," Cornelius answered. "But we could test a few hoodoo spells if you like."

"I thought you're supposed to sprinkle salt around your house for protection." At least that was something Aunt Zoe had mentioned to me before.

"Yes. Putting it in corners will keep bad energy out."

Cooper shook his head. "I don't have bad energy, just bad luck, but I'll tell you what, Curion. I'll get a horseshoe tattooed on my ass and we'll call it good."

"You still see those five specters in their post-death states, right?" Cornelius asked.

Cooper stared over my shoulder. As in right behind me. "Sure."

I spared a wary glance behind me, finding nothing.

"Have you considered that the negative energy surrounding and inside of you is distorting your spectral vision?" Cornelius continued with his inquisition.

Cooper's gaze snapped back to Cornelius. "So, you're saying that with a bit more salt in my life, I'd no longer see ghosts?"

"No. Fortunately, your third eye is wide open now, and there is no closing it short of your own death."

"Fortunately? Ha!"

"However, there might be adjustments you can make that will affect *how* you see ectoplasmic entities." He shrugged, brushing off his coat sleeves. "It's up to you if you're interested in testing some of my theories on which adjustments might benefit you—salt being one of them. In the meantime, that banshee made me hungry. Violet, I need a protein bar."

I looked down at my hands and then back up at him. "Do I look like a protein bar tree to you?"

"You typically carry a bar in your purse. I'd like to eat it."

"My purse is out in Harvey's truck. You'll have to wait until we leave."

I looked at Cooper, who had returned to the steel door. He opened it a crack, listening to whatever was going down on the other side. I tiptoed over to him.

"Do you hear anything?"

"No." He waved Cornelius closer. "I think we should sneak downstairs and into the jail's reception room until we get the all-clear from Nyce or Nat."

"You don't want to wait up here for them?"

He shook his head. "There's only one way out of this room. Down there, we have more options."

"Why are you so concerned about being caught with us?" I asked.

"I know most of the officers on the Spearfish police force, and several of the fire crew members around here, too. The last thing we need is word getting back to Hawke about Curion, you, and me being here at the time of Ewart's death. He'll have come up with fifty new conspiracy theories about the three of us and a new murder case before the weekend is out."

I didn't doubt that for a moment.

"Hawke needs a girlfriend," I said, nodding for emphasis. "Someone who will let him vent some steam and sidetrack him from his obsession with us. It's too bad you had to work your love magic on Natalie. She's great at running distractions."

"Yeah. I know all about her ability to mess with a guy's head. But she's off the market." He grabbed my upper coat sleeve. "Let's roll. Come on, Curion."

The three of us crossed the threshold, but Cooper hesitated at the top of the steps.

"Are you still drunk?" I asked, reaching out to steady him. "Do you need help down the steps?"

"I'm fine." But he didn't push my hand away. "What about you? Can you handle the stairs?"

"Stairs I can definitely handle. But after tonight, I'm declaring banshees out of my league."

Chapter Sixteen

So, let me get this straight, you're telling me that banshees *are* part of my league?" I said to Aunt Zoe an hour later.

She looked up from her *magistra* notebook, her pen hovering over the page. "If one shows up to play, as it did tonight, then yes, dealing with a banshee is one of your responsibilities as an Executioner."

The lines on her face seemed deeper than usual tonight, and her eyes were slightly red-rimmed. Several tendrils of her hair had come loose from her thick braid, giving her a bohemian air. When she'd first started taking notes on tonight's happenings, I thought I saw a tremor in her hand, but after she'd written several lines on the page, it was gone.

I wondered if she'd been working too many late nights recently out in her glass workshop. Or did her current disheveled state have something to do with her dinner guests?

According to Aunt Zoe, Reid and his son had arrived after we'd left for Spearfish. By the time we'd returned, they were gone and the kitchen was all buttoned up, along with her lips. The kids had already been in bed asleep, so I couldn't pester them for details until morning, darn it.

Thanks to Natalie, Harvey, and Doc running interference with the emergency personnel who'd shown up after the docent's 911 call, Cooper, Cornelius, and I made it clear of the mansion without being seen. I'd ridden back to

Deadwood with Doc in the Picklemobile, dozing in and out during the twenty-minute drive. Unlike the adrenaline rush that came with killing a *Nachzehrer*, all of that banshee's shrieking had wiped me out. The others had traveled in Harvey's truck, leading the way to Aunt Zoe's.

By the time we'd rolled into the driveway, I'd caught enough sleep to recharge my brain. I hopped out of the Picklemobile, ready to hash out what had happened in that upstairs jail room and nail down how things had spiraled out of control so quickly.

I was also ready to find out if Reid had made any headway on breaking down the walls around Aunt Zoe's heart. But at the moment, surrounded by a table full of tired and hungry escape room survivors, I didn't want to put Aunt Zoe on the spot by asking about her old flame. That being said, curiosity had me leaning in her direction more than once, something Doc had noticed with one raised eyebrow that soon turned into two, along with a cringe, after I hit him with a super-sized smile.

Natalie dropped into the seat next to Aunt Zoe, a fried chicken leg in one hand and a glass of homemade lemonade in the other. "Are banshees considered to be ghosts or some other kind of supernatural creature?" she asked and ripped a piece of meat off the bone with her teeth.

Aunt Zoe must have made fried chicken for dinner tonight. Wasn't that one of Reid's favorites, along with her three-cheese potatoes dish and homemade lemonade?

"They're fairies according to Irish mythology," Cornelius said while reaching for the Betty Boop cookie jar in the middle of the table. He fished out two cookies, eyeing them suspiciously for a second before holding them up. "Are these blueberry cookies?"

I started to laugh, but then considered that mixed with the right ingredients, blueberry cookies might be pretty tasty.

"They're chocolate chip with butterscotch and toffee

bits," Aunt Zoe said. "I made them earlier today."

"Reid's favorite cookies?" I asked, trying to sound innocent.

I earned a glare from her for my efforts.

"Delightful," Cornelius said and jammed the cookies into the scoops of vanilla ice cream in the bowl in front of him.

"Sparky, was that banshee of yours purty?" Harvey waved for Cornelius to pass the cookie jar. "Or did she look like somethin' the cat drug in and the dog won't eat?"

"She was beautiful." I stood up from the table and went over to the fridge. I wasn't really hungry, but I was terribly nosy. I wanted to see what other leftovers would clue me in on my aunt's dinner with Reid. "She was young and willowy," I told them as I opened the refrigerator door and peered inside. "She had porcelain skin, like an antique doll, and a heart-shaped face." I bent, checking the middle shelf, spying what looked like a bowl of whipped butter. "Oh, and long silver hair." I stuck my finger in the butter and scooped out a healthy fingerful, tasting it. Ah ha! It was sweetened with honey. "She was angelic, even, until she opened her freaky glowing red eyes."

"And her loud mouth," Doc added, joining me at the fridge.

Cornelius proceeded to give them an estimate of the decibel levels the banshee had been reaching, taking the spotlight off of me for the moment.

"Will you hand me one of those pale ales, Killer?" Doc asked in a lowered voice, his back to the table.

I handed it to him, along with the bowl of homemade honey butter, careful not to get what was left on my finger on the sleeve of his black thermal shirt.

"What's this?" He asked, taking the butter. He sniffed it. "Is this the dairy version of Harvey's love goop?"

I cringed. "Don't remind me of that." I pointed at the butter. "Try a little. It's downright sinful. Aunt Zoe makes it

from scratch for her homemade biscuits. There are probably
a bunch of biscuits left over in the breadbox if you're feeling
like a snack." I pointed toward the counter. Aunt Zoe always
liked to make double batches when she baked. "I could sure
use something to munch on after tonight's insanity."

He looked down at the butter and then up at me with a
grin. "Did you use your finger?"

"Yes, but it was clean, I swear. I washed my hands before
I sat down at the table."

"Okay." He set the beer on top of the fridge and then
took my hand, lifting it to his mouth. His gaze had a devilish
gleam as he licked most of the butter off my finger in one
long stroke of his tongue, then sucked on my fingertip to get
the last of it.

"Jinkies," I said under my breath. Even after months of
sleeping with the guy, Doc still knew how to light me up.

"You're right, Boots. This is definitely sinful." He leaned
forward, whispering, "We should take that upstairs later.
There are several more places on your body that could use a
good licking."

I gulped. "I think my unmentionables just caught fire."

"Good." He leaned down and brushed his lips over mine
before adding, "They'll just be in my way."

Mercy me! Had someone cranked up the heat in here?
"You're smoldering again." I fanned myself. "That's not
playing fair. You know that look of yours makes my heart
swoon."

He chuckled, letting go of my hand and taking the beer
from the top of the fridge. I tried to take the bowl of butter
back, but he held tight.

"What are you gonna do with that?" Surely he wasn't
going to hold onto it until we headed to bed? Harvey would
have a heyday at our expense if he caught on to our game.

"I'm going to spread it on your biscuit." Doc headed
toward the counter, leaving me standing there with a damp

finger, as well as other steamy body parts. He opened the breadbox and pulled out a zippered plastic bag of biscuits, holding them up for me to see. "You were right."

Sure, okay, good. I blew out a breath, trying to smack some sense back into my silly heart and wipe the drool off its chin. Where were we? Oh yeah, dinner for Reid. Buttermilk biscuits. Honey butter. Doc licking my finger … No, back to the biscuits.

"Hey, *mon cher*, will you warm up that biscuit in the microwave first?" I asked.

His grin was downright wolfish. "I'll warm up whatever you'd like, Tish."

Cooper leaned back in his chair, glaring over at us. "Don't you two start speaking in French over there. We're not done investigating the crime scene yet."

"Quit your barking, law dog. I'm just getting something to snack on." I grabbed another pale ale and held the bottle up. "Anybody else want a beer?"

"Coop might," Natalie said. "I can tell that his magic buzz has worn off because he's turned back into a cop." She laughed at the mock glare he aimed at her.

"No more for me tonight," Cooper said. "I don't want to end up in another jail with Parker before dawn." He looked over at Doc. "You mind heating one of those biscuits up for me, too? I could use something solid in my stomach."

After scoping out a few more storage containers, I finished my sleuthing in the fridge and returned to the table with a bottle of dark stout beer for myself that claimed to have a hint of coffee taste, according to the label.

"Where did you get this beer, Aunt Zoe?" I asked. It hadn't been in there this morning when I was searching for some creamer.

She shrugged, keeping her nose buried in her notebook. "Who knows? Beer shows up around here like we live next to a brewery most days."

That was sort of true. Whenever we had company over for supper, which was almost nightly these days, someone usually brought beer to share all around. But still, this particular bottle was from a microbrewery out of New Mexico. Where was Reid's son from? I should have asked that when we were out hunting *Nachzehrer* together. I opened the bottle and let the subject drop for now, figuring I'd have to pester her more after everyone left.

Natalie leaned back and tossed her gnawed chicken leg toward the garbage. "I always figured a banshee would be a shriveled-up old lady."

She missed the basket, but Cooper stood and picked up the bone, dumping it into the trash before heading over to open the cupboard where Aunt Zoe kept her over-the-counter pain medications.

"Me, too," Harvey said. "I might've liked to hear her wail, just out of curiosity."

Doc and I exchanged frowns. There was a reason he'd been sitting in that cell with his hands over his ears when Cooper and I finally made it into the jail. It was the same reason I'd taken the nearly identical pose on the other side of a steel door from the banshee right before being dragged from the dark by Cornelius. Her wails had been knockdown, head-poundingly painful.

"Could you hear her, too?" Natalie asked Cooper, as he returned to the table with a glass of water and a couple of pills.

"Yeah, but she wasn't that loud when I was there with Parker. She was just wailing out the docent's name repeatedly." He shot me a smartass smirk. "The sound of Parker's voice hurt my ears far more by that point."

I held up my middle finger, not bothering with any fancy delivery methods. To Natalie, I said, "After Cooper disappeared, which we know was Doc's handiwork, the banshee came out of the cell. She stood not a foot from me and started lifting her veil." I shuddered at the memory of watching the fabric slowly rise, afraid to find out what was underneath.

Doc squeezed my shoulder, setting down a plate in front of me with a steaming buttermilk biscuit cut in half and a healthy dollop of honey butter smeared on each piece. The smell alone had me licking my lips.

I picked up half a biscuit and took a bite, groaning in approval.

Aunt Zoe looked up and smiled.

"Anyway," I continued, licking the sweetened butter off my lips. "It was after the banshee lifted her veil that she opened her mouth and really let loose." I took another bite of buttery biscuit, holding in my groan this time. "I sort of got the feeling she had something to say to me and was going to scream her head off until I got her message."

"Or," Cooper butted in, "she was pissed at you for dragging her to some other realm without having a clue how to return to where we'd started."

I picked up my bottle of beer and pointed it at him. "Like I told you in that jail, it's your fault for not listening to Doc when he told you to let go of me."

Doc set a plate with a biscuit and butter down in front of Cooper. "Eat this. It'll make you feel less growly, you lush."

Grumbling, Cooper took a bite. He closed his eyes for a moment as he chewed. I knew that feeling. Aunt Zoe's biscuits were scrumdiddlyumptious.

"Why do ya think she did that?" Harvey asked Doc after he'd returned to the chair next to me with his pale ale.

"You mean scream like that or show her face to Violet?"

"The face part." Harvey dug into the bag of pretzels he'd gotten earlier from the pantry. "Does her showin' her face have some kind of special meaning? Something to do with Sparky bein' an Executioner?"

"That's a good question." Doc looked at Cornelius. "Did

the banshee show you her face before she started keening?"

Cornelius pulled one of the cookies from his bowl of ice cream. "No. One minute I was telling you I could hear some male voices coming from the other side of the room. The next, a barn owl–like shriek knocked me to my knees. I didn't even have time to catch my breath before the second one hit and bowled me over." He slapped his palm flat on the table as a demonstration.

"Could you feel her sitting on top of you?" Natalie asked, referring to what Doc had told Cooper and me upon entering the cell room that the banshee had Cornelius pinned down.

He picked up the ice cream covered cookie, studying it, then nodded. "I suppose that was what I felt pressing down on me, making it tough to breathe. She'd sunk her claws into me and continued to keen. It was like having ice picks stabbed into my ears. That made it hard for me to focus on much besides trying to block out the sound." He nibbled the cookie. "It wasn't until Violet showed up and lured the banshee away that I was able to breathe freely again and get back on my feet."

I took another bite of biscuit, chewing on my thoughts. Cornelius made it sound like I'd purposely invited the banshee to join me on my surprise journey to the next realm over. In reality, I'd been trying to escape her chilled touch, and ended up accidentally using my physical medium skills to drag her out of there, along with Cooper. At least that was the theory Doc had come up with on our trip back to Deadwood and later shared with the others. Cornelius had agreed with Doc's theory, especially since I had a history of dragging others with me between realms, including him.

"Doc," Aunt Zoe said, glancing up from her notebook. "Cooper said that there were five ghosts standing near you in the cell when he first peeked in the window." She waited for his nod of confirmation before continuing. "You mentioned that you'd picked up their scent *after* Cornelius joined you in the jail room. So, do you think that before Cornelius came upstairs, the ghosts weren't there?"

Doc tipped his head slightly. "I believe that's correct."

"The pied piper strikes again," Natalie said, raising her glass to him.

Cornelius held up his cookie in return before shoving the last half of it in his mouth. "Great Zeus, these are delectable," he mumbled.

"I'd walked around the room," Doc continued, "checking each of the cells for clues, but … Oh, hey! That reminds me." He reached in his front jeans pocket, pulling out a piece of paper, which he tossed in the middle of the table. "I found a clue."

Harvey scooped up the paper and read aloud, "One rubber duckie, two rubber duckies, three rubber duckies, four." He lowered the paper. "What in tarnation is that s'posed to mean?"

Natalie took the sheet. "Each number is written in a different-colored marker—green, yellow, black, and then red." She looked up at me. "It's part of a combination." She pushed back her chair. "I'll be right back."

After Natalie disappeared into the dining room, Aunt Zoe focused back at Doc. "So, were those ghosts trying to pass through you, or whatever you call it when you experience their deaths?"

"Initially, I believe that was the idea, but then the banshee showed up and everything shifted."

"What do you mean, 'shifted'?" Cooper asked.

Doc tapped his finger against the beer bottle. "I have two theories about what happened when it comes to the ghosts and the banshee, and I'm not certain yet which is the most probable."

We all sat still, waiting for him to make sense of the whole scene. Well, all of us except for Cornelius, who was stirring his ice cream into a soupy mess.

"Like Cornelius and Violet said," Doc continued, "when the banshee was keening, her wails were a knockdown, deafening force. In order to block out the sound as much as I could, I had to put up mental barriers. My first theory is that those barriers acted as a mental block that kept the ghosts at bay, as well as muffled the banshee's cries to a small degree."

I considered further ramifications related to that theory. "If that's true, then you might have found a way to keep other ghosts like Prudence from trying to possess you, for lack of a better word, when you're not ready."

He scoffed. "I don't think a concrete bunker buried a mile under the Siberian tundra could keep Prudence out, but maybe the barriers would work with other ghosts."

"What's the other theory?" Cooper asked.

"The ghosts were shielding me from the banshee and her keening to some degree, but not entirely."

"Interesting." Cornelius paused in the midst of stirring. "Both theories would explain why I was knocked out by the banshee while you were able to withstand her shrieks somewhat. However, the second theory means that not only were the ghosts *unaffected* by the banshee, which seems to be the case if you consider the description of the five apparitions according to our specter detector here," he said, pointing his spoon across at Cooper. "But that they also were shielding everyone else in the room."

"But you could hear her screaming in that jail room," I said, trying to keep up. "And so could Doc. It was just Cooper and me who couldn't, so was it a limited shield?"

"Your boyfriend is a *mental* medium, so he's tuned into airwaves you aren't. As for me, my sixth-sense abilities are auditory-based. And let's not forget that the banshee had her claws sunk into my back." Cornelius looked at Doc. "That lack of a ghost shield in the other realms would explain why Violet and Detective Cooper could hear the banshee's shrieks just fine there."

"Exactly. That's why I'm leaning in the direction of the latter of the two theories."

Natalie returned with a piece of paper and pencil. "A ghost shield," she said, dropping into her chair. "Sounds like something out of a comic book." She'd apparently been listening in from the other room.

Doc leaned his elbows on the table, focusing on Cooper. "Did you detect aggression in the ghosts at any time while you were in the room with them?"

"Aggression?" Cooper absently scratched at the table. "No, I'd say they were curious more than anything else. Especially so when it came to Parker."

I froze with the last half of my biscuit held partway to my mouth. "What do you mean when it came to me?"

"I didn't want to tell you while we were in there, but I think two of the inmates took a shine to you."

Harvey chuckled, crunching on a mouthful of pretzels. "Sparky has a way of making an ol' rooster's comb stand up real straight."

"Cock-a-doodle doo," Doc said and kissed my temple.

Aunt Zoe laughed, shaking her head.

"So, were they checking out Sparky's breedin' hips?"

Cooper's face pinched, like he'd bitten into a grapefruit.

"What's with that face?" I set the biscuit down. "What were they doing, Cooper?" I remembered a look he had on his face at one point while talking to me in the jail room, making me wonder at the time if one of the ghosts was standing right behind me.

"One seemed to have a fascination with your hair. He kept trying to run his fingers through it."

I touched my curls, grimacing. "Please tell me it wasn't a prisoner that was burned."

He grimaced. "Sorry."

Oh God. I shuddered. It reminded me of Wolfgang

Hessler and his morbid fascination with my hair.

"Great!" I threw up my hands. "Now I'm going to have to shave it all off."

"Or not," Doc said, wrapping a curl around his finger and tugging playfully.

"What was the other ghost doing?" Aunt Zoe asked.

Cornelius stopped stirring his ice cream and looked up at Cooper, eyebrows raised.

"Kissing her."

I gasped. "He was not!"

"That might explain the moaning sounds I was hearing at that time," Cornelius said, taking a slurp of his ice cream.

Natalie's horrified expression mirrored my own feelings.

Cooper shrugged. "I know what I saw."

"Kissing her what?" Harvey asked with a big fat grin.

I fell back in my chair. "Please tell me it was just my cheek."

"Okay, sure." Cooper was fighting to hold back a laugh, I could tell. "It was just your cheek."

"Was he trying to give her the tongue?" Natalie asked, now obviously stifling some giggles.

"Not in the normal way."

I made a loud, keening sound of my own.

"This ghost was into licking," Cooper explained.

I fake-gagged and buried my face in Doc's shoulder. His body shook with laughter as he rubbed my back, trying to console me.

"Violet, you couldn't feel any cold sensations or anything when this was happening?" Natalie asked.

I sat back upright, still gagging on the inside. "Not a thing." I grabbed my beer and took a long swig of the coffee-flavored stout to wash all of this grossness down. I hoped like hell the licker wasn't the ghost who had an eye dangling. Wait, that had been a guard, hadn't it?

"Your inability to sense ghosts is a good thing in this

case," Doc said, squeezing my leg under the table. "Imagine the nightmares you'd have if you could see what Cooper does."

Cooper shook his head, sobering.

If I could see the ghosts, I'd certainly be more open than he was to trying some of Cornelius's salt experiments.

"Where do you think the banshee came from?" Aunt Zoe asked, focusing on Cornelius this time.

Cornelius crumbled one of his cookies into his bowl of ice cream before answering her. "If my memory of Irish mythology serves me correctly, banshees were originally thought to only show up when members of certain well-known families died. However, which families in particular changes depending on who is telling the story. Being we now know that Mr. Ewart died tonight, it is most likely that his death had something to do with her appearance."

"Ewart is an Irish name?" Natalie asked, scribbling something on the paper she'd brought from the other room.

"It sounds kind of Irish," Aunt Zoe said. "Or Scottish."

"According to Cooper," I told them, "the docent was wearing a green clover pin on his green suit." Which was why he'd initially called the docent a leprechaun when we were down in the basement. Damn, Cooper's eagle eyes worked even when he was plastered.

"But the banshee couldn't have just appeared out of nowhere, could she?" Aunt Zoe asked, looking at me. "Maybe there is a gate between realms in that old jail, like those patrolled by Timekeepers."

I considered that, knowing what I did about Timekeeping, which wasn't much. "If so, that means there is a clock for her, being that she's considered a 'traveler' in Timekeeper lingo."

Cornelius scooped up a chunk of cookie and ate it before saying, "There is also the possibility that a vortex of some sort created by a past mystical event opened a doorway for her to appear."

"Vortex?" Harvey asked. "You mean like the tornado Pecos Bill travels around on?"

"I'm referring to the energy fields in the earth's grid systems and the intersecting ley lines that produce a hot spot of energy."

"In English, Curion," Cooper ordered.

"These intersections produce different effects when it comes to psychic-related activities, several of which are focused along the lines of spiritual healing. However, many psychics believe that vortices are portals to other realms or doorways into other dimensions."

"Swirling masses of electromagnetic energy that pull beings into our realm," Doc added, resting his arm over the back of my chair. "Such as a banshee."

"Speaking of swirlin' occasions," Harvey said, rising from his chair. "I need to go take a leak."

Cornelius nodded. "Another interesting facet about tonight's events is that traditionally in Irish mythology, a banshee does not harm anyone. She merely keens in sadness for the person who is about to die."

"Why is that interesting?" I asked, finishing the last bite of my biscuit, which had gone cold.

"Because she seemed determined to sink her claws into the two of us tonight—but especially *you*. And while I'm no expert on mythological fairies, I've not once come across a tale about a banshee attacking anyone. So what makes you special, Violet?"

Cooper smirked. "Parker has a way of causing friction with all sorts of pains in the asses. Just ask Hawke."

I smirked back. "Doc, the next time I take Cooper with me to another realm, do me a favor and remind me to leave him there."

Doc picked up his beer and pointed it at Cornelius. "You know, I've been wondering about that same thing, Curion.

Why did she go after you and Violet?"

"Did you come up with an answer?" Aunt Zoe asked.

"Possibly." He took a sip from the bottle before continuing. "Maybe the banshee focused on you two in particular because she *really* wanted to deliver her message about the docent's impending death. I suppose it's even possible she could sense that Cornelius had the ability to hear her, and that Violet, being a physical medium, could apport her from the spirit world into ours so that Mr. Ewart might be able to actually hear her wails. Both of you could aid her in carrying out her duties of foretelling his death."

"Poor Mr. Ewart," Natalie said. "He was such a cute little guy."

"I thought banshees were Scottish, too," Aunt Zoe said.

Cornelius nodded. "Actually, there are stories about other beings much like banshees in Norse, Welsh, and a few other cultures. But the banshee is one of the superstars of Irish mythology. Their origins come from the practice of hiring a talented woman singer to come keen at a funeral. The better the keener, the higher the status of the person who died. Of course, the most important families were said to pay the best keeners in the land to show up at the grave of their loved one in order to wail through the night. From that, the banshee myth was born. The fact that many of these keeners were paid in alcohol probably didn't help the banshee's reputation over time, especially when the women eventually became haggard drunkards and were banished from their villages."

Aunt Zoe tapped her pencil on her notebook. "That would explain where the idea for an old, wrinkled version of the banshee comes from."

Harvey returned from the restroom. "What did I miss?" he asked Natalie, sitting back into his chair.

"Banshee History 101. I'll give you the abbreviated version later."

"The stories take different avenues from there," Cornelius continued between bites of cookie. "Some say banshees only showed up for those about to die a violent death. Others talk of the keening only happening at night. And yet others say the banshee would take the form of witchcraft-related animals, like weasels or crows."

Dominick Masterson's words the other day about the truth behind a creature's origins and facts being changed over time came to mind.

Cornelius shrugged. "Some describe banshees as ugly, old haggard women. Others say they are beautiful, like sirens."

I raised my hand. "Beautiful was my experience."

"You do have to keep in mind that the Irish are known for their love of alcohol, so these stories can be wildly varied. However, one common trait is the banshee's haunting wail."

Aunt Zoe leaned back, her mouth pursed in thought. I wondered what all of this was adding up to in her head.

I looked at Harvey. "Did you happen to figure out where the door key was for the escape game?"

"I found a safe behind that framed black-and-white picture of the old jail on the wall when I was foolin' around in there waitin' for you guys, but it had a four-digit combination lock on it. As soon as the paramedics came bustin' through that door between the kitchen and the sheriff's office, scarin' the livin' daylights out of me, the game was over."

"I think I know the code for that lock," Natalie said, sliding the paper she'd been writing on my way. "That clue of Doc's shows a sequence for the colored rubber duckies. Remember how the ducks had different reward amounts listed under their names?"

I nodded, staring at what looked like a complex math problem scribbled on the paper.

"I bet if you take the first number of each reward amount

and put it in the order of the colors listed on Doc's clue, it's the combo." She smiled. "Or something like that. We'd have to go back there to try it out."

"No way in hell is that happening," Cooper said.

"Nope. Never again. Playing the banshee version of the escape room is a once in a lifetime deal for me." I slid the paper back. "I vote we consider your answer right and call it good. Well done, you." I raised my bottle of beer to her and then finished it off.

"Violet," Aunt Zoe said, rejoining the conversation. "You didn't actually execute the banshee, did you?"

I set the bottle back on the table. "Nope. She was still shrieking when Cornelius reached into the dark and pulled me back out." I should have known those bony fingers were his.

Aunt Zoe frowned and then made a note in her book.

"When you say go 'into the dark,' " Natalie said, "you mean only in your mind, right?"

I nodded.

Officially, I'd not actually left my body during the experience. Neither had Cooper, for that matter. We'd been physically in that jail room the whole time. Even though I was a physical medium, I'd somehow taken him along for the ride only in my head. Unfortunately, I'd also taken the banshee. Lucky for us, she was more of a phantom fairy than flesh and blood, so there was no actual body to leave behind.

Earlier, as in shortly after we'd arrived back from Spearfish and settled in here at the kitchen table, I'd told everyone what had happened after I'd panicked and accidentally taken Cooper with me into the dark. When I'd asked Doc why the banshee hadn't been in that bright version of the jail room with Cooper and me, he'd told me he didn't know.

He'd gone on to explain to us that when Cooper had separated from me in the dark version of the jail to look out that square window in the door while I was messing around with the banshee, Doc had been able to pinpoint the source of Cooper's "energy." He had then opened the steel door and pulled him out of there.

I, on the other hand, was not so easy to find, even though we were in the same place. Doc couldn't "see" me due to the blast of energy flowing from me, frying his mental radar. Apparently, screeching alongside the banshee like a pair of baby birds hadn't helped my cause any.

However, Doc was able to find and open the same door he had for Cooper with the hopes that I'd try to follow in his footsteps. That was why the door handle worked when I fell to my knees and the door pulled open for me, which allowed me to slip outside and close the banshee in on the other side. After I'd settled down outside of the room and focused my thoughts on the candle again, Doc found me and sent Cornelius in after me.

By that time, the emergency situation with the docent had grown into a worrying problem as medics and a fire crew arrived on scene and wanted to know how many of us were in the mansion. Since Natalie had hid the registration paperwork sitting on the desk in the foyer before anyone could see it, they had no way of knowing we were in the jail. Harvey distracted everyone while Natalie raced up and got Doc, leaving Cornelius and Cooper the task of getting me back up on my feet.

"You might need to return to that jail again, Violet," Aunt Zoe said, bringing me back to the present with a jolt.

"Why?"

"You left that banshee locked away in another realm."

Yeah, but ... "Do you think I interfered with some process that will keep Mr. Ewart from finding eternal peace?"

Meaning that if Cooper returned to the mansion again, he'd find the old docent's ghost roaming around, looking for clues to escape the place along with other paying guests? The idea of that tugged on my heartstrings.

"Maybe." Aunt Zoe tossed her pen down on the table. "But you can't leave that banshee locked up like that. If she figures out how to escape, or someone else opens that door by accident, there's a good chance she's going to find you and come calling. And when she does, she'll do a hell of a lot more than scream at you."

Chapter Seventeen

Saturday, January 19th

Someone was screaming at me.

I sat up in bed with a gasp, blinking the blur of sleep from my eyes as I scanned my dark room. Who'd been screa …

No, wait, it was just my phone. Someone was calling me.

I looked down at the bed beside me. It was empty. I thought Doc said he was going to hang out at home this morning and maybe head to the Rec Center later.

What time was it?

Too damned early if it's still dark, that's what time it is.

My phone was still ringing.

I leaned over and turned on the lamp on my nightstand. There were two cookies sitting on top of my phone.

I'd forgotten that I'd set them down there before crawling into bed. I smiled and grabbed one, gobbling down the sweet, soft morsel. Chocolate chips, butterscotch bits, and toffee pieces. Yum! I should keep cookies by my bed more often.

Last night, I'd had big plans on sharing a midnight snack with Doc, and maybe another stimulating treat or two before falling asleep. But Doc had pulled me close under the covers and started rubbing my back, whispering sweet nothings in the dark about how much he liked my smooth skin and soft biscuits. Or had he said "soft tidbits"?

I must have dozed off about then because I didn't remember much after he started petting me. Not even any dreams.

The phone rang again.

Damn. It was relentless this morning. Cooper must be on the other end of the line, barking at the end of his chain.

I picked the phone up along with the other cookie and looked at the screen. Zelda Britton's name showed, but I knew better. Zelda would have better manners than to call me before dawn, which meant Prudence the ghost had put her up to this wakeup call.

"Nope. Too early," I told Prudence. I took a bite of the cookie and sent the call to voicemail before setting the phone back on my nightstand facedown. The world could wait another hour for this *Scharfrichter* to roll out of bed and start kicking some ass. I chuckled at how cocky that sounded and brushed the crumbs from my lips.

"Who was that?" Doc asked from the doorway. He had a towel draped around his neck and a pair of cotton pajama pants settled low on his hips.

Oh, good. A cookie and a freshly cleaned stud. My birthday had come early. Now if we only had some honey butter.

"Prudence," I told him and took another bite of the cookie while ogling his eye candy. "She has Zelda calling me, but she can wait. I'm busy."

He closed the bedroom door behind him and leaned back against it, watching me chew with a hooded gaze.

Or maybe it was the dim lighting making him look tall, dark, and hungry.

Or was he staring at my cookie that way? I tucked the cookie closer to my chest, protecting it.

"Is that one of your aunt's homemade cookies?" he asked in a deep, velvety voice.

I nodded, slowly lifting it to my lips. "I'd offer you a bite, but it's really yummy."

He shot from the door in a blink, diving onto the bed and barreling into me. Before I could catch my breath, he had me pinned under him flat on my back as he straddled my hips.

Holding the last half of my cookie out of reach, he loomed over me. "Got it." A victory grin rounded his cheeks. He lifted the cookie toward his lips.

"That's mine, cookie crook." I wiggled my arm free enough to grab his wrist and tug the cookie my way. I leaned up, opening my mouth.

He laughed, letting the morsel brush my lips, but then tightened his bicep, pulling the cookie away.

"Tease!" I tried to pull it back my way, partially sitting up.

His arm held solid. "I'd be willing to share the rest of this cookie with you in exchange for something else."

I quit fighting and fell back onto the mattress, clearly outmuscled, not to mention half-trapped under the covers.

"Like what?" I purred, batting my eyelashes at him. I licked my lips to up the ante.

His gaze got stuck on my mouth. "I don't know, Boots. Get creative."

"Let's see." I walked my fingers up his arm toward his bare shoulder. "If you let me have another bite of that cookie, I'd be willing to …" I paused and pulled my hand away, giving him the come-hither signal with my index finger.

He leaned down.

"Closer. I'll whisper it to you."

He put his ear next to my mouth.

I turned my head a little and whispered sweet but naughty nothings in his ear.

He pulled back and stared down at me with a baffled expression. "You'd do what bunnies do?" he repeated my words aloud as if he'd heard me wrong.

I raised one eyebrow. "Do I need to spell it out for you,

Candy Cane?"

He let out a loud laugh.

"Shhhh!" I covered his mouth. "You'll wake Aunt Zoe and the kids."

"Your aunt is already awake," he said from behind my hand, his lips brushing against my skin. "I heard her making coffee."

I kept my hand over his mouth, smiling up at him. "Your lips are tickling my palm and making my biscuit tingle."

His pupils widened, turning into captivating black holes. Their gravitational pull sucked me into a half-sitting position again, this time propped up by my elbow.

"Violet," he said against my palm. "Lower your hand."

"Not until you give me back my cookie."

He shifted southward, straddling my thighs now, and then leaned over me. One fist dented the mattress next to my elbow as he held the last bite of the cookie above me.

Lowering my hand, I opened my mouth and he placed it on my tongue.

I gave him a fake glare while chewing. "I'm telling you, Oracle," I said after I swallowed. "Burly muscled and rawhide tough don't matter. Never tangle with a *Scharfrichter*."

His other fist pushed into the mattress, imprisoning me. He dipped down, his mouth moving closer to mine. "You're bright and sassy this morning, Killer."

"It's Prudence's fault." I reached behind me and found my pillow. Lying back, I stared up at him, basking in the heat of his gaze. "You smell minty." He must have just brushed his teeth. I gave him a flirty smile. "If I kissed you right now after that cookie, I wonder if you'd taste like a chocolate-butterscotch-toffee-peppermint patty."

He stretched out and settled on top of me, flanked on both sides by my thighs, while sandwiching the goose-down comforter between us. "I'm game to give it a try if you are."

"Okay." I tipped my chin and closed my eyes. "Ready."

I pursed my lips out as far as they would go.

His body shook with laughter. "You look like one of those big-lip damselfish on that documentary about coastal reefs we were watching with the kids the other night."

"I prefer the label 'Kissing Damsel,' please." I cracked one eye. "What are you waiting for, Candy Cane? Kiss the damsel before she turns back into a frog."

His dark eyes gleamed with mirth. "Damsels don't turn into frogs. Princes do."

"Yeah, well I'm not your normal damsel." I made fish lips again.

"No, you're not." He cupped my chin. "Now close that eye."

I did as told.

"Open your mouth."

"Like this?" I opened it as wide as a banshee mid-scream.

"On second thought, keep it closed."

"But how will I—"

He kissed me.

"Finally," I murmured against his lips.

"Shut up, woman," he murmured back. "And let me work my magic." I could feel the smile on his lips.

I kept my eyes closed and waited for the show to start.

He didn't leave me waiting for long, starting with feather-like brushes of his lips over mine while his fingers traced the line of my jaw. His mouth followed his fingers over to my ear and then down the side of my neck.

I giggled. "Your beard is tickling me clear to my nether regions."

He brushed his chin along my collarbone, sending another delicious shiver south as his mouth traveled north.

I moaned. "Keep it up and my bloomers will catch fire."

"*It* has been up since I returned from the shower and saw you sitting in bed looking soft, sexy, and slightly tousled."

"You just wanted my cookie," I teased, my eyes still

closed.

"Yes, I do. And your biscuit, too."

He kissed me again. His mouth was bolder this time. His tongue slid along the outside of my lips, his breath coming faster. I opened my mouth slightly, trying to tempt him to explore further, but he held back. Meanwhile, his body pressed into mine, rubbing in the right places. But not enough.

I groaned in frustration, wanting to feel skin on skin. I shoved the covers down to my hips, where they bunched up and made matters worse.

The bed shifted as he lowered himself onto his forearms, enveloping me in his warm bare skin and the subtly sweet notes from the orange and vanilla soap he'd gotten for Christmas. His tongue delved deeper, finally, encouraging mine to play. I reached up and pulled him even closer.

He tasted good. Like sex in the moonlight on a tropical beach. No, scratch that. Too much sand in tender spots.

I framed his face with my hands, skimming my tongue over his. He tasted minty sweet. I went back for seconds, nibbling and sucking on his lower lip for good measure.

"Touch me," I whispered before going in for thirds.

I could feel his deep, rumbly groan as well as hear it. His hand wrestled with my camisole, tugging it up enough to slide under and find skin.

I stopped thinking then and just floated up to the ceiling while he rubbed his thumb all around. When he shoved my camisole up even further and replaced his thumb with his mouth, I arched my back. Or at least I tried to. But the damned covers were holding me prisoner.

His mouth stopped way too soon. His thumb hovered near my belly button, which was not where I wanted it to be.

"Well?" he asked, his voice husky with need. "Was it a peppermint patty–flavored kiss?"

I opened my eyes and lifted my head enough to frown

down at where his hand rested on my stomach, willing it to move a little more toward my toes. "I'll need to do more testing before I can be sure."

"You'll have to wait." His lips skimmed the side of my neck, leaving a trail of heat in their wake. "I'm busy now."

I scraped my nails along his shoulders. "I should have brought up some of that honey butter."

"You taste better than honey. Especially in certain spots."

I moved my hips under the covers, needing more contact. "Like where?" I reached down and tried to shove the comforter off even farther.

"Like here." He licked the small indent above my collarbone. "And here." His mouth slid down into the valley between my breasts.

I tried to arch into him once more while still struggling with the comforter. "Lick me again," I begged.

He hesitated, then shook his head and started kissing me again instead of licking.

"What's wrong?" I asked, stilling.

"Nothing."

"Doc." I lifted his head so I could look him in the eyes. "What is it?"

"That prisoner ghost was licking you."

I recoiled. "Jeez. Why'd you have to go there right now?"

"I didn't mean to. You said the word 'lick,' and my mind flashed an image of that scene."

I chewed on my lower lip. "Do you want to stop?"

His gaze relocated to my mouth. "Hell no."

"Good." I tried to wrap my legs around him but the freaking covers held me in place. With a growl of frustration, I started thrashing my legs like a mad woman.

He rolled partway off of me, frowning down at my legs. "What the hell? Do you have a charley horse?"

"I can't."

Thrash. Curse.

"Get to."

Writhe. Grunt.

"You."

I sighed and went totally still, my breath ragged. "You need to do something about these covers before I turn into a big green monster and start breaking things."

He chuckled. "Hold that thought."

His feet hit the floor a second later. In record speed, he locked the door, kicked off his pajamas, yanked back the covers, and dove inside, pulling the comforter over our heads.

We lay there facing each other in the semi-dark for a few seconds, just breathing and listening, enjoying a slice of privacy.

"Do you hear that clucking coming from the closet?" Doc asked.

"Yeah, but we're going to ignore it for now. We have some more testing to do."

A smile played at his lips. "So, you're going to need more kissing?"

"And that thing you do with your tongue that shall not be named."

"Right. That thing, too."

He reached up and ran his thumb along my cheekbone. "Have I told you lately how much I love you?"

A liquid warmth filled me from top to bottom, leaving me glowing hot. "Nope. Tell me more."

His thumb traced up to my temple. "I hate it when you go into the dark without me."

"Me, too. It scares the hell out of me thinking I might get lost one of these times and not be able to find my way back to you."

"I would never stop looking for you." He leaned forward and kissed my nose. "Never ever."

I lifted my hand between us, holding out my pinkie. "Pinkie promise?"

He linked his with mine, pulling my hand up to his lips so he could kiss my finger. "Promise."

I tugged free so I could slide my hand around the back of his neck and pull him and his mouth closer. I spent the next several minutes tasting, touching, rubbing while appreciating his magic hands casting spells on my skin.

When we came up for air next, I was under him again. His body was wedged between my thighs, his hips moving against me in a rhythm that had me aching for more.

Finally, there were no covers mummifying me. But my underwear had to go. I'd wriggled partway out of them when a muscle started to cramp in my hip. That would have to do for now. I'd have to practice my under-the-covers yoga later.

I gasped when he sucked on the tender skin under my breast, giving me a love mark that would stick around for a few days. "Doc?"

He lifted his head. His eyes glittered in the shadows.

I shifted my hips, lining up with his body. "Are we going to consummate this relationship or what?"

He grunted, reverting to caveman vernacular, and slid slowly along my tender flesh, sending a wave of delight rippling over my skin.

I wrapped one leg around him. "Hurry before the kids wake and come knocking for you to cook them breakfast."

He didn't dawdle any longer, filling me in one hard thrust. He paused with his forehead pressed against mine, his eyes closed as a low rumble came from his throat. "Christ, you feel good."

"More, *cara mio*," I ordered, moving under him. "Now."

He went up on one knee, angling deeper as he stared down at me, loving me with his eyes as well as his body. The pads of his fingers inched down over my stomach and kept going.

"You first, *querida*," he said in between breath-stealing kisses and then he touched me.

A zing of pleasure jolted a gasp from me. "Doc!" I closed my eyes and reached down, pressing my hand over his to help. "More." My breaths turned choppy, full of cries, pants, and moans.

"Violet," Doc rasped, nuzzling my neck. "I love how tight you feel around me."

Apparently, that was all I needed to hear to freefall into bliss. He kissed me as I bowed into him, muffling the sounds of my delight.

As soon as my body finished its fireworks display, he grasped my hips. "My turn." He drove into me hard, pushing me up the mattress with each growl, until he groaned low and long, fully spent. Then he collapsed on top of me.

It took him a few seconds to catch his breath. "Damn, woman," he said against my neck. "It's never enough." Then he rolled onto his back, pulling me along, too. "Come here." He settled me on top of him.

Tugging the covers back up over our heads, I shielded us from the world again and rested my cheek on his shoulder. "I can feel your heart," I whispered, tracing a heart shape on his arm with my fingernail.

"You should be able to. It beats for you."

I smiled. "If you're trying to woo me, it's working."

"Sexcellent."

I raised my head. "Did you just say 'sexcellent'?"

"Willis was teaching us new words at our last poker night. Although he might have stolen that one from Natalie."

"Dear Lord. You'd better not compare me to a barnyard animal during sex or I might bite you."

"Kinky. That could be fun." He played with my hair, soothing me back down onto his shoulder.

We lay there in silence, listening to the soft clucking sound coming from my closet.

I sighed in defeat. "That fricken chicken."

He chuckled and rolled to the side, scooting down the mattress until we were eye to eye. His dark gaze searched mine as his fingers traveled over my hip. "I have an idea."

I wiggled my eyebrows. "Will I be on top or bottom this time?"

"I don't care as long as I'm inside of you."

"Good answer."

His expression sobered. "Seriously, though, I meant I have an idea about our *Nachzehrer* problem."

I wrinkled my nose. "You want to talk about those creepy bastards right now? Here?"

He nodded. "I've been so busy with work that I keep forgetting to tell you about it."

Before he could get another word out, three light knocks on the door interrupted him.

"Damn," I whispered. "There's the bell. Recess is over."

Doc hopped out of bed.

I sat up and tussled with my camisole, trying to untwist it enough to find the shoulder straps.

Another round of knocking rang out, harder this time.

"Mom?" Addy called through the wood.

Camisole in place, I glanced over at Doc. He was already tugging his jeans over his boxer-briefs. Holy underwear, he was fast!

"What do you need, Addy?" I called back, wrestling my own unmentionables back onto my hips.

"Is Doc in there with you?"

He nodded at my questioning look.

"Yeah, he's here."

"Will you ask him if I should wear jeans or sweatpants today?"

Since when did my daughter consult with Doc on clothing choices?

"Either will work," Doc answered for himself, walking

over to the closet. "Hey, Addy?" He pulled open the doors, bending down. When he popped back up, he was holding a chicken.

"Yeah?" Her voice sounded closer. Lower.

I could see her shadow under the door. She had to be peeking through the crack.

Doc crossed the room and unlocked the door, drawing it open quickly.

Addy squeaked in surprise and scrambled to her feet.

"Take Elvis, would you?" He handed the chicken to her. "I'll be down in two shakes to make breakfast."

Her smile lit her sleep-puffy face. "French toast?"

He nodded once. "And scrambled eggs."

"With lots of cheese?"

"That's a given."

Addy jumped up and down, ruffling Elvis's feathers and earning a loud squawk in the process. Then she raced toward the stairs.

Doc closed the door as Addy's footfalls pounded down the steps, leaning back against it.

"Arrrrgh." I flopped back onto my pillow. "I'm not ready to face this day." After the last two, any hopes I might've harbored of having a normal day had disappeared at the first cluck of Addy's chicken in my closet.

"Come on, Killer. You can do this. After all, I gave you one hell of a jump start."

"Yes, you did, Mr. Cock-a-doodle-doo. You should open the window and crow about it to the neighborhood."

He chuckled. "I'd give Mr. Stinkleskine and his little dog a heart attack." Doc returned to the closet and grabbed a dark blue flannel shirt. He looked at me as he slid his arms into the sleeves. "About the *Nachzehrer*," he started.

"Wait!" I yanked up the bottom of my camisole, flashing my girls at him before pulling the hem back down.

He paused while buttoning his shirt, a wry grin on his

face. "What was that for?"

"I'm trying to distract you from those parasitic creeps."

"It didn't work. Try again."

I gave him a come-hither look. "Hey, big boy," I said in a smokey, pin-up girl voice. "You want to come pet my cat?" I purred at him, although it sounded more like a gargle.

He burst out laughing.

"That was supposed to be a hot invitation to have sex," I explained. At least it was in Jeff Wymonds's porno dreams.

He shook his head, still laughing, and kept buttoning. "Sorry, Killer, but the *Scharfrichter* gets to tangle with the Oracle only once this morning. Now it's time for him to make breakfast for her kids."

I leaned on my elbow and watched him finish buttoning. While sex with Doc was wonderful and his kisses made my delicates smolder, it was moments like this that I loved the best—lying in bed with his scent all over my skin while he dressed in front of me. If only he didn't want to talk about a gangly, sharp-toothed, human-like monstrosity that pined for my blood the same way I craved peanut butter fudge ice cream.

I sat up and wrapped my arms around my knees. "Okay, Oracle. Tell me your idea."

Chapter Eighteen

I wasn't a fan of Doc's idea.

For one thing, it put his neck on the line.

For another, it involved blood—mine.

After a long, steamy shower where I considered the pros and cons of being an Executioner in between wondering why Prudence had called me before the birds had even woken up, I joined Doc, Aunt Zoe, and the kids in the kitchen.

"Coop called," Doc told me as he handed me a cup of coffee. "He wants us at the taxidermy shop at noon."

I nodded and then raised the mug to my lips, taking a sip. "Mmmm. Nice and yummy." I went up on my toes and gave him a thank-you peck on the lips. "Like you, Mr. *Nyce*."

"And morning cookies," he shot back with a wink.

"Come on, Mom," Layne mumbled at the table through a mouthful of scrambled eggs. "I'm trying to eat here."

Doc laughed and returned to manning the stove.

"What's a taxidermy shop?" Addy asked, chomping on an apple slice. "Do you go there to pay your taxes?"

Layne snorted. "No, you bozo." He started to lift a forkful of scrambled eggs to his mouth, but then jerked and spilled the eggs into his lap. "Mom! Addy kicked me."

I grabbed a plate from the cupboard. "Adelynn Renee, keep your feet to yourself." I stabbed a piece of French toast from the serving tray in the center of the table and dropped it on my plate. "Layne, you should refrain from calling your sister names if you don't want to get kicked under the table."

I set my plate down next to where Aunt Zoe was enjoying a cup of coffee with a faraway look in her eyes. I wondered where she was at the moment, and if there were a certain fire captain there with her. And if that fire captain had been tied up on a set of railroad tracks or in a bed.

Before I settled in at the table, I stepped over to Addy and gave her a "good-morning" kiss on the top of the head. *Hold up!* Her hair had smelled earthy. That was weird.

I leaned down and gave her another kiss, sneaking in a good sniff. Earthy *and* musky, along with a hint of pine and … dog!

I tipped her chin up, taking a closer inspection of her face. Her cheeks were pink. Too pink. Fresh from outside in the snow pink.

"Enough already, Mother," she said, pulling free of my grip. "I love you, too."

I focused on Layne, whose food-stuffed cheeks were also rosy, along with his nose. I walked over and kissed him on the temple, letting my lips linger a moment. His skin was cool to the touch.

He pulled away from me. "Mom! I told you I'm trying to eat." He pointed his fork at the mound of scrambled eggs on his plate. "Doc says I have to eat a man-sized portion if I'm going to grow as tall and strong as him and Coop."

I stepped back and looked toward the back door. The dark blue sweater I'd been wearing over my camisole last night hung on the wall peg next to it. That was odd. I could've sworn I'd left it draped over the back of the sofa in the living room last night before heading up to bed with my cookies.

I marched over to the sweater, zeroing in on the long, white dog hairs as I closed in on it. There were also a few darker hairs along with some pine needles and a couple of tiny twigs caught in the weave, not to mention a good helping of dirt sprinkled throughout. I lifted it from the peg. The front and sleeves were damp. I held it up, frowning at a streak of what I hoped was slobber and not snot on one of the shoulders. I leaned closer and sniffed, wincing at the strong *eau de* dirty dog.

Busted!

I whirled around, my jaw clenched.

Four pairs of eyes were watching me.

I homed in on the two kids sitting still as statues at the table. "Where is it?"

"Where's what?" Addy said, her eyes bright. She smiled extra wide, looking a little too much like a miniature, demented, killer clown for my comfort.

I cringed slightly. The poor kid took after me more than I realized some days.

"Where is Rooster?" I asked the two slapdash schemers.

On the way back to the table, I swung by the laundry room door and tossed my sweater in on the washer.

Addy gave an uneasy laugh. "Elvis is a chicken, mom. Not a rooster."

I pointed at her. "Don't play dumb with me, child." When I turned on Layne, he stuffed more scrambled eggs in his mouth, focusing intently on his plate.

I harrumphed and paid a visit to the sink, washing my hands. "What have you two done with that dog?"

"We didn't do nothing," Addy defended.

"Then why does my sweater stink like the dirty mutt?"

A glance in Doc's direction as I dried my hands found him taking great care while flipping pieces of French toast in the frying pan. I looked closer. Was he biting back a grin? No. Maybe. Why? Was he aiding and abetting my children on this dog business? Surely he wouldn't …

I turned to Aunt Zoe. She hid behind her coffee cup.

My jaw clenched. A lot of help she was. This was her house. She should be the one putting her foot down. Then I could be a lazy parent and blame her for not letting my kids add yet another critter to what was becoming the Parker Zoo.

I took a deep breath, taking control of the situation along with my temper before joining them at the table. "We are *not* keeping that dog," I stated in a calm, clear voice.

"But Mom!" Addy wailed, whining at the exact pitch that always made my shoulders scrunch up. Jumping jitterbugs! She could give that banshee a run for her money. "Why not?"

"You didn't even give poor Rooster a try," Layne accused, scowling at me over his eggs.

"I don't need to give that dog a try!" I waved my hands exaggeratedly in the air, losing my grip on that slippery calm. After putting up with *Nachzehrer*, the imp, the banshee, Prudence, Dominick, and that damned licking ghost, I'd reached the bottom of my well of control. "We have already forced Aunt Zoe to accept two messy kids and their crazy mom in her house, along with a vegetarian cat, an escape-artist hamster, and a mother-clucking chicken!"

"Don't forget a large human male," Doc said, placing a bottle of boysenberry syrup in front of me as I huffed and puffed and tried to blow the house down around me.

He gripped my shoulders, squeezing lightly. I wasn't sure if it was to show me some support or to hold me down before I flew completely off the handle. His squeeze turned into a massage, releasing some of my tension.

"I was messy before you two came and I'll be messy after," Aunt Zoe told the kids. She patted my hand. "And crazy, too." Then the traitor smiled up at Doc. "And it's nice to have a man around here, especially these days."

I shoved several curls out of my face that had come loose during my big bad wolf impression and grumbled into my cup of coffee for several slurps.

"See, Mom." Addy grabbed a piece of French toast and dropped it onto her plate, giving me an it-will-all-be-okay look. "Aunt Zoe doesn't mind us or our animals."

I held out my hand, stopping any further animal-related mouth traffic. "No dog."

"Boys are supposed to have dogs for best friends," Layne groused and stabbed a slice of apple with gusto.

It was time to change the subject before my head exploded like a dying star.

"Aunt Zoe, how did things go with Reid and his son?" She'd evaded my questions last night after everyone left, claiming exhaustion and hurrying off to bed.

She avoided my raised brows, but her neck and cheeks darkened.

Doc returned to the stove, stirring some cheese into the skillet of scrambled eggs.

"Do you think Reid likes dogs?" Addy asked Layne in the awkward silence.

Layne perked up. "Maybe. We could ask him."

"If he does," Addy plotted out loud, "we can visit him and Rooster every day."

"Would you look at that," Aunt Zoe said, staring down at her bare wrist. "It's time for me to get to work."

I watched her rise from the table, empty coffee cup in hand, and scowled at her backside as she walked away. "When are you going to tell me about last night?" I wasn't giving up that easily.

"There's nothing to tell." She set her cup in the sink. "Reid and his son came to dinner. The kids and I played hosts. We fed them before sending them on their way." She came back with a washrag and wiped off the table where she'd spilled a drop of coffee.

"You know," I said while slathering some butter on my French toast. "If you won't answer my questions about Reid, I'll be forced to pump my two children for information."

My kids looked from me to her with wide eyes.

She clenched the dishcloth in her fist, squeezing several drips out of it onto the table. "Violet Lynn, there is nothing else to tell."

I uncapped the bottle of boysenberry syrup and drizzled some over my food. "Addy and Layne, what was Reid's son like?"

"Tall and strong." Layne went back to shoveling in eggs.

"I'm pretty sure he likes dogs and chickens," Addy added, struggling to cut her French toast with her fork. "He was laughing at my stories about Rooster and Elvis."

I bet he was. I'd be chuckling too if it weren't my children taking in every other stray animal in the dang neighborhood.

Doc came over with an empty plate and a bowl of steaming scrambled eggs. He spooned some onto my dish before sitting down at the table next to me and loading up his own. "Martin mentioned during our last poker game that his son is a firefighter, too."

"A fireman, huh?" I reached into the middle of the table and stabbed a couple pieces of French toast, unloading them onto Doc's plate for him. "Layne, does Reid's boy look like his dad, only a bit younger?"

Layne swallowed. "His hair was colored more like mine, but his eyes were the same as his dad's."

Doc reached for the maple syrup on the table between the kids, but then paused after watching my daughter struggle with her fork. "Addy, do you want some help cutting that?"

She sighed and pushed her glasses up her nose. "Yes, please." She handed him her plate.

"Equilateral triangles, trapezoids, or rhombuses today?" Doc asked, his knife and fork poised at the ready.

She pursed her lips. "What's a trapezoid again?"

"Two sides are parallel," Layne answered.

"That one, please," she said, stirring whatever was in the coffee mug in front of her.

I pointed my fork at her. "What's in your cup?"

"Doc made the kids hot cocoa," Aunt Zoe said, sitting back down at the table. Apparently, she'd decided to stick around after all.

Addy took a sip, licking the chocolate mustache off her upper lip afterward. "He put some caramel on the bottom and topped it with marshmallows and chocolate chips."

Yowza, that was a lot of sugar.

I aimed a raised eyebrow at Doc. "Are you planning to hook them up to a dog sled and have them pull you around the neighborhood this morning?"

Doc handed Addy back her plate full of trapezoid-shaped pieces of French toast. "We're going to the Rec Center after you head to work. Right, guys?"

"Yeah!" Layne shouted and hopped out of his chair. He jabbed his elbows around in the air several times, like some kind of weird robot dance, and then sat down again.

I gawked at him as I chewed, wondering if he had a kangaroo stuffed somewhere in his pajama pants. "What was that about?"

Doc swallowed a forkful of eggs. "We're going to practice some elbow strikes today when we spar."

"Doc showed us some bruised-knee videos the other night on his computer," Addy explained, digging into her French toast.

"Bruce Lee videos," Doc corrected with a smile. "Although 'bruised knee' works too for that one guy who broke a board over Bruce's knee."

Doc had been teaching my kids some self-defense moves over the last few months at the Rec Center. The kids thought they were learning self-defense for fun, but the rest of us adults knew better. My family was at risk as much as I was when it came to the hazards of my killing profession.

The Executioner gene traveled down through the female line, making Addy the next *Scharfrichter* if I was eliminated from this game before my job was finished. But Layne wasn't free of peril either, even though he was a male. Many, many generations ago, one of my ancestors hooked up with a hybrid male called a Summoner, if I remembered right, mixing together DNA in their offspring and adding the possibility that Layne might turn into something equally as worrisome as Addy.

Doc was doing his best to protect my kids by way of training them how to defend themselves if something came to wipe us all out, like what had happened to Prudence's family long ago.

Me? I was just trying to stay alive long enough to see them into adulthood and keep this "killer" curse from falling on Addy's shoulders before she was strong enough to fight back.

I focused back on Aunt Zoe. "Spill it, darlin'. What happened at supper last night?"

She shrugged. "Like I said before, we enjoyed a meal together and then they left. After the kids and I cleaned up the kitchen, they went to bed and I waited up for you guys to come home."

I shook my head, rejecting her lame answer, and turned to my daughter. "Addy, what happened at supper last night?"

She swallowed her mouthful of French toast before answering. "Let's see. Reid and his boy came over. Aunt Zoe made some really good chicken and biscuits for all of us. She made me wash my hands for thirty whole seconds before we ate because I showed Reid's boy Elvis's pen in the basement. For dessert, we had ice cream and cookies and Reid's boy told me that he and his friends had to rescue a dog and a cat from the same tree once. He said the cat chased the dog up the tree and then they were both too scared to come down." She giggled and stabbed two trapezoids at once. "I would've liked to have seen that crazy cat at work."

Interesting—not just the story, but ... "It sounds like Reid's son is good with kids and pets. Does he have any children of his own?"

"Nope," Layne answered. "He told us that he's not ready

to settle down yet."

A low laugh came from my aunt's direction. "That apple didn't fall far from the tree."

"Reid's son used to be one of those firefighters who parachutes into the middle of a fire," Layne said, pausing to slurp down some cocoa. "He has a bad scar on his arm and leg from a wildfire that nearly killed him."

I looked at Aunt Zoe. "Really?"

She nodded solemnly. "He lost a couple of friends in that fire. I don't think he's made peace with it yet, either."

"How long ago was that?"

"Just last year. He's since returned to working out of a station instead of fighting wildfires."

"He doesn't think he wants to jump into fires anymore," Addy added. "And I'm glad, because he's a very nice boy and I'd hate to see him get hurt again."

I smirked. Addy's use of "boy" when talking about Reid's son sounded like he wasn't much older than my kids. But if my math was right, he must be in his early thirties.

"What's Reid's son's name?" I asked anyone at the table.

"Ox," Addy said.

"That's not his name," Layne said. "It's his fireman nickname." He looked at Doc. "May I be excused?"

Doc nodded, pointing his fork at Layne's dirty dishes. Without a single complaint, Layne took his plate, silverware, and mug to the sink before racing out of the room. I watched the kid go with my jaw unhinged. Had an alien come down to Earth and taken over my kid?

"His name is Oscar," Aunt Zoe clarified. "He's an inch or so shorter than Doc and strong like his dad from chopping down trees and digging fire lines in the forest for the past decade. His hair is sandy brown, like Layne's, and he's handsome in a rugged way that will likely end up breaking many poor girls' hearts in the years to come if hose jockeying continues to be his obsession." She crossed her arms. "Now, can I go to work?"

I held up my finger. "One more thing."

"Only one?" she teased. "That doesn't sound like you."

I chose my words carefully since Addy and her big ears were still at the table. "Does Ox begrudge your past copulatory congressions?"

"What's 'begrudge' mean?" Addy asked, apparently getting stuck on that first big word, as I'd hoped she would.

"Feel bitter about something," Doc explained.

"Oh." She picked up her cocoa. "Ox told me he has a parrot that talks to him while he shaves every morning." She took a drink. "If we can't have a dog, Mom, can we get a bird?"

"You already have one."

"I mean a parrot."

"Nope."

She sighed. "You didn't even think about it before answering."

"I don't need to. There will be no dogs or parrots or tortoises or ferrets or snakes or lizards or fish."

She snorted. "Like I'd ever want a fish."

What? Hadn't she asked for a fish tank for Christmas?

"All they do is swim around and poop." She looked at Doc. "May I please be excused, Doc? I'm super-duper full."

He reached over and mussed her hair. "Sure, kid. Rest up a little before we go work off this breakfast at the gym."

She deposited her dishes in the sink and left the kitchen a little slower than her brother, holding her full belly.

"Well?" I asked Aunt Zoe.

She smirked. "I don't think Ox even knows that his father and I were ever an item."

"Shit." Doc sucked air through his teeth, shaking his head.

Reid had told me yesterday that his son knew a little about "recent history" events, but he hadn't clarified exactly how recent. "So, you think Reid never mentioned anything about you two to Ox back then?"

"Ox didn't act like he knew one iota about our sordid past. But I can't hold that against him. His father, however, has proven yet again what an idiot I'd been before."

Ouch. That had to sting a little. Or a lot. I took a bite of French toast. Why hadn't Reid said anything about my aunt to his kid back then?

"I liked Reid's son," Aunt Zoe continued. "He was courteous and friendly. And he really was genuinely great with your kids."

I swallowed my bite. "Reid probably has a good explanation for keeping you from his son back then."

"Yeah, right." Her expression hardened. "All the more reason to keep this thing with him at 'friend' level for good. I see where I rated then and don't expect anything more if we sailed around the horn a second time."

Doc's phone pinged. He pulled it out of his back pocket. "It's a text message from Coop. He said to turn on your walkie-talkie, Violet."

"I don't even know where it is right now."

He scooted his chair back. "I do." He disappeared into the dining room, returning before I had a chance to console Aunt Zoe anymore. "Here," he said, handing it to me as he returned to his chair to finish his breakfast.

"How do I turn it on?" I still wasn't sure which button did what.

"It's already on. Just push *that* button and talk."

I held it up to my lips. "Uhhh, this is Violet. What do you want, Cooper?" I set the walkie-talkie down on the table.

There was a crackly sound from the speaker and then I heard, "Vi, you're supposed to say 'over,' remember? Over."

Natalie must be listening in on Cooper's walkie-talkie. Or he'd given her one of her own so that she didn't bust a cap in his ass.

I picked it back up. "Shut up, Nat."

"Shut up, Nat. Over." Harvey weighed in through the damned thing. "That's how you do it, Sparky. Over."

Doc started laughing next to me. His funny bone was working overtime already today.

I elbowed him and then spoke into the walkie-talkie. "Does anyone else out there with their ears up want to give their two freaking cents on how to use this stupid thing?" I made sure to add an "over" at the end.

"Violet." Cornelius' voice came through this time. "I believe the saying is 'Got your ears on,' not 'up.'"

I hit the button and growled at all of the buttheads.

"If you're done screwing around, Parker," Cooper came back on the line, "we have a situation in Lead that you need to check out. Over."

Aunt Zoe and Doc traded wrinkled brows.

"What kind of a situation?" I wondered if it had anything to do with why Prudence had called me earlier. "Over," I added before one of the other jackasses said it for me.

"I have a feeling your imp has been at it again. Over." Cooper didn't sound very happy about it, either. Then again, he might just be tired after that disastrous birthday party crashed by a slew of uninvited guests. Not to mention he'd asked Natalie to spend another night with him on their way out the door.

I rubbed my forehead, feeling the beginning of a headache taking hold. "What did the little shit do this time? Over."

"It appears that it tried to eat one of Lead's police cars." There was a long pause and then a very disgusted-sounding "Over and out."

Chapter Nineteen

I was so over this damned imp business. How could something so small cause so much grief? I thought back to my twins when they were in their terrible twos and in the thick of teething and chewing on anything they could wrap their sticky little fingers around. Okay, let me rephrase that. How could something so small be so hard to catch?

I pondered that problem throughout the morning while sitting at my desk at Calamity Jane Realty. Mona and Ben went on with their usual daily activities—Mona typing up a storm in between talking to old clients, current clients, and potential clients on the phone; Ben researching prices, printing MLS listings in preparation for some appointments next week, and just being a nice guy in general.

Jerry showed up midway through the morning, handing out digital, light-up nametags in the shape of stars for each of us and told us to wear them to the premiere party.

Mona beat me to the punch on asking, "For God's sake, why?"

To which Jerry let out a booming, Thor-like laugh. "You're the best, Red." Then he sat at the desk next to her and made a phone call. And then another. And another.

At eleven-thirty, I shut down my computer and grabbed my purse. I told everyone I'd see them at the party tomorrow evening since Jerry was closing the office for the rest of today and all of tomorrow, and then I left out the back door.

Doc was waiting for me in the parking lot behind the wheel of my SUV with the engine running. I slid into the passenger seat, tossing my purse in back, and then leaned over for a quick kiss. "You smell good." Judging by his damp hair, I guessed he must have showered again after sparring with the kids. "How was the elbow-striking extravaganza at the Rec Center?"

"Your kids are mini-ninjas. We practiced saving drowning people in the pool afterward. They're getting good at diving."

He pulled me back for a longer kiss, sucking some of the cherry-flavored gloss off my lower lip. "I don't suppose we have time to stop by my place and bounce up and down on my bed while Cooper and Harvey aren't home."

"Sure, if you want to spend this evening plucking lead pellets out of each other's backsides." I buckled my seat belt. "You and I both know that Cooper will hunt us down and shoot us if we make him wait at the taxidermy shop."

Doc shook his head and shifted into gear. "And here I thought Natalie would take some of the bite out of his bark."

"She's only human, you know."

My cell phone started ringing. "It's probably Cooper wondering why we weren't there ten minutes ago," I said as I fished it out. I looked down at the phone and for the second time today Zelda's name showed on the screen. "Shit, I forgot to call her back."

"Who?"

"Prudence." I held up my phone. "She's going to be doubly pissed now." I stared down at Zelda's name, weighing the pros and cons of taking the call.

"Are you going to answer it?"

"No." I cringed and sent it to voicemail, setting the phone in one of the cup holders. "I'm busy right now. She needs to wait until I can fit 'Get my ass flogged by a dead *Scharfrichter*' into my schedule."

"Which will be when?"

I shrugged. "After I've had a couple of drinks is probably best." I frowned as he turned left out of the parking lot, heading toward Lead instead of Central City, where Jones' Taxidermy was located. "Where are we going?"

"We need to swing by Gold Diggers Automotive Repair up in Lead."

I'd passed by that garage many times, but hadn't needed to pay for their services yet, thankfully.

"Why? Do you need something for the Picklemobile?" Doc had worked for a mechanic years ago when he was still in college. He'd fixed up Harvey's old pickup after he'd borrowed her for the winter so he could store his '69 Camaro SS. Now the Picklemobile ran like she was new again, skipping the exhaust backfires that used to announce her presence with an embarrassing *BOOM*.

"No. I want to take a look at the damage the imp inflicted on that police car Coop was talking about this morning."

I made a face, not sure I wanted to see the destruction that my imp-related negligence had caused. I was sure some guilt would follow, and then more stress, ending with a slight feeling of job incompetence. A visit to Prudence somewhere in that mix would only add to my self-inflicted demise.

Doc leaned his elbow on the center console, kicking back behind the wheel. "How was work?"

"A breeze, mostly. Jerry is pretty jazzed about the party tomorrow night. He thinks it's going to be a huge boost for Calamity Jane Realty's bottom line."

"Not to mention Ben's and your client lists." He glanced my way, his forehead lined. "We're going to have to do something about your face and hair."

We were? Why?

I flipped down the visor and did a mirror check. Sure, I looked a little rough around the edges, and the twisted chignon updo I'd tucked my hair into was slightly messy, but at least I'd added a touch of mascara before leaving work. "What's wrong with my face and hair?" I flipped the visor back up. "We're just going to see a bunch of long-dead animals, right?"

"I meant when it comes to you at work." He caught my hand and married his fingers with mine, settling his elbow back on the console again. "Now that you're a TV star, you're going to have guys swooping in left and right, trying to steal your heart."

I guffawed. "I don't think so. I'm Violet 'Spooky' Parker, remember? It'll be more like a bunch of angry men *and* women storming Aunt Zoe's house with pitchforks and torches. Detective Hawke will undoubtedly be leading the charge."

"Nah. You'll have them eating out of your palm in no time with your natural charisma." He lifted my knuckles to his lips for a kiss. "How do you feel about wearing one of those long-nosed, bird-beak masks that doctors wore during the black plague in Europe?"

We passed the cutoff for US Route 385 and started winding up into Lead.

"That won't hide my hair."

"We could tuck it into a top hat."

"That's a lot of tucking into a small hat."

"How about hiding it under one of those wide-brimmed straw hats that were popular in the 1960s and 1970s?"

"You mean a floppy-brimmed hippie hat?" My mom, the flower child, had several in her closet that I could borrow.

"Yeah. With a daisy pinned to it."

"Sure. And while I'm at it, I could pair it with a tube top and low-rise bell bottoms."

"Exactly."

"That's quite a picture you're painting."

Doc glanced down at my chest. "I'd like to see you in a tube top."

No, he wouldn't. After nursing twins for a year, a tube top rode low on me, sort of like a hula hoop. "I think your rose-colored glasses might need an updated prescription."

"You underestimate the lure of your curls and curves when it comes to the male sex."

My cell phone rang again. I checked it. Speak of the devil. "Crap."

"Prudence again?"

"Almost as bad. It's my mom." I accepted the call, putting it on speakerphone. Maybe if she knew Doc was listening, she wouldn't talk about sex with my dad or my catalogue of past dating mistakes. "Hello, Mother."

"Violet Lynn, where are you?"

I frowned at the tension in her voice. "Doc and I are driving up to Lead, why?"

"Are you behind the wheel?"

"No, Doc is."

"Good. Am I on speakerphone?"

"We're listening to you on the stereo speakers, so yes."

"Hello, Hope," Doc said, slowing for a pickup turning up the hill opposite Gold Run Park.

"Oh, Doc." Mom sighed in happiness at the sound of his voice. "I'm so glad you're still in the picture. Have I told you that lately?"

"Yes, you have, Hope," Doc said, his eyes creased with laughter. "Just the other night, as a matter of fact, when you called to talk to the kids and I answered the phone, remember? You even offered to pay me monthly installments to stay with your daughter if I ever felt like leaving her."

What the hell? "Thanks for that vote of confidence, Mom."

"I was kidding around, Violet Lynn. Mellow out. Don't be such a downer." My mother, Hope the hippie, laughed. Actually, it sounded more like a titter. A drunken titter. At noon on a Saturday?

Once again, *what the hell?*

Doc and I traded worried glances.

"What's going on, Mom?"

"Well … I might have a little bad news for you."

My chest tightened. "Is Dad okay?"

"Your father is fine." Her voice lowered. "And by 'fine,' I mean hot-to-trot and rarin' to go lately, in and out of the bedroom. He's been doing these breathing exercises to increase the circulation in his p—"

"Mom!" I covered my eyes and did a whole body cringe, pressing back into the seat to get as far away from her voice as possible, dreading what might come next through the speakers. "Please! I told you no more talk about your and Dad's sex life within earshot."

Or around Doc, for that matter. I was relatively certain that my boyfriend did not want to think about my parents having wild monkey sex the next time they stopped over for dinner and drinks.

"Oh, get off of it, Violet Lynn," my mom chastised. "You need to chill, baby. And get your mind out of the gutter while you're at it. I was going to say increase the circulation in his *pulmonary blood flow*."

I lowered my hand from my eyes. "Sorry, Mom."

Hold on. Breathing exercises? That rang a bell. "Hey, where did Dad learn about these breathing exercises?"

"Corny told him about them when they went to lunch last week."

Corny? I leaned forward, gaping at the phone screen. "Since when have Dad and my friend become lunch buddies?"

"Violet, Violet, Violet." In my mind's eye I could see her shaking her head. "This world really doesn't revolve around you, dear." She feigned boredom, as if she'd given me this talk once a week for the last thirty-five years.

I shook my fist at the phone.

Doc laughed into his elbow to muffle the sound.

I took a deep breath of my own, trying to find my way back to "fine" and "hot to trot" and "raring to go" in the process.

"Mother, what was the reason you called?"

"Yes, about that …" she trailed off.

About what? I opened my mouth to pester her, but Doc held out his index finger. I scowled and crossed my arms, tapping my foot as I waited for her to get around to finishing her thought.

"Your sister called this morning," she finally said.

I stopped breathing entirely as I waited for the other shoe to drop … right on my head, same as always.

"She's hit a small snag in trying to fix the tiny mess she made."

I looked to the heavens, drawing on the power of the great and powerful Zeus to keep my anger in check and stop me from throwing lightning bolts at the Bitch from Hell, wherever she was.

I cleared my throat. "Are you referring to Susan stealing my identity and using it to illegally marry a sugar daddy older than Julius-frickin'-Caesar? You mean *that* tiny mess?"

"Yeah, that's it," she said, basically blowing off my outburst. "Anyhoo, it turns out that your old man has a nephew."

My jaw clenched. "He's not my 'old man,' Mother, and he never will be!" Lately, whenever I talked to her, she'd been having too much fun with "me" being married to a guy old enough to be *her* father.

"Susan said that his nephew is quite displeased that you are in his uncle's will instead of him."

Doc reached over and squeezed my shoulder as he steered through downtown Lead.

"Did Susan explain to this nephew that there was a mix-up and she is trying to fix it?"

"Well, not exactly."

"What exactly did she say?"

"Doc, you might want to cover your ears," my mother said in a conspiratorial tone.

"Mom," I started in a high, strangled voice and then paused. *Breathe.* "What did Susan say?"

"Nothing. Your sister said nothing."

"Okay, so then the problem is just the small matter of a lack of communication."

"Sort of." Mom sighed. "It's also a small matter of sex."

"You've got to be fucking kidding me."

"Language, dear," said the kettle who taught me most of the swear words I knew—well, Mom was in line after teacher Natalie, of course. Oh, and my neighbor, Claire Morgan.

"Don't tell me Susan slept with this 'displeased' nephew."

"Of course not. Violet Lynn, you have such a jaded opinion of your sister."

A sharp, edgy laugh of disbelief flew from my lips, making Doc wince. "And I wonder why that is, Mom. After decades of dealing with Susan's dick moves, why on earth would I think badly of Satan's concubine?"

"Pish-posh and bygones," she said, dismissing thirty-plus years of putting up with my evil sister just like that. "And your father has talked to you about calling her names in front of me."

Technically, my mother was on the phone, not physically in front of me, but I didn't quibble. "Explain this small matter of sex."

"It seems that Susan wasn't the only woman your old man had married. It turns out he has another wife from a previous marriage he forgot to divorce."

"Wow. Just wow." What a piece of shit my sister used my name and Social Security number to marry.

"And a child, too."

"What? Susan told me he had no kids."

"He lied."

Doc turned, heading up past the high school.

"If he was still married when Susan and he exchanged vows, then her—I mean *my*—wedding is null and void, right?"

"Yes," Doc and my mom said in tandem.

I sank back into my seat, relief making me almost dizzy.

"But the official will is still legal and binding," Mom continued. "According to Susan, he mentioned you by name in it, but not as 'his wife.' "

I frowned over at Doc, who was shaking his head while white-knuckling the steering wheel.

"What's that mean?" I asked.

"It means you're still stinking rich," Mom answered flippantly. "And now your old man's only child *and* nephew are having dying duck fits."

Chapter Twenty

*D*ying duck fits ...
Well, apparently, irritable fowl syndrome was contagious, because after hanging up with my mother, I spent several minutes coughing out curses about my sister's shenanigans while we sat parked outside of Gold Diggers' garage.

Doc held my hand while I steamed up the windows. When I ran out of gas, we strolled over to the Lead police car that was parked off to the side of the lot. The vehicle looked like it had been driven through a steel-brush car wash, with deep scratches in the metal at imp-height all along each side and across the back bumper. One of the tires was missing a big, bite-sized chunk of rubber, too. A peek at the undercarriage made me cringe. The vehicle had been partially disemboweled. Smashed, scratched—even shredded—metal pieces and parts that Doc pointed out by name dangled, dragging on the ground.

Crikey! If the imp was capable of inflicting that kind of damage on a car, I was beginning to understand why Dominick was more than a little concerned about me not making the bugger a top priority on my to-be-caught-and-executed list.

On our way to Jones' Taxidermy, Doc and I grabbed a couple of turkey sandwiches at the Piggly Wiggly grocery store. We were working on the last few bites when we pulled in the shop's drive.

"Look," I said, pointing at the red dually pickup sitting near the front door. "Reid's here."

Doc parked next to it. "Coop must have caught a ride with him."

The only other vehicle around was a white Ram truck with an enclosed trailer hitched to it near the shop's back door. "That must be Garth's truck, then." I pointed at it and popped the last of my sandwich in my mouth, licking a dollop of mayonnaise from my thumb.

Doc nodded. "He mentioned something the other night about needing to take a finished stag and a few other pieces over to a hunting lodge in Wyoming." He handed me a napkin from the grocery sack. "I wonder if he needs some help loading that up today."

The shop's front door opened and Cooper strode out. I knew better than to think he was being a gentleman when he yanked open my door, letting the cold inside. "Parker, you're late."

"So is he," I said, thumbing at Doc. "Bark at him."

"I can't. He's letting me sleep under his roof." Cooper helped me out of the vehicle, holding my arm to keep me steady. "Watch out, it's icy here."

I frowned up at him. "Who are you and what have you done with the real Cooper?"

Doc joined us in front of my SUV. "Natalie spent the night with him again," he reminded me, burying his hands in the pockets of his leather coat.

"Ohhhh." I snickered and elbowed Cooper like we were old chums. "Are you singing happy songs in the shower these days?"

"Shut up, Parker." He scowled at Doc. "And you—don't encourage her." He scanned the hillside behind us, adding in a lowered voice, "Now let's get this walkthrough done before Hawke catches wind that I have you two up here again and pitches a fit."

I grinned. "Like a dying duck."

His gaze locked on me. "What's that supposed to mean?"

"Don't ask," Doc told him. "We stopped and checked out the car at Gold Diggers' garage on the way here. That's why we're running late."

"What do you think?" Cooper looked to me for an answer. "That has to be your imp, right?"

"I think it needs more mead." I'd said the same thing to Doc as we'd driven away from the garage. "And it's not *my* imp."

What was it lately with everyone using the possessive pronoun when it came to bullshit in which I had zero fault? All right, so maybe I had a *teeny* bit of fault when it came to the imp, but I wasn't the one who let it out of its cage.

Cooper scanned the hillside again. "I don't suppose the little bastard left behind any clues that we can use to find it."

Since I was one of the few people around that could see the imp thanks to my Executioner DNA, Cooper had to rely on me to be his eyes on imp-related crimes.

I started to shake my head, but then shrugged instead.

One blond eyebrow lifted. "What's that mean?"

"It left something behind for your Johnny Law pals, but it's not really a clue."

"What was it?"

I tried to hold in my grin, but it seeped out at the corners of my mouth. "A pile of imp crap on the hood."

He leaned back on his heels. "Are you fucking kidding?"

"Yeah, I am. I couldn't see anything more than you could today."

He pulled his coat back and showed me a pair of handcuffs secured to his belt. "Don't push your luck, Parker."

I snorted at his threat. With my best friend keeping Cooper company between the sheets, I had an almost unlimited supply of get-out-of-jail-free passes now. "I'd like to know what the driver of that car did to piss the imp off, though," I told him and Doc.

"You think it had motivation to vandalize?" Doc asked.

"I hope it did, because if that was just a random act of violence, we could have some serious problems heading our way until I can figure out how to catch the slippery hellion."

"Christ, Parker." Cooper huffed out a steam of breath in the cold air. "What's next? Flying monkeys?"

A shrill cackle escaped from my throat before I could lasso it in, scaring a pair of woodpeckers from a nearby tree. "Probably, and my sister would be leading the troupe."

Followed by an irate nephew and my "old man's" kid.

Cooper scowled at Doc. "What's up with her?"

Doc put his arm around my shoulders, pulling me into his side. "She talked to her mom on the way here."

"Are Blake and Hope okay?"

Cooper's familiarity with my parents earned him a hard glare. "Has my mom been calling you?"

"No, but she's sent me a few texts since I got back from Arizona."

Dear Lord. My mother spent one Christmas with my cohorts and now she was practically making friendship bracelets for them.

"They're fine," Doc told him. "But Violet's sister checked in recently. There's a slight problem with cleaning up the mess she made down in the Caribbean."

"There usually is when illegal acts are involved." Cooper crossed his arms, taking the wide-legged cop stance that came as naturally as breathing for him. "What's the deal, Parker? Are you going to be extradited to some tropical island? That would certainly save me a shitload of headaches, especially if this *other* trouble of yours followed you south."

"I've got your shitload of headaches right here." I held up my fist under his crooked nose.

Doc grabbed my hand and pulled it into his coat pocket, warming it with his. "The wedding didn't take," he told Cooper, and then made quick work of explaining my current location stuck way upstream on the left bank of Shit Creek.

"It could be worse," Cooper said, leading the way to the front door a couple of minutes later.

"How's that?" I asked, dreading his answer. Being a detective, he probably knew more about what was legal and what wasn't in this situation.

He shrugged. "Honestly, I don't have a fucking clue. But Nat says I have to be less hostile toward you, so I was trying to find something good to say."

"Seriously? That's your version of cheerleading?"

"Yep. The next time you talk to Nat, make sure you tell her that I was trying to be nice, but you kept threatening bodily harm." He opened the door and ushered us inside.

Jones' Taxidermy still smelled the same as it had the other night—musty with a dose of chemicals. I looked around at the stuffed animals. They weren't so spooky in the daytime with the bright lights on overhead. Someone must have fixed the power.

Several of the pieces that had been bitten were missing, except for Dorothy the camel. She just had a towel draped over her injury.

Reid was leaning against the counter next to the cash register. His thick canvas coat was unbuttoned and his stocking cap pushed back off his forehead.

"Hey, Sparky," he said when he saw me, holding his hand out. "I have a present for you."

I joined him at the counter, taking what he offered. It was a glass eye.

"Boy, you sure know how to make a girl feel special." I held the smooth, domed glass up to the center of my forehead and closed my eyes, speaking in a witchy voice. "Magic eye, don't make me plead. Tell me how last night's date went for Reid."

Reid laughed. "That was pretty clever."

"You should hear her make up nut-shrinking spells on the fly," Doc said from behind me.

Cooper grunted from somewhere nearby. "Or not, especially if Hawke is around." The floor creaked off to my side. "Hey, Nyce. Come check out how sharp the tusks are on this javelina."

"Did you run into one of those down in Arizona?" I heard Doc ask as he moved away from me.

"Well, Fire Captain Martin," I said, opening my peepers. "Let me hear it. Tell me how you think supper went with my aunt." I set the glass eye down on the counter. I didn't need any souvenirs from this place. My memories would be plenty.

"Zo was a wonderful host." He scratched absently at his jaw. "Ox loved her cooking and she had him laughing quite a bit. She took him out to her workshop and showed him some of her pieces, even offered one to him." While his words were all about good vibrations, the tension lines crisscrossing his forehead foretold a not-so-happy ending.

"I heard my kids terrorized him sufficiently."

A smile chased the tension lines away. "Addy and Layne were wonderful. They made Ox feel at home right from the beginning, dragging him by the hand down to meet Elvis."

So, if Aunt Zoe were to ever marry Reid, that would make Ox my step-cousin, wouldn't it? "Doc and I need to meet your son. How soon until he heads back to wherever he came from?"

"He's heading south in a few days, but he'll be moving here for good in a couple of weeks. That's why I wanted him to meet Zo. To break the ice, you know."

Oh, some ice was broken all right. Leaving a big hole to dump Reid into the bottomless lake below.

"Sure. Of course." I hid my squeamish concern about Aunt Zoe's reaction to last night's ending by picking up and pretending to study the glass eye in my hand. "What kind of eye is this supposed to be? A cat's?"

Garth Jones walked out from the back hallway, interrupting us. He was wearing a leather apron that reached clear to his knees and a face shield flipped up. His fat, old bull terrier, Beau, waddled along behind him.

I'd never been so glad to see a taxidermist in my life.

He zipped behind the counter and took a seat on the stool next to the register. Beau just dropped on the floor at the end of the counter, his tongue flopping out, as if he could go no farther at the moment.

"Hey, Martin." Garth leaned on the counter. "I haven't seen you since last month's fire extinguisher checkup. How's that old snowcat treating you?"

"We've had some fun playing in the snow in that girl, haven't we, Sparky?"

I thought back on the trip down to my parents on Christmas Eve. Reid had come to the rescue in the midst of a blizzard, carting a snowcat load of us down out of the hills into Rapid City. "It's a burly baby." I patted Reid's shoulder. "Not even a blizzard could slow it down."

"Why do Reid and Willis Harvey call you 'Sparky'?" Garth asked me.

Reid chuckled. "Because for a while there, wherever there was a spark around town, there was usually a 'Parker,' too. The nickname 'Sparky Parker' was born down at the station and spread from there."

302 ANN CHARLES

I looked at Garth. "I only had a hand in one of the fires, though. And that was an accident." I hadn't meant to knock over the candle in a room filled with mummified little girls coated in lighter fluid. The memory of that flame-filled house of terror still made me shudder.

"Hello, Mr. Jones," Doc said, joining us. He held out his hand for a shake. "Thanks for letting us stop by for another look around in the daylight."

"My pleasure." Garth pumped his hand a couple of times. "I'm a little worried about that long-legged critter coming back around while I'm in Wyoming."

Cooper joined us at the counter. "We'll take good care of the place while you're gone, Jonesy. I already talked to a couple of officers scheduled to work tomorrow night. They're going to come by every hour to check your locks and shine a light in the windows. You know, the usual patrol business."

Garth's relief shone on his face. "Thanks, Detective. And tell your crew that I truly appreciate their diligence."

Cooper glanced at Doc before replying. "Will do. I'll even check in once or twice myself and make sure everything is locked up tight."

"Thanks. I'd hate to have that son of a bitch return and do more damage to poor Dorothy." His gaze fell on me and he cringed. "Sorry about the language, Ms. Sparky."

I waved him off. "Tell me, have you had any other trouble with trespassers or weird sounds out in the trees since Wednesday night? Anything that set off Beau?"

We all looked over at the bull terrier now snoring on the floor. Beau's feet twitched several times, probably chasing a *Nachzehrer* in his sleep. I wish I only had to chase them in my dreams.

"Well," Garth said, scratching behind his ear, "I thought I heard some ruckus going on out here last night while I was putting the finishing touches on that stag in my workroom, but it turned out to be a pair of raccoons trying to get into my garbage cans for a late-night snack."

"You want some help loading that stag into the trailer?" Doc asked.

Garth's face lit up. "By golly, I'd love to have some extra muscle. I put my back out a few months ago and it still twinges somethin' fierce when I lift the heavier pieces around here."

"Coop and I will help you get everything loaded before we leave," Doc said, looking at Cooper, who nodded.

"In the meantime," Cooper said, pulling a small notepad from his coat pocket. Ugh, I knew that pad well, along with the Deadwood Police Department's obsession with clicking pens. "We'll sniff around out here to see if we can figure out a motive for the B&E."

"Sounds good," Garth said. "You guys feel free to touch anything in here. Just be careful around ol' Dorothy. She's not as tough as she used to be."

I looked around at the different animals frozen in attack poses. "Okay. Sure." I tried not to let my grimace come to the surface.

Garth started to walk away, but then turned back. "Martin, when you're ready, come take a look at the work the electrician did on my breaker box so you can check it off on your inspection sheet."

Reid nodded. "I'll be there in two shakes."

After Garth left the room, we spread out under Cooper's direction, each of us looking for something that might give us a clue as to why that *Nachzehrer* would have come to the taxidermy shop in the first place. The bites out of the stuffed critters were self-explanatory in my opinion after seeing the sharp set of teeth on those ugly bastards. This place was basically a big room full of chew toys.

I checked my cell phone to make sure I had no calls from work or home. I didn't, so I stuffed the phone back in my coat pocket and moved over to an open display case near the door. A fox sat on a lower shelf, stuck for all of eternity in head-lowered pose. I slowly reached toward it, curious if the fur on the tail was really as soft as it looked. The glass eyes looked so real, as if it would start snapping its jaws at me any minute now.

"Hey, Parker." Cooper had prowled up behind me.

I stepped back in surprise, coming down on his foot.

"Christ!" He bumped me aside, making a pained face. "What is wrong with you?"

"Me? You're the one sneaking up on me in a room full of creepy dead animals. Didn't you learn your lesson last fall in Mudder Brothers' basement?"

His sneaking up behind me that night had resulted in the notorious nose-breaking headbutt.

He glared at me. "I came over here to show you this." He held out a small, square wooden case with a brass hook latch.

I took it from him, inspecting the box. It looked like some kind of … *Just open it.*

With a flick of the brass hook, the lid flipped open.

It was a compass. And an old one, judging from the fogged glass and what appeared to be a hand-painted compass rose underneath. "Where did you find this?"

"It was on the shelf next to the peregrine falcon over in the corner."

I looked in the direction he indicated, spying the bird, frozen in mid-dive. I'd give Garth this—he was very good at modeling the animals in authentic poses.

"I think it's mahogany," he said, touching the wooden lid. "But look at the markings under the glass." He took out his flashlight and aimed the light on the compass face.

I read clockwise: *Norden, Osten, Süden, Westen.*

"That's German," Cooper said, shutting off the light.

He took the compass from me and flipped it over. There was a word carved into the box surface.

"What's that say?" I asked.

"How should I know?" Cooper said. "I don't speak German."

"But you knew the other words."

"No, I knew *Norden* was German for north from watching documentaries on World War II. Common sense said that being it is a compass, those are cardinal directions." He pointed at the numbers written below the carved word. "That, I believe, is a date."

"1807?"

"I think it's 1801."

"You think this compass was made in 1801?" At his nod, I added, "And maybe this German word is the artist's name?"

"Or the owner's." He shrugged, latching the compass closed. "It's just a guess, but it might be a clue."

I pointed at the small, mahogany case. "I thought we were supposed to look for clues with only our eyes, not our hands." That was what he'd told me down in the basement of that haunted jail last night.

"That's true for you. The rules are different for me."

"Why?"

"Because I've been a detective longer than you've had kids."

I wrinkled my nose. "I like your set of rules better."

"Too bad, Parker. You need to put in more time before you can get your detective badge."

"So, Mr. Super-Sleuth Detective, why might Garth have an early ninetcenth-century German compass sitting on a shelf next to a dead bird? Could it just be a collector's item?"

"Sure, but why would he leave it out on that shelf?"

"He might have misplaced it." I looked around the crowded room. "It would be easy to lose something in a room this distracting."

"That's true. But maybe somebody else left it here by accident and came looking for it Wednesday night."

My jaw fell. "You think a *Nachzehrer* has the brainpower to use a compass?"

"We don't know that the *Nachzehrer* was alone. It might have been used as a distraction, keeping Jonesy busy while someone else took a look around the place."

That was a good point. I needed to broaden my focus if I was going to keep playing cat and mouse with these assholes.

He shrugged. "Or maybe somebody found it in one of the mines around here and Jonesy bought it off of him, leaving it to sit on that shelf for the time being."

"Maybe one of the German miners who came to the Black Hills back during the gold rush days lost it."

"Or that."

I lowered my voice to a whisper, "And maybe that ghost you saw outside is that very miner looking for his compass."

Half of his face scrunched. "Now you're reaching."

"Have you seen the ghost today?"

He shook his head. I couldn't tell if he was happy about the lack of a ghost or not.

I pointed back at the compass. "So, you really think that could be a clue?"

"I think it's worth remembering." He walked away.

A few minutes later, I joined Doc in front of a glass case full of bleached skulls. "You find anything interesting?"

He pointed at one of the midsized skulls with an elongated snout. "Look at the sharp teeth on that one."

"What was it?"

"A fox, I think."

That made two of them here.

He put his arm around my shoulders, pulling me close for a hug. "Reminds me of you."

"Because I'm a vixen?"

He leaned down and whispered in my ear, "Because you're a biter."

"Yeah, but you like it when I sink my teeth in."

His gaze locked onto my lips. "Yes, I do. Especially in certain spots."

Before I could ask him to clarify the parts on his body where he liked my teeth sunk, Reid joined us.

"I'm going to head on back to the workshop and take a look at Jonesy's breaker box. You think you could help me out, Sparky?"

I opened my mouth to tell him that I didn't know anything about breaker boxes, but then realized he might want to talk to me about my aunt without an audience.

"Sure." I pulled away from Doc.

"Hey, Nyce," Cooper said. "Let's get that stag loaded in the trailer before Martin or I get called back to work."

The four of us headed down the hallway leading back to Garth's workshop with Reid out front. Once there, Cooper and Doc joined Garth next to the large stag I saw the other night. It was three-fourths covered with a tarp, only its head and impressive rack of antlers were sticking out.

While the three of them discussed how to move the deer from the workshop up into the trailer, Reid headed over to the breaker box attached to the wall studs above a built-in countertop and started unscrewing the panel cover.

I joined him, glancing around the room. I was too overwhelmed by all of the taxidermy-based chemicals, glues, books, and other odds and ends covering the shelves; the sharp knives, used rubber gloves, stitching tools, and bits of stuffing spread here and there over several long countertops; and the various poised animals staring at me with their creepy dead eyes to see anything *not* out of the ordinary. Then again, I had been a taxidermy shop virgin prior to this past week.

When my focus returned to Reid, he was checking the wiring to each of the breakers. Then he screwed the cover back on and began studying the paper chart on the inside of the breaker box's metal door. While I tried to read the scrawls written on the chart from several feet away, he flicked a few switches, looking around as he tested each.

"Did Zo say anything about last night?" he asked me quietly when he focused back on the chart.

She had, but only after a little blackmail. However, I didn't want to tell him that. He was probably looking for something heartening from me when it came to his future with my aunt, not the cold, hard truth.

I joined him at the counter, keeping my voice low. "She said your son was very nice and good with my kids."

No lie there.

He flicked another switch back and forth.

I wrung my hands, looking for something to do with them. A wide metal box was secured to the wall. The rust-edged door was pockmarked with small dents and scratches. It opened with a creak, and a dusting of rusty powder floated down to the counter below. Inside was an old-fashioned fuse box with colorful, round fuses that screwed into circle holes. Cobwebs were strung between the sides of the box, especially thick in the corners. I remembered seeing something similar in my grandparents' barn when I was a kid.

Several cloth-covered wires stuck out from the box, but had been cut off. Another pair of wires ran out of the bottom. They trailed south behind the counter and wrapped around two white ceramic knobs nailed into the wall before taking a left through the stud inside of two ceramic tubes.

"Check it out, Reid." I pointed at the old fuse box. "Knob-and-tube wiring. When's the last time you saw that?"

"At an old warehouse down near the rodeo grounds." He studied the paper chart again on the breaker box. "The owner started a fire and blamed it on the old wiring, hoping to get the insurance money. Your aunt helped me figure out the truth behind that case."

Oh, right. I remembered Aunt Zoe telling me Reid had asked her for details about the building, which happened to be where she'd had piano lessons long ago. It was shortly after that when Reid finally broke through the wall she'd put up around her heart for the first time and they became a hot mess of a couple, which seemed fitting for a man who dillied with fire and a woman who dallied with a molten glass furnace. But then he'd balked at any sort of commitment to her, and shit went south from there.

"Reid," I whispered, glancing at Doc, Cooper, and Garth over near the head of the stag to make sure they weren't listening. Based on their body gestures, I figured the three of them were discussing lifting logistics. That or they were preparing to perform a three-man version of "YMCA" by the Village People.

"Yeah?" Reid flicked another switch, leaning out to peer down the hallway toward the front room.

"How come you didn't tell your son that Aunt Zoe and you were in a relationship years ago?"

He slowly turned my way, his eyes big and wide. He reminded me of those tiny primates on that show about the wildlife of Borneo that I'd watched with Addy a couple of weeks ago. What was it? A tarsier! That was it. Then Reid looked away, but his cheeks were ruddier, along with his neck.

"It's complicated, Sparky."

I wasn't buying his snake oil. "Complicated how? Is this about your divorce?"

He flicked another switch. The light overhead shut off. "Yes and no."

I waited for him to continue. When he didn't, I poked him in the shoulder.

He sighed. "You're not going to let this go, are you?

"Nope."

He closed the electrical panel and focused on the old breaker box in front of me. "This old wiring is still in pretty good shape. Knob-and-tube was used mainly between the late 1800s through the 1930s, until electrician labor wages grew greater than the material costs, making this sort of labor-intensive installation too expensive."

"Thanks for the history lesson, Fire Captain Martin, but you're still evading the question."

He unscrewed an old yellow fuse, looked at it and then screwed it back in. "I wonder how long ago this building was switched over to the current setup. I'd guess Garth's grandfather was still around, but you never know in these old places. Some folks kept using knob-and-tube wiring into the 1960s and 1970s, until the electrical load grew too great thanks to all of our fancy new appliances and devices."

'Reid, don't make me pinch you to get an answer."

He pulled a small, cigar-sized flashlight from inside his coat and leaned down to look under the counter. "Ox did know about your aunt back then," he said as we walked along, bent over, chasing the old wire through the ceramic tubes in the exposed wall studs.

"Then why did he act like he didn't?"

He frowned up at me. "Who said he acted that way? Your kids?"

"Think taller."

He scowled. "Zo shouldn't make assumptions." Still following the wire trail, he skirted a shoulder-high bookshelf. The wire continued on the other side near the floor.

"So, you had told Ox *everything*?"

"No. You don't tell your kid the whole truth about a relationship after divorcing his mom." He followed the wire around the back corner of the workshop. "There are some things better left unsaid until people cool down and the dust settles."

I followed Reid, bending low, too, so I could keep my voice quieter. "When did you tell your son about her then?"

He shrugged. "A few months after Zo threw me out of her bed. I was pretty miserable, moping around my apartment and Ox came to visit. I tried to pretend everything was fine. When that didn't work, I told him that I was still a little sad about it not working out with his mom after all of the years we put into our marriage. But he didn't buy that either. He'd been there through the yelling matches and rants." His face lined. "My first marriage was hell, and Ox had been singed during the battles more times than I care to remember."

He dropped onto one knee, shining the flashlight under a table filled with jugs of chemicals. Some clear, others milky. I tried to read the words on the labels, but they might as well be German, like the compass out front.

"So, I told Ox the truth at the time," Reid continued. "That I'd been dating a woman, but it didn't work out and I was feeling down about it."

"And?" I pressed.

"And what?"

"That was all you said about Aunt Zoe?"

He glanced up at me. "I didn't figure there was much else to tell since she'd kicked me out and told me if I showed up on her doorstep again she'd fill my ass full of rock salt."

"Yeah, but, don't you think you should've mentioned to Ox before dinner last night that you were trying to woo that same woman back? Maybe fill him in on some of the important events that had happened in the past with you and her?"

"I did."

"But I thought ..."

He moved several feet forward, shining his light under a heavy-duty steel worktable with rusted cabinet doors in the front. "I told Ox she was an old flame and I hoped to rekindle some heat with her. Same as you said."

I slapped my forehead. "That is *not* the same thing."

"Close enough."

"You've been sniffing too much asbestos."

He scowled up at me. "What was I supposed to tell him?"

"How about the truth so that when Aunt Zoe met him, he'd already know some of the details about your history together." I checked to see if Doc and Cooper and Garth were listening, but they were gone and so was the stag.

"But I did tell him," Reid defended. "Like I said."

I crossed my arms, glaring now on my aunt's behalf. "You didn't even give her a name in your version."

He sat back on his haunches. "So, to be clear, now Zo's pissed that Ox doesn't know how much time I spent in her bed way back when?"

"No, you big firebug, she's pissed that you didn't care about her enough *in the past* to tell your son that she was a part of your life."

He scrubbed his hand down his face. "But I did care. It was just … complicated."

"Yeah, love is. Trust me, I know."

"Where do I go from here with her?"

I sighed. "I don't know. Let me think about it."

He stood and grabbed the corner of the steel worktable, tugging on it. The table scraped along the wood floor an inch or so. He got a better grip and put some weight behind the next pull, along with a solid grunt. This time, it slid forward several inches.

"What are you doing?" I asked as he leaned over the table and shined his light down behind it.

"Wondering something," he said, getting down on his hands and knees again to peer under the cabinet doors.

"Wondering what?" I asked, leaning forward to peer behind the cabinet, too. There was a rusted steel plate back there, about three feet wide by four feet tall, half an inch thick, bolted flush against the wall. There must have been an opening there at one time.

Reid sat up. "Why is there a steel plate bolted to the wall right here where the shop backs into the hillside?"

I got down and peered under the cabinet. The plate appeared to be sunk into the floor. How far did it go down?

"You think someone kept a safe behind there?" I asked.

"Maybe. The wire I was following goes through the wall right next to the steel plate. Can you see it?"

"Yeah."

"That wire doesn't come back out anywhere else."

I sat up on my knees. "So, there was power into the space on the other side."

He nodded. "There still might be. Back before there were refrigerators and freezers, people used root cellars and caves in the hillsides to keep things cool year around. Maybe Garth's grandfather kept dead animals in there when there was a backlog of taxidermy work. With some ice or a snowpack, things might last a week or two without too much decay."

I made a face, imagining a cave full of dead carcasses.

Reid chuckled. "You remind me of Addy eating peas when you make that face." He rose to his feet, offering a hand to help me up. "Do you think I should tell Ox all of the details of my past with Zo now? Come clean with him and then let her know what I told him so she understands that I'm not just looking for a roll in the hay with her?"

I brushed the dust off of my pants, weighing my answer. Aunt Zoe had told me more than once in clear English to keep my nose out of her romantic life, including this morning on my way out the front door of her house. If I were to give Reid advice at this point, I'd be stepping over the line she'd drawn in the sand. Especially taking into account her decision earlier at the breakfast table.

"Well … I think …" I looked up into his sad blue eyes.

My cell phone started ringing in my coat pocket.

Chapter Twenty-One

You rang," I said when Zelda Britton opened the front door of the beautiful, historic, Gothic Revival house in Lead that had been haunted by one particular, extremely persnickety ghost for well over a century.

In my imagination, Prudence the ghost hovered over Zelda's shoulder, glaring out at me. Make that me and Doc, actually, since he was standing on the porch behind me.

"Violet," Zelda said, the warmth in her voice taking the chill out of the air. She wore a daisy-covered apron over a black sweater and yoga pants. Her auburn hair was pulled away from her face by a wide headband made from the same daisy-embellished material as her apron. A sprinkle of white powder dusted one of her rosy cheeks while a friendly smile connected both. "It's so good to see you again."

A stomach-teasing aroma seeped out around her, luring me to step foot into Prudence's lair. Zelda must have been baking some kind of sweet bread before we arrived. Cinnamon buns, I hoped. Although my last experience here with her honeybuns still made my cheeks warm. Things in Zelda's house often had a way of leaving me red-faced.

"Please, come in." She stood aside, leaving room for us to slip by her. "Both of you."

"You remember Doc, my boyfriend," I said, leading the way into the foyer.

"Yes, of course." She smiled up at him. "He's awfully

hard to forget."

My heart and soul both agreed with her. I pulled off my gloves and stuffed them into my pockets. I leaned toward the kitchen and sniffed. Definitely a sweet pastry of some sort. Another sniff. Something with apples, maybe, too. My mouth started watering.

Zelda liked to bake. However, her pint-sized stature and tiny waist made me wonder if she ever ate her own cooking, or if her bear-sized husband, Zeke, enjoyed all of her labors.

"Do you want to take off your coats?" Zelda closed the door behind us. "I just finished drizzling some caramel sauce over my apple dumplings."

Jackpot!

I licked my lips and spared Doc a glance, checking to see if Prudence was inspiring any cold sweats in my Tall Medium. He and the uppity ghost had a history of switching places, and sometimes not voluntarily on his part. To be honest, I hadn't been a fan of him coming in here with me this afternoon, and I'd pretty much begged him to wait in my SUV while I found out what had Prudence pawing at the ground since well before dawn. But in response to my pleading, Doc had just kissed my cheek and told me to get my sweet ass out of the vehicle. Then he'd followed me and my sugary buns up onto the wide front porch, knocking on the door for me when I hesitated.

"Do we have time for an afternoon treat?" I asked him. My fingers were crossed all was well on the ghost front, because I really wanted to give Zelda's dumplings a try.

Doc gave me a slight nod and began unbuttoning his coat. I followed suit, handing my indigo trench coat off for him to hang on the rack next to the door.

We followed Zelda into the living room, where she left us while she went to dish up some plates of apple scrumptiousness. I crossed the plush, cream-colored shag rug that protected the original birch wood floor beneath and pulled aside the sheer window curtains to look out at my SUV.

"Plotting your escape?" Doc asked as he settled into the burgundy leather sofa.

"I think I forgot my cell phone in the car," I told him. I'd left my purse in there, too. Prudence had a way of distracting me so that I practically forgot my name when she was near.

"You want me to go get them?" he offered.

"No. But maybe lock the doors."

"This is Lead, remember?"

"I know, but there's an imp running around out there, not to mention *other* creatures can pick up my scent from far away." I scowled out the window. "If that little bugger can tear up the outside of a car like it did, think of the damage if it got inside."

He pulled my keys from his pants pocket and tossed them to me.

After I used the remote to lock the doors, I pocketed the keys and returned to the sitting area, hesitating at the edge of the coffee table.

He patted the couch cushion next to him. "I promise not to bite."

I thought of the many times Prudence had used someone else to hurt me while I was in this house and opted for the leather chair next to the couch.

"Chicken," he said with a teasing glint in his dark eyes.

"I still think you should have waited in the car."

"Nope."

"I doubt anything much is going to happen. Prudence probably just wants to boss me around a little and chew my ass about how bad I'm doing at my job." I looked around the room, figuring she was eavesdropping. "Isn't that right, Prudence?"

Doc and I waited, listening.

Nothing happened.

I smirked. She was probably being purposely quiet now to make me look even more incompetent.

"As I told you on the way here, Killer, for the next two days I'm not leaving your side."

I laced my fingers together in my lap, happy to hog his attention for so long. "Like Cooper said as we were leaving the taxidermy shop, you're going to get tired of me."

"Coop's just jealous I'm not doting on him. He's a needy guy when he's not barking orders at the other cops."

I laughed.

"That's better." He patted the seat cushion again. "Now come sit by me."

"Not a chance in Hell, Candy Cane." I glanced around the room. "Have you picked up any signs of Prudence's presence yet?"

Doc inhaled slowly, his gaze raking the room. "She's here. I can smell her rose-water scent." His focus returned to me, and then he closed his eyes and took another deep breath. After a moment, he opened his eyes. "She's holding back for some reason. I can sense her energy, but just barely."

"Here we are." Zelda sailed into the room holding a silver serving tray with plates on it along with cups of a steaming, amber liquid and a small mountain of cloth napkins. She lowered the tray onto the coffee table and sat down at the other end of the couch from Doc. Her apron was missing, but the dusting of what was most likely flour still remained on her cheek.

A prickle of unease rippled down my spine, followed by a tightening of my shoulders. Something told me Prudence was about to deliver a blow, but I wasn't sure if I should duck or weave first.

I stared down at the serving tray. There were three cups but four plates. And why so many napkins? Was this about the mess I'd made with the honeybuns? Because that wasn't my fault.

"Is Zeke joining us today?" I pointed at the fourth plate.

"No. He's out of town this weekend, surveying some land over in Wyoming for one of the companies he contracts with fairly often."

So, no Zeke. Maybe the fourth plate was an extra in case Doc wanted seconds. Usually Harvey was with me when I stopped by to put up with Prudence's bullying, and nine times out of ten he was ready for seconds before he'd even finished the first round of whatever lip-smacking dish Zelda offered. The dirty bird was going to be bummed he'd missed out on today's treat.

Zelda handed Doc a cloth napkin and a spoon. Me? All I got from her was a pained smile. "I'm so sorry for calling at such an ungodly hour this morning, Violet, but Prudence insisted. She'd been pacing the attic all night and woke me quite early, insisting that I call you immediately. I told her we should wait, but she could not be deterred."

And I'd made her wait longer yet. Oh, boy. Patience was not one of Prudence's character strengths.

I scanned the room, returning to Doc as he draped the napkin over one of his thighs. His movements were smooth, normal. When he looked my way, his dark brown irises were still front and center—no sign of Prudence looking out at me through white eyes.

So where was the antsy ghost?

Maybe she'd worn herself out with all of that pacing and was up taking a nap. Did ghosts need to rest? According to Cornelius, they were energy based, so I would think they'd need to recharge their battery somehow.

In the past, temporary possession often drained Prudence. But she was constantly working to grow stronger in spite of her ectoplasmic nature. There might come a day when Prudence figured out how to recharge by draining the "possess-ee." Or would that be the "possessed"? I shrugged. All of this parasitic talk made me think of the *Nachzehrer*, which made me feel growly about wasting time here with Prudence when I could be out hunting those long-limbed bastards.

"Here you go, Violet," Zelda said, holding out several napkins toward me.

My face warmed. *The stupid honeybuns mess wasn't my fault!* "Thank you."

"Oh!" Zelda reached in her sweater pocket, retrieving a piece of paper. "And here is the list Prudence wanted me to give to you." With a touch of a cringe, Zelda held out the paper for me to take. "It's why she wanted me to call."

I stared at the paper for a moment before reaching out to take it. Accepting a list from Prudence felt like giving in to her pushiness, an act that I did not want to become habit.

Zelda took one of the plates loaded with a golden brown dumpling coated in caramel sauce and handed it to Doc. Steam rose from the mound of heaven. My tongue danced behind my teeth, curling in delight.

But first, Prudence's list …

I recognized Zelda's writing from when she and Zeke had purchased the very house we were sitting in with my help. Her vowels were extra chubby and her overall cursive was quite flowery, like the daisies she and I both loved. This list had been written while Zelda was in control, so Prudence must have only dictated it to her.

Where in the hell was Prudence? I looked up and searched the room again, ending with Zelda, who had grabbed a dessert plate for herself and was settling back against the sofa. She nibbled on a small spoonful of caramel. If the dead Executioner was whispering in Zelda's ear at this very moment, our hostess certainly wasn't acting like it.

"What's on the paper?" Doc asked as he dug into his dumpling, blowing on the steaming spoonful.

"It's a list," I told him and reached for the plate closest to me. "The first word is 'Imp.' "

As my fingers touched the edge of the dessert plate, it slid a couple of inches away.

I frowned at my hand.

And then down at the plate.

And then at Doc.

He held his spoon in front of his face, his lips frozen mid-blow. His gaze narrowed, bouncing back and forth between me and the plate.

Had I bumped the rim without realizing it? I leaned farther, my fingers extended.

The plate slid away from me again, stopping just out of reach.

Doc lowered his spoon, aiming a raised eyebrow at Zelda. "Prudence has a new game, it appears."

She nodded, swallowing her mouthful. "She's been practicing moving things around the house. This morning, I woke up with my cell phone balanced on my forehead. That's when she insisted I call Violet."

So, I wasn't the only one being badgered by a ghost. Poor Zelda couldn't escape from her.

"Tell Prudence that I have office hours she needs to abide by, just like everyone else." Especially on mornings when Doc wasn't going into work. I didn't get many chances to have him all to myself, thanks to the two often-curious kids down the hall.

I shifted to the front of the chair, reaching for the plate.

Prudence slid it to the other end of the coffee table. It would've fallen off the edge if Zelda hadn't caught it.

Zelda pointed her spoon at me. "Prudence says that you need to read that list before you are allowed to eat."

"You're kidding." I half-laughed as I said it.

"Not at all." Zelda collected another spoonful of apples and pastry. "She's still a bit perturbed at you not answering your phone the second time I called, which was made at a more respectable hour, and insists you read her list and take some time to consider the ramifications of your impertinence."

"That's quite a mouthful," Doc told her.

Zelda chuckled. "So is this." She deposited the spoonful in her mouth and smiled at him through closed lips as she chewed.

"You should get to reading, Killer." A teasing grin hovered on Doc's lips. He pointed his spoon at the pile of apple goodness on his plate. "This is really good."

"Thank you." Zelda licked some caramel sauce off her spoon. "It's my grandmother's recipe. Zeke likes it with ice cream, but I think it overpowers the apples too much."

I huffed at their getting to eat while I was being punished. "Fine. I'll read her damned list."

"Prudence said to curb your profanity, Violet. She finds your vulgarity offensive." Zelda raised her hands in a what-are-you-gonna-do-with-such-a-prissy-ghost gesture.

My hands tightened into fists, crushing her list. "Oh, I'll give Prudence something to feel offended about if she doesn't—"

Something pulled my hair. Hard. Yanking my head back even. "Son of a— Ouch!"

Zelda spooned up another bite of caramelly dumpling. "Prudence! Really now," she chastised. "You don't like it when Violet calls you names, so I don't think you should pick on her in return."

I smoothed my hair, rubbing that spot where the haughty old haint had pulled. "She needs to fight fair," I grumbled. "Being invisible gives her a leg up."

Zelda tipped her head slightly, staring upward. "She says that you would lose in a fair fight with her, even if she had both hands tied behind her back." She sighed and shook her head. "Please just read the list, Violet. I don't like it when you two fight."

I wasn't Prudence's bitch, damn it. But fine! Whatever. I

would read the stupid list, but only because Zelda asked nicely and made me feel guilty for being stubborn. I lifted the paper, cleared my throat, and read aloud:

Imp
Duzarx
Caper-sus
Draug
Fhain-Hai
White Grizzly
Guardian Knave

I lowered the paper. "What is this? Prudence's Christmas wish list?"

Zelda set her empty plate on the coffee table. "She says it's an adversary list." She licked her spoon clean and placed it on her plate. "And that they are written in the order that you should hunt them."

"Oh, really." I let the crinkled paper drift to the floor.

I was getting tired of this shit.

Tired of superior-acting assholes telling me what to do.

Tired of sharp-fanged motherfuckers jumping out from shadows at me.

Tired of being backed into corners and having to come out swinging or risk never seeing another sunrise again.

"Violet," Doc warned, setting down his half-empty plate. "Don't." He picked up the list, scanning the page.

Who in the hell did Prudence think she was? Sure, I wasn't the slickest Executioner, but at least I was out there, and as of this moment I was the *only* Executioner in town. Never mind that I had to try to balance this killing bullshit with a somewhat normal life while attempting to raise two children and keep food on the table.

I stood. "Tell Prudence that she's not the boss of me."

Zelda cringed. "Prudence says that you are being

juvenile."

I walked to the other side of the coffee table, snatching up the plate with *my* dessert, and then returned to my chair.

"Tell Prudence that when I want her opinion, I'll rattle her attic chains." I picked up a spoon and buried it in the no-longer-steaming dumpling. "And please remind her that she is a *dead* Executioner while I'm still living. Therefore, it is up to me who gets axed first, not her."

I scooped out a mound of caramel-coated pastry. As I lifted the spoon to my mouth, the blob of food on the end went flying, splatting on the coffee table.

I glared up at the ceiling. "That's real mature, Prudence."

Doc placed the list on the coffee table. "Violet, why don't you explain to Prudence what you've been dealing with for the last couple of days."

"I will if she lets me eat in peace."

I looked at Zelda, waiting to see if loading up another spoonful would be a waste.

"Prudence says you may make your case."

Make my case? That was rich. So, now she was not only trying to boss me around, but playing judge and jury, too.

Breathe, Doc mouthed.

I tried, but the burning fireball of anger expanding in my chest made it tough to take in a lungful of air. "I've killed two *Nachzehrer* over the same amount of days," I said, stabbing my dumpling repeatedly with my spoon, breaking it into tiny bits. "And we're fairly certain there is at least one more waiting for me out under the trees somewhere." I opted out of telling her about the banshee, who was safely locked away in that jail room for now.

Zelda rested her head against the sofa. "Prudence says that if this is true, there must also be a hunter leading the pack."

"I know. I'm going to have to kill the other *Nachzehrer* and then use some sort of trap to lure and catch the hunter."

After another pause, Zelda turned to me with a lined brow. "She says you are not seeing this clearly. That you do not need a trap. It is very likely that the *Nachzehrer* are being used to lead the hunter to you."

"Like a military probe," Doc said, scowling. "Searching the area and gathering information."

"Yes," Zelda said. "Prudence adds that they are likely studying your ways, testing your strengths, and learning your scent."

They'd certainly locked in on the smell of my blood.

"Prudence wants to know what makes you so certain they are truly *Nachzehrer* and not some other foe."

I relayed the pertinent events over the last few days in quick form, starting with the break-in at the taxidermy shop, mentioning Masterson's assessment and advice, and ending with the two kills I'd already made. I didn't mention that I had help during the executions. That would only give the snooty ghost more ammunition for her next attack on my character.

Zelda laced her fingers together after I'd finished. "Prudence believes you are making a grave mistake in trusting Masterson. She says you seem to be forgetting that he was the keeper of the *lidérc* that would have destroyed you if she hadn't stepped in to help."

Of course she would bring that up and take all of the credit for pulling me out of that mess. "Masterson wasn't behind that attack. He was merely keeping the *lidérc* as a pet. But then one of his enemies freed it, so he hired me to catch it for him."

"She believes you're being naïve. A *lidérc* is not kept as a pet for pleasure. It is a deadly weapon. Masterson likely has plans of releasing the devil on an unsuspecting foe—maybe even you."

"Well, whether or not that is true we will never know."

"Why is that?"

"Because I executed the *lidérc*."

Zelda's eyes widened. "She wants to know how you can be sure it is truly gone? You have made mistakes in the past."

Before I could tell Prudence to kiss my ass, Doc spoke up. "It's gone. I was there when Violet destroyed it."

Zelda looked from Doc to me. "She wants to know what Masterson's reaction was to you executing his pet."

"I don't think he's figured out yet that it's no longer caged in the Sugarloaf Building."

"You killed it behind his back?"

"Yes." I loaded another spoonful of apple dumpling. "I decided keeping it around was too big of a risk based on the threat it posed to my family. So, Doc and I took care of it for good." No need to mention anyone else's roles in this in case something was leaked to Dominick somewhere along the line.

I lifted the spoon toward my mouth, pausing to add, "So, you see, Prudence, I'm not the fuckup that you think I am."

The whole spoon was ripped from my fingers this time. It went flying toward the window, clattering to the floor beyond the shag carpet. Apple and pastry globs splattered across the wooden floor and on to the sheer white curtains.

"Dammit, Prudence!"

Zelda gave me an apologetic frown. "She says she warned you not to use obscenities."

I set the plate on the coffee table. "She needs to dial down her sensitivity meter about a thousand notches." I strode over to the mess. When I bent to grab the spoon, it slid out of my reach.

I stood up and growled at the ceiling. That was it! Game over. I didn't have the patience to put up with Prudence's bullshit any more today.

"Zelda, you'll have to pick that up for me. I'm sorry about the mess." I turned to Doc. "I'll wait for you in the car. If you'd like to stay and visit more with Zelda and that invisible horse's ass who needs a lesson on communication and teamwork, by all means, have at it."

"Violet," he said, standing.

I strode past him, grabbed my coat from the rack, and opened the front door.

Only the door wouldn't actually open, no matter how hard I gripped and tugged on the handle.

I checked the deadbolt. Not locked.

I tried again, but the door still wouldn't budge.

"Open the fucking door, Prudence!" I yelled, levering my foot against the wall while I yanked.

"YOU WILL LISTEN TO ME, *SCHARFRICHTER!*" A voice screeched behind me.

I turned, cursing under my breath, and faced off with the whites of Zelda's eyes. "You will treat me with respect!" I yelled back.

She rushed toward me with Zelda's arms outstretched, fingers grasping. Zelda's body moved all wrong, staggering, lurching, looking like a cast member from *Night of the Living Dead*. But her intent was clear—she was aiming for my throat.

"Prudence! No!" I dodged Zelda's hands, body slamming the smaller woman into the wall next to the door hard enough to rattle the sconces.

Zelda gasped for breath.

"Shit. I'm sorry, Zelda." I pulled back to make sure I hadn't hurt the petite woman.

Zelda snarled and reached for my throat again.

I scrambled backward while knocking her hands away, and stumbled toward the living room to escape. But Zelda snagged my shoulder and yanked me backward with a force that lifted my boots off the floor. I crashed into her, knocking her down, squashing the poor thing under my weight. Before I could roll free of her, Zelda's arm snaked around my neck.

"Prudence! You have to stop!" I rolled to the side, taking Zelda's tiny body with me, struggling to break free, but

Prudence had a death lock on my neck.

"You will do as I say!" she hissed in my ear, squeezing my windpipe with far more strength than Zelda could have. "Or we will all die!"

I wiggled one hand between her arm and my neck, gouging my own skin with my nails, frantic for some breathing room. "For fucksake, you are already dead!" I wheezed and snorted, trying to break her chokehold on me.

"PRUDENCE!" Doc bellowed. His deep, gravelly voice raised the hairs on the back of my neck.

Suddenly, Zelda's arms went limp.

I slipped free and scuttled on all fours over to the door, leaning back against it, trying to catch my breath.

Zelda rolled onto her back, blinking up at the ceiling. "What happened?" she asked in her usual voice. "Why am I on the floor? Did I fall?"

Shittle-me-diddle! Zelda had no memory of what had just happened. How was I going to explain this without freaking her out? Or making her feel guilty for something she had no control over?

I looked around the empty foyer. Where was Doc? I could have sworn he was standing over us when he yelled Prudence's name.

Zelda turned her head my way. "Violet, are you okay?" She tried to sit up, but then groaned and fell flat again.

"I'm fine. I'm great." Although my voice came out raspy and my neck felt like I'd been clotheslined by a steel pipe.

"What happened?"

I struggled to my feet, trying to come up with a lie on the fly, something at which Natalie had always been far better than me. "I was heading out to my car for my cell phone and you came along to help me but we sort of got tangled together and tripped."

There, that should do for now.

Leaning over her, I offered my hand, pulling her upright

slowly, gently. "Are you okay?"

I held onto her, afraid her legs might give out. Prudence had forced Zelda to use superhuman strength. That had to leave a lasting strain on her muscles, didn't it?

"I think so." She looked around, chuckling warily. "My legs feel a little shaky. Maybe I should sit down for a minute."

"Good idea. Let me help you."

I led her out of the foyer, only to pause in the living room at the sight of Doc sitting on the sofa with his head in his hands. He'd been sitting just like that in the jail cell the night before. My heart picked up speed. Surely the banshee hadn't come back.

After guiding Zelda into the burgundy chair, I moved over to Doc. I had a history in this house of being hurt every time I touched someone, so I reached out hesitantly.

He looked at me before I made contact. His face was pale, his breath coming fast. Sweat trickled from his temples.

Something was wrong. Either he was allergic to apple dumplings with caramel sauce, or something had happened to him while I was wrestling with Prudence in the foyer.

"Are you all right?" I sat down next to him, risking a touch to his shoulder. His shirt was damp under my fingers.

"Yes." But his hand trembled as he wiped the sweat from his brow. He frowned down at his palms, then flexed his fingers a few times before letting his hands dangle between his knees. He focused on me, his gaze searching my face and then lower. "Your neck …" he started, then his expression hardened. "She went too far."

I snuck a peek over at Zelda, who was leaning back in the chair with her eyes closed. Her chest moved up and down in slow, smooth intervals. She was either sleeping or in some sort of deep meditation by the looks of it.

"Where's Prudence?" I whispered to Doc.

He pointed upward. "She's taking a break in the attic."

I glanced up and then back at Doc. There was something

different about him. Maybe it was his eyes, which were dark, cold, and flinty. I leaned closer. Or maybe it was something lying in wait behind them. Something threatening. Ominous.

"How do you know she's in the attic?"

"Because I put her there."

Chapter Twenty-Two

"How exactly did you put Prudence in the attic?" Aunt Zoe asked Doc later that evening as the three of us finished cleaning up after a late supper.

The house was mostly quiet tonight. Addy and Layne were in the basement playing fetch with Elvis after giving her a bath. Miracle upon miracle, hanging out with that chicken was one of the few things they could do without fighting these days. With the stereo blasting out the Beach Boys down in the basement, Doc and I could finally talk openly with Aunt Zoe about our day's events.

At the moment, the foyer fracas that had occurred at Zelda's house held center stage.

"Is ghost relocation something you've done before?" Aunt Zoe asked, pouring two cups of tea.

"Not blatantly." Doc dried his hands with a dish towel. "This was a matter of channeling focused energy in the right direction." He made it sound like it was a matter of guiding a firehose, but I doubted it was as straightforward as that.

"I'm still amazed how you got her out of there so fast." I smiled up at my aunt as she placed a cup of tea on the table in front of me. "One minute, Prudence—well, Zelda—had me in a chokehold, and the next minute Zelda's arms went lax and I could breathe again." I snapped my fingers. "Just like that."

"I'll give you the short version of the story." Doc draped

the towel over the faucet to dry. "After Violet stormed out of the living room—"

"I didn't 'storm.' "

One dark eyebrow tipped upward. "Raged?"

I was pretty pissed at the time, but ... "Maybe blustered."

"After Violet 'blustered' toward the foyer, Zelda jolted to her feet and chased after her. But her movements were clearly stilted. I knew right out of the gate that Prudence was at the helm and she was furious. I could feel the turbulent energy roiling from her. Given her history of lashing out, I also knew I had to stop her somehow without hurting Zelda. But Prudence is a force of nature—even as a ghost." His lips quirked at the corners. "She definitely 'storms.' "

"Tell me about it." I gingerly touched my neck, wincing.

Earlier this afternoon, as soon as I'd made it safely home, I'd hidden the telltale strangulation bruises as well as my bloody, self-inflicted fingernail scratches with a scarf so the kids wouldn't ask questions. I didn't like to lie to them, even though some things were for their own good. When Aunt Zoe had come in from her workshop, she'd taken one look at me, walked straight over, and gently pulled the scarf away. After several very unladylike curses that would have twisted Prudence's panties in a wad again, Aunt Zoe had given me a kiss on the forehead and promised to brew some lemon-ginger tea to make my throat feel better.

And the tea had. I took a sip of my third cup of the healing elixir, letting the warm liquid soothe the back of my throat before swallowing. I worried for Zelda. She could probably use someone like my aunt to nurse her after being handled so roughly by not just one, but two Executioners.

Doc leaned against the counter, his gaze fixed on my neck. "I knew I had to deal with Prudence from a mental standpoint," he resumed his tale. "So, I closed my eyes, shut out the screaming match going on in the foyer, and searched the ether—for lack of a better word—looking for Prudence's energy. With emotions flying high, it was easy to find. Mushroom clouds on the horizon are less conspicuous."

I grimaced. "I should have kept my mouth shut and just walked away."

"That would have been one solution," Doc said. "But it was probably time for Prudence to realize she's here to help, not dictate and direct."

"What did you do after finding her in the ether?" Aunt Zoe pressed.

He shrugged. "I yelled her name, trying to distract her from punishing Violet and to break her concentration. It worked, giving me an edge."

Interesting that I, too, had heard his yell as if he were standing over me. I wasn't sure what that meant, but I figured that somehow through contact with Prudence via Zelda (or possibly due to teetering on the edge of slipping away into candleflame land myself), I was able to tune into Doc's broadcast.

"Then I tethered to her," Doc continued, "as we had before, and envisioned the attic where she'd assaulted me last fall, taking her there with me."

"Please tell me Prudence was kicking and screaming the whole way." I really wanted her to suffer some sort of retribution.

"It happened so fast, I think she was shocked that I had that power. So was I, to be honest. As I said before, she's very strong."

"But she was attacking Violet," Aunt Zoe said, nodding. "And you, Oracle, are her protector."

"To the death," he said solemnly. His gaze held mine. There was definitely some serious smoldering going on in those dark brown eyes.

My heart fanned itself, looking around for a fainting couch.

Aunt Zoe stirred her tea. "Then what?"

"After I had Prudence in the attic, clear of Zelda and Violet, I told her she needed to rethink her methods of persuasion. That going forward, violence toward one of her colleagues was unacceptable; and if she didn't change her ways, I was going to lock her in that terror-chamber in Cornelius's head until she could promise to play nice." He gave me a wry grin. "I also let her know that Violet was clearly resistant to her leadership style, so Prudence needed to learn to work *with* her instead of being such a pain in the ass."

I laughed and clapped.

"How did she take your reprimand?" Aunt Zoe asked.

"She tried to shove an antique trunk across the floor, but she didn't have the strength left, so she threw an old shoe at the wall instead." He crossed his arms. "I suspect she's always been a bit of a maverick."

Aunt Zoe gave me a meaningful look. "That's a strong trait in most Executioners, no matter where they hail from."

"I left Prudence then so I could check on Violet and Zelda." His eyes locked onto me. "And that's where you come back into the story."

Which explained why he'd been so pale and sweaty when we returned to the living room. "Thankfully, all Zelda remembers is eating her apple dumpling dessert and then waking up on the floor in the foyer."

Doc shook his head. "She was lucky you had sense enough not to hit back while Prudence was using her. That scene would have taken a much darker turn, otherwise."

I sighed, rubbing my temples. "It's partly my fault. I let Prudence push my buttons, even though I knew better. I should have walked away sooner." And taken my caramel-covered apple dumpling with me, darn it.

After all that had happened, Doc had wanted to get the hell out of there ASAP. We'd made sure Zelda was okay and then let ourselves out before Prudence decided to try to come back for more. In my haste to leave, I missed out on dessert, which was a truly heinous crime.

"I don't know," Doc said. "This has been building for some time now. You and Prudence needed to come to an understanding. If you two can ever figure out how to work as a team, you would be twice as deadly."

"I don't think Prudence is the team player type."

"She might have been trained to be a solo killer. Most Executioners are." Aunt Zoe tapped her fingers on the table. "Or she could just prefer to work alone. But being dead has put a crimp in her style, so now she's having to readjust her way of thinking. Change is never easy, apparently not even for a ghost."

"How was she moving things around without using Zelda?" I asked Doc.

"Was it psychokinesis?" Aunt Zoe lifted her cup of tea. "Or would it be considered a poltergeist situation since she's a ghost?"

"Explain the difference, please." I reached for the cookie jar, telling my aunt off to the side, "You really need to quit baking so many cookies, or my curves will be cloning themselves soon."

"Don't bad-talk your curves, Boots." Doc's smolder was back.

"I'm just keeping you at your fighting weight, kiddo." Aunt Zoe set down her cup and pointed at the cookie jar. "You'll like these. They're lemon chiffon. They'll go well with your tea."

Sweet lemony heaven! I deserved at least two cookies after missing out on the apple dumpling deliciousness.

"You're both conspiring against me." I pulled out a handful of cookies. Aiming a narrowed gaze at Doc, I set one aside for later in case a certain Tall Medium felt like tussling for it in the sheets.

Doc eyed the lone cookie and grinned. "Challenge accepted."

"Back to Prudence's new ability," I prompted and closed up the cookie jar.

"Psychokinesis is the ability to move a physical object with your mind," Doc explained. "It's also called *telekinesis* by some. Or TK."

Ah, yes—TK. Moving things without touching them. Saw it in the movies plenty of times. Understood the concept.

"Typically, with TK, the one doing the moving is still alive." Doc paused, staring toward the dining room for a moment with a wrinkled brow. Then he shook whatever was bothering him off. "Poltergeists are when a ghost is believed to be causing an object to move. Although many theorize now that the poltergeist phenomena is actually caused by strong emotions emanating from a living person, especially one with a high influx of hormones like a teenager. But there's no proof either way." He rubbed the back of his neck, glancing toward the dining room again. "In this instance, I would say it's psychokinesis or TK, even though Prudence is dead. She's not your average ghost."

"No, she's definitely not." I took a bite of cookie. The light lemony goodness harmonized with the tea perfectly.

Knocking on the front door turned us all to stone. The steady, heavy-fisted *boom boom boom* almost gave me chills.

I looked at the clock. It was almost nine—late for visitors.

"I think the Grim Reaper is at the door," I whispered.

"Maybe Cooper," Aunt Zoe suggested.

"Same difference." I crammed the rest of the cookie in my mouth. If I'd learned anything today, it was that I needed to eat dessert first, because there was no telling when a pushy dead bitch could knock it out of my hand.

"Yeah, but Cooper doesn't usually knock these days," Doc said, taking a step toward the dining room.

Aunt Zoe's gaze squeezed into a hard squint. "It better not be Reid, Violet Lynn."

I held up my hands. "I'm innocent."

At least I was tonight.

"I'll go see." Doc grabbed the meat cleaver from the knife block. "Something's out there and it's not human. At the risk of sounding like a low-budget sci-fi movie, I sense something … dangerous, but intriguing."

I rose with him, my fingers now tingling. "I think I need to go with you."

Aunt Zoe stood as well. She rubbed her arms. "I feel it, too." She strode to the back door, locking it.

The tingling spread over my palms and up to my wrist. "Watch the kids," I told her and followed after Doc.

He waited for me by the front door. "I tried to look out the window. It's too dark out there to see anyone."

"What about the porch light?"

"It's not working at the moment."

"Shit." I grabbed the baseball bat from the hall closet. Aunt Zoe kept it there just in case Reid showed up and she couldn't find her shotgun. "I wish I had an ax," I told Doc when I rejoined him. "If there's a *Nachzehrer* waiting on the other side of this door …"

"You get the first swing," Doc finished. "Ready, Killer?"

I gripped the bat and nodded as the knocking sounded again. *Boom. Boom. Bo—*

Doc opened the door.

A tall, pale-faced juggernaut with a shock of white hair stood in the shadows, his fist frozen in mid-knock.

"Good evening, *Scharfrichter*," Mr. Black said, lowering his fist. His gaze dipped to the bat and then the cleaver in Doc's hand. "I hope you don't plan to use those on my account."

I lowered the bat. "Can't be too careful these days." I waved my arm toward the dining room. "Do you want to come in, or should we step out there?"

"The former would be preferable, considering the circumstances."

What circumstances? Did he mean the cold air outside on the porch, which was now blowing in around our legs? Or did this have something to do with the *Nachzehrer* probes searching for me in the dark?

Doc held the door wide for him.

Mr. Black brushed the snow off the sleeves of his long coat and then entered. He scanned the room in silence for several seconds after Doc had closed the door, his nostrils flaring noticeably as he sniffed for who knew what. Maybe he was hungry and wanted some of the coconut-chicken curry stew Doc had made for supper. I'd practically licked the bowl when I was finished.

His gaze came back to me. His pupils morphed into snake-like slits for a blink or two as he inhaled again, then returned to a more normal shape.

"Did you bring me another clock to monitor?" I asked, breaking the silence. He'd left more than one "ticking time bomb" on the porch before, which always ended up getting me in trouble with Cooper.

"No."

"A weapon, then?" Like my war hammer, which I'd lost while hunting the *lidérc*, then found buried in the chest of an overzealous monster—this one human.

"You lose the weapons I bring," he said with the faintest of smiles.

"Not on purpose."

"Tonight, I have brought you something far more valued than any weapon or warning." He looked pointedly at my bat. "Do you mind? A *Scharfrichter* is frightening enough without a weapon in her hand."

"Sorry." I set the bat on the dining room table.

"And what would that *something* be, Mr. Black?" Aunt Zoe asked from behind me. She stood under the archway between the dining room and kitchen.

He returned to the front door, drawing it open slowly.

He peered outside into the dark, and then let out a low pulsing whistle.

Yet again, cold air swirled around our ankles.

My neck bristled. I leaned forward, listening for any sound—the crunch of a footfall in the snow, a creaking porch board, a rattling breath.

Silence.

Then I saw something move in the shadows.

My whole body tingled to life, as if I'd stuck my tongue on not one, but two nine-volt batteries simultaneously.

In a blink, a figure rushed through the doorway.

It was a woman.

A tall, willowy woman.

A very pale woman whose long, white-blond hair flowed down over the shoulders of her pearlescent pink coat in gentle curls. The creamy skin covering her cheeks and forehead looked like fresh, untouched snow against the plush, rose-colored velvet collar. The contrast of her dark, delicately arched eyebrows and even darker eyes was startling. Striking. Exotic.

I couldn't stop staring. She reminded me of a younger, softer version of Ms. Wolff. Only, where Ms. Wolff had been cold from her eyes to her touch, this woman's smile wrapped around me like a warm hug on a freezing day. Her charisma practically crackled in the air around her.

Mr. Black closed the door behind her and locked it, leaning against it.

The pale woman's gaze started with Aunt Zoe, lingered on Doc, and then settled on me.

"Violet Parker," she said, her voice as sweet and smooth as pulled taffy. She tugged off her pink leather gloves one finger at a time. "It's a pleasure to finally meet the new *Scharfrichter* in town."

Great googly moogly! How'd she know who I was?

I opened my mouth to say something cool and witty back

to her, but my tongue got in the way and then tripped over itself as I replied, "You ... who ... I don't ... do I ..." I licked my lips and tried again. "Hello," came out this time, only I somehow turned it into three syllables instead of two.

Criminy! It was as if I'd been cast as the bumbling idiot in tonight's production of *Stranger at the Door.*

Her laughter danced through the air around me. I wanted to catch it and laugh with her.

I glanced back at Aunt Zoe. She stared with awe at Mr. Black's visitor, as if peering into a big, beautiful snow globe.

Doc, on the other hand, wasn't nearly so enamored. His gaze was hard, narrowed, darting between her and me.

"Who are you?" he asked, still holding the meat cleaver.

She bowed in his direction. "My name is Hildegard Zuckerman." She turned back to me. "I believe you knew my dear, old friend, Ms. Wolff."

"You're *that* Zuckerman?" I'd heard of her a few times since that unhappy day when Harvey and I had found Ms. Wolff dead in her apartment.

"I believe so." She aimed a chastising look at Mr. Black. "What sordid tales have you told her about me, Ludek?"

Ludek? Was that Mr. Black's first name?

Mr. Black's response was a slight smile and an even slighter shrug.

"He ... he said nothing," I told her. I didn't want to get Mr. Black into any trouble. After all, he'd gone out of his way to help me more than once. "I first heard about you from a friend." Jeff Wymonds, to be exact. "Something about the hard candies you used to make for Oktoberfest."

"Ah, yes. Ms. Wolff and I certainly enjoyed that festival over the years." She tucked her gloves into her coat pockets.

How many years were we talking? The woman didn't look much older than me. Well, me on a good day after getting eight hours of sleep. And not face-buried-in-the-pillow sleep that left me puffed up like a marshmallow.

"I've also been to your store, the Candy Corral," I added. Truth be told, I'd considered taking up residence there in a barrel of chocolate on more than one rotten, stinking day.

Her smile had a wistful air to it. "I've always enjoyed offering sweet delights to weary souls." She looked around the room again, her gaze snagging here and there along the way. "So many protection wards and charms," she said under her breath. Her dark gaze returned to me. "You must feel very safe within these walls."

I did, as a matter of fact, but that was because I'd spent much of my life here, from childhood on up.

To Mr. Black, she said, "It's no wonder I couldn't pick up any signs of her presence in here. It's as if she's hidden within the walls of a stronghold."

"I believe I told you as much," he replied with a raised chin.

She waved him off, focusing back on me. "Are these wards and talismans your doing?"

"No." Aunt Zoe stepped forward. "They are mine." She moved up beside me. "I have sealed the house."

Hildegard tipped her head to the side as she eyed my aunt. "A *magistra.*" She touched her chest. "Amazing! It has not been since my time in the Black Forest that I have come across a *Scharfrichter* and her *magistra* still working together." She shot Mr. Black a sly glance. "You have been wise to keep their secret."

He raised one white eyebrow, but said nothing.

"Why are you here?" Doc asked, his gaze still wary.

Hildegard regarded him for a moment, then took a step closer, sniffing in his direction. Her dark eyes widened. "It's an Oracle, Ludek!" she said in a hushed tone that was filled with reverence.

"I know."

"How could you have withheld this from me?"

Mr. Black shrugged. "You have been busy. And gone.

Besides, I wanted to surprise you."

She took a step closer to Doc, sniffing again in his direction. "You have chosen a *Scharfrichter* as your mate." She squeezed her hands together. "Fascinating! I have not come across such a pairing in all of my years."

Boy howdy, I felt way out of my league here.

Her smile faltered for the first time since entering the house as she continued regarding Doc. "Oh, but this cannot be good." Her voice was solemn.

"What's not good?" I was worried suddenly for no reason. She must be putting out some kind of infectious vibes. Cornelius would probably blame it on her aura and insist that my third eye needed glasses.

"An Oracle and a *Scharfrichter* together in one place."

Doc and I traded somber glances. "Why is that a problem?" he asked.

She frowned at Mr. Black. "You must have realized that this situation is more dire than we'd originally thought."

He gave a single nod.

Of course things were more dire, because a beautiful stranger would never come to my house on a dark, cold Saturday night bearing good news. Why couldn't she have been a damned leprechaun with a rainbow blaring out of her ass?

The thunder of two sets of small feet on the kitchen floor made my heart seize. Crap! *Not now, kids!* I turned just as Addy and Layne ran into the dining room. They skidded to a stop near my side, gaping up at Hildegard Zuckerman.

"Oh my molies!" Addy said, framing her cheeks with her hands. "She's like a snow angel come to life."

"You're not supposed to stare," Layne said, barely moving his lips while openly staring at Hildegard.

I nudged them along, wishing they'd remained hidden in the basement a little longer. "Upstairs now, both of you. Go get ready for bed."

Grumbling about it being a Saturday night and wanting to stay up later, they stomped up the stairs in unison, like tiny elephants on a march.

At the top, my daughter turned, blocking her brother's path. "Umm, Snow Lady, can I have a lock of your hair for good luck?"

Addy must have sensed the same positive vibe that I did flowing from Hildegard. However, wanting a lock of hair sounded a bit creepy, even from a kid.

"Adelynn." I pointed up the stairs at her. "Go brush your teeth now."

Hildegard stared after my two children. Then she turned to me with wonder-filled eyes of her own. "My stars! Another *Scharfrichter* in the making, along with *ein Beschwörer*. This is a very rare treat." She said it as if we'd discovered a cache of diamonds in a hidden cave. "It is no wonder that Ms. Wolff chose to bequeath her timekeeping duties to you."

I blinked a couple of times, finally catching a mental breath. The sight of my children had dragged my feet back down to the ground again. Protecting them came above all else, including this strange woman in our house, her loveliness aside.

"Ms. Zuckerman, why are you here?" I echoed Doc's earlier question, earning a nod from him for asking again.

She laced her long, thin fingers together. "For months now, I've been watching you, waiting to see what would come of your time here. When Ms. Wolff first told me of her plans to make you a Timekeeper, I disagreed with her reasoning. You were a very inexperienced *Scharfrichter*, which makes you more dangerous to those of us here to support you."

"But Ms. Wolff believed in me?" Even back then?

Hildegard shrugged. "I think she believed you wouldn't be able to escape what was sure to befall here. Ms. Wolff, in her wisdom, devised a plan to protect you, so that you could protect us. And now, a *Scharfrichter* is a Timekeeper."

"But I still don't know how to use timekeeping to protect anyone." Including myself.

"Which is something we will come back to shortly."

"So, you're here to see why Ms. Wolff chose me?"

"Not entirely. Ludek has alerted me to a more pressing problem. It seems you have a bounty on your head and it is large, even for a *Scharfrichter.* Alarmingly large. I decided I needed to come here myself and see why the bounty has been set so high. To uncover what or who is drawing these menaces to you in droves."

A large bounty? On *me*? Who put the contract on my head?

"Now I understand," Hildegard continued. "Your daughter is already starting to glow—one of the first signs of an emerging *Scharfrichter.* Can you see it?"

Did she mean like an aura? I shook my head. All I saw when I looked at Addy was my little girl … along with whatever helpless critter she was clutching to her chest while begging me to let her keep it.

"No? Well, trust that I can. Seeing what most can't is what I do best."

Was that some kind of sixth sense? Cornelius would probably have a long-lettered name for it that I'd never remember.

"So, this glow of Addy's," Doc said. "It's drawing the hunters?"

"No. *Der Beschwörer* is the true beacon."

I frowned at Aunt Zoe. "Remind me what that word means again."

"The Summoner."

Right. Layne the Summoner. It certainly had a ring to it. "So you're saying that I'm having extra trouble with these vermin coming out of the woodwork because of my son?" But not Addy?

She nodded. "*Der Beschwörer*, along with the large bounty for your head." She turned to Mr. Black. "I trust you have been watching over the boy."

"Of course."

Knowing Mr. Black was there to help protect Layne was a relief, but … "Has anything come for Layne already?"

"Not yet." His gaze shifted to Aunt Zoe. "He has been shielded by charms, and his power is still awakening."

Okay, so maybe we had some time yet when it came to my kids being in full-on peril. I focused on the snow angel. "So, your purpose in coming here tonight was to meet me and assess the situation?"

In other words, I wasn't in any new extra danger at the moment by yet another creature whose name needed to be added onto Prudence's stupid To-Kill list.

She smiled, once again sending out warm rays of sunshine on a cloudy day. "Actually, I'm here to offer you my services."

"Which are what, exactly?" Doc asked, setting the cleaver on the table next to my bat.

"As I said before, I watch and see what many cannot and do not. I'll make a strong ally, and I have worked with your kind in the past."

I looked her over. "So you're like some sort of spy?" I had to admit, Hildegard in all of her radiance made sexy Mata Hari look like just a coarse Dutch peasant woman.

"I suppose that label works for now." She pulled her pink gloves from her pockets and slid her hands back into them. "But more important, I also believe you need to begin your training as a Timekeeper, so that my dear old friend's life was not given in vain."

She bowed to all of us with princess-like grandeur and then turned toward the door, which Mr. Black held open for her. "I'll be in touch soon," she said over her shoulder, leaving me frowning in her wake.

Chapter Twenty-Three

Sunday Evening, January 20th
Paranormal Realty—Houses of the Dead in Deadwood: Part 1

I frowned at the hideous face staring back at me in the bathroom mirror at Charles' Club. And it truly was hideous, thanks to Aunt Zoe's help adding some latex prosthetic wounds and a little extra makeup to emphasize my actual bruises. We'd left my neck completely makeup-free. After Prudence's handiwork yesterday, along with my scratches, my skin had a natural mottled look that fit right in with the zombie costume Jerry had insisted each of his employees wear to the premiere party.

"Jeez, it's hot," I said to Dead Violet in the mirror, using a damp paper towel to dab at a drop of sweat trailing down from my temple. Zombies weren't supposed to sweat.

There were too many people packed into Charles' Club tonight for the big premiere, turning the swanky lounge into a sauna. I'd escaped to the bathroom to run my hands under cool water—and maybe my feet. But it was even hotter in here thanks to the old-fashioned wall radiator that was working double-time. Apparently, superheating the small, single-stall bathroom was a good way to keep people from parking in here for too long.

Somebody needed to crack a window.

I took it upon myself to be the one, stepping over to the

only window in the room. The digital light-up nametag that Jerry had insisted I wear reflected in the glass like a neon star. I took it off and set it on the sill.

The window's wooden frame looked warped and weathered with paint starting to peel in spots. The radiator ticked away below it, spewing out waves of heat. At this rate, it would have all of Main Street heated up by midnight.

With a grunt or two, I managed to raise the window about six inches. Cold air rushed inside, washing over me. That was a little better. I struggled to raise the window higher, but the old frame was too warped, so I gave up and leaned on the sill next to my nametag while fanning the scoop neck of my black party dress. Maybe I should take off the cashmere leggings I was wearing for the remainder of the party. I doubted anyone besides Doc would notice, since Jerry had insisted the lights be kept low for easier big-screen viewing.

I stuck my arms out the window, enjoying the cold winter breeze. What I wouldn't do to be home with my kids instead of stuck here for another hour or two. The first of the three *Paranormal Realty* episodes would be starting in a few minutes, and I felt like vomiting all over the plush gold-swirled carpet thanks to my frazzled nerves. Something told me that this show wasn't going to be the boon to my career that Jerry thought it would.

If only killing troublemakers paid the bills.

I leaned closer to the window, careful not to touch the sizzling radiator while trying to get more cold air down the front of my dress. Maybe I should dump some ice in my bra after the show started.

I fanned my dress some more, thinking about Hildegard Zuckerman. Aunt Zoe, Doc, and I had stayed up talking quietly in the kitchen about her and Mr. Black long after they'd left. We had so many questions for her. So many questions *about* her. About me. About Doc. About my kids.

About Ms. Wolff, Mr. Black, and Dominick Masterson, to name a few. If Hildegard truly were able to see what others couldn't and didn't, she must have a wealth of information to share about the past, present, and maybe even my future.

Long after we'd gone to bed, I'd spent the night tossing and turning—well, that was after losing the cookie challenge to Doc, but he'd cheated. It had to be illegal to do the things he could with his tongue. Maybe not in Nevada, but surely in South Dakota. Anyway, after he'd drifted off next to me, I'd put a few worry-filled miles on the mattress, eventually sneaking downstairs to the couch so I wouldn't keep waking him.

Then this morning, I'd taken one look at my neck in the hallway mirror and rushed to grab a scarf from the closet. Prudence's reputation as a bruiser still stood strong.

All through breakfast with the kids, I'd tried to pretend that everything in our lives was normal.

Only it wasn't.

It really, really wasn't.

And after tonight's broadcast of *Paranormal Realty*, I had a feeling things might get even worse.

I groaned and took a deep breath of the cold, sweet air.

Actually, it was cold, stinky air.

"Eww." There must be trash bins down below.

I pulled my arms inside and peered out the window into the dark world below. The streetlights adding glowing spots here and there, breaking up the shadows. From my third-floor vantage point at the back of the building, I had a bird's-eye view of Pioneer Way, the Iron Horse Inn, and the Adams Museum. I went up on my toes, trying to see straight down, but I needed a stool to get a little more height.

Across Pioneer Way, I could see my SUV parked in front of the old railroad passenger station. The parking lot was mostly full, undoubtedly thanks to tonight's party. Currently, though, other than an occasional swirl of snow, nothing moved down there, which made sense since it was supposed to dip down to single digits tonight.

Now that sweat was no longer dripping down the side of my face, I returned to the mirror to touch up my makeup. I opened the tiny purse I'd brought along, taking out the tube of fake blood. While I was squirting the jelly-like stuff on my finger, I heard scratching outside the window, sort of like nails on rough stone. Or raccoons scampering around a trash bin.

A car honked in the distance.

A thumping bass rumbled to life outside the bathroom door. The show must be starting. I should probably hurry up and get out there, but I wasn't giddy about seeing myself on not just one big screen, but four. That led to the possibility of four times as much humiliation, especially with some of the ultra-feminine outfits Jerry had insisted I wear for filming. That man needed to seek therapy about his obsession with pink.

I leaned closer to the mirror, slathering the fake blood across the latex cut stuck to my cheek.

The scratching sound came through the window again, louder. Either one of the raccoons was climbing up a drain spout, or there was a loose wire blowing in the wind and scraping over the building's brick exter ...

Something hissed at the window, long and slow.

I glanced over at the old radiator to see if it had sprung a leak and nearly choked on my tongue.

A *Nachzehrer* was at the window.

Correction. A *Nachzehrer* was trying to jam its head through the open window. As I stared, frozen with disbelief, it ate my star-shaped nametag. Then one gangly arm reached through the narrow opening. Its fingers made wide swipes in the air in my direction while its teeth clacked and gnashed.

"Holy fucking shit," I whispered, backing up against the bathroom door.

The ugly bastard turned its elongated head sideways and managed to squeeze partway through the opening, but its ears were in the way. It pulled back and tried to push the window open farther, but the warped frame held it in place.

A wave of stench reached me. The smell of rot and putrescence. I recoiled, lifting my arm and breathing into my elbow.

Somebody knocked on the other side of the door. "Is anybody in there?" a high-pitched voice called out.

Shit! I pressed back against the door, barring the way, fumbling to make sure it was locked.

The *Nachzehrer* gave up on trying to open the window and hissed in at me.

I grabbed the loose roll of paper towels from the sink counter and threw it, hitting the window above it. "Get out of here, you dickhead!"

"How rude," I heard the woman say from the other side of the door.

"Sorry!" I called back. "I wasn't talking to you."

Silence.

The lady must have left. Good. Although, if she went to get the manager, I was screwed.

I scowled at the *Nachzehrer*. It was trying to shove its head through the open window again, struggling harder than before.

I had to do something. Get rid of it somehow. But I needed a weapon.

I glanced around the room.

A plastic vase with flowers—nope.

Spare rolls of toilet paper under the sink—nope.

A plug-in air freshener—nope.

A plastic spray bottle with blue liquid in it—maybe.

Come on, Violet. Think!

The *Nachzehrer* growled, its nails scraping on the brick outside as it tried to get more leverage. A trail of something dark ran down over its hollow cheek and dripped onto the radiator, where it sizzled into steam.

Blood.

Hell's bells! It was tearing off its own freaking ear. This jerk was really determined to get to me.

The frame creaked as the *Nachzehrer* pushed again. Then its long tongue unrolled from between its pointy teeth and aimed straight at me.

I ran my hand down the side of my face, coming away with a piece of jelly-covered latex stuck to my palm. Ick! I flung it to the floor.

What a hellish mess. What was I going to …

The *Nachzehrer* shoved again, whining as its skin pulled

back from its teeth, showing me its blackened gums.

The window glass cracked. The outer frame splintered, and a piece of wood flew off, landing on the tiles between us.

I stared at the splintered wood. It was only about a foot long, but maybe if I could get close enough to the bastard, I could jam that thing down its throat.

Although those were awfully sharp teeth.

It hissed again, its long fingers reaching up to grab at the frame.

I was out of time.

"Oh, fuck me." I rushed toward the piece of wood on the floor. As I bent down to grab it, the *Nachzehrer* lunged and swung for me. Its fingers snagged my dress, catching hold.

"Let go, damn it!" I struggled to pull free as it tried to haul me closer, dragging me inch by inch along the slick tiles toward its gnashing teeth.

Crap! This was going south fast … but I did now have the rather solid piece of wood in my hands.

Suddenly, I realized what I had to do. Instead of pulling away, I changed course and charged toward it, taking it by surprise. I held onto each end of the wood and rammed it flat against its teeth.

Its head reared from the blow, wrenching out of the window. As its weight shifted backward, its arms flailed, its fingers scratching at the brick as it started to slide down the side of the building.

"Yes!" I cheered. "Good-bye, you bast—"

One of its hands caught hold of the brick sill outside the window. The ugly jerk popped up again on the other side of the fractured glass, its black eyes glaring in at me.

I grabbed the top of the window and tugged down, trying to close it, but the damned thing was stuck.

"Come on!" I grunted and pulled down again.

Something hot and wet touched my chest. I looked down

and let out a small shriek. Its tongue jutted through the open window, slithering up along my neck.

"Oh, hell no." I yanked down with everything I had.

The window slammed shut with a solid thud.

The *Nachzehrer* screeched and fell backward into the night.

In the sudden silence that followed, the radiator sizzled.

I looked down. "Oh, gross!"

Part of the thing's tongue lay on the radiator, cooking at a low sizzle.

I grabbed the roll of paper towels from the floor and gave it a couple of pokes. It didn't move. I looked around, frantic. I couldn't just leave it here for the next person visiting the ladies' room to find. God, it was really starting to stink, too. But what …

Screw it. I was a mom. I'd handled plenty of disgusting crap in my life. I grabbed a bunch of toilet paper from the stall and carefully picked up the tongue, gagging when it stuck a little to the radiator. Then I dropped it in the toilet and flushed it away.

After I scrubbed my hands twice with soap and water, I returned to the window, peering through the fractured glass. Where had the *Nachzehrer* gone? Back into the trees? I needed to find it and finish it off before someone else saw it. I tried to look straight down again, but it was no use.

I saw something move near the Adams Museum. Framing my eyes with my hands, I searched for the creature under the glow of the streetlights. Where was that long-legged asshole?

What I saw instead made me gasp.

Or rather *who*. Sporting a top hat, black coat, and cane, Cornelius danced along the sidewalk like he didn't have a care in the world. Along with Harvey and other property owners of the haunted locations starring in the *Paranormal Realty* show, Cornelius had been invited to attend the premiere as a special guest, so he was most likely on his way here. It was a bad night to be running late.

I watched as he paused near the front of the museum to twirl not once, but twice.

Who did he think he was? Fred Astaire?

I tried to lift up the window to call out a warning, but the sucker wasn't budging now without a wrecking ball.

Across the way, in the parking lot in front of the old train passenger station, I saw a long-limbed, spidery figure slinking in and out of the shadows between the vehicles parked in the lot, heading toward my SUV. Once there, it rounded to the driver's side and started rubbing its head against the door. At least it looked like it was rubbing. Maybe it was licking with a bloody half-tongue.

I shuddered and focused back on Cornelius. He had stopped at the front corner of the Adams Museum and was beating on the museum signpost with his cane. No. Wait. After pressing my nose closer to the glass, I could see that he was actually sword fighting with the sign.

That meant he was making noise.

How long until the *Nachzehrer* heard him? Could it hear him? The first two I'd run into had been deaf. It didn't matter, because Cornelius would be into view soon for the nasty bastard.

"Cornelius," I whispered, my breath steaming the glass. I tapped on the window. "Cornelius! Get out of there."

Of course he couldn't hear me from this distance. Not to mention that his inner sixth sense was tuned to the whispering dead, not the loud-mouthed living.

Another check on the *Nachzehrer* sent my heart tumbling. It was no longer loving up to my vehicle. Instead, it stood on the roof and was peering toward the Adams Museum.

"Shit!" I had to go. I had to get to Cornelius before the *Nachzehrer* did.

Grabbing my purse from the sink counter, I unlocked the

door and ran out, running into someone waiting in the shadows.

"What the hell, Violet?" Natalie asked, pulling herself up off the floor. "You've been in there forever. I was coming to see if you died in there."

"Almost."

I started down the narrow hallway toward the restaurant's main room, but she caught my arm.

"Hold up. Where's the fire?" she joked.

"Outside! Cornelius!" I shook free, and raced out into the restaurant.

The overhead lights were all off as the *Paranormal Realty* show played on the big screens. I heard the familiar voice of Dickie Dowdin, the host, going on about how haunted Deadwood was as I scanned the room for Doc and Harvey in the dim light coming from the televisions. I couldn't find them in the sea of bodies, though, and there was no time to search for needles in the haystack.

"Violet," Natalie whispered, grabbing hold of my arm again. "What's going on? Is Cornelius hurt?"

"Not yet. But he will be if I don't go get him soon." I handed her my purse. "Find Doc. Meet us in the parking lot."

"Vi—"

"Now!" I shoved her toward the bar where I'd left Doc before my escape to the bathroom.

I started to weave through the crowd toward the front doors, but then I noticed a lit exit sign by another door off to the side. When I pushed through it, I found myself in a stairwell. These must be the back stairs, which should dump me out next to Pioneer Way—perfect!

I started down the steps and then stopped and backed up. On the wall at the top hung a fire extinguisher. Next to it, in a glass case with a bright red metal frame, was an ax for emergency use.

"Hello, gorgeous," I whispered and pulled open the door

to the case. The ax was actually more of a long-handled hatchet, but beggars couldn't be choosers.

Ax in hand, I rushed down the stairs and blasted through the steel door at the bottom, racing out onto a gravel pad. A big green trash bin sat front and center. Ha! I was right on that count, at least. But as it turned out I'd probably been smelling the *Nachzehrer*, not the garbage.

I looked up at the building, locating the bathroom window overhead. Holy flippin' flap, it was high up. How did that bastard fall from there and not leave a splat of blood on the ground? I shook off the thought. Now was not the time to play Cooper's crime scene game. I had to get across Pioneer Way and help Cornelius.

I turned back toward the road and cursed. I'd forgotten about the concrete jersey barrier that lined the four-lane street, and how high the street was compared to the building's bottom floor. I'd have to be eight feet tall to pull myself up to the street level from here, and that was if I were able to do a single pullup, which I wasn't.

To my right, the way was blocked by another building. To my left, I'd have to run almost a block to Lee Street, where the road leveled out with the ground, before I could cross.

Clack-clack, clack-clack, clack-clack.

What was that? Was it the creature's nails on the asphalt? No, it sounded more solid.

Above the repetitious clacking, another sound rang out in the cold calm—an accordion. Then a trumpet. Then drums. And maybe a tuba. Was that …

Jumping Jesus on a pogo stick! It was polka music.

That was why Cornelius had been dancing and twirling. He was listening to polka music, which he'd once told me revs him up and opens his psychic ears. I thought he usually saved polka tunes for the morning.

Beneath the polka beat I heard something else—ragged

pants of breath mixed with guttural growls.

Chills drag-raced up and down my spine. That damned polka beat was like a freakin' beacon.

I took off toward Lee Street at a dead sprint. As soon as I came level with the street, I hurdled the jersey wall and crossed the empty four-lane road. I clambered over the jersey wall on the other side of Pioneer Way, cutting through the parking lot in front of Iron Horse Inn.

Cornelius was in my sights now. His sword fight had ended, but he was still hanging out next to the snow-covered lawn by the Adams Museum, bending down to tie his shoe from the looks of it.

I couldn't hear the *Nachzehrer* over the steam train of my own breath, but I saw it slinking in the shadows underneath the old railroad station. It appeared to have zeroed in on Cornelius, which would explain why it was still oblivious to my presence. That or the fact that I'd chopped off its tongue, which it might use to help sniff me out.

The creature moved out of the shadows for a split second as it loped toward a panel van parked near the back of the museum, giving me a clear view of it for the first time.

I didn't like what I saw. At all.

This one was noticeably bigger than the last two. Far more hulking, too. Christ, it must have been a defensive lineman when it was a human.

The *Nachzehrer* slipped into the shadows on the other side of the van, where it was probably waiting for Cornelius to come into view.

I had five seconds to intervene. Maybe less.

"Cornelius!" I yelled, racing full bore at him across Deadwood Street.

He stopped in the midst of another twirl and looked my way. His eyes widened. His jaw dropped. He stared at me as if I were a stark-raving mad zombie bearing down on him with an ax.

Crud. I hadn't thought that part through.

"Run!" I pointed my ax at the van the *Nachzehrer* was hiding behind.

At the sight of me, the creature crept into view. It tipped its head up and let out a hair-raising yowl.

Cornelius jumped in surprise, turning toward the *Nachzehrer*. Instead of backing away from the creature, he stumbled toward it.

What the hell was he thinking? I pushed my legs faster, harder.

Out of the corner of my eye, I saw the *Nachzehrer* leap into the air, reaching those long gangly arms out to snare Cornelius.

I dove head-long toward the polka king and slammed into him at chest level, knocking him into the snow-covered grass. The creature flew over us, its fingers almost snagging my dress. It tumbled across the road, coming to a stop in the gutter.

I pushed up onto my hands, frowning down at Cornelius. The polka music continued to emanate from his coat pocket, slightly muted by the snowbank below us.

He blinked up at me and then patted my head like I was a good dog. "Heel, Violet. You're a tad terrifying tonight."

"I aim to thrill." I scrambled up off the snow and grabbed him by the front of the coat, yanking him upright. "Get behind me."

The *Nachzehrer* was on its feet already, lurching toward us across the brick street.

"Do you see that?" I asked Cornelius.

He scoffed. "How could I not?"

"It's another *Nachzehrer*. I have to kill it by severing its head before anyone else sees it." Or sees me holding an ax, the sight of which would take "Spooky Parker" to a whole new level.

Cornelius reached down beside me and grabbed his cane

from the snow, tapping it twice on the salt- and slush-covered sidewalk. "So, we're partaking in gladiatorial combat tonight, then?"

"Something like that."

"Brilliant. And are you experiencing the urge to eat my brains?"

"What? No. Why would I—" Oh, right. My costume. "Maybe later. One pain in the ass at a time."

The *Nachzehrer* charged on all fours, hurtling at us like a four-legged spider with sharp, gnashing teeth.

I shoved Cornelius out of the way. "Stay back!"

I gripped the ax, but before I could brace for impact, it was on me with its foul breath and snapping jaws. I swung the ax, but it dodged my blow. The creature leaned into me, sending me stumbling backward on the sidewalk. I hit a patch of slush and slipped, falling on my back in the snow.

The son of a bitch pounced, pinning my legs under it, leaning over me. Its jaws descended toward my face. I reached up and gripped its neck with my free hand, pushing it away while trying to wiggle free. The skin under my hand was loose and slippery, like a sheet of pliant rubber.

"Get off!" I bucked my hips, but it was too heavy. I sank deeper into the snow.

I managed another swing, but the ax blade glanced off its shoulder.

It raised its head up to the stars and started to howl.

A cane swung into view before it managed more than a note and whacked it upside the head. Something cracked. The *Nachzehrer* swayed to the side, its eyes rolling lazily, unable to focus.

That was the break I needed. I shoved upward again, knocking it off balance. It tipped sideways, but the thing was too damned heavy. I let go of its neck and gripped the ax with both hands, swinging with all of the strength I could muster while half-pinned to the ground.

The blade sank into the crook of its neck.

The *Nachzehrer* let out a shriek of pain, spraying my face with spittle.

"Gah!" I yelled, cringing, trying again to buck it off.

It bobbed sideways, almost keeling over.

But then it leaned back my way, opened its mouth, and spewed green, vile goop down the front of my dress.

"Noooo!" I looked down in horror. "You douchebag!"

I gagged on the rancid fumes of decay surrounding me.

Cornelius came up behind it, grabbing it by the shoulders and hauling it off of me. The *Nachzehrer* fell onto its back on the sidewalk, its arms and legs paddling in the air like an upside-down beetle.

I staggered to my feet and then leaned over, hands on my knees, dry heaving. After a few deep breaths, I wiped the snot from my nose and glared down at it. "You parasitic jackass."

I dodged its arms and tugged the ax free of its neck. Black blood poured from the wound as the creature stared up at me with its dead dark eyes. It continued to gnash its teeth slowly, still trying to reach for me. But it was struggling to even move. I must have cut its version of the carotid artery.

I heard an engine growling, coming closer. Damn it. Someone was coming.

"Violet," Cornelius said, looking toward the sound of the approaching vehicle.

"I know. I hear it." I tried to line up the ax for another blow, but the *Nachzehrer* kept moving its head back and forth. "I need you to hold it still for me."

"And how do you propose I do that? Sit on it?"

"No, smartass. You need to grab it near the ears and hold its head still."

"How many chickens have you had on the chopping block?" he asked.

Chickens? What? "None. Why?" Oh, I got it. "How many have you?"

"I lost count after twenty-three."

"Criminy. Did you use to work at a chicken farm?"

"No, my grandmother down in Louisiana had chickens, and we ate some. Others we sacrificed—and then ate."

I frowned at him, shaking my head. I needed to keep an eye on him when he was around Elvis. "Okay, we can talk about chickens later—but not around Addy. Now hold its head so I can get a clear neck shot."

"Maybe I should do the swinging, not you. Natalie has mentioned your shortcoming."

"Which one? I have many."

"The ax-related one."

I glared at him. "Trust me, I'd love to hand this job off to you and go take a stroll through a car wash right now, but I have to kill this bastard so it disappears, or we'll have a very weird body to bury somewhere in the hills and neither of us needs Detective Hawke sniffing around."

"Good point." He cradled the creature's head and tipped its chin up, giving me a clear target. "Give it one hard blow. Severing the spine will be tough with such a small ax. You don't want to make it suffer."

"Yeah, right." That was easy for him to say. He hadn't been front and center while it tried to reach through the bathroom window and tear me to pieces.

I tightened my grip on the handle.

He cringed, pulling back slightly. "And don't miss and cut off my fingers. I have grand plans yet for them."

I lifted the ax. "I offer no guarantees."

Chapter Twenty-Four

"Hey, you didn't miss," Natalie said several minutes later, standing over all that was left of the *Nachzehrer*, which was just a small pile of dust on the sidewalk.

"Third time's a charm." I shivered in the freezing breeze, wishing I had some of that heat from the bathroom radiator baking me right about now. On top of leaving my coat and gloves up at the party, my dress was wet from my attempts to clean off the nasty thing's green barf with snow.

Doc tipped my chin up toward the streetlight. "It's hard to see if you've sustained any more injuries with this zombie makeup." He tilted his head. "I think you actually look *less* beat up than when we left your aunt's house."

"I lost one of my latex cuts up in the bathroom when the *Nachzehrer* stopped by to wish me good luck on the premiere."

He sniffed, taking a step back. "And that smell?"

"The creature deposited a green, gelatinous liquid on her dress after Violet delivered the first blow," Cornelius explained.

"The first blow? So, you did miss." Natalie grinned.

"It was hard to lop its head off while I was pinned on my back by the big motherhumper."

"And then it puked on you."

"You're enjoying this way too much." I grabbed another handful of snow. My hands trembled as I scrubbed down the front of my dress. Stupid, weak-stomached creepster. I gasped as a bit of snow trickled down the scoop neck of my dress.

Doc shucked his coat and draped it over my shoulders. The spicy scent of his cologne almost overshadowed the creature's stench, but not quite.

"Did you bring my keys?" I asked him.

"Yes." He jammed his hands in his pockets. "But you can't go home yet."

"Why not?"

"You have to go back inside."

"No." I groaned. "Why?"

"Because the television show is almost over and your boss is going to want you to be there for the post-show song and dance."

"Yeah, but look at me." I thumbed at my sodden dress.

"Actually, babe," Natalie said. "With your hair a mess and your leggings torn, you look even more zombie-ish than you did before. It's a good look on you."

"Shush, smartass." My leggings were torn? I looked down. Sure enough, there was a rip below my right knee. I didn't even remember that happening. "Criminy, these are cashmere. It's not like I have an unlimited supply of clothing for these dickwads to keep ruining."

"Bollocks," Cornelius said.

"Exactly."

"That wasn't about your leggings, Vi," Natalie said. She pointed at Cornelius, who was holding up what looked like a bent stick.

"I broke my favorite cane."

An accordion struck up a tune from his pocket, joined by a tuba.

"Does anyone else hear polka music, or am I losing my shit?" Natalie asked.

"Did you know that polka was created around 1830 by a

female farm worker in Bohemia?" Cornelius asked her.

"*Nyet.*" I held my hand in his face. A drop of ice-cold water ran up my sleeve.

He leaned to the side to look at me around my hand. "That's Russian, Violet. Bohemia is actually now part of the Czech Republic, not—"

"No more polka tonight, music man," I cut him off. "You and that crazy beat almost got us killed by a *Nachzehrer.*"

"Maybe it just wanted to dance," Doc said, chuckling.

Cornelius reached into his coat pocket and the music stopped, leaving the night as quiet as it was cold and dark.

I scrubbed my freezing hands together. My fingertips were numb.

Doc took my hands in his, warming me up. "What do you say, Killer? How about we go back inside together and wrap up this party, and then I'll take you home and ease you into a nice, hot bath."

"A bath, you say? Will there be back scrubbing involved?"

"And front." He winked. "Then, after you're all pink and wrinkly, I'll wrap you up in a warm blanket and sing you a lullaby."

My teeth started to chatter. "My favorite one?"

He nodded. "I know how much you love to put the lime in the coconut and drink it all up."

"And you'll use Kermit the Frog's voice?"

"Of course."

Natalie hooked her arm in Cornelius's and pulled him toward the restaurant. "Come on, you guys, before Jerry realizes we're not there. Harvey can only stall him for so long."

"What am I going to do with this?" I held up the ax. "It belongs in the back stairwell."

Natalie took it from me and tucked it inside of her coat.

"I'll put it back while you work your magic in the spotlight."

Doc put his arm around me and urged me along when I continued to drag my feet.

As soon as the four of us stepped inside Charles' Club, the television show's credits started rolling on the four televisions and the lights came up.

Damn it, I was hoping to have a few minutes to swing by the bathroom again and try to make repairs to everything south of my scalp.

Jerry walked in front of one of the big television screens as a round of applause filled the room. He was so tall he didn't need a podium to be seen.

"I would like to thank everyone for coming tonight to share this important event with all of us from Calamity Jane Realty. I'm sure you all will agree that we have some amazing agents who are here to help you with all of your real estate needs, big or small."

Another round of applause spread throughout the room.

I slipped off Doc's coat and handed it back to him now that we were back in the sauna. Thankfully, my wet dress was now acting as a cooler.

"Violet," Jerry called out. "Where are you?"

When I tried to blend in with the wallpaper, Doc took my arm and held it up.

"Come up here. Ben, you too."

My feet didn't move. They wanted to go back down the stairs and head for home.

Doc nudged me forward. "Go get it over with, superstar. I'll make it up to you later."

I groaned and then forced one foot in front of the other. When I reached Jerry, he glanced down at me and then did a double take. Lucky for me, his shout of laughter was drowned out by the din of conversation in the restaurant.

He leaned over and said in my ear. "Violet, you really went all out on the costume tonight." He sniffed and his smile slipped as he recoiled slightly. "Although you could have gone easy on the zombie perfume."

I patted him on the sleeve. Silly man. It was *Nachzehrer* vomit, not decaying zombie flesh.

"Hey, where's your nametag?" he asked.

"It got eaten," I told the truth with a straight face.

He laughed. "A zombie joke. I love it."

"What did you think of the show?" Ben asked me as he joined me up front with Jerry.

"It was …" I thought of the *Nachzehrer* trying to squeeze its head through the bathroom window and then licking my neck. "A bit nerve-wracking."

Jerry clapped us both on the shoulders. "Take a bow, you two. You did the team proud."

Before I had a chance to do as told, a piercing whistle rang out over the clapping. In the back, Natalie waved at me from on top of a table.

I waved back, smiling. If she thought we'd be doing any table dancing tonight, she was in for a letdown. My body had done enough shaking, rattling, and rolling outside on the ground.

She frowned and shook her head. Then she held up a yellow and black walkie-talkie and waved again, more frantically this time.

"Now what?" I muttered under my breath. After taking a bow to make Jerry happy, I threaded back through the crowd toward Natalie. Doc and Harvey were there with her.

"What's going on?" I asked the three of them.

"Coop just called in for backup," she said.

I looked to Doc for a less cryptic explanation.

Doc handed me my coat. "We have to go, Killer. Duty calls."

That didn't clear up things yet. I turned to Harvey. "Go where?"

Harvey hooked his thumbs in his red velvet suspenders.

"Go back huntin' over at Jonesy's. That three-limbed critter of yers came back for seconds."

I scowled. "You're kidding."

"Nope," he said with a happy grin.

Natalie pulled on her coat. "Hurry up, Vi. I don't like Coop being alone out there with one of those things." She looked at Doc. "I'll go tell Cornelius to run interference for us with Vi's boss and coworkers." She hurried off across the room.

"But my dress is a wet mess." And so was I. Mentally, I was hanging on by my fingertips at the moment.

Harvey looked me up and down. "Yer fine. Quit yer caterwauling and let's hit the road."

I turned to Doc. "Please tell me this is a practical joke and you're really going to take me home and read a sexy book to me while I soak in a tub full of bubbles."

Doc took me by the elbow. "Sorry, Killer, but it appears your work isn't done yet tonight."

A hop, skip, and a round of grumbling later, Natalie, Doc, Harvey, and I reached my SUV in the parking lot.

"Watch out for that door," I told Doc as he rounded the front, keys in hand. "I think the *Nachzehrer* was rubbing on it earlier. Or licking it."

"Gross," Natalie said, climbing in the backseat.

"I don't see anything," Doc said through the open driver's side door while taking off his coat. I watched from the passenger seat as he pulled his shirt free of his pants and started unbuttoning it.

"What are you doing?" I asked.

"I have an idea." He took off his shirt and handed it to me, leaving him standing there in a white undershirt. "Take off your dress and put that on instead."

"Hurry, Vi," Natalie said, covering Harvey's eyes. "Coop could be in trouble."

"Come on, let me peek," Harvey said, trying to knock

Natalie's hand away. "An old man like me doesn't get many peep shows these days. Doc doesn't mind, do ya?"

Doc just chuckled and slid his coat back on.

"Okay, okay." I shrugged out of the wet, stinky mess and slid on Doc's shirt quick as I could. I hugged the warm cotton to me, soaking up his heat.

"Give me your dress," Doc said.

I wadded it up into a ball and gave it to him.

"I'll buy you a new one," he said and jogged over to the trash can near the corner of the lot, tossing it away for good.

"Good riddance," I muttered and sniffed the collar of Doc's shirt. Yum. Spicy, musky, with a blend of cedar. I should wear his shirts more often.

A minute later we were off, rolling toward Central City and Jones' Taxidermy. My fingers were crossed that the other *Nachzehrer* had already left the scene and Cooper would tell us to head home and eat some cake. What cake? I didn't care. Pie would work, too.

When we pulled up in front of the taxidermy shop, Cooper's Deadwood Police rig was there, but he wasn't inside of it. The hillside behind the building was full of shadows, the moonlight unable to pierce the thick tree cover.

"Where is he?" Natalie asked, reaching for the door.

"Wait!" I said, hitting the door lock. "We need to have a plan." I looked at Doc. "Don't we?"

"You're calling the shots, Killer. You've taken on three already. What do you think we should do first?"

I turned to Natalie. "Try Cooper on the walkie-talkie. We don't need to accidentally sneak up on him and wind up with a bullet in the kisser."

"But keep yer voice low," Harvey added. "Just in case he's in a pickle at the moment."

She nodded, lifting the walkie-talkie. "Coop, come in," she whispered. "Over."

I waited, my breath held.

Come on, Cooper. Where are you?

"Try again," Harvey told Natalie.

She closed her eyes. "Coop, we're here. Where are you? Over."

I stared out the windshield at the shop. Garth had left some lights on, probably so the cops doing drive-bys could see inside. I watched, waiting to see any movement.

A *tap-tap-tap* on my side window made me jump.

Cooper stood outside, peering in at us.

Open the door, he mouthed, and pointed in Natalie's direction.

Doc hit the unlock button. Natalie scooted toward the middle as Coop slid in next to her, quietly closing the door behind him.

"Where's the *Nachzehrer*?" I asked.

He pointed toward the dark hillside behind the shop. "It made its way up into the trees about five minutes before you guys showed up."

"So, we're too late?" Natalie said.

"No, I'm pretty sure it's still up there. I followed it and watched it slide into a crevice in the rocks."

"You followed that thing on your own?" Natalie gaped at him as if he'd sprouted a pink unicorn horn. "It could have turned on you."

"Sure, if it'd heard me, but I made sure it didn't."

When her eyes narrowed, he added, "Nat, this isn't my first manhunt."

"Yeah, but that's not a man. And you're the one always saying to never go in without backup."

"Well, I'd called in backup—you. I knew you'd be here soon and I didn't want to lose sight of that thing." He glanced at me. "It's tall, like Jonesy said. Must be over seven feet when it stands upright."

I wondered how it compared to what Cornelius and I had just taken whacks at. "Tell us what happened."

"I stopped by to check on things, like I told Jonesy I'd do." Cooper rubbed his hands together to warm them. "I was about to take off when I thought I saw movement near the side of the building. I drove closer and that's when I saw him."

"The *Nachzehrer*?" I asked.

"No, the ghost I told you about before."

I grimaced. "The one missing half of his head?"

"Yeah." Cooper's grimace was twice as deep as mine. "He waved for me to follow him, so I did. He led me partway up the hillside and then put up his hand for me to stop and wait." He frowned out the window. "It wasn't more than a minute or two before I heard something coming slowly up the hill. That's when I saw it, the three-limbed perp, making its way up toward the rocks. It was hard to see fully, but I caught a couple of glimpses of it in the shafts of moonlight coming through the trees." He looked at Doc and then me. "I think that fourth limb has partially grown back."

"Maybe it was a different *Nachzehrer*," Doc said.

"Maybe." Cooper shrugged. "Anyway, it didn't come out from that crevice in the rocks during the time I waited for you guys to show up."

"So, it's either hiding in there," Natalie started.

"Or there's a cave or an ol' mine on the other side of those rocks," Harvey finished.

Cooper nodded. "We need to go check it out. If that thing is still in there, we need to finish it off."

I looked out at the dark hillside. "You want to follow it into what might be its lair?" Criminy, walking into a grizzly den in spring seemed less hair-raising.

"We could try to draw it out," Doc offered. "They can't resist *Scharfrichter* blood, right?"

In other words, go back to his earlier idea involving my blood and his neck that I'd rejected.

"I say Sparky goes in after it," Harvey said. When I

frowned at him, he shrugged. "You bring it out here in the open and it'll be like tryin' to catch a butterfly with a baseball bat."

"Let's not forget that the bounty hunter could be watching and waiting somewhere around here," Doc said.

I groaned. "Oh, yeah." What kind of creature was responsible for creating and controlling each of these *Nachzehrer*? Something even more hideous and horrifying?

"I don't think the bounty hunter is here yet," Cooper said. "That ghost only showed me the *Nachzehrer*."

Natalie scowled at him. "You of all people are going to rely on a ghost as a bounty hunter barometer? Who are you and what have you done with Detective Cooper?"

He pointed at me. "It's Parker's fault."

I wasn't even going to try to defend myself because that was actually true. Although he'd been following me too closely yet again when he'd been "blasted" open to the ectoplasmic world, but now was not the time to fling monkey poo back at him.

"What if the bounty hunter is waiting inside the cave for me along with the *Nachzehrer*?" I asked. "What if it's just one big trap?" The one Reid and I had taken out had been trying to lure me in, too.

"Yer best chance is still to go in after it," Harvey said. "It's like wranglin' lost cattle. Best to lead them into a box canyon where you can corner the critter."

Doc stared at me, his brow tight. "Well?"

I sighed. "So, what's the plan, Cooper?"

"I'm thinking that you, me, and Nyce go in after the *Nachzehrer*." When Natalie started to protest, he held up his hand for her to let him finish. "Nat and Uncle Willis wait out here in case it manages to get past us."

"Or in case we need to make a run for it," I said. "You guys can have the getaway vehicle running and ready to tear ass out of here."

"Ah, damn. I left Bessie at home," Harvey said, sounding forlorn about it.

Cooper nodded toward his police rig. "I have a couple of my own personal firearms I can lend you two."

"Okay, fine," Natalie said quietly. "But how will we know what's going on? I doubt the walkie-talkies will work from inside a cave."

"You won't," Cooper said, taking her hand in his and giving it a squeeze. "You'll just have to keep an eye out, be ready for all hell to break loose, and shoot straight if anything comes barreling down the hill toward you—especially if she has crazy curls and screams like a baby." He gave me a smartass grin.

I glared at him. "I'm going to feed you to the *Nachzehrer* before I kill it, Cooper."

Harvey snickered. "It'd probably spit him back out. The boy's too hard and gristly."

Doc peered out the windshield at the hillside. "If we're going to do this, let's get it over with."

Five minutes later, I gave Natalie a hug and patted Harvey's shoulder. "Be safe, you two." I looked at Natalie. "If that thing comes at you, it will move fast, same as last time." To Harvey I said, "Aim for the head, like Reid did."

Cooper gave a handgun that he'd pulled from the back of the police rig to his uncle. "You know how to use that, right?"

"Well, I should smile," Harvey said with a big grin.

Cooper groaned. "You and that damned Zane Grey book."

He handed Natalie a shotgun. "I *know* you know how to use this."

"How does he know that?" I asked her. "Is playing with shotguns one of your weird sex games?" Instead of a black cat suit, did she dress in some camouflage-print negligee and blow a duck whistle at him while cracking the whip?

"No, you big dork. Coop and I went to the shooting range together, remember?"

Oh, yeah, I'd forgotten about that. I really wished Cooper hadn't blabbed about their sex life in that haunted jail the other night. That was going to plague me more than dealing with that banshee.

"Switch me coats," Natalie said. "You don't need to ruin your Christmas present from Doc."

I shrugged off my trench coat and took her fleece-lined parka. It smelled sweet and citrusy, her favorite perfume. I hoped it would disguise my scent from the *Nachzehrer*.

Cooper gave Doc another handgun. "You've used this one before."

Doc checked the safety on the weapon and then put it in his coat pocket.

Criminy. Cooper was giving guns away like they were party favors. "Did you bring a portable armory along?"

"In my line of work, it pays to be prepared for the worst."

I crossed my arms. "We can't fire guns in a cave."

He held up his own Colt .45. "This is in case we end up back outside chasing after that thing."

"Fine." I held out my hand. "Where's mine?"

"Right here." Doc handed me the ax that he'd stored in the back of my SUV after Reid's and my run-in with the *Nachzehrer*.

I made a face and took it. "It's not fair, you know. I always have to get my hands the dirtiest."

"You're the one always saying that bullets are no good against these creatures," Cooper reminded me, stuffing his police baton in his belt holder next to what looked like a stun gun.

"Shut up, Detective Know-It-All."

Doc held the mace he'd bought me for Christmas in his other hand. "Ready if you two are."

"You have your Kevlar vest on just to be safe?" Cooper

asked him.

Doc patted his chest and gave a thumbs-up. He must have had that stored in the back of my SUV, too.

I felt underdressed for the party in just Nat's coat and Doc's shirt.

Doc looked at me. "Do you want to wear my Kevlar vest?"

I shook my head. "You and I know that will just slow me down in the thick of battle. Besides, I got it for you, not me."

Cooper grabbed Natalie and pulled her close. "Don't be a hero," he told her and gave her a quick kiss.

"Same goes for you," she whispered up at him with a worried brow.

"Hey, where's my smooch, boy?" Harvey said when Cooper let her go.

"I'll let Nyce give you a good-luck kiss tonight," he said, and clapped his uncle on the shoulder.

Natalie turned to me. "You know what you need to do."

"Strike first, ask questions later?"

She hugged me. "Just keep your eyes open when you swing."

Doc caught my hand and tugged me toward the trees. "Come on, Killer. Let's go wrangle a *Nachzehrer*."

Chapter Twenty-Five

We let Cooper lead the way to the *Nachzehrer* hoedown. He kept his light on the ground as we hiked in silence up the hill. Too soon, we stood at the base of a large rock outcropping, two stories high.

I shivered, probably as much from the task before us as the cold wind rattling the trees overhead.

"Can you smell anything?" Doc whispered to me.

"That's funny. I usually ask you that." I sniffed, shaking my head. "Just pine trees, fresh air, and Natalie's perfume on the collar of her coat."

Cooper aimed his flashlight beam on a dark opening between two very large rocks that were leaning against each other, like huge, crooked teeth. "It went in there."

The crevice was about four feet wide at the bottom, tapering to an arm's length over my head.

I took a step toward the opening, trying to gear up mentally for what might be waiting for me in the dark. "I'll go in first."

"No." Doc caught my arm and tugged me back. "I'll go. When I give you a signal, then you'll follow." He didn't wait for a committee vote. Leading with his flashlight, he turned sideways and slid between the rocks. And then he was gone.

"I shouldn't have let him go first," I said, worrying my lower lip.

"He's a big boy."

"Yeah, but—"

"Make sure your cell phone is on silent mode," Cooper said, checking his walkie-talkie. "We don't want that thing to realize we're in there until we know the lay of the land."

I checked and tucked my phone away in Natalie's coat pocket. "There's a chance it can't hear anything. Maybe the implantation of the *Nachzehrer* egg in the human ear causes deafness, I don't know. I think the tongue is used as one of its senses, though, sort of like a snake."

He grunted. "Best to be safe. Act as if it can hear us."

"All clear," Doc whispered from the shadows.

"Did you hear what Parker just said about its hearing?" Cooper asked Doc.

"Yeah. Let's go."

He lit the way for me as I slid between the rocks. On the other side was a narrow passageway that required Doc and Cooper to duck slightly. There were no timbers holding up the ceiling or any other sign of mining activity. Maybe this was a natural cave. There were a bunch around the hills, several of which doubled as popular tourist attractions.

Doc gave us a hand signal to follow and started down a long slope. Cooper brought up the rear. We moved without a sound through the rock-lined throat, heading into the bowels of the Earth. The air was warmer in here than outside, at least, but still cool and damp and musty. Sounds were muted, like we'd been closed inside of a big coffin in the ground.

I shuddered and tried to think of something less macabre.

The tunnel sort of reminded me of the one between Calamity Jane Realty and the courthouse, via what had come to be known as the "Hellhole." Only that tunnel had more width and formal arches ... and a couple of creatures that I hoped not to run into ever again. Especially that one with the red arm.

And I was back to thinking about the macabre again.

A minute later, we rounded a bend and the tunnel opened wide. Doc stopped short, holding up his hand for us to do the same.

I peeked around him and my breath caught.

Holy shit. What fresh hell had we stumbled into?

Doc shined the light around the cavern, which was about the size of the dining room at Bighorn Billy's. Mounted on the walls throughout the place were heads of all shapes and sizes. Some of the creatures I recognized as the usual predators found in many hunting lodges and wildlife exhibits—a bear, a mountain lion, and a wolf, to name a few.

But most of the creatures I hadn't seen before even in books, and I hoped never to run into them in the future. Like that shaggy beast with two pointy horns poking straight out of its forehead. It reminded me of a Scottish Highlands cow in coloring, but it had three white eyes, a round flat face, and two long tusks reminiscent of a sabretooth tiger.

Next to it was a Bone Cruncher's head. Its milky eyes stared out into the cave, its toothy jaws frozen in mid-crunch on a human skull.

I grimaced, recalling the night I'd faced off with one behind Harvey's barn. I was still waiting for the second Bone Cruncher to come calling, since Mr. Black had warned me they typically hunted in pairs.

Across the room, stood a stuffed chimera. Its feathery black mane and long snout brought back visions of Slagton and the battle we'd gone through back there on that bright, sunny day … and then a short time later facing off with *Kyrkozz* in the dark once again. Lucky for me, Harvey's old stick of dynamite had saved my bacon on that trip. The chimera in front of us was bigger than most we'd dealt with, though. The pack alpha, maybe. A true hunter's prize.

As we tiptoed deeper into the cavern, I shined my cell phone light around, bouncing from one creature to the next. Cringing. Wincing. Swallowing gasps.

Several more creatures stood in attack poses. Some of them had four legs, a few had six. One looked like a centipede, but it was the size of a bobcat with a hyena-shaped head turned inside out and a slimy, scaly body.

There was a spider-like beast that looked to have been mixed with a bighorn sheep—its legs spindly and jointed, but its back broad and muscled. There were talons at its feet, rather than hooves. Talons with one especially long, sharp claw.

Standing next to that was another mid-sized creature that had scales down its neck and back, huge pointy ears, and two huge bulbous eyes—like a fly.

I blanched and switched my focus to the gremlin-like creatures positioned throughout with their wrinkly gray skin, thick flappy lips, and pinched angry faces.

Doc pointed out a mounted two-headed serpent with a cow-like tongue and what looked like extra-large gills for cheeks.

Next to it was a bat creature with wings and big ears on a small human body. White fur cascaded down its back and along its whip-like tail.

And then there was a raptor-looking creature with spikes on its beak.

And an imp-sized beast with floppy ears, a pig nose, and red eyes that glowed in the flashlight's beam.

And below that, I spotted a wooden cask. Cooper joined me and shined his light into it. Shrunken human heads nearly filled it. At least I thought they were human. The faces of the poor victims were scrunched into exaggerated frowns. *Skull raisins*, I heard Harvey say in my mind and quivered. There must have been twenty heads in the cask, maybe more.

I hurried along, cringing at some of the creatures, trying to make sense of others. Things with tusks. Things with horns. Things with rows of sharp teeth. Things with deadly claws. Things with too many eyes. Things that didn't even look like they had faces, just a conglomeration of fur, spikes, and antennae-like feelers.

"Help me," a raspy voice whispered.

I froze.

Slowly turning, I looked from Doc to Cooper. Both were checking out different creatures with looks of wonder on their faces—not the good kind of wonder, either, like that inspired by a newborn puppy or a piece of pizza dripping with cheese fresh from the oven. Neither of them seemed to have heard anything.

Huh. Maybe that was the voice of reason in my head, reeling from horror overload.

I turned back to a mounted head that was surely some sort of troll with its wide, flat face; thick, fleshy lips; and tiny round ears. Or maybe an ogre. What was the difference between the two? I hoped to never find out firsthand.

"Help me," the voice said again.

I hurried to Doc's side. "Do you hear that?" I whispered in his ear.

His forehead wrinkled and he shook his head.

"Someone is calling out for help," I told him.

"I don't hear it. Which way is it coming from?"

I pointed toward the other side of the cavern.

He firmed his grip on the mace and eased across the rock floor, keeping me behind him. Cooper followed, armed with his police baton.

A narrow tunnel led into thick shadows.

I sniffed and grabbed Doc's arm, pulling him back. When he looked at me, I pinched my nose and mouthed *Nachzehrer*, pointing into the shadows. He nodded and then continued.

The stench of rotten flesh and sulfur grew with every step, making me glad I'd skipped the fancy *hors d'oeuvres* at the party. Although that caramel pecan–baked brie sure looked finger-licking good, and I'd never met a meatball I hadn't liked.

I could see the glow of dim light up ahead, which made my heart rock and roll. I doubted a *Nachzehrer* used a flashlight, so maybe we were finally going to meet the bounty hunter. I had a feeling it was behind all of these freaky monster trophies.

Slurping and crunching sounds, along with grunts and snorts reached my ears. What the hell? Had we caught the hunter on lunch break?

We moved slowly, carefully, silently, watching where we stepped. I clutched the ax handle like my life depended on it, which it did at the moment, along with Doc's and Cooper's.

Then we rounded a corner and stopped on a dime. In front of us was a small room lit by a single lightbulb dangling from a hook in the rock ceiling. A worktable sat against the wall, cluttered with jars and hammers and picks and knives, along with a collection of tweezers, scalpels, stained rags, clippers, and sharp fishhooks on chains that still had pieces of something on the pointy ends. I didn't want to know what those pieces were. Ever.

Help me, the voice wheezed in my head.

I stared at what looked like a body, mummy-wrapped in white gauze on a rock platform.

White gauze ... Make that a cocoon.

Oh, dear Lord. There it was, just as Masterson had described. A *Nachzehrer* in the making.

Kneeling next to the cocoon with its back to us was the three-limbed creature. It was chewing on the lower half of the body like it was an ear of corn. Cooper had been right. The fourth limb was growing back. In fact, it was nearly half-sized now, and its burned skin looked mostly healed, as far as I could tell. How was that possible?

Oh! Suddenly, it all made sense.

Eating the nutrient-filled cocoon.

Regenerating a limb.

Growing stronger.

Only the three-limbed bastard was devouring the shroud of another soon-to-be *Nachzehrer*.

I covered my mouth, gagging behind my hand.

The *Nachzehrer* paused and lifted its head. Its tongue uncurled and moved about in the air.

Oh damn.

It whipped around, staring right at me with those flat black eyes opened wide. Its jaw unhinged, and then it hissed at me.

I should have been scared, but I was far more disgusted by the stringy pieces of cocoon stuck to its face and dangling from several of its teeth.

I stepped out from behind Doc. "Hello, asshole."

The *Nachzehrer* lunged at me.

Doc bumped me aside and swung the mace at it, delivering a skull-cracking blow to its forehead that sent it reeling backward.

The creature hit the wall and slid to the floor of the cave. Its head tilted to the side as blackish blood trailed from its lips down its fleshy neck.

"Your turn, Killer," Doc said, patting my shoulder. "I told you my plan would work if you'd just give it a try."

I resisted reminding him that his so-called plan had also included my blood, because I was glad we were able to skip that element this time.

We eased up to the creature. It was gnashing its teeth slowly, as if still chewing on the cocoon.

"I need a clear shot at the neck."

Cooper grabbed it by the ankles and pulled so it lay flat. "There you go. On a silver platter."

I stood over it, taking aim.

Gah! I hated this part.

"Hurry up, Parker. I want to get the hell out of here before something else shows up to the party, or we get stuck down here."

"Quit yer caterwaulin'," I told him, stealing his uncle's line, and swung the ax. This time, I nailed it on the first try. Natalie would have cheered. We watched as the head and body quickly withered, leaving a small pile of dust amidst the pebbles.

"Damn," Doc said. "We forgot to put a coin in its mouth to test the myth."

I grimaced. "I wasn't going near those teeth."

"That's some weird shit," Cooper said, rubbing the back of his neck. "One minute it's a huge pile of flesh and bones and teeth, the next it's nothing more than dustpan filler."

"Tell me about it."

Kill me, the raspy voice said.

I turned back to the cocooned body. "Did you guys hear that?"

"Hear what?" Doc asked.

When I looked at Cooper, he shook his head. "I'm not hearing anything."

I walked over to the cocooned body, leaning closer.

Kill me, I heard again. *Kill me. Kill me. Kill me.*

I pointed at it. "It's coming from this."

"What's it saying?" Doc joined me.

"First, when we were in the other room, I heard it say, 'Help me.' Now, it's saying 'Kill me' over and over."

"You're sure it's coming from this?" Doc pointed down at the cocoon.

I nodded. "It's a *Nachzehrer* in the making." I shivered, aware of the whole horrifying process taking place under the layers of cocoon.

"There must be just enough of the human left in it to realize what's going on," Doc said.

My eyes watered. "What a horrible way to die."

"And then to feel that bastard eating on you." Cooper cursed under his breath, muttering something about "fucked-up shit," and walked over to the worktable. He started poking at some of the tools with the end of his baton.

Doc looked at me. "You know you're going to have to take care of this one, too."

I groaned. This was different. Inside that cocoon was some poor soul who still seemed to have an ounce of humanity left.

Leaving Doc standing there, I moved under the light bulb, frowning up at it. "Where's this electricity coming from?"

"Good question," Doc said. He joined me and we traced the cloth-covered wire over to a thick steel plate covering a hole in the wall behind the worktable.

Hey, I knew that steel plate! "That leads to the back room in Jones' Taxidermy. Reid and I were looking at the other side of this yesterday." I touched the cloth-covered wire. "It's knob-and-tube …" My voice trailed off as I tried to make sense of it.

"What is it, Parker?"

"So, Garth, or one of his ancestors, must have known that this cave was here. Does that mean Garth is an *other*?" I shook my head. "No, he couldn't be. I would have sensed that somehow. Unless he's the bounty hunter and very good at cloaking."

Doc walked over to a hole carved high into the rock wall. He aimed his light into it.

If Garth wasn't the bounty hunter, how could he *not* know about what was behind the steel pl …

"Hey, Killer," Doc called, his voice scratchier than normal. He pulled out a small, clear glass decanter with a fat base and a cork stuffed in the opening. "Take a look at this."

As I stepped closer, he shined his flashlight through the glass. Inside, it was partially filled with what looked like white rice. But on closer inspection, the rice pieces were moving. Vibrating. Twitching.

"What the hell are those?" Cooper asked, peering over my shoulder.

Kill me, I heard again from the cocooned body.

I reared back, bumping into Cooper, who grabbed my shoulders to steady me.

"Oh, Jesus," I whispered. "Those are *Nachzehrer* eggs."

Doc carefully set the glass decanter on the worktable and we all took a step back from it.

"We need to get out of here," I said.

"Not yet." Cooper pointed at the cocooned body. "That thing will be roaming the hills next if you don't finish the job."

"But it's not fully turned." I shook my head, clutching Doc's coat sleeve. "There's still a man in there."

"Not really," Doc said. "It's too far gone to ever be human again."

I looked from Doc to Cooper and back. Both wore haunted expressions.

We all knew what I had to do.

My gut sank. Returning to the cocoon, I stared down at where the head most likely was.

"Goddammit," I whispered, blinking the tears from my eyes.

"Violet," Doc said, "if you want, I can help with—"

"No." I sniffed. "Enough of this shit."

Keeping my eyes open, I swung the ax.

Chapter Twenty-Six

"And then what happened?" Aunt Zoe asked, looking up from her notebook.

Once again, we were sitting around her table, enjoying a few nightcaps while we rehashed the evening's events with her. Only the word "nightcaps" made it sound sexy and sophisticated, when in truth I'd stumbled over the threshold earlier and quickly locked the door behind us. If I'd had a metal portcullis to block the entryway and a drawbridge to raise, I would have.

"Then the cocoon and the body within it turned to dust," Doc told her, sipping on the hot buttered rum Harvey had set in front of him a moment ago.

"Same as the other *Nachzehrer*," I added.

Doc pushed back from the table. "I'm going to go check on the kids and say good night. Be right back."

"What about that voice you kept hearing?" Natalie asked after Doc had left, scooping out a bowl full of caramel corn from the huge tin in the center of the table.

Aunt Zoe had made the kids' favorite Saturday night treat, even though it was Sunday. With Martin Luther King Jr. holiday tomorrow, they had a three-day weekend, so she'd let them eat and be merry a little later tonight before shipping them off to bed. I'd stopped by their rooms long enough to steal kisses before hopping in the shower to wash the last of the *Nachzehrer* puke off of me. Now, sitting here in my fleece pajamas, surrounded by friends and family, I could almost forget that I'd killed not one, not two, but three *Nachzehrer* tonight.

I scooped some caramel corn from the tin, too. "It was the end of the voice, as well," I told Natalie.

She winced. "What a horrifying way to go out."

Harvey set down two more mugs of hot buttered rum—one in front of Aunt Zoe and the other in front of me. "So, you think ya got every last one of those buggers?"

"I hope so."

The old boy scowled. "Ya should have saved one for me and Bessie."

Cooper, Doc, and I had hightailed it out of the cave after delivering that final ax chop. We'd been more than ready to breathe fresh air and escape from all of those creepy, stuffed monsters in the outer cavern. Natalie and Harvey had been waiting with guns drawn when we'd come crashing down the hillside. While Natalie had been happy to see us, Harvey had looked a little put out, telling Cooper that he'd wanted a chance to fill a *Nachzehrer* with some hot lead. On the drive home, he'd gone on to complain that he'd felt left out, since he'd not gone along to hunt a single long-limbed bastard with me, unlike everyone else.

"I'm sorry we didn't save one for you," I told him. "But we did save the eggs. You want me to let you play with those? They sort of look like maggots."

Harvey shuddered, making a gargling sound in his throat. "When the Rocky Mountains go flat." He returned to the counter where Cornelius was pouring hot buttered rums.

To my surprise, Cornelius had been waiting here at home with Aunt Zoe when we'd arrived. After the party, he'd caught a ride here from Rosy, the camerawoman who'd helped film much of tonight's premiere episode of *Paranormal Realty*, not wanting to walk without his cane. When he'd arrived, he'd told Aunt Zoe he figured we'd be returning with a tale to tell, and he'd been right.

According to him, Jerry had come around looking for me after I'd left. Cornelius—in all his wisdom—had explained that my root chakra was blocked, causing me to be constipated, so I'd needed to leave the party and go work on "flushing out" the problem.

When I'd heard Cornelius's excuse, I'd considered giving *his* root chakra a swirlie in the toilet. However, he went on to clarify that Jerry had promptly ended his search for me and hurried away, so I just rolled my eyes and crossed my fingers that Jerry never asked me for more "flushing" details.

"Where did you put the eggs?" Cornelius asked me.

"Cooper took them."

He'd left the taxidermy shop with them, promising to store them in a safe place for now. Since I wasn't interested in keeping them anywhere near my two curious children, who had a history of shoving peas and Tic Tacs up their noses and in their ears, I was happy to have them somewhere other than here.

"Why didn't you guys just destroy them right there in the cave?" Natalie asked.

"Because we weren't sure how," I told her. "Aunt Zoe, do you have any ideas how to get rid of them?"

She shrugged. "I suppose you could try burning them."

"Yeah, but burning didn't work for a live *Nachzehrer*, so we thought it might not work for the eggs, either."

"That's true." She rubbed her chin. "I suppose Masterson might have an idea, but the last thing we want is for him to know we have them. He tends to like to keep troublemakers as pets."

I nodded. "That was our thought, too."

"I suppose you don't want to take any chances with doing the job wrong." Natalie stuffed a handful of caramel corn in her mouth.

"You could drown them in a bottle of whiskey," Harvey

suggested, setting two more mugs of hot buttered rum down at the table, this time in front of Natalie and his own chair. "Enough hair of the dog will kill anything. Hate to waste the whiskey, though."

"Yeah, but maybe they like whiskey," I said, taking a sip of the sweet buttered rum, which warmed me from the inside out. "For all we know, it could start the growth process."

Cornelius joined us at the table with two more drinks. One he set in the middle of the table. The other he sipped.

"Who's that for?" I asked, pointing at the one in the middle. Was Reid coming over?

Natalie plucked a piece of popcorn from her bowl. "Coop is on his way. His shift is over. He radioed in on the walkie-talkie while you were in the shower."

"Maybe we could freeze them for a length of time, starve them of oxygen," Aunt Zoe suggested.

"Yeah." I cringed. "But look at how things often 'wake up' after being frozen for hundreds and thousands of years."

"Like what things?" Aunt Zoe asked.

"Like *other* things that perform cell reproduction after being plucked from the ice in the Antarctic."

Natalie snorted. "You're talking about the movie *The Thing*, aren't you?"

"No. Maybe." There could be truth to that. Hadn't Layne recently told me about some documentary on the permafrost melting in the Arctic Circle, citing something about there being potential viruses waiting there that could give modern humans some trouble? Or had I dreamed that?

Doc returned, scooping up some caramel corn before sitting down next to me. "What are we talking about?"

"Getting rid of those eggs. So far, we've covered burning them, drowning them in whiskey, and freezing them."

"I say we take them into the dark and leave them somewhere else," he said.

"Another realm?" Aunt Zoe tapped her pen against her

cheek. "But doesn't that open up the risk of someone else finding them there? Someone looking to cause more trouble?"

Doc shrugged. "The dark is vast. It could take a long, long time for anyone to stumble onto them."

"We could leave them with that banshee," Harvey tossed out. "She could sing them lullabies night after night."

I groaned. "I hope to never run into her again."

Knock knock knock.

We all looked over at the back door. Cooper stood outside, pointing down at the doorknob.

Harvey hurried over and opened the door for him.

"The front door is locked," he told us, taking off his coat and hanging it by the back door. He stopped by the kitchen sink and washed his hands before joining us at the table.

"That was me," I told him, lifting my mug. "I'm feeling a bit paranoid tonight."

Doc frowned at me. "Because of the eggs?"

"Because of the bounty hunter." I looked at Cooper. "Did you find anything out about Garth's history?"

He shrugged and took the chair next to Natalie. "Only the regular stuff—date of birth, location of birth, driver's license information. He's got no crimes on record beyond a single speeding ticket from ten years ago." He reached forward and grabbed the mug of hot buttered rum, raising his brows at Natalie in question, who nodded back. "I don't think Jonesy is your bounty hunter."

"So, you believe it's just a coincidence that his shop abuts that cave and powers it with electricity?" Aunt Zoe asked, her brow lined.

"Probably not." Cooper stole a piece of caramel corn from Natalie's bowl. "But I think he might not have been the one who had anything to do with it."

"What do you mean?" Natalie asked.

"I did some searching on his grandfather, old Jeb Jones.

Turns out that he met his demise when his shotgun jammed while he was out hunting in the hills behind the shop. It blew up in his face—well, blew off his face to be more accurate, and took half of his head with it."

Harvey sucked air through his teeth. "That's a quick way to change out yer banjo for a harp."

Doc nodded. "So, that's who you've seen roaming around there."

"It appears so." Cooper took a drink of the rum.

"And this half-headed specter," Cornelius said while inspecting a piece of popcorn. "It showed you the location of the cave?"

Cooper nodded.

"Hmmm." Cornelius looked across the table at Doc. "Did the specter try to reach out to you at all at any time you were in or near the taxidermy shop?"

"No." Doc's mouth tightened. "Nor could I pick up its scent."

Now that was odd. Normally, Doc was a bloodhound when it came to ghosts, and they flocked to him because of it. "What do you make of that, Cornelius?" I asked.

"I don't know. Something certainly feels peculiar about this ghost. Maybe we can do a séance in that cave of horrors and see if we can draw it out."

"No!" Doc, Cooper, and I all rejected the idea in unison.

I didn't know about the other two, but Cornelius would have to drag me there in a straitjacket. I had my limits, and that cave was well beyond them.

"We're going to need to do something about that place and all of the creatures you three saw in there," Aunt Zoe said. "We can't let anyone else stumble across that."

"Maybe this is something Mr. Black could help with," I suggested. "Along with getting rid of the eggs. I could try to contact him in the morning." I wasn't sure how, but Eddie Mudder seemed to have a direct line to him.

"Where did you put the eggs?" Aunt Zoe asked.

"Somewhere safe," Cooper said. "Trust me, until we figure out what to do with them, they're locked up tight."

I was sort of leaning in the direction of Doc's idea—removing them from this realm. That or shipping them into outer space, along with my sister. Just knowing the eggs were close by made me nervous. I crossed my fingers that I didn't dream about them tonight. Those tiny suckers were fodder for horrific nightmares.

"So, how was the premiere party?" Aunt Zoe asked me. "Besides the part about the *Nachzehrer* showing up in the bathroom window."

"To be honest, I don't know. I missed the actual show and was only there for about ten minutes after it was all over."

"I recorded it," she said with a smile. "The kids and I watched it and thought you might want to rewatch it eventually. Your children were bouncing at the sight of you on the television screen."

"I'm glad they enjoyed it, but ..." I made a face. "Maybe I can handle watching it some night after a few tequila shots."

"There are going to be two more shows, right?" Natalie said.

"Yeah, but Jerry's not planning on having a party for those."

"Are you sure?" Doc asked.

"No, but he hasn't mentioned anything about it."

"He probably wanted to wait to see how tonight's shindig went," Harvey said.

"God, I hope you're wrong," I said, taking another drink from my mug. Thinking about Jerry reminded me of Ray and his note. What the hell was that about, anyway?

"So, what about the bounty hunter?" Natalie asked. "If it's not Garth, then who is it?"

I looked around at each of them. "We'll have to keep our

eyes and ears open, I guess."

"Maybe it left this plane again," Aunt Zoe said, scribbling something on the page.

"I doubt I'm that lucky."

"We need to check on that particular traveler's clock," Doc said. "Doesn't Mr. Black have that one?"

"I can't remember."

"So, we're stuck waiting." Natalie sighed. "I hate waiting."

"Yeah, I've noticed that about you," Cooper said, his grin flirty as he captured her fingers and lifted them to his lips. Meanwhile, he reached out with his other hand and stole more popcorn from her bowl.

"You dirty law dog," she joked, catching his other hand and forcing him to put the stolen popcorn in her mouth. She held on to his hand, taking extra care to suck the caramel off his fingertips.

He gulped visibly.

Harvey watched the two of them with puckered lips, then snorted and turned to Aunt Zoe. "I think I'm gonna need to crash on your recliner again tonight, Zoe."

She nodded without looking up from her notebook. "It's all yours, Willis."

Cornelius took another drink from his mug, licking his upper lip afterward. "Did you know that hot buttered rum dates back to the colonial days? Early Americans believed rum had medicinal properties that would strengthen the body. Turns out they weren't wrong. Rum is good for the heart and arteries. It's also good for the bones, alleviates arthritis, and can be used to clean wounds."

I smirked. "I'm surprised you didn't say it's good for nose erections."

"If it's good for the heart," Cornelius said, lifting his mug to me in a mock toast, "it's good for all sorts of erections, including nasal and penile. So, drink up, Tall Medium and

Bristly Detective."

Cooper groaned. "You had to go there, didn't you, Parker?"

"Violet has a way," Aunt Zoe said with a wink in my direction.

"Drinking rum always makes me feel like a pirate," Natalie said. "Is that a hornpipe in your pocket, Coop, or are you just happy to see me?"

Cooper's cheeks reddened slightly, which made Natalie laugh.

"I think he's happy," Aunt Zoe said, teasing him along with Natalie.

"Well, it certainly makes everybody purtier when I drink rum," Harvey said. "I mean, look at you, Coop. Yer downright knee-wobblin' handsome at the moment. I'm startin' to feel the urge to hug you and give you some wet, sloppy kisses."

Cooper pointed at his uncle, his eyes narrowing to gunslinger slits. "Don't even try it."

I looked at Doc. "How about you? You finding Cooper extra pretty now, too?"

Doc eyed Cooper with a grin. "He's a fine, handsome man with or without the rum. How about you speak some French to me, Coop?"

"Shut up, Nyce, or I'll shoot you."

Chuckling, Doc clinked his mug against mine. "Coop is mighty fine, but you, me proud beauty, leave me shiverin' in me timbers," he said with a gravelly pirate accent. "You have the finest booty I ever laid me eyes on. How about I haul you upstairs later, plunder yer wares, and fire me cannon through yer porthole?"

I snorted and then choked, coughing in laughter.

"Plunder her underwear, ya say, you salty dog?" Harvey asked, snickering. "Or plunder her under *there*?"

I reached over and snapped his suspenders. "Zip it, dirty

bird, before I plunder your derriere with my size eight boot."

He wiggled his bushy eyebrows at Doc. "I got yer heifer all heated up and ready for mountin', Captain Doc. You owe me another bottle of rum."

Doc lifted his mug to Harvey and said to me, "Prepare to be boarded."

"Sparky's gonna get heiferized!" Both of Harvey's gold teeth shined back at me.

"That's it," I said, starting to rise. "I'm going to kick your butt until those gold teeth fall out."

Harvey tee-heed and hopped out of his chair, racing out of the room.

"You better run, old man!" I called after him. I turned back to the rest of the table, finished off my buttered rum, and set the mug down with a hard *clunk*. "Now, what are we going to do about those eggs?"

* * *

Monday, January 21st

I didn't dream about the eggs, thank God. However, I did dream about cows, and for that, I was going to pinch Harvey several times today.

Doc's side of the bed was empty when I sat up, but I could hear the shower running, so he hadn't left for the Rec Center yet. I decided to surprise him and get some coffee brewing in the kitchen. Pulling on some pajamas over my camisole and underwear, I headed downstairs.

By the third step down, I could smell that somebody had beat me to the coffee maker. But the kitchen was empty when I got there. Where was Harvey? He hadn't been in the recliner when I peeked in the living room.

I poured some coffee and stood in front of the kitchen

sink staring out into the gray and dark blue of early dawn. Movement next to Aunt Zoe's workshop drew my gaze.

A dog appeared from behind the shop, sniffing the air. Then it slinked over near the front of the shop and nosed at something on the ground. Was that a … Crap, it was a bowl of food. The kids must have put that out there yesterday for the dog, even though I'd explicitly told them not to feed it.

I set my coffee down and grabbed my thick cardigan sweater from the peg next to the back door, sliding into Aunt Zoe's snow boots. Quietly, I eased out the door and tiptoed down the porch steps, pausing at the bottom to glare at the blue-handled digging shovel partially blocking my path. I sighed. Darn kids never listen to me.

I picked up the shovel, planning to put it back inside Aunt Zoe's workshop. Halfway across the yard, the dog looked up from the bowl of food and stared at me. Its white and tan hair was matted and dirty. One ear stood high and mostly straight, the other flopped over. It lifted its snout, sniffing the air.

"Hello, Rooster," I said, trying to figure out what breed he was. He looked long in the "mutt" department and short on pedigree papers. I held out my hand, palm up. "Come here, boy."

The dog whined and took a step back.

Then I remembered the shovel in my other hand. I planted the blade in the snow and held out my hand again. "Come on, Rooster. It's okay, it's just me and my smell."

The dog glanced left and then right, and then it let out a small bark and took a hesitant step toward me.

"That's it, buddy." I crunched through the snow, easing closer. "Let's get you cleaned up and we can see if the shelter can find a forever home for you. Somewhere other than with us."

Rooster took another step, and then stopped. He started to shiver visibly. I couldn't blame the mutt. My nose was nearly frozen already, along with my fingers. It must be ten degrees out here, maybe five. The snow had that hard crust that comes with ass-freezing temperatures.

I inched closer, both hands out now, palms up. "Come here, Rooster. I promise not to hurt you."

He lowered his head, looking up at me submissively and whimpering softly.

Something in my chest tightened and then reached down into my stomach. A wave of nausea crashed into me. I stood up straight and swallowed several times. What in the …

Snap!

Rooster and I both looked toward the trees behind the workshop.

Crunch, crunch, crunch.

A cloaked figure stepped out from thick shadows under the trees. It moved like the Tin Man, stiff-jointed and wary. In one hand, it held a bow. In the other, a small ball of fire crackled.

Rooster started to growl and hustled over to stand next to my leg.

The figure stopped just this side of the tree line. Bright yellow eyes glowed out at me from under its wide hood.

"Who are you?" I asked.

It spoke in a guttural growl that made the hairs on the back of my neck rise. Whatever it had uttered, I couldn't understand the language, but I thought I heard the word *Scharfrichter*.

Rooster let out a sharp bark. The hairs on his back were raised, too. He and I were in agreement—this was not a friendly wood sprite here to wish us a happy winter morning. Unfortunately, I'd shown up to a bow-and-fireball fight with nothing more than fuzzy teeth and a stray dog.

After another bark, Rooster took off running across the snow. He disappeared around the other side of Aunt Zoe's glass workshop and into the trees beyond.

"Thanks a lot, Rooster!" So much for filling that guard dog position. Now all I had left was my fuzzy teeth for defense. "The kids should have named you 'Chicken.'"

I turned back to my morning visitor and froze.

It had raised its bow and had the fireball aimed at me like an arrow. It spoke again in that guttural growl. This time, I thought I heard the word *Nachzehrer*.

I lifted my hands in the air. "Are you here for me?"

It grunted and pointed where its ear would likely be under the hood. "*Eier! Nachzehrer!*"

Eier must either mean ear or eggs. I really needed to learn some other languages besides English and pig Latin. "You want your *Nachzehrer* eggs?"

It nodded, that ball of fire still trained on me.

Here I was, standing face-to-face with the bounty hunter that had unleashed those long-limbed bastards on me and my friends. I tightened my fists. If only I could destroy its precious eggs in front of it while laughing maniacally.

"Too fucking bad. I don't have them. And if I did, you'd be the last one I'd give them to."

"Mine!" it snarled, pounding on its chest.

Ah, so it did speak some English. I shrugged. "Not anymore. Now they belong to me." I pounded my chest back at it.

It roared and pulled on the bow string, drawing out the fireball until it looked like an arrow.

But before it could let go, a streak of white and tan fur came from the trees and slammed into it. The fireball veered wide, hitting in the snow next to me and sizzling out.

Rooster snarled and yipped through clenched teeth, playing tug-of-war with the hunter's cloak.

I raced over and grabbed the blue-handled shovel standing in the snow. When I turned back, Rooster had pulled the cloak half off the hunter, giving me a clear picture of its curled horns, wide gray forehead and glowing yellow eyes.

What in the hell was that thing?

The tightness in my stomach, along with a fresh batch of raised goosebumps down my back, said it certainly wasn't friendly. I raced toward it as the hunter shook free of Rooster and kicked out at the dog, who yipped in pain and ran off.

The hunter drew its flaming arrow again and sent another fireball at me.

I gripped the handle and swung the shovel, hitting the fireball right back at the hunter.

It dodged, its yellow eyes widening in surprise.

"That's right, cocksucker. All-star softball team." I tromped through the snow toward it. "Come on. Hit me with another."

It took aim again.

BOOM! A shotgun blasted, echoing off the hillside.

Birds screeched around us, fluttering away from the trees.

The fireball missed again, landing several feet to my right.

"Get it, Sparky!" Harvey cheered from behind me.

The creature looked over my head, taking aim at the back porch.

"Don't even think about it!" I raced at it, moving like the wind, and swung right as it let go of another fireball. The shovel blade nailed the fireball, bashing it back into the hunter's face.

It screeched in pain and stumbled, crashing into a tree.

Before it could lift the bow again, I grabbed the shovel handle in two hands and skewered the son of a bitch, jamming the pointed blade through its chest.

Its mouth gaped, and then it crumpled to the ground. Brown fluid dripped down its furry chin as it stared up at me with those wide, yellow eyes. Bubbles sputtered from its lips. The hunter appeared to be trying to speak.

But I didn't feel like listening. This fucker liked to infect humans with parasitic nightmares so it could use them as pack hunters to kill my kind instead of fighting me one-on-one with its own two hands. There was only one thing to do with the chickenshit dickosaurus.

I tugged the shovel free of its chest. It lay gurgling in the snow as more dark fluid trickled from its mouth.

"You picked the wrong *Scharfrichter* to hunt." I stood over it and raised the shovel. "To Hell with you."

With a loud grunt, I brought the blade down hard, aiming right below its furry chin. A sickening crunch filled the air, and then the fireball in its hand spread up its arm and quickly engulfed its torso. The head combusted next, burning bright blue and white. I stepped back, shielding my face from the searing heat.

And then it was over, leaving smoldering bluish corkscrews of ash on the snow.

I stood huffing down at what was left of the hunter. Something nudged my leg. I looked over to find Rooster panting up at me, his tongue hanging from the side of his mouth again.

"Thanks for coming back, Rooster," I said, reaching down and scratching the mutt between the ears.

He barked once and walked over to what remained of the hunter. He circled the ashes, sniffing at them, and then lifted his leg.

"You're kidding me," I said as he splashed some piss on the blue ashes and the snow around them.

He finished peeing and then wagged his tail, seeming quite pleased with himself as he kicked snow onto the ashes.

"Criminy," I said, shaking my head. "How am I supposed to give you away when you pull that kind of heroic dog crap?"

Grumbling, I trudged toward the back porch where Harvey stood waiting. Doc had joined him at some point, probably after the shotgun blast that most likely woke up the whole neighborhood.

"Nice job, Killer," Doc said as I crested the steps. His

hair was still very wet from the shower, his breath steaming. He grabbed me by the sweater collar and pulled me close. His dark eyes searched mine. "You okay?"

I nodded up at him, my body still humming from the post-killing adrenaline rush.

"Sorry I wasn't here faster. You caught me mid-shower."

"You smell good." I thumbed toward the trees behind me. "That was the bounty hunter."

"I figured."

"It wanted its eggs back."

"Did it, now?"

"Yeah, but it didn't say 'please.' "

"How rude." He leaned down and gave me a hard, fresh kiss. "Never a dull moment with you, Tish."

Harvey rested his shotgun on his shoulder. "Well, I didn't get to kill any bad guys, but at least Bessie got to clear her throat."

"That reminds me," Doc said, stepping back from me. "Cooper radioed on the walkie-talkie as I was throwing on some clothes, wanting to know if that was Bessie he heard squawking bright and early on a Monday morning."

Harvey grunted. "I suppose he's on his way over now to give me an earful."

"Pretty much, yep." Doc pointed down at the base of the steps. "Who's your friend, Killer?"

I looked down at the dog, who'd apparently followed me back to the house. "Doc, this is Rooster. Rooster, say hello to Doc."

The dog barked up at Doc.

He laughed. "The kids must have taught him how to speak on command."

I cursed.

"So," Doc said with a grin. "Do we have a dog now, too?"

"I don't want to talk about it."

He put his arm around my shoulders and kissed me on the temple. "Have I told you lately how much I'm over the moon about you and your kids and all of their pets?"

"Sure, you say that now, but when I have ten cats …"

Aunt Zoe met us at the door with the phone in her hand. "It's for you," she said to me. "It's Masterson."

I took the phone. "Violet speaking."

"Good morning, *Scharfrichter*," he said in his usual charming drawl. "I hear you've been busy."

Did he mean killing *Nachzehrer*? Or had he heard Harvey's shotgun blast a few moments ago? "A little here and there. What do you need?"

"My *lidérc* is missing."

"Oh, really?" I winked at Doc. "Have you filed a missing *lidérc* report with the local law enforcement?"

Doc's forehead lined.

Harvey snickered. "Here we go again."

Meanwhile, Dominick huffed in my ear. "If you happen to know where it is, *Scharfrichter*, I strongly recommend that you tell me at once."

"Is that some sort of veiled threat?"

Aunt Zoe's gaze hardened as she stared at the phone.

"It's not veiled," Dominick said, his voice deadly serious. "That *lidérc* belongs to me. I don't like it when someone takes something of mine without my permission."

"Duly noted, and I wish you luck finding your no-good, pain-in-the-ass Hungarian devil."

"Violet," Dominick warned, the charm gone from his tone, leaving a hard edge behind. "Don't you dare …"

I hung up and handed the phone to Aunt Zoe. "Dominick sends his love. It's a bit prickly this morning, though, sort of like Cooper's before he's had any coffee."

"You know that's not the end of Masterson," she said.

"It is at the moment." I linked my arm with Harvey's while Doc held the door wide for us. "Now, what's for breakfast, you ol' buzzard? Killing assholes first thing in the morning makes me hungry enough to eat a cast-iron skillet."

The End ... for now

Ann Charles is a USA Today bestselling author who writes award-winning mysteries that are splashed with humor, romance, paranormal, and whatever else she feels like throwing into the mix. When she is not dabbling in fiction, arm-wrestling with her children, attempting to seduce her husband, or arguing with her sassy cats, she is daydreaming of lounging poolside at a fancy resort with a blended margarita in one hand and a great book in the other.

Facebook (Personal Page):
http://www.facebook.com/ann.charles.author

Facebook (Author Page):
http://www.facebook.com/pages/Ann-Charles/37302789804?ref=share

Instagram:
https://www.instagram.com/ann_charles

YouTube Channel:
https://www.youtube.com/user/AnnCharlesAuthor

Twitter (as Ann W. Charles):
http://twitter.com/AnnWCharles

Ann Charles Website:
http://www.anncharles.com

More Books by Ann

www.anncharles.com

The Deadwood Mystery Series

WINNER of the 2010 Daphne du Maurier Award for Excellence in Mystery/Suspense

WINNER of the 2011 Romance Writers of America® Golden Heart Award for Best Novel with Strong Romantic Elements

Welcome to Deadwood—the Ann Charles version. The world I have created is a blend of present day and past, of fiction and non-fiction. What's real and what isn't is for you to determine as the series develops, the characters evolve, and I write the stories line by line. I will tell you one thing about the series—it's going to run on for quite a while, and Violet Parker will have to hang on and persevere through the crazy adventures I have planned for her. Poor, poor Violet. It's a good thing she has a lot of gumption to keep her going!

The Deadwood Shorts Series

The Deadwood Shorts collection includes short stories featuring the characters of the Deadwood Mystery series. Each tale not only explains more of Violet's history, but also gives a little history of the other characters you know and love from the series. Rather than filling the main novels in the series with these short side stories, I've put them into a growing Deadwood Shorts collection for more reading fun.

The Deadwood Undertaker Series

From the bestselling, multiple award-winning, humorous Deadwood Mystery series comes a new herd of tales set in the same Deadwood stomping grounds, only back in the days when the Old West town was young.

The Jackrabbit Junction Mystery Series

Bestseller in Women Sleuth Mystery and Romantic Suspense

Welcome to the Dancing Winnebagos R.V. Park. Down here in Jackrabbit Junction, Arizona, Claire Morgan and her rabble-rousing sisters are really good at getting into trouble—BIG trouble (the land your butt in jail kind of trouble). This rowdy, laugh-aloud mystery series is packed with action, suspense, adventure, and relationship snafus. Full of colorful characters and twisted up plots, the stories of the Morgan sisters will keep you wondering what kind of a screwball mess they are going to land in next.

The Dig Site Mystery Series

Welcome to the jungle—the steamy *Maya* jungle that is, filled with ancient ruins, deadly secrets, and quirky characters. Quint Parker, renowned photojournalist (and lousy amateur detective), is in for a whirlwind of adventure and suspense as he and archaeologist Dr. Angélica García get tangled up in mysteries from the past and present in exotic dig sites. Loaded with action and laughs, along with all sorts of steamy heat, these books will keep you sweating along with the characters as they do their best to make it out of the jungle alive.

Made in the USA
Columbia, SC
17 August 2022

65437739R00248